RESURRECTION PASS

RESURRECTION PASS

KURT ANDERSON

PINNACLE BOOKS
Kensington Publishing Corp.
www.kensingtonbooks.com

PINNACLE BOOKS are published by

Kensington Publishing Corp.
119 West 40th Street
New York, NY 10018

All Kensington titles, imprints, and distributed lines are available at special quantity discounts for bulk purchases for sales promotions, premiums, fund-raising, educational, or institutional use. Special book excerpts or customized printings can also be created to fit specific needs. For details, write or phone the office of the Kensington sales manager: Kensington Publishing Corp., 119 West 40th Street, New York, NY 10018, attn: Sales Department; phone 1-800-221-2647.

This book is a work of fiction. Names, characters, businesses, organizations, places, events, and incidents either are the product of the author's imagination or are used fictitiously. Any resemblance to actual persons, living or dead, events, or locales is entirely coincidental.

ISBN-13: 978-0-7860-3681-3
ISBN-10: 0-7860-3681-8

First printing: April 2017

10 9 8 7 6 5 4 3 2 1

Printed in the United States of America

First electronic edition: April 2017

ISBN-13: 978-0-7860-3682-0
ISBN-10: 0-7860-3682-6

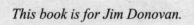

This book is for Jim Donovan.

The wind had dropped with the sun, and in all that vast world of branches nothing stirred. Any moment, it seemed, the woodland gods, who are to be worshipped in silence and loneliness, might stretch their mighty and terrific outlines among the trees.

—ALGERNON BLACKWOOD, *The Wendigo*

He woke with a start and sat blinking, trying to conjure reason out of the cold and dark air. His lungs burned as though from some deep-seated respiratory infection, and his feet were a throbbing mess, tacky with blood. The light around him was negligible, and although he had hoped for a moment that it was dawn, he knew now it was not. Knew that he had slept for minutes rather than hours, and the night still held the land in her silent, black fist. The only light was that of the stars, burning their thin alien light down upon the land. He was burrowed in under a fallen spruce and he was very cold, and as his consciousness returned, so too did his panic, for he could hear the sound of something making its way along the pine needles of the forest floor.

Something was coming toward him in the woods.

Prologue

The moose was going to die soon.

Ben Splithand knelt near the reddened grass, the stock of his 30-06 resting on the ground. The blood formed a tacky mat under a balsam fir, and when he glanced to the south he saw the moose had chosen this spot so it could watch its backtrail. He reached down and touched the sticky grass. Thirty minutes since the moose had left? An hour? He had not seen it nor heard it leave. The only indication of its watchful presence was this, an oval of blood-dampened grass drying to brown in the afternoon breeze.

The moose was much wiser than it had been in the morning, when it ambled through the sparse stand of alders fifty yards from Ben, steam rising off its back. It stood broadside and unaware, pushed out of the dense tangle of brush by Ben's grandfather and uncle. It was not panicked, just moving away from yet another danger, a *yikihcawases* that would go seven, eight hundred pounds. Ben had been caught by surprise, looking up from the bright rectangle of light from his phone, his text message to his girlfriend half finished. He had shrugged the rifle off his shoulder as the moose started quartering away through the thicker scrub. It was a bad shot, a low-percentage shot. He had taken it.

Now, five hours later, he held his reddened thumb up for inspection. The blood was clean, no flecks of pink lung tissue. Brighter than the darker maroon color of a liver hit. No surprise; the moose would have died long before this had Ben's slug struck the vitals. There wasn't any partially digested grass or shit in the blood, so at least it wasn't a gut shot. About the only good thing he could salvage out of this situation.

He stood. The wind was blowing crossways, west to east, and the moose was headed north, into the bad country. His uncle had thought the moose had been hit in the leg; his grandfather opined it had been struck somewhere low in the belly. "You were thinking about your own dick, after all," the old man had said to Ben. "That must have been where you aimed."

Ben followed the blood trail down the slight decline, hoping the death he read in the moose's resting places would hurry along and make its claim.

Now the night was coming down on the land, the shadows under the hazel and mountain maple taking on substance, congealing around him. The mosquitoes hovered, landing on the backs of his hands, stinging him through his blue jeans. He was very thirsty.

The blood trail was easy to follow even in the low light; something had happened after Ben had spooked the moose from its last bed, and what had been dribbles of blood were now freshets. A bone end must have splintered, the sharp edges severing an artery. The moose was just ahead of him, leaving a wake of blood as it crashed into a long, deep valley.

The valley was several miles wide, the bottom shrouded in fog, with the tops of the balsams and white pines that lined the side slopes jutting out of the mist. The bottom was hidden in the fog, but the far side was visible, the granite bluffs rising almost vertical out of the mucky ground. Evening thermals rose from the valley floor, carrying a thick, funky odor up to Ben. He stood at the top of the valley. It would be another story for him to tell, one of the few living Cree in Highbanks who had visited Resurrection Valley. He worked his tongue around his mouth until he could spit, then let the little globule of saliva drop to the ground. He had less than an hour before the Canadian twilight would swallow up the trail.

The brush crackled less than a hundred yards away as the moose's hooves dragged through the underbrush. Ben held his 30-06 up and peered through the Leupold scope, pausing when the scope passed over a jack pine stump, the budworm scars like tiny rivers. There was still plenty of shooting light left.

Ben moved slowly down the valley slope, eyes scanning the brush, looking for a darker brown leaf that might be an ear, a sweeping limb that might be the curve of an antler. There was a flat bench carved into the side of the valley, and he crossed it and descended down a steeper grade. He made sure his heel touched first, followed by the rest of the foot; he was much quieter than the moose, whose movements had become sloppy as death neared. The ground grew softer as he descended, and the moose's hooves made a series of sucking, squelchy noises ahead of him.

Then the noises stopped. Ben paused, his head cocked to the side, finger resting lightly on the curve of the trigger. After a moment, a long, low bawl issued from a tangle of alders. He took a step back, his finger creeping toward the rifle's safety. The moose cried out again, louder this time. Ben took a deep breath and waved aside the cloud of mosquitoes in front of his face. It was the moose's death cry, nothing more. He had heard it before, but for a moment all the old stories about Resurrection Valley, which the Cree called *Asiskiwiw*, flooded his mind. Stories about the moss eater, the devil's first cousin, who lived in the low, wild places with his curved, filmy-green teeth, whose laughter sounded like a cross between the cry of a loon and the howl of a wolf.

All was quiet now, except . . . except something moving in the brush, barely audible. A leg, perhaps, twitching in pre-death spasm.

He glanced up. The last light from the setting sun was a red smudge. It would be darker inside the bush, too dark to even properly field dress the moose. The mosquitoes would be drawn to the fresh blood. Other reasons to delay, with no need to name, tumbled through his mind and were accepted without question. He slowly backed away, the 30-06 held in front of him, and scrambled up to the flat bench. He paused there and took several shuddering breaths, then continued to the top of the ridge, where the ground was dry and flat.

He would wait for morning to claim his kill.

Dawn was just a gradual lightening of the clouds in the east. Ben rubbed his face vigorously, then took a few minutes to wipe the dew off the rifle's barrel with his shirt. Even here, the damp air of the valley was pervasive, the smell and the moisture like an old towel wrapped around his head. When the barrel and receiver were dry, he kicked dirt over the remains of his fire and stood looking down into *Asiskiwiw*.

It was not the first time Ben had slept under the stars by himself, but he swore it would be his last. Every time he drifted off, the moose would bawl, a choked, warbling sound that turned into a moan as the night wore on.

Ten minutes, he thought. Walk down, finish it off. He would pack out the backstraps and the liver, leave the rest for the wolves. He had no children of his own, but his parents had been dead for almost a decade, and his sisters, eleven and thirteen, needed the protein. He supposed by now both of them were frantic with worry after he had failed to return home. No time to think about that now.

He thumbed back the bolt on the rifle. He had never unloaded it and he knew there was a live cartridge in the chamber, but the bright brass of the casing made him feel better, the gleam of metal like a bit of missing morning sunshine.

He started down the valley. The fog was still heavy, and even the tops of the trees were covered. He stood in his boot prints from the night before and slowly scanned the trees until he was certain he knew where the moose had fallen. Then he started forward, clicking the safety off the 30-06.

He had not gone very far when he saw pockmarks from the hooves pressed deep in the soil, filled with water. There was no blood. He followed the little potholes, pushing aside the low-hanging branches. The leaves were dew-laden, and his shirt was quickly soaked. He felt a strong desire to see the sun, to feel its heat on his skin.

Twenty yards later he stopped, his own feet slowly sinking deeper into the ground, fingers digging into the walnut stock of the rifle.

The moose lay on its side in front of him, half-buried in the spongy earth. For a moment he thought it had been killed by some predator and the remains cached—bears, as well as the occasional cougar or wolverine, would cover whatever they couldn't eat with leaves and duff and return later. But the material covering the moose seemed part of the earth itself, as if the ground and roots had risen up to swallow it. There were only minimal signs of struggle; a few overturned leaves, and a long yellow scratch in a small poplar sapling, probably from a flailing hoof.

Ben moved a step closer. One of the roots was twined around the moose. It wrapped around the knobby spine, pressed against the long, flat shoulder blade, and entered the hide. No, not a root, some sort of thick tendril. Gray and smooth, absent the hair-like offshoots a root would have.

The moose's eyes were open and covered with a fuzzy gray mold. The left eye had burst, and the mold followed the vitreum down the side of the muzzle. The antlers, still covered with blood-rich velvet, were coated with a mold so thick they looked bloated, cartoonish. Another tendril snaked into the moose's open mouth, past the jutting yellow teeth, and disappeared into its gullet. There was still no blood.

Bile rose in Ben's throat. He tried to step backward, but his boot was mired in the soft ground. He pushed down with his other foot, the mud forming a vacuum around his boots. He grabbed a sapling and pulled his leg up. The ground gave off a low sucking sound as his foot slipped free of the boot. Ben hopped to the side, his white sock a splash of brightness, as the mud around his submerged boot began to contract. Ten long miles of hopping along the unbroken trail back to Highbanks with one boot flashed through his mind.

"Goddammit."

He knelt down and plunged his hand into the hole. The mud was cold and fetid, like reaching into the inside of a long-dead animal. The back of his hand brushed something hard and he reached for it. The object moved under his hand, and Ben recoiled.

He looked at his mud-streaked hand, then down at the closing hole, the edges already folding in on themselves. He tentatively reached back in, and again something closed around his wrist. He grunted and reared back, his knees digging into the soft ground. Whatever was holding him gave way, and he held up his hand to wipe the mud away. There was a pink welt across his wrist, and his hand was already numb and discolored from lack of blood.

He glanced over at the tendril snaking down into the moose's throat, his mind starting to make the connection. As he studied the moose, he caught the tiniest of movements. It came again, a slight bulging under the mat of growth on the moose's intact eye. It took Ben a moment to process what he was seeing: the moose was moving its eyeball, looking for the sound of the commotion. As he watched, a long, low bawl sighed out of its mouth.

"No," Ben said.

Still kneeling, he brought his rifle to his shoulder, disgust and horror and sympathy all mixing together. The rifle was a semiautomatic, and he emptied the clip without aiming, bone and antler and brains flying backward, splattering the brush. The head of the moose disintegrated, torn apart by the 220-grain slugs, but the tendril that had been down its mouth didn't move. It hung there, suspended, the pale material deepening into a rosy color near the tip.

Ben set the rifle down and tried to get to his feet. He couldn't; tendrils the size of garden hoses were wrapped around both ankles. He struggled for a moment, realized he was not going to break free with brute strength alone, and pulled his knife from the sheath. The pale flesh (*and it is flesh,* Ben thought frantically, *not roots*) separated easily under the sharp blade. Ben sliced the tendrils off one ankle and kicked them away. The cross sections of the tendrils were waxy, with no arteries or veins. Within seconds the severed ends turned a sickly gray.

He moved to his other ankle. The remaining tendril was already contracting, as though it expected the blade. It made the cutting easier, and he sliced through it in one quick movement.

He pushed himself to his feet but only made it halfway to a standing position. Another tendril had wound through a belt loop on the back of his jeans. He reversed his grip on his knife and hacked at it blindly. A sharp pain bloomed across his lower back as he cut himself, and almost immediately something cool and insistent pressed against him, nestling into the cut. He made another vicious swipe, and the pressure released.

He straightened. More tendrils had coiled halfway

to his knees while he had been distracted. There was no pressure until he tried to move. Then they constricted instantly, and he felt his shin bones crack. He moaned and stood still, searching the ground for his rifle. He finally caught a gleam of blued steel and picked out the outline of his 30-06 a few yards off, nearly sunken into the ground, its length wrapped inside more waxy loops.

The tendrils crawled over him, and when Ben looked down at his hands he saw a gray, fuzzy growth on his skin. He leaned down with his knife again, then was jerked to a stop, an involuntary scream coming from his mouth. He had felt nothing until he moved. But when he did, the tendril that had wound around his shoulder pulled his arm so far back he felt his muscles separate.

Ben stood, motionless except for his heaving chest. The tendrils advanced steadily, climbing up his body like vines. He did not move and there was no more new pain. He craned his head upward, hoping for the sight of the morning sun. The sky was still gray; it would likely drizzle later. He hoped his sisters had found breakfast.

He weighed his options. He flexed his legs the smallest of degrees, and the pressure and pain from the constricting tendrils made him moan. He looked at the moose, thought of what it had been, of how it had not quite been dead. When the main mass of tendrils reached his waist, Ben brought the knife forward, very slowly. Someone would take them in; someone always took in orphans.

"I'm sorry," he whispered, and pressed the blade against the skin of his left wrist. He pulled hard, with downward pressure, as if cutting through a length of thick rope. He tried to transfer the knife to cut his other wrist, but he had severed the tendons and the knife fell from his grip. No matter; blood was burbling out of his open arteries, driven out of his body by his hammering pulse.

A tendril rose out of the mass around his lower body and twisted along his arm. It paused just above the cut, then circled his forearm and squeezed. The blood slowed to a trickle, and the end of the tendril pressed itself over the cut, its waxy end taking on a rosy glow.

Two hundred yards up the slope, on the ridgeline, a gray jay rummaging through the remains of Ben's paltry campfire cocked its head to listen. The screams came in waves, the voice growing hoarse and then choking off.

The jay hopped to the far side of the campfire and, finding nothing, flew up into the branches of a spruce tree. It could hear moaning now, low and plaintive. After a while the sound changed, became almost conversational. The jay listened for a few more seconds and then grew bored and flew off into the woods, still looking for its morning meal.

THE BAD COUNTRY

Chapter 1

"We've got to do something."

Jake Trueblood watched the meadow below them. It had been a beaver pond at one point, but the dam had long since been breached and the water was gone. Waist-high grass grew inside the acre-sized depression, a dozen dead and limbless trees amid the yellowing stalks. On the far side of the meadow a jumble of sticks marked the remains of the lodge, and backed against it was a young woodland caribou, panting, its hind end streaked with blood. Three timber wolves paced around it, cutting in lightly when it tried to escape, but not attempting to close in.

"You have a rifle," the girl said, touching his shoulder. Her name was Rachel Bell. Not a girl, he thought, but a young woman, part of the group but not its leader. "Shoot over their heads."

Jake turned back to the meadow.

Two of the wolves were young, born that spring, and the mother was pulling double duty, keeping the caribou at bay and making sure her pups didn't do anything stupid. The caribou would only get weaker as the day went on. The alpha female had already bought their dinner when she had bitten through the big muscles on the back of the caribou's leg; now they just had to wait for it to be served. Of all the lessons she would pass on to her pups, Jake thought, patience would keep them alive the longest.

Remember that.

"Sorry," he said to Rachel, then turned to address the rest of the group. There were six others, rigged out in new clothes, top-quality gear, and big backpacks full of equipment. "I thought they already had it down."

He'd heard the yipping early that morning as he fed twigs into the breakfast fire. He recognized the tone and the chatter of a hunt in progress and listened carefully, tracking the chase through the woods, hearing it stall out less than a quarter mile away. This was their second morning in the brush, and he'd been brusque with them the night before, their banter around the fire turning quiet at his one-word answers to their myriad questions. Well. They were silly questions.

So this morning, when he was sure that the hunt had entered its final phase, he snuffed out the fire and went to each of the tents, and instead of telling them they were leaving he'd asked them politely, each one, if they wanted to see a pack of wolves on the hunt. They had, and he'd led them here, to this everyday desperate scene, a temporary stalemate that wouldn't make the highlight reel on The Nature Channel.

"Can you?" a tall, bearded man named Cameron Fairchild asked. He stepped next to Rachel and placed a hand on her shoulder. "We're far enough away from . . . everything, right? One shot won't matter."

"I can't scare them away," Jake said. "Not for good, unless I shoot one. And maybe not even then."

"Don't shoot them," Rachel said. "Just fire over their heads."

Jake turned to her. That open face, those untested eyes. *Patience,* he thought again, *patience and temperance.* No reason for him to paint this situation with reality, broad strokes or fine. No need to explain that even if he went down and scared the wolves away and wrapped the caribou's leg in goddamn gauze it wouldn't help. The wolves would find it, or other wolves or a bear would find it, and the caribou would die alone and in pieces. There was nothing to gain. *Patience. I might not be working for tips, but I've got another ten days with them, and if they get what they need—*

"No gunshots," Warren Campbell said, stepping through them. He smiled at Rachel, eyes crinkling, the silver hair around his temples reflecting golden in the morning sunshine. "I think what Mr. Trueblood is saying is that wolves need to eat, too. Which of course you understand, Rachel. You're a biologist."

"Ecologist," she murmured, her eyes flitting to the meadow and then back to Warren. "And I know they need to eat, just not . . ."

Just not before she's had her own breakfast, Jake thought. Then: *Christ, what's wrong with you? She was probably playing on swings and going to the mall when you were out trapping muskrats, skinning them in the shed under the kerosene lamp Henry got from the railroad. And hoping the son of a bitch inside Mom's bedroom was too drunk to come out to the shed and tell you how you were doing it all wrong.*

Jake walked out a dozen steps, picking through the

screen of hazel and onto the edge of the meadow. The two wolf pups continued pacing, tongues lolling. The female went very still, her yellow eyes locking in on his shape, then quickly flitting around him, picking out the other shapes. Not counting, but something close. Assessing.

"Go on," Jake whispered.

She melted into the brush, not running or even trotting, just turning away like a dog disinterested in a situation. The pups, each pushing sixty pounds already, continued to haze the caribou for a few moments before realizing they were alone. Then their ears cocked forward, their heads swiveling around and then locking in on something deeper in the alders, something that only they could see. They trotted off. The caribou watched them go, neck bent, with the tines of its velvet-covered antlers pointing at the departing wolves, its sides bellowing.

The conversation behind him fell off. Then the slow footfalls of Warren—he didn't know all of their footstep patterns yet, but he knew Warren's, surprisingly light for a big man, surprisingly quiet—coming up behind him. *Here it comes,* he thought. *Was that an Indian thing, communicating with your eyes? Did you talk to it, somehow?*

Warren's voice was low. "You could have done that five minutes ago."

Jake looked at the meadow, at the caribou whose death had been extended by a few minutes, maybe an hour. Then back to Warren, a man perhaps a decade older than Jake, thick but not yet gone to fat, his eyes dark and intelligent. He was after something buried in the Canadian soils, something that Jake knew little about. But he could tell Warren was going to get it, or know the reason why he couldn't. Warren looked like a guy used to getting what he was after.

"You ready?" Jake said.

Warren held his gaze. "Next time you want to veer off course, check with me first." He glanced at his watch, which looked like it cost more than Jake wanted to know, the only watch in this group of seven, who had not brought phones or handheld GPS units or anything other than their fine camping equipment and silly questions. "Better yet," Warren said, "how about we just skip the sights?"

Jake adjusted the straps on his backpack. It afforded him three long breaths, and when he looked up his face was calm. "Fine with me."

Ten minutes later he was sweating, the weight of his pack nearly seventy pounds, as he led the once-again silent group deeper into the brush.

He pushed them harder that day than he had the previous. It was purposeful, meant to stretch out muscles that were unused to rugged terrain, to keep the chatter down. He increased the pace steadily, and a break that might have lasted ten minutes the day before was seven today, and they came spaced further apart. There was some groaning, but not much—soft as they might look, they were in pretty good shape. Runners, he supposed, or maybe treadmillers. They could handle it.

He felt good himself, only the usual aches and pains. The other pain had been silent for a while, weeks stretching now into months. Gone for good, perhaps.

When he talked, it was about water. Making sure

they drank enough, that there wasn't too much in their socks. Sweaty feet were more than an unpleasantness— he had learned that much, at least, at Dwyer Hill. Had learned how blood blisters and fungal infections could combine into something that would make feet and ankles swollen purple nightmares. Finding water was not really a problem in this sprawling wilderness of lakes and rivers and swamps, and they all carried iodine tablets and ultraviolet decontamination units. But the treated water tasted bad, and he noticed several in the group were reluctant to do much more than wash their mouths out when they stopped for a canteen break.

"Not quite up to your standards?" he asked Jaimie Bednarik. She had just spat out a mouthful of water.

Jaimie wiped her mouth with her forearm. She was as tall as Jake, with broad shoulders and a finely sculpted face Jake thought of as handsome rather than pretty. "Tastes like boiled shit," she said.

"Maybe so," Jake said. "But you're a big girl, you need to drink." He leaned forward and tapped the jugs in her backpack. "Drink two of these a day, I don't care what it tastes like. You get dehydrated you won't die, but you will slow us down." He started away, then turned back and said in a lower voice, "We might find some better water up ahead."

She nodded. "So you do know where we're going?"

"More or less. Do you know what you're doing?"

Her eyebrows dipped for a second, and then she relaxed and flashed him a smile. It transformed her face, and Jake found out he was wrong: she wasn't pretty or handsome. She was beautiful. "More or less, Mr. Guide," Jaimie said. "More or less."

Two hours later he stopped at the far edge of a long,

low alder thicket. It had been a decade since Jake had been through this section of woods, and that had been in the winter, running a marten and fisher trapline, when the ground was frozen and he had broken a trail with his 1978 Ski-Doo snowmobile. It had been a slog then and it was far worse now, traveling in the tag end of the warm season, especially after a wet summer like this. It would be impossible in the spring, or the autumn if the fall rains came like they used to. But this was the only way he knew to approach the destination from the eastern route.

He wiped his brow and glanced at Warren, who was staring at him, his shirt collar soaked through with sweat. Warren arched an eyebrow. Jake turned away, took a drink of water.

They went on. After finding the pass between the flowage and the spruce bog, Jake knew he was in the right general area, but now he needed to make it overland to the small drainage coming out of the blackwoods, a massive forest of black spruce that covered dozens of square miles. The drainage had no formal name, but he called the small seepage blackwoods spring, no capital letters; it wasn't big enough or important enough for that. But blackwoods spring would take them a good five miles in the right direction, and it was far more efficient to follow the mini-floodplain it had carved through the forest than it was to go overland. Time was of the essence—he'd heard it from Warren enough to know it wasn't something he said lightly. In quickly, do whatever they needed to, and out before the fall rains swelled the rivers and swamps. Following blackwoods spring was one way he knew they could save some time.

The problem was coming in from the east. Well, one problem. The other was finding the rest of the equipment, which had come in three months ago via chopper, the equipment set down on high ground. The crew—maybe this crew, maybe another, Jake didn't know and hadn't been able to get more than the barest of details—had been scheduled to come in a few days later. That didn't happen, and his understanding was that someone had fired a high-velocity slug through the chopper's cockpit on its return flight. The slug hadn't damaged anything critical, but it had sent a shard of metal through the pilot's hand, making him reconsider his career of flying covert operations in broad daylight. So no more chopper flights.

Jake was deep in his thoughts when he felt someone come up beside him. The woods had opened up, and there was enough room to walk side by side. He turned and saw ash blond hair hanging over blue-gray eyes.

"I wanted to say thank you," Rachel said.

"For what?"

"The wolves. Getting them to leave the caribou alone." She took a deep breath, as though to confess something. "I know they'll probably be back."

Jake swatted at a deerfly on his arm. "Welcome."

He turned back to what passed for a trail. There was a patch of mature sugar maples to his left with minimal undergrowth, and he had to consciously make himself steer clear of the big timber. The constant crush of close-set trees and the low brush made a person want to veer away from the line they needed to follow, to follow any trail where your face wouldn't get slapped by branches, or where the ground wouldn't suck at your feet. But the easiest path never led to where you wanted to go. You had to bust through the thick parts, had to get your boots—

She was still talking. "—and you forget there are places where we don't matter."

He nodded.

"You weren't listening to me, were you?"

He glanced to his side. "Thinking about where I need to go."

"Sorry," she said, and he could see she was hurt, a little at least, from his lack of attention. A girl used to two guys comforting her.

He turned to the rest of the group trudging along behind them. They were ready for a break. He saw it in their sidelong glances at each other, but he wanted to get to blackwoods spring first. Or at least get to a spot where he knew he had missed it. If they hit the spring close enough to the place where it burbled out of the ground, they would be able to fill up their canteens without using the water filtration pumps. Saving minutes, saving hours. Maybe make Jaimie smile again.

"It's going to die anyway," she said, and now her tone was different, softer. "Isn't it?"

"Yes," he said. "Everything does."

She looked up sharply. "Is that supposed to make me feel better?"

Jake reached up and once more tightened the straps on his backpack. "I thought we were talking about the caribou."

An hour later he found the spring.

Chapter 2

The two men glanced at each other through the haze of cigarette smoke. It was dark, and they had just pulled into a driveway etched into the endless expanse of spruce and alders. At the end of the drive was a trailer house, flanked by a dozen cars. The girls, huddled in the middle of the Crown Vic's backseat, leaned forward to inspect themselves in the rearview mirror, one set of lips painted a deep crimson, the other a shiny black. Vanessa and Sharon, local girls, the kind who truly appreciated a free drink at the Caboose back in town. The kind who wanted to *pahhhty*.

Dragon girls, Byron thought. He turned back to the double-wide. *And yonder's their lair.*

The house was three miles north of Highbanks. In the Crown Vic's headlights they could see the siding streaked with rust below the window frames. The driveway was not much more than a wide spot in a weedy yard, lined with pickups and the same sort of long old cars they were in. It was Vanessa's car, but neither girl could drive tonight—the local constable had walked right into the Caboose, done a quick assessment, and told them as much. Byron and David had agreed to drive them home. Gentlemen of the first order, knights among men. It was their first night back in the village, and the girls had been in the bar when they'd walked in.

"Screw bear hunting," David had said after his sixth or seventh drink, watching the two girls dancing to an old Shania Twain song. "Tonight I'm hunting local."

"I hear they don't shave this far north," Byron replied, his eyes tracking the girls as they sashayed across the grimy wood floor, leaving little pieces of peanut shell and popcorn in their wake. They weren't bad looking.

"I been in the bush for seven days," David said. "I ain't scared of one more night. And that one on the left, she looks like she'd be . . . adventurous."

That was four hours ago, and the girls were drunker now, and he and David were plenty buzzed, too, but not so drunk as to miss what looked like a bloody tissue plastered against the windowpane set into the screen door, illuminated by a bare yellow porch light. Several fading yard toys were parked between the weeds, and from somewhere behind the house a dog was barking. They could hear the music through the vinyl siding, a steady thumping. David listened for a moment to see if the *woofs* followed the rhythm, maybe a woof every four beats, but they didn't.

"Pull up through them trucks," the girl with black lips said. "Weasel and Garny always leave an open spot for us."

"Weasel and Garny," David said. He took a sip from the Labatt's nestled between his legs. "Tell you what. Byron and I'll go borrow a truck from camp, drop your car off back here." They had been driven to the Caboose by their guide, Jimmy, who had promised to retrieve them at midnight.

"Oooh, Van, I think the city boys are scay-*ered*," Sharon said. "Way out in the country, who knows what'll happen?"

"You ain't driving off with my car," Vanessa said, checking her lipstick in the rearview mirror. She opened her lips, then rubbed at the smudge of black on her front tooth with the corner of her shirt. "Come on, have a drink, say hi. They're harmless."

David rolled the Crown Vic up through the parked vehicles, the headlights illuminating a mixture of Ontario, Manitoba, and First Nation license plates. There was indeed an open spot near the porch, and David pulled onto a patch of weedy gravel and killed the motor. The dome light came on as the girls got out.

David took the keys out, considered them for a moment, then tucked them in his pants pocket. "Don't give me that look," he said to Byron. "You didn't think it was going to be that easy, didja? Come home to an empty trailer house, you banging away in one end, me in the other?" He grinned. "See if we could get it to rock back and forth on the cinder blocks, like a teeter-totter? We might get a chance yet."

Byron scratched behind his ear. "I'm not that fired up about it anymore, tell you the truth."

David nodded. "You got that reluctant, *I'm-thinking-about-my-baby's-momma* look to you, all right. But we can't sit out here in the car."

They opened the screen door, and Byron saw that the bloody tissue was actually some sort of homemade flyer, advertising an upcoming powwow and a First Dance, whatever that was. There was a keg just inside the door, and next to it a plastic pitcher filled with an assortment of Canadian bills and loonies and toonies, one- and two-dollar coins. David threw in an American ten-dollar bill and plucked two red Solo cups off the stack. They stood to the side of the keg, sipping the beer and looking out over the small living room to their left, the kitchen to their right. Not quite wall-to-wall with people but close enough, the air thick with tobacco and marijuana smoke, the music thudding. It was too loud to talk, so they communicated by glances and expressions, same as they did on the job, knowing which parts of the day were going to be shitty, which apprentice wasn't going to cut it.

After a while, Vanessa appeared out of the crowd and latched onto David's arm. "There you are," she said, nudging the toe of his Danner hunting boots. "You better be able to dance in these shitkickers."

They moved off into a small cluster of people in the center of the living room, weaving to a song Byron remembered hearing at the construction site a few months ago. He studied the wall, looked at his phone. Another song came on and David and Vanessa stayed where they were, bumping into another couple. David said something to them, all of them laughing, Vanessa slapping David's chest and throwing her head back.

Byron drained the last of his beer and refilled his cup. When he turned around, there was a man wearing a camo shirt and a headband waiting in line, a cigarette dangling out of the corner of his mouth. He was in his mid-twenties, a few inches taller than Byron, and rangy. He had a tattoo on his left forearm, *Okit*-something, the rest of the word disappearing up under his sleeve.

He said, "You leave any for me?"

Byron stepped out of the way. When the man finished filling his cup, he motioned Byron toward the door. Byron glanced at David, then followed the man out onto the porch and into the yard. The only other people outside were a couple making out against the side of the trailer house, the girl with one leg wrapped over the guy's hip.

The man leaned against a truck. "You get your bear?"

Byron cocked his head. It wasn't the question he'd expected; then he realized there was probably only one reason an American in camo would be out here, at this trailer house, in these clothes. "I missed."

"With a rifle?" Eyebrow arched—*just how the fuck you miss a bear with a scoped rifle?*

"No, with my bow. Twenty yards, broadside. It came in right at dusk and my arrow hit a twig, or something I couldn't see. It ran off."

"Big?"

"Yeah." He took a drink. "I don't know, seemed big to me. Two-fifty, three hundred? Seeing it that close, I'm probably overestimating."

"You're good with a bow to hunt bear, you got good eyes. Probably know exactly how big it was."

"Well, it's still just as big," Byron motioned toward the darkness of the woods, "somewhere out there."

They both stared off into the woods, blackness broken only by the occasional flicker of a late-season firefly. The man turned back to Byron. "You hunted the same bait after that?"

Byron nodded. "Five more nights. Nothing but skeeters."

"You with that Davis bunch, then? Hunting up north of the Little Glutton River?"

"How'd you know that?"

The man smiled. "Jimmy Davis is the laziest guide around. He don't know how to set his baits up right for bowhunters, or don't care, I guess." He glanced up at the night sky, where faint aurora shafts danced. "There's so many bear around here, his guys sit there and shoot 'em off the pile like dogs coming in to their bowls. With rifles, you know? Archery hunters, they might get one chance, but Jimmy ain't got enough stations lined up to set you up with one that's got the right wind." He held out his pack of Marlboros. "I'm Billy."

"Byron." He took a cigarette. "You a guide?"

"Nah. I don't like bear; too greasy. Most of the time guys who come up to hunt 'em are greasy, too."

"Yeah, well, there's some doozies at camp. There's one guy, from Texas I think, he—"

"You come here with them Fineday girls?"

Byron nodded, suddenly cautious. The guy couldn't have been more than twenty-five, and his northwoods accent and relaxed manner had lulled Byron into bullshitting mode. And this guy, Billy, he was still relaxed, leaning against the rusty quarter panel of the Ford F-150, his cigarette held lightly between his index and middle fingers. Relaxed, but getting to the point.

"Sharon and Vanessa?" Byron said. "Yeah, we ran into them down at the bar. The Caboose?"

"You ran into them? So you already know them, eh?"

"Met them, I mean. If they're with you—"

Billy held up a hand. "Hey man, I don't care. They're kinda wild, you know? Always cadging drinks, and when there's new guys in town they like to party. We don't get much of a chance to get out of Highbanks. Everyone knows their game, it's usually not a big deal. Just, you know. Be nice to them."

"They're not your sisters or something, are they?"

Billy laughed. "No, I'm a Martineau. You ready for another beer?"

As they went back into the house, Byron reached forward and tapped Billy on the shoulder. Billy turned. "What do you mean, it's usually not a big deal?"

Billy shook his head, still smiling. "Man, you better have a shot with that beer—relax a little. You're on vacation, ain't you?"

It was after three in the morning, and the party had changed, the pace becoming frenetic and then slowing, picking up again and now almost dead. The people had changed, too, some leaving, others slipping off to one of the small bedrooms down the hall, several more passing out on the stained carpet or the shiny vinyl couch. A few others had come in, more sober than the rest of the party, four serious-looking guys, each one holding bottles of Budweiser. It was the only American beer Byron had seen in this land of Labatts and Molsons.

Byron stared blearily at his cards. They were playing a game called smiley, and the lowest hand won the pot, which was now just under twenty dollars, Canadian. He had a pretty good hand, but he couldn't remember what the other guys had in their hands, even though they'd shown each other after the last round of betting, per the rules. He couldn't remember what was in the dummy hand, either—*stinky*, they called it—and when he closed his eyes for a moment, he couldn't remember what he was holding in his own hand.

"Eh, lookit Sleepy over dere," someone—maybe Weasel?—said. The accents got thicker as the night went on, and Byron himself seemed to have lost control of his mouth. Not what he said, just how he said it. A grin and a slur. "C'mon, Sleepy, your turn."

"In and good," he said, slapping his cards down. *Inanngoo*. If he won he would take the pot; if he lost he would pay the pot. Someone handed him the bottle of cinnamon whiskey. He held it up to the kitchen light, sloshed it back and forth, took a drink. He wondered if they were trying to get him drunk so they could take his money, but he didn't think so. They'd already taken plenty of his money earlier in the game; if anything, he was getting better at this smiley game the drunker he got.

"In and good," Weasel chirped. He was small and thin, so white as to be albino-ish, except for his dark eyes. "Doesn't even look at his cards and he's in and good! Moose nuts on this one."

"Mooose nuts," Billy said, drinking down the last of the cinnamon whiskey. "I'll take a card."

Byron blinked several times. They were looking at him, heads cocked. For a moment he wondered what he'd done wrong, and then they started laughing and he realized he'd fallen asleep.

"Turn your cards over, Sleepynuts," Weasel said. Byron flipped them over, saw with relief he had lost to Billy—he couldn't quit after winning the biggest pot of the night, but he could quit honorably after losing—and dropped a twenty on the pile. One way or another, he was going to find a ride back to town; let David figure out his own logistics. He was pushing himself up to a standing position when someone screamed from the back bedroom.

The door flew open and a bottle careened through it a second later, shattering against the thin wallboard and knocking a framed picture to the carpet. David stumbled backward out of the bedroom in his underwear, arms covering his head. A glass ashtray shot out of the doorway next, striking him in the forearm. He swore and stumbled away, this time avoiding a throw pillow.

"Piece of shit perverted motherfuck!"

Vanessa charged out of the room in her bra and panties, eyes wide open with fury, and swung a roundhouse punch that connected with David's ear. He tripped over the pillow, one hand slipping along the wall as he tried to keep from falling. Vanessa swung again, reaching way back, and hit him high on the head. One breast had fallen out of her bra with the last punch, and Byron could see there were red welts on her chest. Not scratch marks—more like hickeys, or burn marks.

David uncovered his head and looked up. "Hey, listen—"

Her left fist caught him in the mouth. As Vanessa reared back for another punch, David reached out, his hand flat against her sternum, and shoved. She flew backward, her feet skimming across the short pile carpet, her shoulders smacking into the wall. Her head snapped back after her shoulders hit, and she fell to the ground, a dish-sized indentation in the wallboard. Then the trailer house was silent.

Shit, Byron thought, and burped up foul-tasting cinnamon breath.

David started to get up, saw men staring at him, and went to a knee next to Vanessa instead. "Hey, come on, I'm sorry," he said, touching Vanessa's shoulder. "Wake up."

Vanessa's hand waved feebly at him, pushing him away. Sharon emerged from the other bedroom, saw Vanessa on the floor, and immediately advanced on David, who reared backward, avoiding her nails by a fraction of an inch. Sharon paused, shooting David a murderous glance before dropping to the ground next to her friend. She started slapping Vanessa's cheeks, first one side and then the other. "C'mon, honey," she said. "You're all right."

Byron noted that her slaps were keeping time with the beat of the music. *Finally got some harmony*, he thought. *Man, I wish I wasn't so drunk.*

Sharon looked up. "Get me some water, you limpdicks."

Someone pushed past Byron and filled a glass with cloudy water. Sharon dumped it over Vanessa's face, and she spluttered and pushed herself up on her elbows. Sharon reached over and tucked Vanessa's left breast back into her bra. From behind Byron, the screen door hissed as someone quietly left the house.

"Wha'tha fuck?" Vanessa said, one hand creeping around to touch the back of her head. Her palm came away sticky with blood.

"You okay, hon?"

Vanessa blinked twice, her eyes coming into focus. "Yeah, shit. I'm okay."

David disappeared into the bedroom, and Byron could

hear him rummaging for his clothes. The trailer house was still very quiet, and to Byron it felt like the air had been replaced, simultaneously charged and stale. The room was like an animal's den, one he had stumbled into and one in which the denizens were just now becoming aware of his presence. Well, not *his* presence, not yet. Nobody was looking at him. They were waiting for David to reemerge from the bedroom. But there were two strange animals here, two things that were not like the others, as the song went.

One of the men got up from the couch, his shoulders sloped into powerful arms. He held a bottle of Budweiser by the longneck between his thumb and forefinger and swung it back and forth like a metronome, his eyes assessing the room. He was wearing fatigue pants with a wide utility belt, a knife strapped to one side and a phone on the other. He turned to look at the table, and Byron could see where the man's nose had been broken, probably more than once, the line of cartilage zigging first to the left and then the right. There was a semicircular scar going through and above his right eyebrow, the scar tissue still pink.

"Billy?" the man said.

"Yeah, Darius."

"How long it take you to put on *your* pants?"

"What do you mean—oh shit."

Billy crashed through a couple men and threw the screen door open, while another man ran to the bedroom. The others were moving too, Weasel and Garney following Billy, the remaining men moving away from the kitchen table and toward Darius. Byron stood where he was, wishing David hadn't run, wishing there was a way they could take their beating and be done with it. That he would be exempted never crossed his mind.

"Fuck!" someone shouted from inside the bedroom. "Window's open!"

Darius waved his beer bottle at the rest of them. "Go on, help Billy-dog. He runs fast, but he ain't a fighter."

"Which way?"

"Use your goddamn ears," Darius said. For the first time there was annoyance in the clipped voice: *Youse your gott-dam ears.* "Go!"

The men streamed down the porch steps and onto the weedy drive. There they paused, silent as attentive hounds, and from farther down the road came the sound of a man's grunt. They raced down the driveway, the dark knot of men spreading out and disappearing from the rectangle of view afforded by the screen door.

Darius looked at the open door and back to Byron. He inclined his head slightly and cocked an eyebrow. Byron sat down.

Darius crossed over to the two women and conferred with them in a soft, almost paternal voice, kneeling next to Vanessa and taking her hug when she offered it. He stood and watched as the two girls went into the back bedroom, the lock clicking behind them, then walked over and sat opposite Byron.

They said nothing for a minute. Byron found he wasn't scared, just disgusted that David's little fetish— he'd heard rumors about his partner's sexual bent through friends of his girlfriend, had caught some hints about it from David's offhand remarks from time to time—had come out at this inopportune time. He didn't know exactly what his fetish was—not exactly—but he'd also heard David didn't always try to ease his partners into the concept. He'd chalked it up to different strokes for different folks, figured it was none of his business.

"He your brother?" Darius said after a bit.

Byron shrugged. "Sure."

"Like blood brother, I mean."

Byron considered the question. "Tonight he is."

"Yeah, okay." Darius leaned back in his chair and looked at the yellowing ceiling, flecked with flyshit and laced with darker brown from leaks in the roof. "Hunters."

"Hunters."

"You didn't come up here to check out the land, maybe buy a piece of property?"

"What?"

"You know," Darius said. "Maybe invest in some property, see if it gets more valuable over time? Cree land, the stuff we own outright, ends not far from here. There's plenty interest in Crown land lately, maybe you and your brother are like that. Hunt a little, prospect a little? There's money in the ground, is what we hear. Something special."

"I don't know what you're talking about."

"Yeah, maybe not." He leaned forward on the table and smiled, his eyes lighting up. "Hey, why you want to come up here, shoot one of our bears? You don't got no bears where you're from?"

"Not very many. What are you going to do with David?"

"That his name? David?" He leaned back in his chair. "Man, these bears up here, I feel bad for 'em. Dig around all summer for bugs and worms, maybe a few blueberries, always hungry and the food tastes mostly like shit, 'cept for the berries, and it's goddamn hard to get full from berries. Then one day he smells something and be like, what the *fuck*? Someone left some goddamn *doughnuts* out in the woods? And what's this—oatmeal and honey?" He laughed. "Holy shit, what's the catch?"

Byron could hear the men outside, yelling encouragements at each other somewhere down near the end of the driveway. Another grunt, then a strangled call for something—help, mercy, maybe God's intervention; Byron didn't know. He closed his eyes, then flinched back when Darius flicked his earlobe.

"Sleepynuts," Darius said. "Come on, you gotta stick with me. So these bears, man, they finally, *finally,* find something good, right? You know how it feels, a long day in the woods and you got a hollow belly, all shrunk up, even your mind a little messed up 'cause there's not enough sugar in your blood? Bear be like that for four, five months and then all of a sudden, one day, boom! Manna from heaven."

A burning trickle of acid was working its way up Byron's throat. He fought to swallow it back down.

Darius took a swig from his bottle of beer. "They go on like that, up to the minute somebody blasts them. Okay, fine—there's worse ways to go, right? But bears are smart, man, they *know* there's a catch, they know it from day one. Maybe he ain't a brother to man, but a bear's different from a moose, different from lots of things. Smart and mean and sometimes silly. Even grown bears get silly."

They were coming up the driveway now. He could

hear feet dragging in the gravel, the panting of the men, one of them breathing wet and gurgley, like he was trying to hold in a mouthful of fluid.

Darius leaned forward. "See, that's the part that's hard to think on. It ain't that they get baited like a dog and then shot like a dog. The bears *know*, they *know* that there's a catch, but they keep coming back. They eat the little bit that's given to them and they know it's gotta end bad, but they still play the game. Can't help themselves, you understand?"

The men dragged David inside and propped him against the wall next to the keg. Byron looked at his friend. One of David's eyes was swollen shut, and his left earlobe was ripped and hanging from the side of his head. Blood streamed from his ear onto the collar of his shirt. His hands were pressed over his groin, and there were boot prints etched into the fabric over his ribs. David had made his own marks: Billy had a swollen cheekbone, and one of the others had a bloody lip. They were all looking at Darius, and Byron had a sense that if Darius had given a nod, the men would have fallen on both of them like a pack of wolves.

"And then," Darius said, "one late summer night, some asshole with a thousand-dollar rifle knocks the doughnut outta his mouth mid-bite. And the bear knew it was coming, and when he dies, he's embarrassed. That's the sad part, friend. The part that makes me sad."

David mumbled something.

"What's that?" Darius said.

"He says they're bowhunters," Billy said.

Darius raised his eyebrow, and the pink scar stretched

like a small mouth making a grimace. "Not tonight they're not."

Now they were in the backseat of Vanessa's Crown Vic again, he and David sandwiched in the middle of the back seat, the spruce and aspen rolling slowly past them in the spray of headlights. Weasel was on one side of them, Billy on the other, with Garney driving. Darius was in the front passenger seat, silent except for the occasional *left* or *right*. They had left the main road fifteen minutes earlier—if you could call a rutted two-track with a few sprinkles of class 5 gravel the main road—and the Vic was screeching and scraping its way over the rocky forest trail.

"I'm gonna be sick," Byron said.

"Don't puke in here," Garney said. He was thickset and nearly bald, and Byron could see a patchwork of scars across the folds of skin at the base of his neck. "They puke in here and Vanessa's gonna be pissed."

"I can't hold it," Byron said. He could feel the bile building up in his throat again, the slow rolling of his stomach.

"Stop," Darius said. "We're close enough."

Billy pushed the car door open and Byron stumbled after him, going to all fours on the rocky ground and arching his back, the hot churn boiling out and out and out. He crawled to the edge of the road and vomited again, his entire body convulsing, the smell of beer and cinnamon and inhaled smoke rolling out of him. He heaved until the convulsions stopped and he was spitting out bile. When he looked up he saw they had David pushed up against a tree on the other side of the road, his arms tied behind the trunk. He looked sick and weak, smaller than Byron had ever seen him.

Darius said something, and Billy and Garney walked over to Byron, crossing through the headlights and casting long-legged shadows on the road behind them. They pushed him against a poplar tree, seized his wrists, and yanked them behind his back. Something hard and thin was wound around his wrists and cinched cruelly tight. A second later Billy passed a loop of wire over his ankles and repeated the process. Then Billy wound a length of wire around Byron's forehead, cinching it so his face was pointed directly at David. The wire cut into his brow, and a line of blood trickled down his nose and fell to the ground with a steady pattering. More blood soaked into his eyebrows, which Billy wiped away with the pads of his thumbs.

"Good," Darius said. "Make sure he can see."

There was a knife in his hand, Byron saw, a hunting knife with a five-inch stainless steel blade and a molded plastic handle. A practical knife, nothing showy. And in that instant everything Byron had told himself over the past hour, every assurance that the Budweiser men weren't going to really hurt them, fled.

"Back the car up a few feet," Darius said. "Light 'em up."

"It's good where it is," Billy said. "They can see."

Darius stared at him for a second, his expression flat, then walked over to David and pushed the knife into his right side, almost casually, sticking the blade in up to the hilt and then pulling it back out. David inhaled sharply, his eyes bugging out at the monstrous and sudden pain come alive inside him, and began to scream. His screams went on for a long time, eventually turning into a rapid mewling. The bottom of his shirt was drenched with blood, soaking into his jeans.

Darius handed the knife to Weasel.

The small man stalked around David, then poked the knife into David's belly on the other side. This time David's scream was higher, raspy, and went on for even longer. Byron closed his eyes and Billy slapped him. When he looked up again, Weasel was grinning at Darius and pantomiming a twisting motion with his hand and wrist, showing him the technique. Now Garney held the knife and he was prodding David with it, saying something Byron couldn't hear. For a minute David's pain-crazed eyes settled on Byron, and somewhere inside his blood-streaked face came that curious tilted expression, the look they had given each other for years, the look that made Byron love the man through all his faults. *We doing things right?*

No, Byron thought. *We sure didn't do things right on this one.*

Then Garney stepped between them, and the night air filled with more screaming.

This time Byron didn't open his eyes when Billy hit him. He kept them closed for a long time, but when he opened them he had to look, his eyes wouldn't *not* look, and David was pressed against the tree like a bloody scarecrow held captive, his eyes glazed and staring off into the night forest. Denied even the ability to slump his head.

Then Darius was poking Byron in the belly with the point of the knife, not hard enough to draw blood but painful, like a hornet stinging him again and again. He was talking, and Byron knew he had to listen.

"Yeah, there you go," Darius said. "You not feeling too good about your friend?"

Byron mumbled a reply.

"No," Darius said, and his voice was sad. "We aren't the fuckers, By-*ron*. You and your buddy are the fuckers. You think I don't know?" He stepped closer, his features largely lost in the shadows, the lights from the car backlighting his head. "I see the truth." Behind him, Byron saw three heads bob up and down in agreement.

"You want to know the truth?" Darius said. "You *knew*, like the bear knows. Knew there was something wrong with him." The pressure from the tip of the knife eased. "Knew it for years."

Byron's eyes opened wider, and Darius smiled, his stained teeth yellow in the headlights. "I see far and I see deep, By-*ron*. All of you guys want to come up here, sample what we have. Shoot our bear, mess with the women, okay? Take what's in the woods, in the ground. Okay. But you don't got no respect; I see that too. This land just something you visit, the people just jackpine savages, eh? It's only interesting 'cause you wanna take something from it."

The knife pressure was back, just below his belly button, light but constant pressure. "Tell me it's true."

Byron wondered where his inner steel was, why it didn't rise up, tell this guy to kiss his ass. There was nothing inside of him except for terror and a deep, inconsolable sadness.

"Fine," he said. "It's true."

Darius's eyes squinted shut. "Oh man, that's the wrong answer. You shoulda said it *was* true, that now you learned better. You can't learn, can you? Like a goddamn puppy so retarded it pisses in its bowl, then drinks it." Behind them, one of the men giggled. It sounded like Weasel, the man who an hour earlier had given Byron a nickname, had passed him a bottle of whiskey to share. Darius motioned behind him, jabbing at the night air with his knife. "Your friend's dead, Byron."

"I know."

"You gonna die, too, Byron."

Spit in his face. Come up with something to say. Try to get his face a little closer, then bite off his nose. These thoughts came and went, and in the end he simply said, "I don't want to."

Then the knife pressure was back, scalding his belly. "Man," Darius said, "I wish *I don't want to* meant something in this world."

By the time Byron's screams had faded and they had finished the rest of the beer, the eastern horizon had turned gray. They took turns standing or sitting on the trunk, occasionally looking at the two bodies wired to the trees. Weasel wanted to take pictures with his phone, but Darius wouldn't let him, not because he was worried about evidence, but because he felt a picture wouldn't be as powerful an image as the memory of this sight that they would keep in their heads. When the sun had nearly broken the horizon Darius deemed it light enough to work, and they cut the wires and lowered the bodies to the ground. Garney looped short sections of rope around the bodies' ankles, leaving ten feet of slack and then tying the other end to a stout dead limb Billy salvaged from a blowdown. Then, with one man on each side of the limb, they began to drag.

They stopped several hundred yards from the car, where the flinty ground dipped into a spruce bog. The trees were mostly dead, but the ground was a deep and vibrant green, covered with a thick layer of moss and Labrador tea. Weasel and Garney cut through the moss with a spade from the trunk of the car, severing the green carpet and the thin roots underneath, carving out large sections to expose the dark and acidic soil underneath. The openings immediately filled with brown water. Darius and Billy dragged the bodies into the carved-out graves and heaped the moss over them, the resulting bulges no different in appearance than the hundred other moss-covered hummocks in sight.

"Man," Garney said when they were done, wiping sweat from his brow. "All this work—shit, and for what?"

"Because," Darius said, resting a hand on his shoulder and gesturing around them with his other hand. "They're coming, Garney. Like we always knew they would. Coming for what we have." He paused, surveying his bloody hands, then dropped to his knees and scraped up a bit of the dark loam. He rubbed the dirt in to his stained hands, rolling it back and forth, then let it drop back down to the pine needles. "They might take it," he said. "I know that. But when they do, they'll pay full price."

Garney looked at him. He nodded, slowly at first and then with more emphasis, and Weasel and then Billy followed suit, the three of them nodding at Darius as the sun broke over the horizon, their long shadows stretching out to the west, to the swamp where the acidic waters had already begun the long, slow decomposition of the two corpses.

Chapter 3

They stood on the ridge above the valley, gathered in a semicircle. It was noon and they were soaked with sweat, their shirts darkened all the way through. Jake could remember only a few days warmer in his time in this area, and none this late in the summer. *That has to be the reason,* he thought. *This much warmth, this much moisture, things are going to happen that normally don't.*

Before them, in a broken circle of brush, a fuzzy mass pushed up from the ground. Cameron Fairchild squatted next to it, head cocked, his lanky frame less than two feet from the mold-covered mass. It had structure under the growth, perhaps something that had once been alive. Hard to say what that might be except . . . except it wasn't alive anymore. The material covering it was thick, a sickly whitish-gray color, like congealed wax or animal fat. Cameron reached out and then pulled his hand back, wiping his fingers on his pants even though he hadn't actually touched it.

"Rachel?" Warren said. "Is it from the . . . ?"

"The reaction?" she said. "I don't think so."

She stepped forward, plucking a branch out of the pine needles and prodding the mass with the stick. It dimpled under the pressure, and when she pushed harder the end of the stick broke through. She levered the stick upward, trying to break off a piece of the moldy exterior, and the wood snapped. She leaned in closer, using the butt end of the stick, and pushed harder. The material parted around the stick, but did not break off.

"There's something in there," she said. "Looks like fabric of some kind." She poked again. "The biological material grew around it, so it's some kind of saprobe."

Warren tapped her on the shoulder. "Plain English."

"Just a mold," she said. "Typically these kind are black in color, and we call them sooty molds. They form a carpet over the material, like this one did, and break it down for the nutrients. But this is white, like a *Penicillium* genus, which are dry molds. This is a wet one. Gelatinous." She dropped the stick and stood. "It's nothing. Nature's Jell-O."

"You said there was fabric inside it?" Cameron asked.

"Hard to tell," she said, then suddenly became aware everyone was looking at her, waiting for more. She blushed. "Relax, guys. Something died here, and this fungus is breaking it down. Happens all the time."

"But there's fabric inside," Jaimie said. "That means—"

"Nothing," Jake said. He could feel the tension ratcheting up, and he wondered if it was because they were out here, finally, at their destination and hadn't found the gear, or if it was due to some other reason. He did know that they were on edge as a group, and a panic could start as easily as a brush fire in an old pine forest—and would be just as hard to put out. "It's a gutpile," he said. "Somebody put on gloves to keep their hands clean, then threw them on top when they were done."

"You've seen this before?" Jaimie asked, eyebrows furrowed.

"All the time," Jake lied. "I'm going to go look up top again."

Jake left the small copse of alder and walked to the top of the ridge. The X on Warren's laminated map led to an open patch of rocky ground. There was nothing there but stray lichens and long inch-deep furrows where glaciers had scraped over the rock surface millennia ago. They had been searching in concentric circles since the previous evening, combing the brush along the ridgeline. From what Jake understood, the equipment should have been easy to spot: a diesel-powered Geocore pneumatic drilling rig, ten six-gallon fuel containers filled with stabilized diesel, a bundle of ten-foot-long core tubes, and seven diamond-tipped drill bits encased in plastic sheaths; $2.3 million of equipment, according to Warren. And Jake's own worth, according to Warren, was less than two shits if he couldn't find something that big in this little patch of godforsaken wilderness.

Jake looked around the woods, a mixed stand of mature hardwoods and pine with narrow stands of alder and poplars running down the drainages. Open country, at least for this area of the bush. Warren was right. He should have been able to find the rig within an hour.

"Someone took it," Warren said. He had joined Jake

on the ridgeline and stood looking at the woods and brush with an expression of barely controlled fury.

"Who?" Jake said. "Why?"

Warren turned to look at him, his face smoothing out, becoming unreadable. "Who knows?" He looked down at his rolled-up cuffs, frowned, and rolled them back down to cover up his wrists, taking time to button each cuff before turning back to Jake. "The world is full of people who don't like explorations of any kind."

"Maybe," Jake said. "Who was the pilot, again?"

"The pilot?"

"The one who took a round through his hand."

Warren studied Jake for a moment, impassive. "Who told you that?"

Jake turned away, moving to a slightly higher point to survey the valley. Far below them, the slow, tannin-stained water reflected the granite outcroppings on the far side of the river. The ground leading up to the river was fairly open, pockets of wetlands mixed with granite outcroppings. The only tall vegetation was along the fringes of the river, a dense stand of sedge grass and cattails.

"I hired him out of Vancouver," Warren said from behind him. "He has a reputation for discreet work." He paused. "And it was a piece of shrapnel, not a bullet."

Jake turned. "How shaken up was he? After he took fire, I mean?"

"Plenty," Warren said. He was watching Jake closely. "What is it?"

"Let me see one of your maps."

Warren shrugged his backpack off his shoulder, rifled through several scrolls of laminated paper, and selected one. He unrolled the map, revealing a multicolored contour map. Warren placed a finger—no dirt under the fingernails, Jake noted, the cuticles neatly trimmed—on a location that Jake understood to be the spot where they were standing. The landscape around them was shown in a series of lines, evenly spaced to the south, then changing direction in the area around Resurrection Valley, switching direction to run north and south, then breaking off the linear lines into strange swirls. To Jake it looked like someone had stuck a giant spoon in the earth and done some mixing.

Warren saw him squint. "It shows geomagnetic signatures," he said. "Not topography. Lots of people think the underlying rocks follow the same pattern as what we see up here. Not necessarily so."

"We're here?"

"Yes." Warren removed a pen from his backpack and carefully placed an X on the map. "You want the flight path, don't you?" Without waiting for an answer he drew a dashed line to the southeast. Jake and Warren turned in unison to the direction that the helicopter had taken into—and presumably out of—the coordinates they had been given. Jake oriented himself along the line, then looked up. The vector Warren had drawn on the map led to a dense tangle of brush, then more woods. Beyond that was a small, flat-topped hill, perhaps a quarter mile away. It was rocky and barren, with only a few wispy cedars clinging to the edges

"You thinking what I'm thinking?" Warren said.

"He wasn't shot at on the way out," Jake murmured. "He took fire on the way here."

Warren nodded, excited, but for a moment Jake had seen something flash through his eyes. A recalculation, perhaps—Jake not quite the simple-minded country Indian Warren thought he had hired. "You military?" he asked. "Putting that government training to good use?"

Jake looked back at him. "What reaction were you talking about, earlier?"

Warren cocked his head, smiled, then shouted out for the group to stay where they were. Jake was already moving, and Warren followed him. They found a game trail and wove through the brush, not talking, Jake caught up in the same excitement as Warren: the pure pleasure of seeing the mystery, any mystery, dissolve before your own reasoning.

Yeah, yeah, Jake thought, as they climbed the hill. *We get on top, there'll be nothing but some lichen-covered rocks and a strong breeze.*

He heard the flapping before he crested the hill, and quickened his pace until he and Warren were nearly running up the incline. Jake pulled himself up the last ten feet and stood on top of the rock outcropping, panting and happy. The ground in front of him was about a thousand square feet of basalt rock, with a large, tarped bundle smack dab in the middle. The bundle had been covered in a heavy-gauge camouflage tarp, but one of the stones used to weigh it down had rolled off, and the corner of the tarp was snapping in the stiff southwesterly breeze. He turned and held out a hand for Warren, pulling him over the last lip of rock.

Warren took a moment to get his breath, then walked over to the bundle. He stood for a while, as if afraid to look underneath, and then peeled back the rest of the tarp. The rocks slid off the other corners, and Warren let the breeze carry the tarp across the rock face until it wrapped around a cedar tree. He ran a hand lightly over the equipment, spending more time on the cans of diesel fuel than anything else, tipping them up to check the seals. Gradually, his shoulders relaxed, and he turned to Jake.

"That short-dropping son of a bitch," he said. "How'd you figure it out?"

Jake shrugged. The pilot had done what any smart man might do after taking fire. Stop a little ways off from the preset delivery location—four, five hundred yards. Not an impossible shot if there were other guys waiting, but most guys up here typically carried brush guns designed to hit their targets at under a hundred yards. Maybe the pilot knew that. He sure as hell knew he wouldn't get paid if he returned with the equipment still in the cargo bay, so he dropped the equipment close enough to call it an honest mistake, and walked away.

Behind them, the tarp flapped in the wind.

"You play it close to the vest, huh?" Warren said.

"Just glad we found it, Boss."

"There'll be a bonus for this, you know. And you don't have to play Tonto."

Jake walked over to the tarp and pulled it loose from the tree. He shook it out, letting it unfold in the breeze. Warren joined him, and they worked together to fold the tarp into a square bundle. It was an oddly intimate exercise, coming together to join the ends, flipping it over, and then coming together again. Jake noticed that Warren's eyes never left him while they were folding and refolding, studying Jake with the same type of expression he'd had when inspecting the equipment and the fuel tanks. Making sure that the tools he had purchased were in the expected condition.

Jake almost laughed at the thought, because that's what he was, a tool. No matter what he did with the money—and it was more money than he could make in five years up here, guiding or trapping—that fact would remain. He was a tool, and his master was right here, wielding him as he saw fit. Perhaps it was not such a big deal.

"Something funny?" Warren asked.

"Yeah," Jake said. "A saying from moose camp."

"What's that?"

Jake motioned at the equipment, then at the valley below them. They could see the rest of the group through the treetops, watching them. Jaimie's tall, broad-shouldered form stood out in front, her short dark hair contrasting with her pale skin. He studied the route back down to them, the steep slope followed by the thick brush, a route that was difficult enough without carrying long core tubes, drill bits, or, god forbid, a small diesel engine. "He who finds the moose gets the lightest load home."

"That's a good one," Warren said. "Too bad this isn't moose camp."

He woke in the predawn gray of the following morning and knew immediately what kind of day it was going to be. He could feel the pain forming in his body like a thunderstorm, throbbing but not yet fully awake. Stirring, pacing, winding around his elbows and knees and shoulders, around the sockets of hips, deep in his core. It was not the ache of sore muscles, although there was plenty of that as well. This was the other, the sporadic and malicious visitor, the one that came and went . . . and sometimes came and stayed. It was in his chest, too, wrapping around his ribs and spine, and causing his heart to hammer. He could almost taste it, a bitter presence running through blood and lymph.

He had brought himself to this point, pushing his body too far and too fast. Moderate exercise was okay—was good—but exhaustion could trigger an episode. And he was exhausted, exhausted from hauling the heavy equipment down all day long and into the twilight hours, exhausted from the pace and the load on the trip in, and more than a little worn out from biting his tongue in the presence of strangers. Add in lying on the cold, hard ground for three nights—he had not made a browse bed from balsam branches as he normally would, because they had not camped in areas where there were enough balsam boughs for everyone—and waking up to this state of the body was not unexpected.

He reached out, stifling a groan, and felt inside his canvas Duluth Pack. From a side compartment he withdrew three pill bottles, shaking out two capsules from the largest and singles from the others. He dry-swallowed the pills, feeling them make their slow way down his esophagus. There was a thermos of water a few feet away, but it may as well have been a hundred miles. He worked his throat, forcing the pills down. He knew it was silly to swallow the prescription pills before the others, the ones he bought from a friend of a friend. Eventually he would abandon this self-imposed policy, as he had so many others, but for now it held. Prescriptions first, then the others; the ones that actually did something.

He waited. His temples were throbbing, and it took

some time for him to realize that there was another noise to the morning; the low rumble of the Geocore's diesel engine. It ran for a moment, then stopped. Nobody tried to restart it. A test run. That was good. The first drilling location was only a few hundred yards down, in the valley, where the steep sides mellowed out into the floodplain along the river. The rest of the crew would be able to move the drill cores down there, along with the remaining gear, by themselves. Perhaps the other pill could wait.

It was the only real self-delusion he allowed himself, that the other pill, or pills, could wait. It was part of his policy too, he supposed—not only waiting for them to be the last ones he took, but pretending they might not even be needed.

Five long minutes later he reached out again, this time unzipping a separate side compartment. Inside was a small generic aspirin bottle with the cap's plastic safety mechanism long since carved away. He untwisted it and laid there with his eyes closed, and tried to remove any emotion from his self-assessment. Was it a three-pill day? No; three-pill days were the kind that made carving away the safety latch on the pill bottle a necessity, and he had opened the container easily enough.

He shook out two small white tablets and opened his eyes, gazing at them blearily. He put them in his mouth and swallowed, and closed his eyes.

Two minutes later he was sleeping.

He woke to the sound of the drill rig's engine again, coupled with a sound like sandpaper rubbing against a hard-grained wood. He straightened one leg, then the other. Pain flared and subsided. He did the same with his arms, then craned his neck from one side to the other. It was okay. Not good, but this far away from home and a warm bed, okay was perfectly acceptable. He managed to get partially up, knee-walked over to the thermos, and twisted the cap free. The lukewarm water was flat and tasted of pine needles, and he drank until the water poured down the sides of his face and soaked his collar.

He took his time getting his boots on. His job was largely over for now and there was no hurry, no need to embarrass himself by stumbling from the tent or leaning against trees. He took another drink of water. His head was fuzzy, and he felt fairly serene. Neither of the conditions were his natural state, and it was his best indication that the pills, the second set, had fully kicked in. He did not like the false sense of well-being, at least not much, but there would be a time for pain and clarity. It would come for him within twenty-four hours. For now, the boots.

He stepped from the tent and squinted into the late summer sun. Below him, the diesel engine purred. It was a strange contraption, several hundred pounds of anchoring legs and infrastructure, the engine itself another four hundred pounds, squatting over the river floodplain like a mechanical spider. They had delivered a tripod and winch with the rest of the gear, as well as an industrial-strength dolly fitted with wide, all-terrain tires. Without the winch and dolly there would have been no way to move or position the equipment. Warren had thought of everything, and the team seemed to know their exact roles and responsibilities. With the exception of Warren and a crew member named Andy

Parkson, they were all younger than thirty, probably chosen for their physical stamina as much as for their technical skills.

He stood blinking outside the tent, watching the core tube slowly rotating below him, the technicians hovering nearby to monitor the gauges. Warren had said they would gather samples for two or three days, max. From what Jake could glean from the group's conversations, the stratum they wanted to pull samples from was close to the surface.

Jake made his way down to the valley floor, the ground squelching under his boots as he descended, hopping from one island of rock to the other when he could, trying to avoid the worst of the boggy ground.

What the hell were they after?

He paused a short distance back to watch the two technicians work. Dyson Greer was the lead technician; tall, with a shaggy beard and knobby shoulders, he talked in a slow, easy tone that reminded Jake of a cross between a stoner and a Buddhist monk. Andy Parkson was the auxiliary tech, a thin and quiet man in his thirties who dry-shaved every morning and quietly pitched in to help with whatever task needed doing. They were both wearing mud-splashed hip boots, methodically drilling anchors for the rig's legs, using a combination of the tripod, dolly, and brute strength to position the Geocore rotary rig.

They continued drilling down into the rock, a slurry of dark loam and rock chips building up at the base of the core tube. Parkson stopped the drill rig about four feet down and then pulled a lever to retract the drill bit. Once it was free of the hole, Greer swung the rig away, and Parkson threaded an anchor rod into the hole. Jake knew the rods well; he had carried four of them, each close to eighty pounds, down the hill yesterday afternoon on separate trips. Each one was fitted with an expansion tip, and now Parkson used a small sledgehammer to slam the upper end, causing the embedded tip to balloon and anchor into the rock. The hollow clangs echoed back to them from the other side of the valley.

Jake's gaze drifted across the slow-moving boggy river fifty yards away, flanked with sedge grass, to the rock bluff that framed the north end of Resurrection Valley. The bluff was nearly vertical, except for a narrow hogback ridge that cut diagonally down across the face. A few wispy cedars clung to the lichen-encrusted rock. The valley bottom was pockmarked with strips of wetlands, low boggy stretches between the rocks. Pocket wetlands, Rachel had called them. The swampy ground grew even wetter next to the river, which lacked a defined shore. Instead, the land seemed to dissolve into water, a blurry transition between terra firma and the river.

"Strange place." Rachel had come up behind him while he surveyed the valley, partially lost in the painkiller's pleasant haze. She was dressed in light nylon pants and a microfiber shirt, and held an iPad in a leather case in one hand. "You can tell there's something interesting underground."

"Mmm," Jake said. "I thought iPads were a no-no."

"It doesn't have a 3G connection," she said. "And the GPS has been disabled. Warren cleared me to use it."

"Good for you," Jake said.

They watched as Parkson and Greer drilled another anchoring hole into the rock. The Geocore rig's diesel engine rpms climbed mildly as the bit chewed through the stone. A cloud of gray dust rose up from the ground, clinging to the mud on their hip boots.

"Good thing there's some bigger rocks," Rachel said, tapping her foot against the rock they were standing on. "Not the bedrock they'd like, but at least they can anchor to it. The rig can float on the ground if it has to, but it's so wet down here that Warren thought they might bend a core tube or something."

"He doesn't take too many chances, does he?"

She huffed air out through her nose. It reminded Jake of the way a whitetail doe would puff when she was angry. Probably something he shouldn't say to her, although the reason for that escaped him at the moment. He smiled, mildly amused at his attempt to identify his political incorrectness. Yup, it was certainly a two-pill day, and he was just floating along, talking with a pretty, spoiled girl about geotech exploration in a valley his father had once called the single most uninviting place he'd ever visited. Resurrection Valley, or simply *the bad country.*

"What?" she said, seeing his smile.

Jake shook his head.

"Are you ready to go, then?"

"Go where?"

"I have to gather some data," she said. "Remember? Warren said you'd come with me."

"What kind of data?"

"Well, I'm an ecologist, so . . . ?"

He looked at her blankly.

She sighed. "Plant and animal survey, see if there's anything endangered or threatened. First level due diligence. For you, just a walk in the woods."

"Warren didn't say anything to me about this."

She shrugged. "What else are you going to do? C'mon, Cameron and Jaimie are going to be collecting core samples, Dyson and Greer will be running the rig, Warren will be getting in everyone's face about being more timely." She poked him lightly in the arm, her eyes gleaming. "By comparison, I'm pretty good company."

He rolled his shoulders, feeling for the pain he knew was lurking underneath the opioid cloud. He felt a twinge and he used it to focus, to clarify his thinking, to pull himself out of this damned false happy place. "Why'd you get into ecology?"

"For the stimulating company, obviously," she said. "Come on, Grumpy, let's go check out the neighborhood."

"No," he said, his voice stopping her as she started away. "I want to know. Why?" He waved a hand toward the drill rig, welcoming the pain that twisted through his knuckles and wrist. "Why ecology? So you can let some suits know how much damage they can do without getting sued?"

She gave him a patient smile. "It's not like that."

"If you're in it for the money, I can understand. But you're an afterthought, right? They can't be paying you as much as those guys. So what, this is the only gig you could get, figuring out how much good ole Ma Nature can give up? Some sort of ecology pimp?"

Very slowly, the animation that had been in her face drained away. Her mouth pursed twice, but each time the words she was about to speak retreated back inside her. After a moment she turned away and started picking her way down the valley. Jake watched her as she moved from rock to rock, moving quickly at first, then slowing. She stopped near a small swamp (a pocket wetland, he thought) and took out her iPad, snapping pictures of the plants on the fringe of the marshy ground. Her face was red, her lips pursed.

Too much, he thought. *Jesus. A little push would have done it.*

And on the heels of that: *Oh, Deserae. I'm sorry, babe. Sorry I even looked at that dipshit little girl, or at Jaimie.*

Deserae, who he had first met in the city when they were in college. It was a mid-December night, and the snowflakes were cartwheeling through Rice Park in downtown St. Paul, catching the glow from the Christmas lights strung up in the trees. He had come to the coffee shop to get out of the wind, his mind too cluttered to study for his upcoming finals, and when he went up to order his coffee he couldn't decide what to get and was too embarrassed to admit he didn't know a cappuccino from a latte. As he stood there trying to look indecisive rather than clueless, she had moved alongside him and said it was a French press sort of night, didn't he think? He ordered two, and although she insisted on paying for her own, she allowed him to sit at the small table with her. He had tried to talk. Hard to do without studying her face, the kind of sight he thought people should have to stand in line to see.

They met in the city, but neither one was made for it. He could still see her on a crisp September evening three years after they met, standing at the edge of the marsh with the sun setting and the massive full harvest moon rising in the east, Deserae swinging her little twenty-gauge in a smooth arc and tumbling a canvasback, almost squealing in pleasure at the thought of the roast duck dinner it would provide, then turning to him and telling him someday he might grow up and learn how to shoot, too. She was as lovely then, her cheeks smeared with mud to hide her face from incoming ducks, as she had been in the coffee shop in her merino sweater and silk scarf, in the dim light of their apartment with clothes melting away, in the bright spring days when they walked everywhere, broke and happy and the world there just for them. Perhaps more lovely then than anywhere or anytime.

And what would she think of him now? Creeping through his thirties, trying to cobble something together for a life, alone and growing more and more ornery with every passing day. He knew. He knew what she would think: his fate was far worse than hers.

He heard the diesel engine rev again and turned. They were still anchoring the legs, but later that day they would begin to drill down into the ground, probing into the area where Warren had shown him those strange geomagnetic swirls. In a day, maybe two, it would all be over. He would have his money and he would go on to the rest of his non-life.

One of these days, he thought, *I promise, honey, I'll start working on being who I was again.*

He started after Rachel, trying out different apologies in his mind as he walked.

It was late afternoon and she had still not spoken to him. The different things he might have said had remained inside him, curdling in the back of his mouth after her first withering glare. He stayed back, shadowing her as she moved through the marshy ground, then up through the sides of the valley, snapping pictures, occasionally plucking a leaf to study against the key on her tablet. She took nothing with her, no samples, just cataloging what she saw and marking down her observations. They were almost two miles from the drill site.

"We need to start heading back," he said.

She kept walking, moving even farther away. Jake sighed and followed her in silence. It was very quiet; he couldn't hear the drill rig from here, or much of anything else. There were few birds and no animals in the valley, and the plant life was mundane. He supposed that was a good thing for Warren, because bringing along an ecologist on an exploratory mission obviously meant there was the potential to develop this site. The idea of development seemed farfetched to him—the site was far from anything and everything—but perhaps it would not be so hard to carve a road through the swamps and brush. From a pure civil engineering perspective, he supposed it was actually quite simple—the hard part would be convincing the locals that it was a good idea. And convincing the banks it was worth the investment.

The bottom of the sun was almost touching the horizon when Rachel finally tucked her tablet into her backpack and headed back to camp. Jake followed her, as he had most of the day, his hips aching and the beginnings of a headache forming at the base of his neck. He didn't feel as bad as he'd thought he might. There were some days when he would be relegated to his bed by the dinner hour, pills or no pills, a cobweb of pain spreading over his body joint by joint.

It took far less time to make it back to camp when they didn't have to stop at every patch of vegetation. Warren was talking with Cameron some distance from the drill rig and the rock dust it was generating. He waved them over.

"Well?" Warren asked. "Any indications?"

Rachel shook her head. "Nothing," she said. "It's pretty sterile around here, biologically speaking. I need to find somewhere with some active life."

"Okay," Warren said. "We're about ready to start drilling, so go get some rest. It took a while to get everything aligned, but we should be able to collect our first sample before it gets dark." He turned to Jake. "Everyone is pretty hungry."

"It'll have to be freeze-dried stuff," Jake said. "No game around that I can see." He turned to Rachel and tried a smile. "It's pretty sterile around here, is what I'm saying."

She ignored him, moving up the slope to the campsite and slipping into her tent.

"Christ, you're a charmer," Warren said. "And no shooting—I told you that. I don't care if a goddamn bear wanders into camp. The drill rig makes more than enough noise."

"Why the big hang-up on a little bit of noise?" Cameron asked. His beard was covered with flecks of mud, as were his clothes, except where he had pulled off his hip waders to reveal clean blue jeans. Cameron's eyes were the same shade of blue as his jeans, bright and inquisitive within that shaggy face. "They're not actually monitoring us, are they?"

"I don't know," Warren said. "But we keep it under eighty decibels, no matter what. And if someone complains that we're spooking game, we need to pack up and leave. Right away."

Cameron reached up and scratched at his beard, looking around him at the barren valley, then up to the pines at the top of the ridge. "Who's going to complain out here?" he asked. "Environment Canada? One of the First Nations?"

"Could be either one," Warren said. "I signed on the dotted line that we wouldn't disturb their hunting land to the west on our way in, and that we would be under eighty decibels the entire time. I also confirmed drill holes would be sealed and covered, and any spills would be reported immediately through this." He patted his vest pocket containing one of their satellite phones. "We're going to respect each and every one of those requirements."

"Well, that Geocore is a pretty tight little unit," Cameron said. "No spills unless we tip it over. And she's anchored down real nice."

"You ready to pull a sample?"

Cameron grinned. "Absolutely." He twirled his finger in the air for Greer, who gave him a thumbs-up and depressed one of the levers. The drill bit ground through the overlying rock, moving slowly, almost imperceptibly. The hollow core inside the wider drill bit spun slowly, reflecting the setting sun.

"What's that?" Warren said. "Three inches a minute? We'll be down into the good stuff in less than an hour."

"If it's there," Cameron said.

"It'll be there," Warren said.

They watched the drill rig slowly bore into the

ground. It was like a giant straw, Jake thought. Plunge it into the ground, but instead of holding your thumb over the top the way you kept liquid in a straw, the hole-sawing bit was retracted, allowing small drilling teeth on the inside of the bit to unfold. When the drill rig began rotating again, the teeth cut sideways into the bottom of the core, severing it for extraction.

From thirty yards away, Greer held up one hand, indicating five feet of progress. As the sun slid completely below the horizon, he held up two hands, fingers splayed.

"Almost into it," Warren said. It was as talkative as Jake had seen the man, almost giddy, and Jake had to admit to a certain level of excitement himself. Dinner had been forgotten. It didn't matter to him that whatever they pulled from the ground would likely be unremarkable, at least visually. There was, perhaps, something extremely valuable right under their feet. The fact it would come from Resurrection Valley, from the bad country, only added to its allure. It would be like finding a diamond in the trash.

We're not after diamonds, though, Jake thought. *Not copper or silver or gold, either, I think. Something different, something that causes a reaction.*

He had no idea what that meant, and he didn't really care. He was so captivated by watching the core rig that his pain was forgotten, and he shrugged off the first trembling as the shaking of his exhausted leg muscles. Then he noticed the leaves on the poplar trees near the top of the slope, already yellowing, had begun to shower down, the thin trunks shaking back and forth as though under a high wind. "What's going on?" Rachel called out from above them, emerging from her tent. Cameron raced up the slope to her and put an arm around her shoulders, which she shrugged off.

"Warren?"

He held up a hand, his eyes never leaving the drill rig. The tremor grew, rippling under them, and Jake had to take a step to steady himself and keep from falling. The ground was trembling, the leaves and grasses shuddering. One of the rocks in the soft ground slowly slid out of the earth, like a tooth popping loose from a gum. The trembling intensified, and Jake was about to retreat back up the valley slope, away from what he guessed was one of the first recorded earthquakes in this area of the world. Back into the woods, which to him always meant safety, his natural refuge in this world, more so than the city or the hot desert sands where he had spent three years of his life being someone else entirely. The only other place he had ever felt as safe was with Deserae, and that was a safety that had turned out to be fragile, as delicate and beautiful as the tiny iridescent scales on the back of a butterfly's wings.

Then the shaking stopped.

Warren glanced at Jake, who shook his head. "No idea," he said.

Greer had already shut the rig off. Warren and Parkson walked over to him, Cameron still at the top with Rachel. Jake stayed back, watching as the three men inspected the drill rig, which seemed undamaged as far as he could tell. Jake scanned the valley, now darkening, as still and silent as it had been all day. The only indication of the temblor was the mud-streaked boulder that had popped out of the ground and the fresh carpet of yellow poplar leaves farther up the slope. After a bit, Greer and Warren produced small LED flashlights to continue their inspection, and Jake made his way back up to the campsite.

"What happened?" Rachel asked.

"I don't know," he said. "Do you? Is this the reaction you were talking about?"

"No," Rachel said. "I . . . I don't know what that was."

Jaimie had joined Hans, the diesel engine mechanic, at the small campfire. She looked up from the aluminum pot in which she was boiling water for their freeze-dried meals. She seemed to be the least concerned of all of them regarding the event—Jake wasn't sure what else to call it; earthquake seemed a bit dramatic—and again he was impressed by her calmness. "Maybe Mother Nature doesn't like to be poked and prodded," she said.

"Maybe not," Jake said. "But something tells me we're not done with her yet."

Hans, a short, prematurely balding man who carried a laminated service manual and a pocket-size Bible with him, had been sleeping in his tent and was awakened by the shaking ground. He was anxious to know if the temblor had damaged the drill rig's engine.

"Ask them," Jake said, motioning toward the men laboring up the slope into camp. He could smell the rehydrated food, and his mouth was salivating. Sometimes the pills drove away his appetite as well as his pain, but tonight that wouldn't be the case.

"Is the engine okay?" Hans asked. He patted the small rectangle the Bible made in his front pocket, something he did constantly.

"It seems to be," Warren said, closing his eyes and

rubbing his forehead. "But the core tube is bent, and the drill bit is trapped underground." He glanced at Greer. "I doubt we can salvage either one."

"Anchors are bent, too," Greer said. "Let's cut them all off and start over."

"What if it happens again?" Hans asked. "You get too much vibration coming up the core tube, that little engine is going to rattle apart."

"I was thinking about that," Greer said. "This time we'll let the legs float on top of the ground. That way, if we get another shaker, we'll move with it." He held a hand out, shaking it and moving it along an imaginary plane. "Sometimes you gotta roll with the flow, man. Right?"

"Sure," Hans said, patting his Bible again. "Thank goodness everyone's okay. I think I heard a tree fall back in the woods a bit when the shaking was at its worst." They all looked around them, as though the ancient white pines around their campsite might suddenly topple over.

"Did we cause this?" Rachel asked quietly.

They all looked to Greer, who shook his head. "Highly doubtful," Greer said. "Only time a drill rig is going to cause movement is if you're near some sort of geothermal activity, drill into some felsite, and release pent-up steam. We're way too shallow for that—up here, the real pressures are way down in the guts of the earth. We're barely punching through the skin."

"So it's what?" Jaimie asked. "Coincidence?"

"Who knows?" Greer said. "We probably drilled into a minor pressure plate, jump-started a process that would have happened in the next few hundred years anyway. It's a unique place, geologically speaking. Lots going on, even as shallow as we're operating."

"But nothing to worry about," Warren said.

Greer glanced at Warren, then turned to the rest of the group. "No, nothing to worry about at all," he said. "Just a little shake and bake. Tomorrow morning we'll reset and give her a good poke."

"Good," Warren said. "Get something to eat, all of you."

They ate their meals straight out of the packets, tossing the containers and plastic forks into the small fire. There was little talk, and after a few minutes they began to straggle into the one-man tents. Jake waited until all had left and then pushed the coals into a small, concentrated pile with one of the half-burnt sticks. In the morning, he would spread the coals out again and supply some twigs and fresh air. It was something he always liked to do when he was out in the brush, coaxing life out of what appeared to be dead gray ashes. He sort of hoped that Jaimie, or even Rachel, might be awake to see him perform the old trick. The thought simultaneously amused him and disgusted him. Well. It had been a long time since he had been around women, and longer yet since he had been around women quite like Rachel and Jaimie, intelligent and strong and a bit exotic, in different ways.

Easy, he thought. *They're not exactly looking for a northwoods love affair, and you need to keep your mind focused on the job.*

Later, as Jake tried to position his body on the hard ground so he could sleep, his mind kept returning not to the women but to the trees, the way they had twisted and shuddered, how the leaves had come down from the poplars like . . . well, shit. Deserae had always said the way the leaves would fall on a windless day made her imagine the trees weeping, crying at the approach of winter, at the departure of warmth and rain. Her analogy had disturbed him, for reasons he couldn't quite fathom, and it bothered him more now, thinking about this early leaf fall. His thoughts followed him into his dreams, where aspens and balsam firs and white pines twisted and swayed all night long. He woke once and understood, in a moment of clarity that sometimes comes after a dream, why their movements had bothered him so much. For it was not as though the earth had been moving the trees, or that the trees were crying. It was as though the trees themselves, long anchored in this remote valley, had been trying to claw themselves out of the ground so that they might escape.

Chapter 4

He woke long before the others, chased out of bed by his pain. By the time the sun had crested the horizon, he had the fire going and the water simmering in the aluminum pot. The coffee had already percolated, and the soot-streaked pot was resting on a large, flat rock at the edge of the fire. He was hurting, but his joints weren't on fire as they had been, and he'd elected to try making it through the day with a double dosage of ibuprofen. The pain could return quickly, sweeping in and taking over his body and his thoughts in less than an hour, but for now the sun was warm and the smoke was blowing away from his face.

Warren emerged from his tent, fully dressed. He had stubble on his cheeks but he had taken the time to comb his hair, and he was wearing a clean shirt and pants. He nodded at Jake and walked off to the bushes. From somewhere deeper in the forest, a woodpecker's jackhammer issued.

"You feeling better?" Warren asked when he returned.

Jake poked a stick into the edge of the fire. There was mostly softwood up here, poplar and balsam deadfall. It burned hot but didn't last long. "What do you mean?"

"You walked down to the drill site yesterday like you had glass in your joints," Warren said. "Coffee ready?"

Jake tossed him a cup from the backpack that served as their mess bag and took one himself. Warren wrapped his sleeve around his hand and poured Jake's cup full, using the metal ring on the back of the pot to steady the percolator. The coffee steamed into Jake's mug, thick and black. Warren filled his own mug and set the pot back down on the edge of the fire, turning the spout away from the fire so the smoke and ash wouldn't fall into it. *He's had campfire coffee before,* Jake thought, blowing at the top of his mug. *Good for him.*

Warren inspected his fingernails, his coffee mug cooling beside him. After a while he looked up. "What is it? Arthritis? Something more serious?"

"Nothing," Jake said. "A couple nights on the hard ground."

"Don't bullshit me."

Jake locked eyes with him for a moment, then crossed over to the meager woodpile and picked up a piece of dry, barkless aspen, smooth as a baseball bat. He twirled the stick across the back of his hand like a baton, then tossed it into the fire. Warren covered his coffee mug as a small shower of sparks erupted. "I got us here," Jake said. "I'll get us out."

"You weren't much of a guide yesterday, from what I understand."

"My contract was to get us here, then out," Jake

said. "Us lazy Indians make a point of only doing what we have to."

Warren drank his coffee. The woodpecker continued its work in the distance, the hammering going on for a minute or two in one area, followed by silence as it went to another tree. There was stirring from the tents now, the nylon bulging out as the team struggled into their day clothes.

"We can get along just fine," Warren said, his voice soft now. "You keep being a good boy, you'll get a nice little surprise at the end of this. But if you compromise our schedule, if you don't play nice, then we're going to have a discussion. We're already a half-day behind, maybe more."

"I'm here," Jake said. "Anything anybody wants, all they have to do is ask."

Warren drained the last of his coffee and threw the dregs into the campfire. "Anything?"

Jake stared at him. "Within reason."

"Okay, good." Warren tossed him his empty mug. "Then quit being a dick."

It took most of the morning to cut the core tube loose from the drill rig. Once it was finally free, all eight of them lifted the rig, legs still splayed out over a ten-foot radius, and carried it fifteen yards away. It was much faster than disassembling the rig and moving it piece by piece, and Greer and Warren looked pleased. Jaimie seemed happy to have the physical work, even playful, flexing her muscles for Cameron to feel, who patted her not inconsiderable biceps and murmured something about an arm-wrestling contest later on that night. Rachel watched their exchange with interest, smiling, but despite her good humor there was an underlying tension, her too-polite smile hinting at something between her and Cameron. Her calves were tense little balls of muscle, swelling out against her nylon pants.

"They are pretty good legs," Hans whispered as he went by. "But we ain't been out here long enough to stare that hard."

Jake gave him a flat stare, and Hans laughed and opened the service manual for his prework check. Greer and Parkson were already positioning the new core tube and drill bit, and Cameron and Jaimie were set-ting up the small shelter where they would archive the samples. There didn't seem to be a lot of measuring equipment that Jake could see. He supposed most of the samples would be analyzed back in the lab, wher-ever that was. Not Canada, he presumed, and maybe not the States. His contract and nondisclosure agree-ment were with GME, Global Metallic Endeavors, a Toledo firm he had never heard of, and one that didn't show up on Internet searches. Before he signed the contract or the NDA, he asked Roger Collingsworth, an old friend still working out in Toronto, if he could find some more information for him. Roger had called him back an hour later and told him GME appeared to be a shell corporation, possibly funded not by one of the major mining corporations but rather by the United States Department of Defense.

"It's not a bad thing to work for DOD," Roger told him, his deep, slightly nasal voice softened by the land-line telephone. "They pay up, and you're not going to be working with a bunch of stiffs. If the money is good . . . ?"

Jake affirmed it was good enough and asked about Roger's kid.

"Seventh grader," Roger said. "Can you believe it? Everything I tell him, he says 'I know' and then does it different. But hell, he's a good kid, playing football like he was meant to do it." A pause, and Jake smiled, knowing that Roger was pushing up his glasses on his nose, something he did every few sentences. "Marie's a bitch about everything else but letting me see him, so we make it work." Another pause, longer this time. "Are you . . . ?"

Jake shuffled his feet, waiting for Roger to finish the question. He had called from the Whitehorse general store, one of the only places in Whitehorse that had a phone he could use, and the owner was watching him out of the corner of his eye. Outside, a late spring flurry was showering snowflakes down onto Main Street.

"Are you okay?"

"Hanging in there," Jake said. "Thanks, Roger."

"Sometimes it's beautiful," Roger said, the old words sounding the same as they had back in the days when they both had been young in body, their minds and souls aging faster every day, baking in the hot desert sun. Roger hadn't had glasses then, he'd had goggles and a Kevlar helmet, and his son had still been in diapers.

"But usually it's shit," Jake replied automatically, and hung up the phone.

Now he walked up to Rachel. If he'd had a hat, he supposed he would have been holding it in both hands.

He had to step around in front of her to make her look at him. As she did, her face lost its careful, cheery look. "What?"

"Upstream?" he asked.

"I can manage," she replied, slinging her backpack over her shoulder.

"Okay." He turned and gestured upstream. "A little feeder creek comes in upstream; I can't remember how far. If you follow it for a ways, it opens up and there's a little wetland, different from this." He gestured at the low, boggy ground leading down to the river. The dark green tamaracks were starting to turn yellow, and behind them the gunmetal river lay flat, without so much as a ripple. "There were some marsh marigolds, a few ladyslippers around the edges. Seemed a lot more colorful than what we have here." He toed a group of small mushrooms that had emerged overnight, a fairy ring of gray-capped fungi. "You want some animal life, too, right?"

She nodded cautiously. "You've been here before?"

"Years ago. Scouting for a trapline. It's one of those places not many people visit. I thought I might take a pile of fur."

"Did you?"

"I didn't set a trap," he said. "There's not much here to hold critters."

"Did you ever . . ." she paused, chewed at the bottom of her lip. "Did you see anything unusual when you were here? Animals acting strangely?"

"How do you mean?"

Behind them, the diesel engine started, and a faint whiff of exhaust passed over them. He stepped out of the plume and she moved with him. "How much do you know about what we're after?" she asked. "Has Warren briefed you, or are you just . . ."

"I'm just the help," he said. "I don't know anything."

"I can't tell you specifics," she said, "but you should know how important this is." She leaned in closer to him, close enough that he could smell her, a bit sweaty after several days in the bush but pleasant nonetheless.

Concentrate, Jake. Jesus.

"The material we're looking for has incredible biomedical potential. It interacts with living tissue, particularly the nervous system. If I can find evidence that the phenomenon is occurring naturally, we can use that information as a boilerplate for duplicating it in the laboratory."

"Regenerative properties?"

Rachel's eyes opened a bit. "You're not just the help."

"I am," Jake said. "I just have some experience with nerves and the brain. Personal experience, nothing professional. Anytime someone says 'biomedical' and 'nervous system,' the Holy Grail is always trying to repair lost connections. Deserae's doctor always said . . ." His sentence trailed off. He had not said her name aloud for over a year, not since the last time he had seen her. "Never mind."

She stood looking at him. "I'm not here for an environmental review," she said at last. She glanced behind her, saw that Warren was busy talking to Greer, and turned back to Jake. "And we're not just taking samples. Every ounce we take out of here could save thousands of lives, could help people walk again. And it's more than regenerative, Jake. It's transformative."

"How do you mean?"

Her eyes flitted across his face. "I'm being literal. The material we're after has a carrying capacity, a way to retain properties from one medium to the other. Or from one organism to another. And it not only transfers the properties, in certain cases it magnifies them."

"I'm not sure I follow."

"Think about scar tissue," she said. He could tell she was impatient, not necessarily with him, but in the way that all intelligent people could be when forced to explain something they already knew and accepted as basic fact. "It grows back to replace damaged tissue. But it's stronger, has a different cellular composition. In a way, it demonstrates that our body has *learned*. Learned it is susceptible to damage, so it makes sure we don't make the same mistakes. Do you understand?"

"We won't get fooled again," he said, nodding.

"The Who? Really?"

"British band? I'm Canadian, Rachel. Come on, put two and two together."

"I'm being a bit of a nerd, aren't I?"

He had to smile. "Nerds are usually a bit . . . softer . . . when they're lecturing us rubes."

"Geek, maybe? No? An ass, then. I'm sorry," she said, "I just get excited about this. See, the material not only imprints properties from one organism to another of the same kind, it can transmute. So the properties of a highly mobile organism can be transferred to a more stationary one. When the trees started shaking . . ." She paused, smiling at herself, at her silliness, her teeth flashing. Jake felt his breath shorten a bit. "I thought that it was what we were looking for."

"The reaction."

"Yes."

"You thought the trees had come alive."

She glanced at him, searching for mockery, and found none. "We've seen it in the lab. Not trees, but algae."

"No shit?"

"No shit. We set up different nutrient concentrations. When they're exposed to the material—we only have a few grams—they actively seek out their food. But only when the material is exposed to bacteria or invertebrates first. It takes the neurological properties from the first organism it's exposed to, the sensations and processing abilities, and transfers them to other organisms." She paused. "It turns them into sentient beings."

They were quiet for a moment. Behind them, voices from the crew came through the purr of the diesel engine and the soft scraping of the new core tube. Far off, a raven croaked its news into the azure summer sky.

"Can I ask you another question?" he said.

"You can ask."

"Are you working for the military?"

She held his gaze. "I'm working to advance the science," she said at last. "That's enough. Now me."

"Go ahead."

"Will you help me?"

He moved slowly, not dawdling but giving her enough time to survey the land. There was little to be found in the way of life on the valley slope, sentient or not, just lichen-covered rock and sedge grasses, the occasional stunted birch, more of the gray-colored fungi.

He was glad he had sprayed his hiking boots with water repellent before they'd left. It had been unusually wet this summer, and the ground around the valley was a combination of clay and gravel that held moisture like a sponge. Their boots squelched as they walked upstream, the sound of the drill rig growing fainter behind them.

He found the feeder creek within an hour, the water clear and cold where it cascaded out of a notch in the valley slope. Alders clung to the creek edges, and he backtracked a few steps to more open ground, then turned upstream. The wetland was less than a hundred yards away, an acre-sized marsh dotted with color. The marigolds were no longer blooming, but there were irises and lilies near the edges of the water, and farther back Jake could see a small patch of what looked like pink ladyslippers. There were ripples on the far end of the little pond, and he held up his hand. They waited, and a moment later two green-winged teal emerged from the vegetation, the drake with a bright orange head streaked with stripes of green over its eyes, the hen drab but exquisitely feathered. They saw Jake and Rachel, frozen at the far end of the pond, and swam back into the reeds.

"Those ducks used to be cattails," Jake whispered.

"Shut up," she said, slapping his arm. She looked at the water's surface, which was marked by water striders and other bugs. "This is perfect. I'm going to be here awhile."

She was excited, he saw. Not just by the place but by the chance to test out her hypothesis. Jake leaned back against a tree, watching. She moved slowly, snapping pictures and consulting her field guides, tapping notes into the tablet at regular intervals. She reminded him of a blue heron stalking the edge of the water. He smiled and sat down against the trunk of the tree, and dozed. He woke in the mid-morning sunshine and saw her on the far side of the pond, her boots off and her pantlegs rolled above her knees. He waved at her, but she was intent on some plant lying flat on the surface of the water. He slept again, and when he woke she was sitting a few yards away, pulling her socks back on.

"*Mibosa candelabra*," she said excitedly. "Can't be sure, but I think I'm right. Also known as the candleflower."

He blinked, looking at her sample bags. "Where is it?"

She gestured to the far side of the wetland. "*They* are over there. A few dozen, all past bloom, so I can't be completely sure of the species. But they *moved*, Jake. I'm almost certain of it. I even have video."

He stood, feeling oddly off-balance by her presence. "They moved?"

"As I was approaching." She pulled her boots on and stood. "They're anchored by their roots, but they swiveled away from me. The levels of . . . the levels of the material up here, in this end of the valley, are very low, if the geomag pattern from the satellites is correct. But it's still a high enough concentration to allow the candleflowers to take on the evasive response of the insects in the pond. Or the fish, or the ducks. My god," she said, flopping back on the ground and clenching her fists. "Do you know what this means?"

"I don't think so."

She sat up. "If we can take the material back and replicate this, then we can take something slow and make it fast, or take something growing too fast and slow it down. That's just the beginning. Jake, we might be able to take something that's stopped entirely and make it start back up again." She paused, looking at him and frowning. "I shouldn't be talking this much."

"Like someone with a spinal injury, you mean?"

"Yes," she said. "And we could take something that is moving too fast and make it slow down."

He considered this. "Now we're curing cancer," he said at last. "What else can we get done this afternoon? We need to keep going, Rachel. Quit resting on your laurels."

"You know it's not that simple," Rachel said.

"I know," he said. "Congratulations."

"If we do make a breakthrough, it won't be for years."

He nodded, staring at the far end of the pond. The ducks had not reemerged from the reeds, and he wondered if they had taken flight while he was sleeping. It had been years since he had taken a true nap, and to do so now in this wilderness, with a near-complete stranger as his only company, was odd. Perhaps it was the ibuprofen, or the reprieve from the inflammatory pain. Or perhaps it was simply feeling comfortable, and content. And he *was* content, working on something other than guiding outsiders to the next walleye, the next moose.

"Who's Deserae?"

"What?"

"You mentioned her earlier. Something about her doctor."

He brushed the leaves and dirt from his clothes and stretched. "You want to keep going up the valley?"

"No, we're good for the morning." She looked at him. "I'm sorry, Jake. I didn't mean to pry."

He waved it off. "Is there anything else?"

"No. Thank you so much. I mean that. This could be the beginning of something very big."

He slung his backpack over his shoulder. It was the first time she'd said thank you, the first time he'd heard someone else say Deserae's name in a very long time. "Let's go."

When they crested the next slope, they saw the crew huddled around the drill rig, the core tube retracted so that it looked like a single large antenna poised above the main structure. Jake paused, Rachel beside him, catching her breath from the ascent. They were less than two hundred yards from the drill site. Cameron and Jaimie were still inside the tarp lean-to Jake had constructed using the camouflage tarp that had covered the drill rig and fuel containers, their heads bent over as they worked inside the shadows. Warren's voice came floating to them, the words indistinct but the tone insistent, barking some order or another.

"Looks like he finally got some samples," Rachel said, watching Cameron and Jaimie separating out several lines of dark brown soil, or mineral.

"Samples of what, exactly?" Jake asked. "Some kind of ore?"

She turned to him. Her hair was tangled, and she was sweating a little in the afternoon heat. "Have you heard of Prometheus?"

"The Greek god?"

"Close. He was a Titan, the creator of man, the one who breathed life into creation. The one who supposedly stole fire from Mount Olympus and gave it to mankind, instead of only the gods having it."

"A socialist god. Okay."

She smiled. "We're looking for a form of promethium. It's a rare earth element, usually used to make magnetic imaging devices. The particular mineral it forms here makes this type of promethium very, very special."

Jake looked out across the valley, passing over the unremarkable river to the steep bluffs on the northern end. To the south, there was just the green swarm of northern forests and bog, the same bush they had waded through for days. The sky above them was unmarked by jet contrails. The closest thing to civilization was the village of Highbanks seventeen miles away, his hometown, where he'd lived until he was sixteen years old. "And this is the only place you can find promethium?"

"No," she said. "China has some significant deposits. Russia and Iran, too."

"Ahh, all of our good friends. I bet they like sharing. Tell me something, Rachel."

"I've already told you too much. If Warren finds out—"

"He won't," Jake said. "Tell me, are there other applications for promethium?"

Below them, the diesel engine hummed back to life and the core tube descended quickly, pausing with two feet of tubing above the top of the rig. She turned to watch, and Jake studied her face, then turned back to the operation. Greer threaded a new tube into the one already in the ground, and the next section of tubing went down, moving faster, almost plunging into the earth. Whatever stratum they were in now was much softer than the soils above it.

"Rachel?"

"Yes," she said. "There are other applications. Can we get back to camp, please? I'm tired, and I need to log what I've found while it's still fresh in my mind."

They started toward the drill site. They were half-way down the valley slope when the ground began to tremble. At first he thought it was a landslide and he craned his head upslope, an old mountain habit. But there weren't any rocks coming down on them. It was another shaker, a mini-earthquake, similar to what they had experienced the night before.

"It'll pass," he said. "Just wait it out."

The shaking intensified, the rumbling growing, and then the ground rippled under them, lurching one way and then the other. Rachel slipped and he reached out and caught her by the sleeve, the jackhammer vibrations from the ground almost tearing her from his grip. There was a small copse of stunted birch rooted into a ledge of bedrock nearby, and they stumbled toward it, the ground convulsing beneath them.

"Grab on." He motioned toward the largest birch, only about four inches in diameter. He grasped a slightly smaller tree a few feet away, the trunk shaking wildly. He noticed Rachel had wedged her boots against the base of the trunk of another birch, and he did the same. From downslope they could hear Warren's frantic cries for Greer to shut the machine down.

"Jake?"

"Hold on," he said, his voice shaking from the constant thrumming coursing through his body. "I don't know."

Greer lurched to the drill rig, which was now tilted at a ten-degree angle. He was only a few yards away when the ground buckled under him and he pitched forward. The drill rig tilted at a steeper and steeper angle, the diesel engine sending a plume of clear, rippling exhaust into the air. The core tube shrieked as the metal crimped, then sheared off. Greer got to his feet, his beard wet with blood, and stumbled forward for the kill switch. The ground jerked violently and he pitched forward, his forehead striking the corner of the rig's frame, tilted two feet off the ground. Greer fell to the ground, shuddering either from his injury or the gyrations of the ground. Parkson had been crawling toward the rig but now seemed frozen, crouched on his hands and knees and staring at Greer. Warren was trying to get to his feet but seemed to be stuck. A small seam of mud had appeared next to him, the slick brown earth quivering and rippling.

"Jake?" Rachel asked again. "It's an earthquake, isn't it?"

"I don't think so," Jake said. The diesel engine, no longer laboring against the bent core tube, was revving at a much higher rate than it would normally idle, and the angle of the rig kept increasing. The exhaust was turning dark as engine oil spilled into the cylinders. "Stay here, Rachel."

He shrugged off his pack and started running down the slope. Muddy water was oozing out of the ground, and he was halfway to the rig when he slipped on the mud and his feet went out from under him. His boots left long red streaks in the clay as he tried to regain his balance, and when he fell the next time, the left side of his body was drenched from the saturated ground. He scrambled to his feet and slowed to a jog, alternating glances between the drill rig, now belching great clouds of black smoke, and the ground liquefying under his feet. He stepped over a long pale root that lay atop the ground, then another. The second root, almost as thick as his wrist, quivered as he leapt over it.

What the hell?

Then he was at the drill rig, fumbling for the kill switch. The rig was almost at a forty-five degree angle, and he had to climb onto one of the tilted anchoring legs to access the control panel. The cylinders were grinding and shrieking like living things. He hit the kill switch and the grinding stopped, but black smoke continued to spew into the clear blue sky. From somewhere inside the machine, the grinding was replaced by a dull roaring sound, as if another engine were caught inside the cylinder walls.

It's on fire inside, Jake thought. *Sorry, Warren, your baby is toast.*

He dropped down to the ground next to Greer. There was a pool of blood under Greer's face, and he made a burbling sound each time he exhaled. Jake could hear Hans cursing at someone to help him, his voice colored with pain. Warren was saying something too, impossible to hear above the sound of the still-burning engine.

"Greer?"

He was unconscious, but his body didn't have the

slack look Jake associated with vertebral trauma. He would have to take a chance and flip him over before he drowned in his own blood.

He grabbed Greer's shoulder and pulled. Greer flopped over on his back, his leg twitching. Jake used the cuff of his shirt to clear the blood from Greer's face. There was a laceration just above his right eyebrow, pink bone visible underneath the blood pouring out of the wound. Jake pulled his hunting knife out of his sheath and cut a sleeve off Greer's shirt, then wound it around Greer's forehead. Greer's leg continued to spasm, and when Jake looked down, thinking maybe it was the start of a seizure, he saw that one of the long pale roots was wound around Greer's ankle. The end had crawled inside Greer's pants, forming a bulge under the denim. As he watched, the root slid higher inside Greer's pant leg.

"Jesus Christ," Jake said.

He brought his knife down on the exposed root. The knife blade sliced through it easily, and Jake ripped the severed root out of Greer's pantleg and threw it on the ground. It did not look like a root. He didn't know what it looked like exactly, just something that had long been underground, something on the edge of rottenness. Greer mumbled something through the blood.

"Easy," Jake said. "Try not to move, okay?"

Hans cursed again from behind them, and when Jake stood and turned, he saw the mechanic kneeling in the soupy ground, two of the tendrils wrapped around his left arm, one wound around the bicep and the other encircling his wrist. They seemed to be pulling at opposite angles, and Hans's bald head had turned cherry red. Another tendril emerged from the ground behind him and started creeping toward Hans's free hand. Its movements were slow, measured, like a cat stalking a bird.

"Behind you!" Jake shouted.

Hans either didn't hear him or was too lost in his own struggles to respond. Underneath them, the shaking was getting more intense, water oozing to the surface and turning the ground into soup.

He looked down. Greer's eyes were cloudy, and he held out a trembling hand. Jake squeezed it, then placed Greer's hand back on his chest. "I'll be right back," he said.

Jake ran toward Hans, the ground dissolving under his feet. *Static liquefaction*, he thought, as he leapt from one rock to another. *Enough water and the soil loses its strength. Same thing that causes mudslides.*

He skidded to a stop next to Hans, his knees sinking several inches into the muck. The tendril that was creeping toward Hans's other hand paused, seemed about to reverse motion, then fell to the ground as Jake chopped it off. At the same time there was a muted pop, the sound of someone snapping a wishbone, and he saw the tendrils around Hans's arm cinched cruelly tight. He wedged the knife blade under them and turned the edge up, severing the tendrils in one slice. Hans's arm fell limply to his side.

"How bad?" Jake asked.

Hans didn't reply, instead tucking his arm in to his body, mewling with pain.

Broke, Jake thought. *Christ, we're dropping like flies.*

"Come on." Jake helped him to his feet. He needed to get back to Greer. He pointed toward a small escarpment of rock, roughly fifty feet square, elevated a few feet from the rest of the valley floor. A single cedar grew from its center, and the brown detritus of dead needles wafted down as the tree shuddered. But there was no mud on the rock, no water. He hoped that meant no tendrils, either. "Get in the middle of that rock pad," Jake said. "And stay there." Hans stumbled off. Jake jumped onto one of the small boulders that dotted the valley bottom and balanced atop the shaking rock. Parkson and Warren were both fighting against the tendrils, the ground bubbling mud around their struggles, each man slowly sinking into the earth. Cameron was struggling against a single large tendril wrapped around his ankle, but as Jake watched, Jaimie bent down and ripped it in half with her bare hands. They stumbled backward through the sucking mud, retreating to the shelter of the tarp.

"Not there!" Jake hollered. He gestured toward the rock pad. "Over there!" Jaimie nodded, and they sprinted toward Hans, the tarp lean-to collapsing behind them.

Jake eyed the ground. It had turned into a bubbling cauldron of mud, and long sinuous shapes twisted in the muck. There weren't enough rocks to allow him to navigate without touching the spongy ground, but there were enough to avoid wading through most of it. He started toward Warren, who was closest to him, holding the knife at his side. Warren was half-submerged in the mud, and when he looked up and saw Jake beside him, he clutched his shoulder like a drowning man.

Jake shrugged him off. "I gotta cut you free," he said. He leaned down, keeping his feet moving constantly, feeling the tendrils moving through the supersaturated soil. There were three tendrils around Warren's ankle, and when the first one was cut he saw the other two contract, tightening their grip. Warren grunted in pain, then released a long hissing breath as Jake severed the other two. Fifty feet away, Parkson was still on his hands and knees, but he had sunk into the ground. His elbows and knees were completely submerged in the muck.

"Come on," Jake said, hauling Warren to his feet. "You're okay. Help me with Parkson."

He hopped from rock to rock, taking no more than three steps at a time in the oozing ground. He was so intent on avoiding the muddy ground that it wasn't until he reached Parkson that he realized Warren hadn't followed him. Jake turned and saw the crew chief stumbling after Cameron and Jaimie, fleeing to the rock pad. *Okay,* Jake thought. *Probably better for him to go there anyway.* He didn't care; his only thought, his only driver, was to remove his people and then himself from danger as soon as possible. He had fallen back into his old habits, and there was a certain comfort in that.

Parkson looked up, his face pale. "If I don't fight it, it doesn't hurt as bad."

"Where does it have you?"

"Everywhere."

Jake inserted his hand into the muck, feeling the long, slimy segments quivering under his hand. There was a mass of tendrils around both of Parkson's feet, twined above his knobby anklebones. Jake slid the knife under the mud and severed the tendrils around his right ankle. Parkson sucked in his breath, his eyes bugging out, as the other tendrils constricted around his left ankle. He yanked his free foot out of the muck.

"Keep it high," Jake said. "Jesus, the ground is alive with these things."

He reached into the mud under Parkson's other ankle. The mass of tendrils pulsed and slithered, growing taut under Jake's palm. Parkson whimpered as they contracted.

"One sec," Jake said, still feeling in the mud. He wanted to cut them all in one slice if he could. "Hang on, Parkson."

There seemed to be just the one bunch, three wraps wound tightly above the ankle. He brought the knife blade down, his index finger resting on the back of the blade for extra control. Parkson's whimpers subsided as Jake carefully ran the edge of the blade down his shinbone, the tendrils falling away. More had emerged on the ground around them, like earthworms coming to the surface after someone stuck an electric probe into the ground. The last tendril was moving as Jake cut, and he had to chase it in the muck, all the while feeling more lengths crowding alongside his own knees and feet.

So this is why they call it the bad country.

And on the heels of that thought, a glimmer of doubt. The men his father had hunted with had rarely spoken of this place. But when they did, it was in reverent tones, reserved for preachers talking about the Book of Revelation, or scientists pondering a latent volcano, one which should have exploded and had not. He did not think earthquakes, mudpots, or even these insistent, clutching tendrils would have caused those men to speak that way. But then again, he had been very young. After his father was gone, those strange, hard men of the bush no longer gathered at Jake's house on cold winter nights to tell their tales and speak of places where men should not go.

Parkson quivered and gurgled behind him.

Jake turned. A large tendril had jammed itself into Parkson's mouth, and Parkson's terror-stricken eyes were watching in horror as the tendril wormed its way farther down his throat. His right hand, which Jake had just freed, was now held by another tendril, and it contracted, twisting Parkson's arm around behind his back. Jake reacted without thinking, bringing the knife out of the mud and then down in a quick motion, severing the tendril. He yanked the end out of Parkson's mouth and flung it away. Before it even reached the ground, Parkson was yanked backward by the other tendril, and his cry turned into a full-throated scream, spittle flying from his mouth.

Jake hacked at the tendrils that had swarmed back around Parkson's foot. Something cold and wet wrapped around his wrist and yanked him forward. Jake pitched forward into the mud, and more tendrils pressed against his face, wiggling towards his eyes, his nostrils. He pushed himself up, stabbing blindly at a serpentine shape just under the surface.

He scrambled to his feet, blowing mud out of his mouth. "You free?"

Parkson pointed at his ankle, still submerged in the mud. Jake jammed his knife under it, turned it sideways, and hacked. There was a sudden release of pressure, and then Parkson was up, all of his weight on his left foot. Seventy yards away, the team members who had climbed onto the rock pad were waving at them. Jake could see their mud-streaked faces: Warren, Hans, Jaimie, and Cameron. Their expressions were frantic with fear, but there were no tendrils around them. He pointed Parkson toward the rock. "Go."

Parkson stumbled toward the rock pad, limping badly but making progress. Jake wiped the mud from his face and swept his eyes across the valley.

"Shit."

He began slogging through the mud, back to the drill rig. Flames were dancing over the structure, and the dense, oily smoke formed a black pillar rising high into the sky. The long reed canary grass next to the rig was singed, and fluttered from the movement of air feeding the flames. And beneath the smoke and flames lay the inert shape of Greer, wrapped in the embrace of dozens of tendrils.

Chapter 5

Jake stood ten yards from the drill rig, unable to move forward. The flames had spread out over the bottom of the rig, fed by a ruptured fuel line, and the heat washed over him, taking his breath away. Sweat dried on his face, and his skin felt suddenly tight, stretched over his cheekbones. Only thirty feet away, Greer was almost completely entombed in the tangle of tendrils, which were moving slowly over his body, prodding, assessing. One of the coils had wound itself under the bloody bandage on Greer's forehead.

It didn't make sense. The tentacles—which was how he thought of them now, not roots—should have withered under the heat. Greer's face should be blistered and peeling. Then it came to him: *They're on the ground. All the heat's up high.*

He dropped to his belly and began to wriggle forward. The heat did not dissipate entirely, but it became manageable, about at the upper end of what he had experienced in various saunas and sweat ceremonies when he was younger. He inched toward Greer on his stomach, his knife out in front of him. He could feel the ground vibrating under him as the inferno raged ahead and above him. He didn't like being on the ground at all, and he supposed Greer was already beyond help. It was the sight of the coiled growth under Greer's head bandage that propelled Jake forward, the indecency of it, like a hand thrust under a lady's dress.

As he neared, the coils around Greer contracted, tightening their hold. At the same time, he felt something ripple under his belly, under the ground. He pushed himself to his knees and was immediately met with a wave of heat. He flattened again, falling to his elbows. It wasn't just the heat; the air was noxious and unbreathable just inches above his head.

"Greer? Greer, can you hear me?"

Greer's head moved a fraction of an inch, and then it snapped back into its previous position, the coil under Greer's bandage contracting. The blood that had plastered his face was gone, and even his beard seemed cleaned of the gore it had been streaked with only minutes ago.

It drank it, Jake thought. *It's a goddamn bloodsucker.*

"Easy," Jake said. "I'm going to cut you loose."

The knife blade had no more than touched the surface of the first tendril when the entire mass of gray coils surrounding Greer contracted. Greer's scream was overlaid with the sound of cracking bones and joints. Jake withdrew the knife, and the coils relaxed.

All except one. A thick ribbon emerged from underneath Greer's belly, slightly darker than the others. It moved upward, the pointed end nosing along Greer's flannel shirt and coming to rest at his throat. It lay there, pressed against the throbbing pulse under the stubbly skin of his neck. It was a threat, simple and awful: *Leave me to my feeding.*

Jake glanced around him. The tripod lay on its side a few yards away. Perhaps he could get the harness around Greer and yank him free. No, he would never be able to get the harness through that Medusa's head of writhing tentacles. And even if he could, it seemed the tentacles would simply crush Greer before he could be pulled free. What, then? The drill rig was engulfed in flames, and there was nothing there but hot steel and flaming paint and fuel oil. His eyes happened across one of the cans of diesel fuel on the far side of the rig. He squirmed over to it, Greer groaning some entreaty to him as he crawled away. Jake couldn't tell if he was asking for help or if he wanted Jake to save himself. It didn't sound like either request, though; it sounded like a different kind of entreaty. Two small words, choked out of Greer's tortured body.

"Kill me."

No, Jake thought. *We're not there yet.*

The plastic fuel container was hot to the touch, the sides bulging out from the interior pressure. Jake shook it, and dark fuel sloshed against the sides. A quarter full, perhaps a couple of gallons. He dragged the container back to Greer, who was still moaning, his fingers twitching inside the grip of several smaller tendrils. Jake unscrewed the spigot and hot air rushed out, the smell of oily hydrocarbons so thick he thought the can might explode in his hands. But that was the thing about diesel; it didn't explode as easily as gasoline. It burned, though. It burned very, very hot.

He crawled around Greer, soaking the ground with the fuel oil about three feet from his body. When he had completed the circle, he crawled back toward the flaming rig, trailing the can behind him. Greer moaned something at him again, but Jake didn't turn around. If the tentacles crushed Greer, so be it; this slow consumption, if that's what it was, was more awful than the quick crushing death the coils could obviously deliver. And Jake thought the threat was simply that—a threat. Whatever this creature was, it obviously preferred to keep its prey alive so that it could feed at its own pace. It might kill Greer, but it would only do so if there was no other way to keep him in its grip.

Jake took a deep breath and got to his feet, then threw the last dregs of fuel in the can into the inferno. The yellow container crumpled instantly in the heat, and the flames danced outward, flickering at the trail of diesel. For a moment Jake thought that was it, that the ground was too saturated with mud and water. Then the trail lit up, starting near the rig and quickly racing around Greer's body, a low, guttering flame like St. Elmo's fire. The heat spiked up, and even lying flat on the ground, Jake had to wriggle backward, gasping for breath. The grass around him burst into flames. The diesel had done more than he'd thought it would, acting as a thermal catalyst for the superheated grasses that hadn't yet burned. Greer screamed again, braying in pain; it was as though he could finally get enough breath in his lungs to make the kind of noise his body demanded.

I killed him, Jake thought. *I just burned him alive.*

But the flames died down as quickly as they had sprung up, and when they had subsided, he saw that Greer, his face and arms red and covered with heat blisters, was very much alive. And the coils were almost gone. All but one had retreated into the ground. The remaining tendril was shriveled and darkened, no more threatening than a dormant grapevine. Jake waited a moment to let the heat dissipate, then crawled forward and clutched Greer's wrist. The skin slid over the flesh of the wrist, bunching under Jake's hand, and Greer's screams went up an octave.

Jake wormed backward, yanking Greer after him. The ground was cooling rapidly, and he could feel the earth moving under him again, rapid and erratic movements, nothing like the smooth rippling he'd felt moments earlier.

He kept moving, trying to ignore Greer's screams. He needed to get Greer into the river, to stop the heat from destroying any more of his tissue. The air reeked of diesel smoke and burnt hair and skin. He didn't look at Greer's face, instead focusing on the wrist and arm he held in front of him. His lungs were scorched, and his throat and mouth felt like he'd gargled boiling liquid. They went forward in lurches; Jake first, then yanking Greer along behind him. In a moment or two he could risk getting to his feet, and then he would be able to hook his arms under Greer's armpits and—

Greer's scream turned into a garbled choke. Jake spun around and saw a tendril already retreating back into the ground, the tip soaked with blood. It had punched a ragged hole in Greer's windpipe the size of a quarter, the open wound spurting blood into the air. As soon as Jake stopped pulling him, more tendrils swarmed over Greer; others moved toward Jake. There was nothing erratic in their movements now; they had been momentarily disoriented, but now the mission was clear: they would not have their prize taken.

A small puff of dust erupted from one of the darker tendrils and spread into the air.

Jake got to his feet, dizzy and nearly blinded from the heat. Greer would soon be dead; the blood was coming out at an incredible rate, squeezed from his body by the coils of tentacles encircling his body. Jake stumbled forward a few steps and looked back. The tendrils were not pursuing him. They were bunched around Greer's throat, twisting and coiling around the crimson pool. Jake backed up, watching through watering eyes as Greer's lifeblood drained from him and was just as quickly absorbed into the gray coils, which changed color as they swelled from their feeding.

He gagged, breathing in more of the dust that had come from the tip of the darker tendril. It tasted bitter, like bile. He turned to wobble across the valley, trying to stay on the rocks wherever he could. The ground was very soft.

He could hear Warren and the others calling for him, but he couldn't see them. He swiveled, feeling as though his brain was lagging a quarter second behind his eyes. What vision he had left continued to narrow, two long tunnels of light surrounded by a pitching and whirling darkness. The ground tilted underneath him, and his legs felt suddenly weightless. He had felt this way only once before, hit in the head by a binder chain in a logging camp in Whitehorse.

He forced one foot in front of the other. He wasn't sure what direction he was going, but he needed to keep moving or he would be pulled into the earth, embraced and devoured as Greer had been. He moved onward but his pace slowed; he had wandered into a stretch of softer ground. He labored to free one boot, then the other. He could feel his strength fading as his vision shut down. Did it matter? If he had seared his eyes, if he was going to wander through the world blind, did it matter whether he died now or later? Anger at his own weakness surged through him, and he yanked his boots free and stumbled forward. A second later he felt someone at his side, propping him up.

"Come on," Rachel said, turning him ninety degrees to the right. "Follow me."

When he woke, it was to darkness, and for a moment he felt the panic close in over him, smothering him with a blank and awful certainty; he had indeed gone blind. And then bits of light appeared in the darkness, pinpricks of brightness. After a few seconds the panic retreated, and he saw that the bits of light were in an old and familiar pattern: the long handle and scoop of the Big Dipper. His eyes drifted up, tracing the line from Merak through Dubhe, the last two stars on the Dipper, which led to Polaris. From there he picked out the fainter stars of the Little Dipper, Deserae's favorite, Polaris forming the end of its handle. She had even written a poem about the North Star shortly after they had moved north, the words scribbled on the piece of paper that was still tucked inside Jake's pack.

> 'Round and 'round its eternal pivot,
> the star that guides the world its anchor.
> Scooping up the darkness one night at a time,
> twirling around the center of us.

She was not a poet by nature, although he had told her more than once that she saw things more clearly than most did, that she had within her some keener perception of the world worth sharing. She scoffed at this, but did not object when he retrieved the little poem from the wastebasket, smoothed the wrinkles, and tucked it into his pocket.

The aurora was out, a thin green glow over the rocks to the north. There was no moon.

"Jake?"

He turned his head and saw Rachel and Cameron squatting next to him. Their faces were covered in shadows but their features were clear; he had not cooked his eyeballs, then. Warren and Parkson stood a few paces back from the edge of the rock pad, talking in soft voices. Hans and Jaimie were huddled together, not moving, the starlight and aurora shimmering off Hans's balding head. Jake swallowed, wincing from the pain in his throat, and pushed himself to a sitting position. It felt like he had a terrible sunburn.

Rachel held out a canteen. He took several small swigs, grimaced, and handed it back. She dabbed a piece of cloth into the throat of the canteen, upended it, and handed him the damp cloth. He dabbed at his face, then his arms. His skin was streaked with mud, and he reeked of fuel oil.

"Greer?" Jake said.

Rachel looked away. Jake turned to Cameron, who shook his head. "We can't even see where he was anymore."

Parkson had to be in pain from his dislocated ankle and possibly a broken arm, but he was upright, balanced on one leg as he talked to Warren. Hans's shoulders were hunched over, and he hissed in pain as Jaimie adjusted the crude bandage around his arm. Everyone is doing something but me, Jake thought. He pushed himself to his feet and the world tilted. He lurched forward, pitching into the outspread arms of Cameron and Rachel. The dark northern night revolved around him.

"Hey," Rachel said. "Where do you think you're going?"

He shook his head. "Dizzy."

"You breathed in too many fumes," Cameron said. "Your throat was almost closed up by the time we made it over here."

"We?" Jake said.

"Cameron came out and helped," Rachel said, "and if he hadn't been carrying an EpiPen, you'd be dead right now."

"Huh?"

"I'm allergic to wasp venom," Cameron said. "I carry a pack of epinephrine with me when I'm in the field. You must have breathed in so much smoke that the toxins were closing up your throat."

Jake let them set him back down onto the rock slab. This time when Rachel handed him the canteen he drank deeply. His stomach felt queasy as it filled with water, and he inhaled, letting it settle. Making it settle. He took another drink. He was dehydrated, and burn victims needed lots of water to heal, to get back to full physical and mental capacity. He would be of no use to the group if he couldn't move or think clearly. He took stock, moving his ankles and knees, then his wrists and elbows. His skin was bunched and red, but they looked to be first-degree burns, more an annoyance than an actual injury.

Boots scraped on the rock and he looked up. Warren stood a few feet away, his hair plastered with mud. His face, however, was wiped clean, and his expression was calm, almost serene. "You going to be all right?"

Jake took another drink, then screwed the cap onto the canteen and handed it back to Rachel. "I'm fine."

"Good," Warren said, and crouched down on his knees so that he was face-to-face with Jake. "You want to tell me what the hell that was out there?"

Jake looked from Warren to Parkson, who stood a few feet off, then over to Cameron and Rachel. They were all looking at him as though he was going to let them in on a really good secret. "Serious?"

"Listen," Warren said. "There won't be any repercussions; we just want to know what we're up against. Greer is . . . missing, Jake. This is serious."

"Are you for real?" Jake said, pushing himself to his feet. Warren's face tilted and straightened, and the rest of Jake's vision came into focus a second later. He felt his legs gaining steadiness underneath him. There was really only one thing better than water for clearing his head, and he felt it coursing through him now, anger turning into rage, hot and bright. "Stand there, tell me this is serious?"

"If you knew about this—"

"If I knew about what?" He took a step forward, the sound of his boot hitting the rock very loud in the silence. That was followed by another scrape as Warren fell back a step. "You think I would've been wandering around this valley like a goddamn tourist if I knew it was going to rise up and try to fucking eat us?"

There was no sound except for their breathing. Warren had reset his feet and seemed ready to step back up into

Jake's face. Jake waited for it. He kept seeing Greer's eyes bugging out in pain and surprise as the tendrils punched through his trachea and gathered around his lifeblood like hogs at a trough. Warren had been somewhere in the distance, safe on his rock pad. Now here he was, telling Jake he would be forgiven if he would just pony up some information.

"He doesn't know any more than we do," Cameron said at last. "Back off and let him get some rest, Warren."

"He knows something," Warren said. "As soon as I told him where we were going, that I wanted him to lead us to Resurrection Valley, his rate doubled."

Their eyes, lit only by starlight and the faint glow of the aurora, swung back to him. Jake felt his anger spike up another notch. These city people, with their suspicion and their need for information, their need to assign blame, as though he was the one who had suggested going into this godforsaken wilderness in the first place. They were like children, blundering around in the woods with all the answers, then bawling when the real world didn't play by the rules. He felt rage building up inside him, the culmination of his irritation and anger, an eruption that would lead to action that would simultaneously distance himself from this group and set the matter straight on who was in charge.

"It's alive," Jaimie said. Her voice was calm, almost serene. They turned to her.

"What?" Warren said.

"There's life underneath us," she said, looking up. Her handsome face looked even stronger in the shadows of the starlight, but her eyes were very shiny and wide, and at the moment she looked like a young, scared girl. "More life below than above, sometimes."

"Enough," Warren said.

"It knows we're here," Jaimie said, her voice still calm, but her eyes darting out from the group to survey the wet, boulder-filled valley. "And now that it has a taste, it's not going to stop."

"Tend to Hans's arm," Warren said. "And shut up with that nonsense."

Parkson stepped into the middle of the rough triangle that had formed between Jake, Jaimie, and Warren. "Everybody needs to settle down," he said. "Jake saved my life, got me loose from whatever the hell is out there." He gestured out over the valley floor, silent and barren. "If he was watching all of it happen from up on the ridge, I might think differently. But he was right here, down in the slop with us."

Cameron cleared his throat and looked at Jake. "So what do we do?"

Jake looked out over the valley. From somewhere deep in the woods above them came the baritone call of a great horned owl. The air still smelled of fuel oil and smoke, but Jake couldn't tell if it was from his clothes or the remains of the drill rig. His shoulders settled a fraction of an inch. He turned and looked up the side slopes of the valley, which were streaked with mudslides. His eyes went back to the group, Parkson with his bad foot dangling off the ground, Hans with his dislocated shoulder. "What time is it?"

A green glow on Warren's wrist lit up his bearded face. "A little past midnight."

Jake did the math. The long days of summer had been shrinking for over two months, and it would not be light enough to see well for five hours. It would be a cool night, but not dangerously cold.

"Your satellite phone," Jake said to Warren. "Call in for help."

Warren shook his head. "It's on the solar charger, back at camp."

"Then we stay here until it's light enough to see," Jake said. "At dawn, I'll go for the campsite, see if we can get in touch with someone."

"Who did you have in mind?" Warren asked.

"Well," Jake said, "we got a dead guy half-buried out in the mud out there, and two men hurt. You got a chopper in here to drop off the drill rig, you can get another one in for medevac."

Warren turned away, looking up the slope toward the tents. Jake waited for him to say something, but Warren was silent. Jake followed his gaze up into the darkness. The camp was over the lip of the ridge, not visible from the bottom of the valley. No more than a couple hundred yards. He'd be able to stay clear of the softer ground if he took his time and waited for good light. There were several stretches where he would have to cross without relying on rocks for stepping stones, but he would be able to cross those quickly. Whatever was in the ground did not appear to be especially quick.

The owl called again, booming out the question its kind had been asking for countless millennia.

Who? Who?

Cameron and Rachel sat down on the rock, huddled close for warmth. Parkson sat down a little way off, and Rachel motioned for him to move closer. He slid his butt along the stone until he was against Rachel's other side, who put an arm around him and said something about a sandwich that caused both men to laugh softly. Warren stood off on his own, still looking up the valley. Jake was tempted to sit; huddling close to a stranger for warmth would not be a new experience. But the night air was clearing his mind even more, and he knew if he warmed up he would relax slightly, and that meant he would lose some of the edge he was just starting to regain. Even half-loopy and sunburned, he was best prepared to stand watch for the night.

Stand watch. And against what?

He looked down at the mud-splattered group. Somebody's teeth were chattering, and the sandwich pressed tighter together. After a few minutes the chattering subsided. Warren was still standing on the northern edge of the rock pad, and Jake supposed that was a good place for him. He didn't know if the tendrils would seek them out, if they could sense the vibrations the group sent down into the earth, or could feel the warmth of their bodies. He supposed anything was possible. He supposed, also, that some of the stories he had heard as a child were not entirely fiction after all, that the bad country was not named that because it was muddy or devoid of game. That his father's people understood there were places in the wilderness it was best to avoid, and if you had to visit them, it was wise to tread softly.

There's life underneath us. He heard Jaimie's words again, echoing in his mind like the calls of the owl. *More life below than above, sometimes.*

Above them, the Little Dipper scooped away at the darkness.

He had no watch and knew only that it was somewhere in the deepest part of the night when he heard the voice.

Warren was still standing guard on the north edge of the pad. He had been pacing from one edge of the low escarpment to the other to stay warm, and now he paused at the same time the sound reached Jake's ears. Warren was nothing but a silhouette, the black shape of a man backlit by the meager starlight, his head cocked to the side. The aurora had either faded or had been covered by clouds to the north. Rachel, Jaimie, and Cameron were breathing deeply in their small huddle. Parkson was still sitting with them, but Jake heard his breath catch for a moment and knew he was awake and had heard the noise as well.

Warren's head pivoted. "Was that—"

"Shhh," Jake whispered. The hair on his forearms and the back of his neck, already pushing out against the cold, began to tingle. Up until now the night had been very quiet; the only sounds were the breathing of the group and the light rustle of the northwest wind through the long grass. There were no sounds of the night creatures, as common in the northern woods as the constant hum of traffic had been in his campus apartment in St. Paul, the freeway only blocks away. His uncle Henry had told him that most animals had once slept at night, eons ago, and it was only when people learned to kill them so well that they were forced to adjust to moving about on the dark side of the earth's turn. But there was nothing prowling tonight. Even the owl had fallen silent.

Jake took in a shallow breath, then another. His pulse was pounding in his ears.

"Helllp."

Warren sucked in a breath and took a step back from the edge of the rock pad. Jake hissed at him to be still.

Parkson, who had twisted around at the sound, went motionless as well.

"Helllp meeeee."

It was coming from the darkness to the north, somewhere in the direction of where Greer had fallen. A scabrous, coarse whisper. Warren reached into his pocket and produced a small LED flashlight. The thin beam swung out into the darkness, tracing the contours of rocks and casting long fingers of shadow where it passed over the tall grass. The beam paused at a lump in the ground, just at the edge of the flashlight's power. The whisper came again.

"Pleeeessse helllp."

"Jesus Christ," Warren whispered, steam puffing from his mouth. He looked up as Jake joined him. "I thought he was dead."

"Give me that." Jake took the flashlight from Warren and trained it on the lump. It was fifty yards away, only partially visible through the matted grass and low rock outcroppings. It was impossible to see any details, but the voice was clear enough, if raspy and weak. Jake's mouth went sour as he thought of the hours-long struggle that had occurred in silence out in the soggy floodplain, Greer slowly pulling himself free from those waxy snares, half drained of blood and burned across his body. Clinging to the stubbornness of life.

Jake felt for his knife. He had spent a good hour sharpening it against the smooth edge of a stone, straightening out the invisible teeth until the edge bit into the back of his thumbnail without slipping.

The whisper came again, this time slurred and without meaning. *More of a whimper than a whisper,* Jake thought. *He can't have much left.* Greer must have crawled a good distance toward the rock pad, but he was either out of strength or he was ensnared by more tendrils. Jake started forward. Warren caught his arm.

"Give me the light," Warren said, his words smoking out into the night air. "I'm coming with."

"You leave me out there . . ."

Warren kept his hand extended.

Jake stared at him, but there was nothing to discern except the faint white of his eyes, the same intense but fundamentally calm expression. It would be difficult to carry Greer back alone and keep the light on the rocks. He placed the flashlight into Warren's palm. "Let's go."

They stepped from rock to rock, Warren lighting the way behind him so that the flashlight beam cast long shadows from Jake's legs out in front of them. Behind them they could hear Parkson rousing Rachel and Cameron, followed by Jaimie and Hans. Jake followed the flashlight beam from one rock to another, moving a few feet ahead of Warren. Moving this way reminded him of when he used to traverse the Little Glutton River in the summer with his friends, the rocks slimy and slippery at first when the river dropped, then crusting over. These rocks were slimy, too, and they weren't very large. The rock pad was the only area large enough to serve as a haven. Once they freed Greer, there would be no place to rest until they made it back to the pad.

Just keep moving, he thought. *It's strong but it's not fast. You'll be back before it even knows something is moving.*

"There he is," Warren said, jabbing the flashlight beam. "My Christ."

Greer was entombed in a nest of cobwebby filaments. He lay on his stomach with his arms outstretched and his head facing away from them. The filaments were much smaller than the tendrils they'd encountered earlier, no thicker than pencils and fuzzed over with a moldy growth. Thicker coils encircled his legs and torso. His neck and head were crusted over with a furry mat, creeping over the burnt skin on the back of his neck and into his heat-crinkled hair. His clothes were half burned off, and patches of heat-damaged skin showed through the holes, revealing more gray tentacles under his shirt.

Jake knelt down and gripped Greer's shoulder, where the mold was not too thick, and shook him. There was no response. He scrambled around to the other side. Warren followed, stepping lightly from one rock to another and then training the beam directly on Greer's face.

Jake recoiled. The mold had grown deep into Greer's eye sockets and nostrils, and the flesh on his cheeks was dissolved, eaten away almost to the bone. A few stray hairs from his beard were encased in a jellylike substance. The muscle that remained was devoid of blood, almost translucent, as though he had been lying there decomposing for weeks instead of hours. Behind him, the flashlight beam went bobbing off into space as Warren made a series of retching noises.

"Greer?" Jake shook him lightly, peering closer in the sudden darkness. "Can you hear me?"

Warren spat several times behind Jake, and the flashlight beam came back, wavering over Greer's ruined face. Greer lay there openmouthed, his tongue and teeth still intact, the rest of his face unrecognizable. Jake touched a finger to the side of Greer's neck, where several larger tendrils were still pressed tightly into the wound in his throat. The flesh under his fingers was cold and still.

"He's dead," Warren said. "Let's go, for Chrissakes."

Jake withdrew his hand and wiped his fingers on his jeans. There was nobody else out here who could have called for help, and even if there was . . . it had been Greer's voice, a gravelly baritone with a Southern accent, unmistakable, even in a whisper from death's door.

Jake held out his hand for the light. Warren protested again but Jake did not respond, just remained there with his hand outstretched behind him. After a moment, Warren placed the flashlight into his open palm.

Jake passed the light over Greer's chest. Two thick coils were looped under the smaller filaments, pressed tight against Greer's ribs. Another tendril snaked inside the entrance wound in Greer's throat. Jake saw Greer's throat bob, and a wild thought raced through his mind, simultaneously filled with relief and horror:

Alive! He's still alive!

Then the tendrils moved again, and he understood.

The two coils on Greer's throat contracted, squeezing stale air out of his mouth. At the same time, the tendrils wound inside his throat flexed and twisted, making Greer's pale throat bulge. A second later Greer's mouth opened grotesquely, the mandible creaking. Without thinking, Jake brought the flashlight up and saw the tendrils working inside the back of Greer's throat, spread out in his larynx like tiny, pale tentacles.

"Helllp mee-eeee."

Like a puppet, Jake thought, feeling blood draining from his face. *Except the strings are on the inside.*

"Helllp mee-eeee . . . plllleeeeassse . . ."

Now the tone seemed different, no longer pleading but sly, mocking, as though Jake were in on some great joke, an inside joke that only the two of them could fully appreciate. The mouth closed and opened, and it came again, the same plea, the coils around his chest squeezing out more air. No puffs of steam came from Greer. *Dead man's breath.* Jake's thoughts were wild and jumbled. *Dead man's breath and dead man's words and my Christ it's inside him and eating him and—*

More life below. More life below than above, sometimes.

Warren's hand was on his shoulder, jerking him back. Jake fell on his butt, and he saw one of the tendrils in the air where his face had been a second ago. The tentacle slithered back into the dark ground. Warren helped him up and they stumbled backward, their feet seeking purchase on the rocks. The flashlight beam swung crazily in the night air, and all Jake could think was *get back, we need to get back—*

Behind them, a scream cut through the night air. There was a thud and a grunt, and then another scream. It was Rachel's voice.

"No! Oh my god, it's got him!"

In front of them, Greer's voice huffed out something that sounded like laughter.

The scream came again, and then Warren gave Jake a rough shove and they were running back toward the rock pad, to the sound of something being dragged very fast over the stones in front of them.

Chapter 6

Cameron and Rachel were gone.

Jaimie had a larger, more powerful LED flashlight, and she was painting the valley floor with brilliant white light. In the slanting beam the small boulders and rocks looked like irregularly spaced headstones. Warren was sweeping his own flashlight over the same area, still panting from their flight. Jake did a quick scan and saw Parkson and Hans standing next to Jaimie, the two injured men standing very close to her, as though for protection. Jaimie was screaming for the two missing people, her strong voice booming out over the valley.

"What . . ." Jake said, trying to catch his breath, "what happened?"

"Rachel!" Jaimie shouted over the top of the flashlight beam. "Cameron!"

Jake grabbed her shoulder. "What happened?"

She shrugged him off and pointed the flashlight beam to the right, toward the river. "There!"

Jake saw them for a split second. Cameron was lying flat on his back, feet pointing away from them. He was struggling to sit up even as he was being dragged, and as they watched, his feet jerked farther into the darkness and he slipped back down, his head banging against the ground. Rachel was bent over his feet, working desperately on something, her face set in concentration. In the flashlight beam her sweaty face was pale, colorless; the world had gone black and white. Then Cameron's body jerked again and he disappeared into the darkness, Rachel scrambling after him.

"It's got him," Jaimie said. "We need a knife."

Jake stepped away from her as she swung the flashlight to Parkson, then Hans. Neither one had a blade. She turned to Warren, who just shook his head and pointed at Jake.

Jaimie swung around to Jake. "Give it to me," she said. "They need help."

Hellllp mmmeeee, Jake thought.

"It's a trap," he said. "It's trying to draw us off, one by one."

"Give me the fucking knife!"

Jake placed a hand over the hilt and took another step back. Jaimie's eyes widened, flashing at him in the backsplash of dim light. He held up a hand as she advanced. "We go together," he said. Jaimie stopped and cast an anxious look behind her, at the darkness where Cameron and Rachel had just been.

"Okay," she said. "Let's go."

"All of us," Jake said. "That way if one of us gets stuck the others can—"

"I can't," Hans said, his voice little more than a squeak. "I got a busted arm."

"He's right," Warren said. "Parkson's hurt, too."

"They're *dying* out there," Jaimie said. It was almost a scream. "Give it to me *now*."

Jake sized her up. The flashlight in her hands was the long-handled variety, and he supposed she wouldn't be averse to swinging it to get what she wanted. She would not be trained and he could take her, almost certainly, but why? She was right; they couldn't just leave Cameron and Rachel to fend for themselves. He wondered why in the hell it was taking him so long to go after them.

Hellllp mmmeeee.

It was not just the risk of dying that was paralyzing him; it was the dread of infestation. His father's people were adamant that the bodies of the dead remain intact, no autopsies, no burials. Jake had never felt strongly about it one way or another, but now he understood. It was one thing to be dead. It was another thing to be relegated to a piece of meat, a medium for others to poke and prod at, to remove the last shreds of dignity from the temple. And he knew that death waited for him out there in the darkness, had known it since he had looked inside Greer's mouth, had heard that sly, crackling whisper. Death, followed by the greatest horror of all, infestation.

Hellllp mmmeeee.

"Watch your feet," he mumbled.

"What?" Jaimie said. "Speak up!"

Jake cleared his throat. "When we find them, don't forget to keep an eye on your feet. It likes to distract you."

Jaimie regarded him for a second, and then the flashlight, which had been halfway raised, went down. Then she pivoted and swung the beam back to where it had been. There was a flash of movement behind one of the boulders, and then she was off, sparing one backward glance to make sure Jake followed. He ran after her, hand still on the hilt of his knife.

The ground grew wetter as they neared the river. There were several long furrows, and mud had splashed up against the boulders where Cameron had been dragged. Rachel's boot prints dotted the area at crazy angles, as though she had been doing some bizarre dance. Jake tugged at Jaimie's shoulder and motioned for her to shine the light on the ground. Jake leaned down, trying to discern something from the jumble of blurred footprints. In the middle there was a long, shallow depression, which must have been made by Cameron's body. The depression led farther west, paralleling the river.

"That way," Jake said, putting a hand on the flashlight and guiding it to the west. The rocks had grown larger closer to the river, but they were spaced farther apart. The flashlight beam went between two large, jutting boulders. In the LED light, the mud sprayed along one of the boulders was plainly visible. Beyond it, hidden somewhere behind the boulders, they could hear someone grunting with effort. Jaimie started to move toward the noise, and Jake grabbed her shoulder again.

"What?" she asked.

"Slow," Jake said. "Careful."

She waved a hand at him and took off, her boots squelching in the mud. Jake followed, calling after her to slow down. Jaimie kept going, casting the flashlight beam across the broken ground, bellowing for Rachel and Cameron. There was no answer. The ground grew soggier, yet he could see the trail plainly now through the boulders; a shallow rut pockmarked with footprints and the long grooves where Cameron's fingers had sought purchase in the mud. Jaimie stopped for a moment and trained the flashlight on the ground, letting Jake catch up to her. There was a splotch of red splashed across one of the boulders. Perched on top of the rock, at the terminus of the short crimson trail, was a fingernail, the base splintered and bloody.

Something wet and pale was wiggling out of the ground, stretching up toward its bloody prize.

Jaimie bolted forward, now in a full-fledged run, still bellowing. Jake followed, but she was long-legged and was quickly outstripping him, the flashlight beam bouncing farther and farther ahead. The little bit of light it cast behind Jaimie diminished. He dug in, tried to find another gear. He went a few more steps before his foot caught on an unseen boulder and he pitched forward, arms thrown out in front of his face. He landed on the soft ground with a splat, the cold mud enveloping his face and torso. He scrambled onto one of the boulders, kicking his boots hard against the ground like he was still playing fullback on the JV team, his coach hollering at him to pick up his goddamn feet. There was nothing there, no tendrils, just mud and rock. He took a deep breath and looked out over the valley.

Jaimie was invisible, but the flashlight beam showed intermittently between the rocks, already a hundred yards or more ahead. Jake balanced atop his tenuous perch, straining to see what direction she was headed. He heard someone call out in the darkness and Jaimie's bellowing reply. Something brushed against his boot, and he kicked it away, shuffling to the other side of the boulder. It was not much of a sanctuary, barely large enough for his size eleven boots.

"Over here!"

This time Rachel's voice was clear, but there was no answer from Jaimie. Jake closed his eyes against the meager starlight and took several deep breaths. Something rasped against the side of the rock, scraping along the surface as it crept upward.

Come on, he thought, trying to pinpoint the location of the voice. He closed his eyes. *One more time.*

There was no sound except the scrape of the unseen tendril, climbing higher on his perch, and the faint sigh of the breeze, carrying with it the sour smell of the river. And then, less than a hundred yards off, he heard Rachel's voice again. He turned toward the sound and opened his eyes. It was very dark, but his night vision had been calibrated against the back of his eyelids and he could see, faintly, the boulders and the muddy ground between them. Rachel and Cameron were now far to the south; whatever was dragging them along had not followed a linear path. It had taken a left turn, curving away from the river.

Jake kicked at the tendril that was nestling against his boot and leapt down from his rock perch. He trotted for a bit, then slowed into his still-hunting gait; neither fast nor slow, a steady heel-to-toe walk that produced minimal vibration and sound. He had used it with success on deer, on moose and caribou. Once on a sleeping black bear on the side of a greening valley in late April, the bear enjoying the sunshine that bathed the lush valley, its belly full of the fresh greens. Its exhalations were coming out in something close to snores, paws stretched out in front of it, claws retracted. It was too early for mosquitoes or blackflies, and the bear was dead to the world, winter-skinny but with a full belly. Jake had been just as quiet when he slipped away, the sound of the bear's snores making him grin for days afterward.

Something swung over him in the night, very low. He hunched his shoulders instinctively and looked up. It was a large owl, winging through the constellations and swinging low over him, its head swiveling, perhaps the same owl they had heard earlier. The owl was gone as quickly as it had appeared, its head still casting back and forth, in the exact same direction Jake was headed.

He paused, thinking. Then he turned and started down a different path, one that would bring him to the left of where he had heard Rachel's voice. His own nonlinear route.

In a few minutes, he heard noise ahead of him and slowed again, then stopped. Rachel was panting, her breaths interspersed with a chopping noise. He was almost even with her position, roughly 180 degrees from the angle Jaimie had approached. The ground was harder here, and in the starlight he could see he was on a wide outcropping of stone tilting out of the ground at a gradual angle so that he was now several feet above the ground. The surface under him was jagged and uneven, and he picked his way across the fissured rock, careful to avoid a fall. The urge to call out to Rachel was very strong, but he remained silent. Jake had known some old trappers from Highbanks who would drag a lure-soaked piece of rabbit skin behind their snowmobiles, a scent trail that eventually led to the prize, the bloody flesh inside the wooden box cubby, the entrance guarded with cold steel. This situation reminded him of that trick, pulling the unwitting pursuer into a deadly little cul-de-sac.He peered into the darkness, Rachel some unseen yards ahead of him, panting and chopping, Jaimie quiet, either in her own stealth mode or off the trail.

He worked to steady his breathing, steady his thoughts. The animals that always gave those old trappers fits were the fishers and wolverines, the smart ones that attacked the back of the fortlike cubby. They knew the front entrance was too good to be true.

He waited. A meteorite carved a brilliant yellow slash across the firmament. Some time later another meteorite flashed, the arc shorter and furiously bright, blasting straight into the atmosphere instead of following the oblique angle its brethren had taken. Jake was motionless, his breath smoking in front of him. In the light of the second meteorite he had seen the landscape in front of him clearly, marked by numerous rock formations, jagged triangles and smooth domes. The chopping continued but was slowing, the sounds echoing faintly inside the labyrinth of stones. Rachel's breathing had grown ragged, desperate. Above Jake the night sky was scratched by lesser lights, the tail end of the Perseids.

Wait, he thought. *Wait.*

The chopping stopped suddenly. "Jaimie?" Rachel's voice was wheezy. "Where are you?"

She was closer than Jake had thought, but he could tell from the projection of her voice that she was facing away from him. He turned his head and saw the thin white cloud of her breath rising above a jumble of stones.

"Jaimie? Please say something."

From the darkness came a wheezing reply, indecipherable. Rachel began to sob. "Jaimie, is that you? I . . . I can't tell."

This time the silence was longer, and then he heard movement. When Rachel spoke again her voice was clearer, and he could tell she was standing up. "Okay, I'm coming."

Shit.

"No," Jake said. "Don't move."

He heard the scrabble of feet on rock, the voice now close by. "Who is that? Jake?"

"It's me," he said, just loud enough for her to hear. "Don't move."

"You have to help us," she said. "It has Cameron in a choke hold and I can't"—she grunted, and the chopping sound came again—"I can't get him *free*. He's not breathing, and Jaimie's out there somewhere and she sounds hurt—"

"Listen," Jake said. "Whatever has a hold on Cameron has Jaimie, too. It wants all of us."

A strained breath, another chop. "If I could just—"

"Rachel." His voice was not much more than a whisper, but firm. "Move to high ground—now. Trust me."

"High . . . high ground?"

"The tallest rock you can climb."

"What about Cameron?"

"I'll take care of him."

A pause. "I'll help."

"Rachel—"

"I'm not leaving him. His face . . . purple."

Jake picked his way forward, moving through the stones, many as tall as he was. The ground between them kept changing from hard to soft, sometimes from one step to the next. It was like wading the Hellshair Creek for brook trout, never knowing what the next step would bring—gravel, sand, or simply a crevice between two rocks, all of it hidden by the frothing, swirling water. One misstep and you were stuck in the freezing water, pinched between two boulders or mired in quicksand. He always fished the Hellshair alone, and there was nobody to help free him if he became trapped. Well. They were very big trout.

C'mon Jake, concentrate.

"What?" Rachel said.

He had not realized he'd spoken aloud. He looked up from his careful surveying of his path and saw her outline ahead of him. Her head was steaming from exertion, and she held a rock the size of an ax-head in her right hand. All around her were more man-sized boulders, the jagged peaks like crude teeth encircling her. There was a human shape huddled at her feet, one foot twitching. One of the tallest rocks also had the flattest pitch, ending in a rounded point. There was a small ledge halfway up, and he motioned her toward it, unsure if she could see him. It was the only haven he could see.

"Get up on that rock while I cut him free."

"I'm not leaving him."

"Get up there," he said. "It's going to do something when I cut it. It's going to react, and you need to be out of the way."

She stared down at Cameron for a second, made as

though to toss the rock she held, and instead kept it in her grip. She turned and scrambled up the side of the boulder, coming to a rest with her feet on the small ledge, her arms wrapped around the peak. The sanctuary would be of little help if one of the tendrils—some of which seemed to be hundreds of feet long—decided to reach up and pluck her off of her perch, but it was better than standing on top of them.

Jake stepped, heel-to-toe, over to Cameron. Cameron's face was dark purple, his teeth bright in the starlight as he fought for breath. Somehow, he still wore his glasses, although the frames were bent and mangled, and one earpiece hung down his cheek. The lenses were intact, however, and behind them his eyes were very wide. The tendrils had him at the throat and the ankles, but nowhere else that Jake could see, the coil around his neck just loose enough so that Cameron could draw in meager breath. This tendril was dented and bruised, but the places where Rachel had struck it seemed to have scabbed over, the gray mold he had noticed before filling in over the damaged tissue. Jake knelt down. Feet or throat first? He thought of Greer as he lay under the burning drill rig, the way the tendrils had crushed him when Jake had tried to take their prize away. They seemed to be growing stronger, and their ability to drag a full-grown man hundreds of yards spoke to their size and power. It would only take one contraction and the powerful tendril would snap Cameron's neck. The length around his feet was even thicker, leading off into the darkness. It flexed and loosened, as though it were taunting Jake, or waiting for him to make his decision.

"You son of a bitch," Jake breathed.

The tendril around Cameron's throat constricted again, harder this time, and Cameron's eyes bugged out in pain. Jake brought the knife down, severing the tendril wrapped around his neck. It fell away, and Cameron managed one deep inhalation before he was jerked, screaming, out of the rock circle by the tendril around his ankles.

Jake raced after him, shouting at Rachel to stay where she was. Cameron was only a few feet in front of him, turned on his side, his hands reaching out for Jake. His body was sluicing through the mud, slaloming off boulders as he careened through the narrow openings. He started to pull away and Jake leapt for him, his left hand extended. His fingers slipped over Cameron's chest, grazing over his shoulders and neck, then down one trailing arm as Cameron was pulled out from underneath him—

Cameron's hand encircled Jake's wrist. They went skidding along the wet, hard ground together, the pace never slowing despite Jake's added weight and friction. They hit a low rock and Cameron grunted with pain, and a second later Jake collided with it and felt a searing pain along his ribs. Cameron's grip held but Jake could already feel it weakening; there was no way he could maintain his hold, and Jake would never catch him again. He couldn't get close to Cameron's ankles to cut him free, and there were only a few seconds left before his grip would fail—and another moment after that before Cameron would be dragged, alone, into the darkness.

Jake brought his knife hand up and over, rotating the grip slightly as he positioned it over Cameron. He tapped Cameron's chest with the flat side of the blade.

"Take it."

Cameron's free hand closed over the hilt. A second later they hit another boulder and Cameron's grip loosened, his fingers breaking contact with Jake's fingers one by one. They were hooked, index finger to index finger, for a moment. Jake's tendon felt like it might pop. Then the last connection broke and Jake fell onto the wet ground.

Cameron, no longer screaming, disappeared into the night, Jake's knife held tightly in his hand.

YESTERDAY'S WARRIORS

Chapter 7

They found him by the river, and right away Billy knew they shouldn't have come. Darius was sitting cross-legged on the ground, looking out over the water with his back to them. There was a low smudge fire going in front of him, a small pile of balsam boughs over a bed of coals. Darius was wearing jeans but no shirt, and other than his bare torso the only thing different about him, at least from outward appearances, was the absence of his cell phone. His knife was stuck in a stump next to him, and Billy could see the blood on the hilt even from where he and Garney paused, twenty yards away.

Garney stepped down hard on a dead branch, the noise like a small firecracker under his boot. Darius didn't turn around. Garney looked at Billy, eyebrow raised. He was sweating heavily, the rivulets of sweat running down his broad face and soaking into the collar of his shirt.

Beyond Darius, the Little Glutton River swirled around the granite rocks, the river very high for the late summer. Garney circled wide around Darius and looked out over the swollen river, his shirt back with a V of sweat running all the way from his broad shoulders to his equally broad waist. Billy joined him, grateful for the fire's smoke after the long, buggy walk to the river. The deerflies were thick, and he swatted several off his arms even standing directly downwind of the smudge fire. After a little while, because he couldn't not look, he looked.

The largest cut ran from Darius's left shoulder diagonally down his chest, ending just under his right nipple. Two scars were above it, running in parallel like a scratch from a bear. His belly was covered in blood, and it had soaked into the waistband of his jeans. Billy looked at Darius's face, expecting his eyes to have the faraway, dreamy look he associated with holy men and their visions—the look also of crazy men and their visions. But Darius's eyes were hard and focused, looking out over the river as though some enemy were wading toward them.

Billy followed his gaze. The water was stained brown from the heavy rains that had swollen the wetlands. In a normal year, most of the base flow was from groundwater, cool and untainted by the touch of the land. Now it was just tea-colored water, nothing out there to glare about that Billy could see. Then again, Darius saw a lot of things to be angry about. Sometimes it took the rest of them a little time to catch up.

"We got news," Garney said.

Darius stood. He was built as solidly as any man Billy had ever seen, including his football teammates at the community college in Regina. Darius had never lifted weights that Billy knew of, but he was well-muscled, especially his shoulders and back. He wasn't defined—he liked his beer, and he never ran or did anything aerobic—but there was nothing soft about him either. His eyes were still very hard, and Billy looked away. After a moment, Darius eased himself down the bank of the river and waded out to wash the blood off his chest.

Garney paced the riverbank. Billy stood next to the stump, watching Darius ladle water over his chest, wondering if this was the man he wanted to follow. Wondering if there was anywhere Darius could lead them that Billy couldn't get to himself. The river water washed away the blood, and more welled to the surface, running down his stomach. Darius stared at the water, which was turning pink as he cleaned himself.

Go ahead, Billy thought. *Get mad at the water; see if it helps your mood.*

Garney moved next to Billy, breathing through his mouth. "We shoulda waited."

Billy didn't say anything. Garney was right, but he was also wrong. There was no right time; had they waited, Darius would have been equally furious. Billy walked over and carefully kicked the smudge fire apart. With the woods this green, the chances of wildfire were low, but it was something to do besides watch their great leader standing in the river in the middle of the woods, staring at his own blood spreading in the water.

After a few minutes, Darius climbed back onto the bank and pulled his shirt on. The cotton clung to his skin and turned red.

"We didn't know if we should bother you," Garney said.

"I'm guessing it's important."

Billy looked to Garney, who was still standing there

mouth-breathing, wiping mosquitos off his forearms. "His brother was out hunting," Billy said, "a few miles north of the Braids. He saw a plume of smoke, not far from where the chopper was going earlier this summer."

Darius frowned, rubbing at the pink scar above his eyebrow. "Wildfire?"

"No," Garney said. "Russel said it was black and thick, like a tire burning or something. Right up near Asiskiwiw."

"Resurrection Valley," Darius said. "He didn't go look, eh?"

"No," Garney said. "He was a good three or four miles out when he saw it, up on top of that big hill this side of the Braids. He didn't want to cross the river by himself."

"He's sure it wasn't from a brush fire?"

"Not sure," Garney said. "But you told all of us to watch out for anything different, and Russel said the smoke looked man-made. If it was a brush fire, somebody threw a tire in there, too."

"Asiskiwiw," Darius said.

He laced his fingers together and closed his eyes. His nostrils flared, and after a moment a line of sweat appeared on his brow. The low rumble of a passing logging truck came from the provincial road, three miles away. Billy watched as a mosquito landed on Darius's eyelid, its abdomen swelling with blood. After thirty seconds it lumbered back into the air, her belly filled with enough fuel to make another thousand just like her. More mosquitoes landed and drank their fill, stepping delicately around the drops of sweat rolling down Darius's face, landing on his shirt where the blood was seeping through the cotton. Another logging truck went by, the metal stakes rattling in the bed sockets.

Finally Darius opened his eyes, and Billy saw a bit of something in those dark brown orbs he hadn't seen before. Not fear, exactly, but a close cousin.

"Okay," Darius said. "We have to go see her."

They dropped Garney off at his girlfriend's house and headed west out of Highbanks. The gravel road was muddy and rough, beaten into uneven lanes by the logging trucks. They passed the meadow that housed the annual powwow and First Dance ceremonies, a huge pile of tamarack and balsam logs drying out over the summer for the big fire. Billy smiled, thinking about all the babies, ranging from a few weeks old to a year, crawling and spitting and crying and giggling in their little ceremonial dresses. There was supposed to be a bumper crop of First Dancers this year, a couple dozen babies from all the surrounding area.

They passed an active timber cut a few miles down the road, a hundred-acre clearing filled with mud-splattered brush. A clam-bunk skidder was perched on the near edge of the clear-cut, arranging the long aspen trunks for the forwarder. Billy craned his head to watch as he and Darius drove past, trying to make out the operator behind the mesh-covered glass.

"I think that was Weasel's cousin."

"Marvin?" Darius said. He shook his head. "He's up in Potowatik. Sixty days. Couldn't come up with the fine money after he punched that constable."

The drive got smoother as they passed the logging operation, and the road closed back in on them. After another couple of miles, the gravel turned to something closer to dirt, and mud splattered against the bottom of Darius's truck as they headed north. The aspen forest turned to black spruce, the deep ditches full of brown water.

"You going to log with Garney and them this winter?" Darius asked.

Billy took awhile to answer him, a good half mile of corduroy road passing under them, graded into a series of bumps. "I don't know," he said at last. "Maybe."

"You don't think it bothers me, do you?"

"Why would it bother you?"

Darius cranked his window down and spat into the slipstream of air. He turned to look at Billy. "There's folks around here think I'm against everything."

Billy opened his own window and cocked his elbow outside, studying the black spruce forest. There was a market for these scraggly trees, too, mostly for their pulp. Logging was one of the few professions around Highbanks that allowed a man to make a decent wage, and it was the only way Billy had been able to overwinter himself the past couple years. He didn't mind the work, and the money was good. Christ knew they had enough trees to go around.

He glanced over at Darius. "You think calling the Blacksky crew a bunch of earth-rapers could have possibly had anything to do with that?"

"That was different," Darius said, "and you know it."

"Okay."

"They were using wheeled rigs in early May," Darius said. "The frost was barely out. You walk out there you can still see the ruts. If old man Blacksky had used his tracked rigs instead—"

"I get it." Billy put his hand outside the window, palm flat, and moved it up and down on the air currents, banking left and right. He thought it must be how a hawk felt when it soared on the thermals. Darius turned down a rutted track, and the trees closed in again. They rattled up a steep hill, the shelves of bedrock like giant, tilted stairs. The truck's frame scraped against the rocks as Darius eased it up the hillside. "How come Garney couldn't come with?"

"He ate today." Darius downshifted into low gear. "You haven't."

"Serious?"

"She thinks it matters. And don't even think about coming out here with liquor on your breath."

"How'd you know Garney had eaten and I hadn't?"

"Because you never eat breakfast," Darius said, "and Garney smells like he took a bath in maple syrup."

Billy laughed. "He always smells that way."

"Listen," Darius said, pulling to a stop in front of a tarpaper shack. "I wanted *you* with me, not Garney and not Weasel. Never Weasel. You got your doubts about me. It don't take any touch, any sight, to know that. But I don't have any doubts about you."

They got out of the truck and started toward the house. There was no lawn, and tall grass and brush grew right up to the walls. Close to the house, the grass had turned yellow and the brush was dead, denuded of leaves. Billy supposed it had been sprayed with some sort of herbicide, or maybe salted. The house was small, twenty feet by sixteen feet, not much more than a shack covered with peeling tar paper, the asphalt shingles cracked and curled. The south and west walls were faded gray by sunshine. The tar paper on the east and north walls was still black under a crust of grayish-green lichen. There were two small windows, curtains drawn on the inside. The grass was matted down along the western side of the shack, and small bones were strewn in a pile in the middle of the clearing. There was still flesh on some of the bones.

Just rabbit bones, Billy thought. *Or maybe grouse.*

And on the heels of that thought, another: *Why in the hell haven't the bones been scattered by predators?*

He turned to Darius. "You come out here alone?"

"It's not as bad as you think," Darius said, absentmindedly. He stepped on the pallet in front of the door, his normally rough voice meek. "Elsie?"

There was a low yowl from inside the shack, and the sound of something heavy hitting the floor. Billy saw the curtain flutter slightly and scrambled back, his heart rising up in his throat. He caught himself before he turned and ran for the truck. The pale yellow eyes he'd seen belonged to a cat, poking its enormous black head through the curtains to inspect the visitors. It withdrew slowly, its eyes never leaving Billy's face until the curtain fell back across the window.

"You okay?" Darius asked.

"That's one big fucking cat," Billy said. "Ready to go?"

"We aren't leaving," Darius said. "She knows we're here."

"What do you mean?" Billy asked. He looked at the shack again, and then let his eyes roam over the forest that surrounded them. It was mostly balsam fir and spruce, grown so closely together there was no way to walk through them except for several twisting trails lined with brown needles. The cat yowled from inside the house, deeper this time, almost a growl. "She could be anywhere, Darius."

"Yes," Darius said. "Exactly."

"Quit being a goddamn creep."

Darius turned to him, unsmiling. "We'll wait in the truck."

They were almost out of cigarettes, the windows rolled up to ward off the mosquitoes, when they saw the shape standing at the edge of the overgrown lawn. It was twilight, and all they could see was a silhouette, a wizened figure clutching a bucket in one hand, the other hanging loosely at her side. She was looking not at them but rather at the grass at the edge of the lawn, a few feet away. She crossed over to it and knelt, plucked a strand of long grass with her free hand, and held it next to her mouth. When she stood again, they could see her licking her lips.

"That's right where I pissed," Billy said.

"Quiet," Darius said.

"Does she even know we're here?"

"Yes." It was the woman's voice, Elsie's voice, high and strident, loud enough to be heard through closed windows. "Yes and yes. Come on, boys. Help an old lady clean some cranberries."

Billy stepped out into the tall grass. Elsie was moving toward the shack, her back to him, and he saw just how small she was. For some reason, he had always imagined her to be tall, stringy but strong, the kind of woman who would grab you by the shoulders and curse at you face-to-face. This woman was not much bigger than a sixth-grader, and, carrying her bucket into the shack, she reminded Billy of just that, a farm kid coming in from the evening milking.

They followed her, the wind sighing in the firs and spruce. Billy fell into line behind Darius as they stepped onto the pallet and into the house.

Elsie was already sitting at the kitchen table. The smell was intense, the sour stench of unwashed bodies and cat piss, of leftovers scraped onto the floor and not eaten. The only thing he had ever experienced that rivaled the reek inside these cloistered walls was the fur trader's building, the flensed skins and the barrels full of carcasses in various states of decomposition. He saw Darius stiffen a bit in front of him when the smell hit him, then square his shoulders and keep going.

There were several sections of newspaper spread out in front of Elsie, and she had dumped the contents of her bucket atop the yellowed paper. A small single-mantle lantern hung on a hook above them, illuminating the sprawl of highbush cranberries that covered most of the table. There were some leaves and twigs still attached to the berries, and Elsie's fingers, disproportionately long compared to the rest of her, picked and plucked even as she surveyed her visitors. Her fingertips were stained red by the juice, the nails long and yellow. She motioned to the chairs.

They sat down and started picking, pulling the clusters apart and setting the cleaned fruit back into the bucket. It was tedious work, and Billy was glad for it—the kind of busy work he had always enjoyed when his mind was in turmoil. There were long oval pits in the cranberries, and the flesh was incredibly sour, not the kind of fruit his family had ever bothered with. Wild strawberries and raspberries were a treat growing up, but blueberries were always the main show. He glanced up and saw that Elsie was staring at him, her hands working below, never pausing even as she surveyed him. She was old, but he had no idea what decade of life might be hers; this far north, fifty years could look like eighty. Her eyes were sharp but rimmed with gunk, her skin mottled and touched by past frostbite. Her teeth were mostly hidden behind the cracked lips, but those he could see were yellow and worn. He looked back down.

"You brought me a Thomas," she said at last. Her voice, which Billy had only heard when she called out to them, was not unpleasant. "Why?"

"It's not just you he doubts," Darius said.

Elsie slid her chair next to Darius and laid a hand on his leg. Billy watched as her red-stained hand roamed over him, up and down his legs, twisting momentarily in his lap, her face intent, studious. Darius sat unmoving, a clump of cranberries in his hand. The cat, which Elsie called Piss-Whiskers, padded into the kitchen to watch. Its head was almost the size of a basketball.

"You're cloudy, Darius," she said. "But not completely dark." She reached down and squeezed the cranberries he held, then traced a line through the bright red juice. "This is not the first time your hands have been red this month, is it?"

"No." Darius's voice was little more than a whisper.

She leaned in close, as though she were going to kiss him. "And what did that do for you?"

"It was needed."

"It was?"

"They came to take. Like you said they would do, Elsie. Take and take, and never give back."

"And now?" she asked.

"Now we must do what is needed again."

"Ahh," she said, then pulled back and withdrew her hand. "I see you leaving soon, Darius, perhaps as early as the coming dawn. Five of you." She gestured toward Billy. "Even if this one could learn our ways, his own doubt is like a blanket over his head. It would take months, years, to open his eyes."

"No, I didn't bring him here for that," Darius said. "I brought him only to meet you, in case there is a need for . . . guidance . . . in the future." He took a deep breath. "I cannot see myself returning, Elsie."

She leaned in close and sniffed, her nostrils flaring. "Have you smelled its breath?"

"No," Darius said, drawing back. Billy could see him suppressing a shudder, not sure if it was from Elsie's presence, inches from his face, or her question. "I smell *nothing*, I see *nothing*. Not my death, not my return. And the place where we must go is—"

"Speak not of it," Elsie said. "Bad enough that I have seen it in your mind."

"We have to go," Darius said. "We both saw this, Elsie. That which is ours being ripped from the earth."

She traced a finger through the berries that remained on the table, staring at the path she created.

"Others have gone there and returned," Darius said.

Elsie leaned back, her arms falling to her sides. After a moment, Piss-Whiskers padded over and nudged his enormous black head into her palm. Elsie stroked him absently. "Yes, but this is not a hunting trip. You go with the red haze in you. To a place we are better off to not visit."

"What? We just stay here, then—let them do what they want?"

She chuckled. "Your anger is admirable, Darius. This other, this Doubting Thomas, has some of it as well. A fine group of young men. Of warriors?" She sighed. "You want my counsel?"

"I do, old mother."

"Take the middle path. Wait for them to leave that place, and then butcher them in the forest." Her eyes gleamed. "String their guts from the branches for the crows to peck on and the marten to gorge himself on. Throw the rest into the swamp. This you know how to do."

Darius said nothing. Above them, a moth almost the size of his hand circled the hissing lantern. Billy had never seen one like it before, black all the way through except for a band of iridescent blue along the edges of its wings. Its shadow danced along the walls, flittering across shelves filled with jars full of meat; canned venison, the meat gray, floating in its own liquids. The cat watched it with him, the irises in its yellow eyes narrowed to slits.

Darius leaned toward her. "If we wait, they may escape. If we take them in the valley—"

"Yes," Elsie said slowly. "And yet my counsel is to stay in the forest. They may not even find anything worth returning for, Darius. Wait for them, and they will carry answers with them." She paused, her tongue flicking at the corner of her mouth. "If they even make it out."

"Can you see if they will?"

"Ah." She smiled. "So that is what you ask of me, then. Your own blindness makes you hard to read, Darius."

"Can you see?"

Elsie stood and lifted the bucket of cleaned berries from the table. She set them in the sink, then poured some water from a jug into a cloudy glass. She drank deeply, her scrawny throat convulsing. When she turned back to them, water had run down her face and soaked into the collar of her shirt. She glanced at the moth, still circling the lantern, and muttered something under her breath. The moth's circles around the lantern widened, and a moment later it lit atop one of the jars of canned venison to rest. Billy turned back to Elsie's face, now even harsher in the slanting lantern light.

"I won't turn my eyes to look upon that place, Darius," she said. "Lest something looks back."

Darius looked to Billy, then back to Elsie. He nodded.

Elsie sat back down next to him. "Wait, and take them in the forest."

"Old mother, I promise nothing."

She mumbled something again, and stared at one of the narrow windows. Through the crack in the curtains Billy could see the night sky had gone completely dark. The wind was rising, and he could feel the breezes working through the numerous chinks in the shack's walls. How she spent a winter out here without freezing was beyond him; the small wood-burning stove in the corner would struggle to keep temperatures above freezing most days. There was no woodpile, just some deadfall she had broken off from the lower branches of the spruces and firs. *Maybe she hibernates,* Billy thought. *Squeezes down into the mud and muck for the winter.*

"You said you saw us leaving," Darius said after a while, "at dawn."

"Yes."

"There are four of us, four *Okitchawa.* Who is the fifth you mentioned?"

She was still looking out the window and spoke without turning. "I send you young fools with an old fool. But one who has been there before, one who has fasted in the forest. He will have counsel for you, Darius."

"Henry? Henry Redsky?"

She scratched at a patch of scarred skin on her cheek with one long fingernail. "Tell him *osikosa* says it's finally time for him to be the wise man he always thought he would be."

"You said there would be five of us," Darius said, "before you knew my decision."

"It is you who are blind," Elsie said slowly. "Not I."

Darius stood, and Billy did the same, his knees popping loudly in the little room. Instead of moving toward the door, Darius stepped behind Elsie's chair and began to knead the back of her shoulders. Billy watched as Elsie's faraway look contracted, became focused. She turned to look at him, her mouth parting, a line of saliva suspended between her cracked lips. One of her hands creeped up and entwined with Darius's, their fingers lacing together. The cat, which had been sitting on the floor watching them, gave a low, displeased yowl and scurried into the back room.

"Go wait in the truck, Billy-dog," Darius said, then grinned when he saw Billy's expression. "Unless you want to join in."

Billy fled into the night.

Chapter 8

Jake stood atop the boulder they had chosen for their refuge, the early sunlight filtering through the dense morning fog. He pried a piece of granite from the rock and heaved it into the distance. It splatted down in the mud forty yards away, no bounces, no movement from the saturated ground. Nothing at all.

"Be ready to move," he said.

Rachel was sitting with her knees drawn up to her chest, her arms wrapped around her legs. They had been on this boulder for two hours, ever since Cameron had disappeared. As the blackness softened into gray, the landscape had taken focus around them, a strange rock garden that looked like the carnage resulting from a mudslide. Stones ranging from the size of a man's head to some as large as a pickup truck were strewn throughout the river valley. The boulder they stood on elevated them six feet above the ground, giving them a clear view of the river, a flat, gray expanse just to the north of them. The water was fringed with a sparse stand of cattails, which gave way to sedge grasses and then mossy, muddy ground next to the water. The ground dipped behind them before it reached the valley slope, and it was covered in mud slicks and puddles. Far above them, they could hear birdsong drifting down.

"Are we even going to look for them?"

Jake looked up again at the top of the valley, only a few hundred yards away. If they could thread their way around the soft spots and make it to the top, the satellite phones could bring help. Just as important, they would be on dry ground. Whatever creature was out there, it seemed to be able to move easily through the soft mud of the valley floor, but it could not move through rock or harder ground. It could move on top of the rock, yes, and he suppressed a shudder as he thought of how it could move through the human body as well. But one thing seemed clear; the higher they got, the less likely this thing was to wrap its tendrils around them.

"What are we dealing with, Rachel?"

She looked at him, lips pursed. "I don't know."

"Bullshit," he said. "This is the reaction you were talking about, isn't it?"

"No," she said, "nothing like this." Her eyes drifted over the broken ground, then back toward the rock pad where Warren, Hans, and Parkson were still presumably waiting for them. Jake watched her, studying her face. He believed her when she said she didn't know what was happening—she was in as much shock as anyone—but she had expected *something*.

"When we were coming back from the pond, you said there was something more the promethium did, besides just transferring properties from one organism to the other."

"Jake, I can't—"

"You want to get out of this valley?" he asked. "I can help you do that, but you have to give me intel."

She took a deep breath, then exhaled. "It's selective in the properties it transfers. The most basic, the most primal tendencies tend to get transferred first."

"Eat, sleep, screw?"

"No," she said. "Survival instincts. I saw the candle-flowers take evasive action when I approached, which was transferred from something. Water bugs, or maybe those ducks. There's one other reaction they could have had."

"Fight or flight," he murmured. "And we just rammed it several times with a drill core tube."

"Yes."

"And what is it?" That was what he really needed to know, because whether it was people or animals, once he knew what he was up against, he could kill it.

Maybe.

"I'm not exactly sure," she said. "It's enormous, obviously, and it can release toxic spores. It has long tendrils made of fleshy material. You said Greer had mold on him?"

"Yes."

"I think it's some kind of fungus," she said. "Certain ones that are underground can extend for miles. A honey mushroom in Oregon is the world's largest living organism, Jake."

He turned, almost spat, and swallowed it instead. "You saying we're being hunted by some kind of pissed-off mushroom?"

"That's not—"

"Because it *is* hunting us, Rachel. It's ambushing us and luring us out, picking us off one by one. And it's doing a damn good job of it, too. The most action I've seen out of a mushroom before is when one flipped over by itself in a hot frying pan." He turned, and this time he did spit, angrier than he had been. "And I blame that one on the butter."

"Okay," she said. Her eyes were ringed by purple shadows, but her gaze was steady. "Fine. What's your explanation?"

He held her gaze for a second, then looked away. There was another explanation, and it was even more ludicrous than Rachel's. It was the reason this territory was called the bad country, *macimaliki*. The place where the *Whitigo* had been buried, even though he— it—wasn't quite dead. Nobody came here, not from Highbanks or any of the other scattered Cree villages, ostensibly because there was no game. As Rachel had noted, the area was mostly devoid of animal life, as certain sections of the bush would sometimes be after a pack of wolves moved through it. But whatever the local people blamed it on, they all knew the story, the legend of the valley that had two names, English and Cree.

Resurrection Valley. Asiskiwiw. The heart of the bad country.

"I—"

His voice broke off as the sound came to them, distorted as it bounced off the rock. It was laughter, or perhaps weeping, the thin, high cries coming from the boulder-strewn country to their south. It came again, a gibbering that was impossible to pinpoint. They looked at each other, listening as the cries came again, then slowly faded away.

"Was that . . ." she swallowed hard. She stood clutching her forearms, her skin covered in gooseflesh. Behind her, the bottom of the sun was just separating from the horizon, a pale orb behind the heavy river fog. A ghost of a sun. "Was that Cameron?"

"Rachel," he said. "Don't move."

A small tendril had emerged from the soil at the base of one of the rocks. It was dark, almost black. It rested against the rocks just below them, and for a moment Jake had the distinct impression that it was listening to their conversation; it even looked like a small microphone. Then the top of it split open, and a cloud of dust spread from its ruptured tip. The cloud drifted upward, spreading over them in a hanging cloud. They stepped back to avoid it, and more dust settled over them, emanating from somewhere behind them. Rachel waved at the dusty air with her hands. Then her look of mild annoyance changed to one of painful surprise, and her hands went to her throat, as though she were trying to choke herself.

"Come on," he shouted.

She stumbled toward him, out of the cloud. Jake caught her hand and turned to escape, feeling the burn in the back of his throat. More clouds were rising into the air all around them, enveloping the small rock formation. There was only one open escape route, a patch of relatively uncontaminated air leading down into an open stretch of muddy ground.

Rachel was clawing at her throat. The clouds of dust (*Spores,* Jake thought—w*e're breathing in part of this goddamn thing*) were increasing, and he could hear more tendril ends splitting open, a soft *thooooptt* as they ruptured, the gray dust hanging in the foggy air. He stripped off his shirt, ripped it in half, and wound one end around Rachel's face.

"Not there," he said, tugging Rachel away from the open path. "We go into it."

She tried to pull away from him. "Can't breathe."

"Rachel!" He took a loose rock and flipped it down the alley of clear air, using the same sideways arm motion he'd used to skip stones across the river. The rock bounced three, four times, skittering across the surface into the muddy ground. The mud rippled underneath its path, the earth bulging and then flattening. The ground shuddered twice more, while around them more tendrils split open. The sunlight was now partially obscured, and Jake's vision was blurry through his watering eyes. Rachel's eyes were almost completely red, and she reached for his face as though trying to confirm his identity. Instead, she reached around behind him and pulled the ends of his torn shirt into a knot, cinching the fabric over his mouth and nostrils. Then she gave him a single nod, her throat convulsing as she struggled for breath.

They went north, through a thick cloud of spores, and leapt from one rock to the next, dropping down to the muddy ground only when they had to, staying in the rocks when they could. Rachel was beginning to flag, her face almost purple. Jake stopped on a flat rock and ripped the shirt bandanna from her mouth. He shook it out, then did the same with his own, sending out a thick cloud of gray; the fabric was almost entirely plugged with spores. Rachel sucked in a long, whistling breath, her chest heaving but only a little bit of air moving into her lungs. She whispered something he couldn't hear, and a moment later her eyes rolled back in her head.

Jake caught her as she fell, then slung her over his

shoulder. He regarded the countryside in front of him. He could hear Rachel's tortured breathing, a raspy inhale followed by a quick, huffing exhale. Her windpipe was almost closed. For a second he considered a tracheotomy, and then he remembered he'd given his knife to Cameron.

Cameron, who had saved Jake the day before.

You must have breathed in so much smoke that the toxins were closing up your throat, Cameron had said. Except it wasn't from the smoke, Jake realized. It was from the spores, which caused some kind of anaphylactic reaction. And the EpiPen, like his knife, was still with Cameron. Ten yards away, a black tendril was poised three feet above the ground, the tip arched backward like a snake ready to strike.

"Where did you take him, you son of a bitch?" The tendril seemed to regard him for a moment, and for one crazy second Jake thought it might actually speak to him, or at least nod its head or make some kind of acknowledgment. Instead, it split open and sent more spores into the air.

Jake turned and ran back toward the river, eyes trained on the ground, trying not to breathe as he ran back through the cloudy air. In thirty yards he saw a wide, shallow rut in the mud and turned down it. The spores were still very thick, and he had not put the bandanna back over his mouth. His throat was burning, his vision starting to close in. He kept running, Rachel bouncing on his shoulder. The rut curved through the boulders, slaloming left and right. Here was the sharp heel print of a boot, digging into the ground; there, the severed stump of a tendril, no larger than a parsnip, black with decay. He rounded another corner and stopped in cleaner air, gasping for breath. Rachel's struggles had ceased entirely.

Cameron lay entangled in coils just a few yards away. The gray lengths that held him were now a pinkish, healthy color. His eyes were filmed over, and one of his hands was pressed over his chest, as though he had died pledging allegiance to some entity. His hand was curled around the hilt of Jake's knife, at the center of a dark maroon stain that covered most of his torso. His legs were splayed open, his boots crusted with mud. There were several more sliced and decaying ends around him, and the large coils encircling his torso were marked with long slashes. One of the tendrils had curled around his neck and crawled up his face to enter his ear, the lobe split open to reveal pink cartilage. Another tendril was twined around his forearm and wrist, just a few inches away from the knife handle.

Jake draped Rachel across a four-foot-high boulder and staggered forward. The tendrils were motionless, but he could feel their aliveness, their awareness. He stepped carefully over one tendril, then the other. There was a soft rustling, a muted crackling noise. Close to the hum of electrical current going through wires but somehow biological, instead: Something exploring and moving, pushing its way through stiffening flesh. He leaned forward and unbuttoned Cameron's shirt pocket, withdrawing a black plastic case. He tucked it into his own pocket, staring at Cameron's hand, still wrapped around the hilt of Jake's knife.

Another trap, he thought. *Let it go.*

No. It's distracted. This . . . portion . . . of it is distracted with its feeding.

He pried Cameron's fingers free and set the cold,

claw-shaped hand down to rest on Cameron's belly. He yanked the knife out of Cameron's chest. It had gone in between the ribs, and it pulled out with a wet sucking noise, the blade streaked with dark heart's blood.

The tendrils around him tensed, repositioned. Jake held still, not even breathing, his throat throbbing with his hammering pulse. One of the tendrils, large and pale, wormed forward along Cameron's ribs and began to explore the gore around the entrance wound. Jake watched as it found the blood, as the pointed end entered the narrow wound. From behind him, Rachel gave a long, tortured wheeze.

He waited.

The tendril had been elevated an inch above Cameron's chest. Now the length of it settled down on his shirt. It entered the wound several more inches, paused, then slithered forward. From inside Cameron's wound came the crackling again, and a moment later Jake heard the wet snap of a rib breaking. Something bulged across Cameron's stomach and the pale tendril began to darken. Around Jake, the rest of the tendrils, which had risen up as though in expectation, settled back down. He backpedaled slowly, careful not to tread on the other tendrils. When he was free of the tangle, he picked Rachel off the rock and staggered away, into a patch of air that was relatively clear of spores. He had not heard Rachel breath since her last wheezing exhale.

He staggered twenty steps and laid Rachel down on the stony ground. Her neck was twitching with an erratic pulse, but he felt no breath when he placed his hand in front of her mouth. He opened the plastic case and withdrew one of the pens, flipping the protective end off of the short needle. He inspected it quickly, released the safety latch on the end, and paused. Where to inject? Leg, heart? He looked at her swollen throat, and inserted the needle directly into the throbbing vein in the side of her neck. A small fountain of blood jetted out around the tip as he depressed the plunger.

His sweat dripped, pattering down onto her upturned face. Nothing. After a moment, he leaned down and tilted her head back, digging his fingers into the back of her mandible to force her mouth open. He pressed his lips against hers and exhaled, feeling the air push back against him, nowhere to go. He waited ten seconds, tried again. Some of the air seemed to make its way down her trachea this time, and he thought he felt her chest expand slightly under his hand. He breathed in more air through his nose, trying to filter out the spores—he thought he may have acquired some kind of immunity after his first exposure—and pushed what he hoped was clarified air out through his mouth. This time he felt her chest swell. He pulled back, watching her throat. It looked the same, the pulse still hammering erratically, but now there was movement in her throat muscles. Then she gave a strangled wheeze, her mouth open and sucking for oxygen.

"Good girl," he breathed.

He heard a sound and looked up. For a moment he saw nothing, just mud and lichen-crusted rock, and then he caught movement out of the corner of his eye. More tendrils, light- and dark-colored, were swarming toward them. Jake looked down at the open case and the three needles that remained. Then he closed the case and picked Rachel up again, dabbing his finger at the

thin trickle of blood on her neck, and began to labor his
way toward the thin spire of smoke that rose above the
last of the morning fog.

They were on opposite ends of the rock pad, Warren
on one side and Parkson and Hans huddled together on
the other end, the lone cedar tree in between them like
a referee. They were not looking his way and Jake
stopped for a moment, watching them. Behind them,
the drill rig was still sending smoke into the air, the fire
inside the piston sleeves still burning.

Christ, what happened between those three?

Jake hollered, and Warren's head jerked up. He had
a long red welt along his cheek, and he held a chunk of
rock in one hand. Parkson and Hans looked up as well,
Parkson's face colored an ashy gray, Hans's countenance dark. Each man held his own rock: blunt, fist-
sized weapons. There were no signs of the tendrils
around the rock pad, but he could see the tension in
their postures and knew they had endured a long night
as well, if not with the tendrils or spores, then apparently with each other.

"Jake?"

Jake started at the sound of Rachel's voice, then carefully lowered her to the ground. She wobbled for a moment and he held her shoulders, studying her face. Her
color was okay, and her eyes were clear. She rubbed absently at the puncture in her neck, then reached out and
touched the plastic case in Jake's shirt pocket.

"You found Cameron's EpiPens."

"Yes."

"Is he dead?"

"Yes." He felt her shoulders shake under his grip and squeezed her gently. "I'm sorry, Rachel."

She closed her eyes. "Did he suffer?"

He saw the tendril snaking its way into Cameron's ear, rupturing the eardrum, sending those searching fingers into the pink brain tissue, then into the chest, breaking ribs as it sought out the organs . . .

"He had the knife," Jake said. "He used it on himself."

She opened her eyes. Jake was struck by the intensity in those dark blue-gray eyes, the color he associated with the deepest, coldest parts of the trout lakes he fished. "Did it get Jaimie, too?"

"I don't know. Probably."

"And she doesn't have a knife."

"No," Jake said.

Rachel looked to the rock pad, at the three faces watching them. She drew in a deep breath, held it, stretching her lungs back out. He wondered about Jaimie. Greer had been bait, and Cameron . . . Cameron had been sustenance, plain and simple. Such restraint with Greer, and then such single-mindedness with Cameron.

"Who are you people?" Jake asked. "What are we doing out here?"

She looked at him, lips trembling. "It's a military contract. Department of Defense. We need to harvest the promethium, Jake. The Chinese research is years ahead of us. They have a different grade of it, not nearly as pure as what's up here. They haven't been able to transfer more than a few basic properties so far, and not with any consistency. But they will, soon enough."

"What are they trying to do?"

"We've heard . . ." her words trailed off. "I shouldn't tell you any more."

"I think you better."

She sighed. "Doesn't matter much now, does it? Greer's dead, Cameron's dead. Jaimie too, probably." She rubbed at the small bump on her neck where Jake had injected her with the EpiPen. "The most aggressive tendencies, the hunt and kill tendencies, are easy to transfer once you get the promethium refined. Or, if you can find it in a pure form, the transfer happens by itself. If you . . . if a government . . . found someone with the right tendencies, a super warrior, they could use the promethium to transfer those properties, to make a legion of super warriors. All you need is a host to transfer it to." She paused. "Or a thousand hosts."

"A million hosts," Jake murmured. "A million natural-born killers."

"No," she said. "Not natural."

Jake looked out over the valley, at the high stony ridge on the far side of the river. The boggy river wound through the rushes and sedge grass, the brown water devoid of shorebirds and ducks. Once again he recalled his uncle's words as Jake, only seven years old, peeked into the kitchen from his hiding spot in the little living room, the Franklin wood stove roaring against February's bitter cold. The kitchen table was covered with beer bottles, ashtrays, coffee mugs, the men speaking in soft voices, their words hard to hear above the wind in the eaves and the crackling of the spruce logs in the fire. They were talking of travels to the north, beyond the Braids. About a long, dead-looking valley, where the old ones had done certain things to each other after particularly long and cruel winters, a place nobody visited anymore. Asiskiwiw. The muddy valley, a place where people were not meant to be.

"Jake." Rachel put a tentative hand on his forearm. "I didn't know it would be like this."

He looked down at her mud-streaked hand. "I believe you."

"What should we do?"

He was thinking about the stories, about what they had done. That had not been hunting; it had not even been cold-blooded killing. It had been something far worse, a response to the long, bitter season of starvation and terror. If Rachel was right, whatever element was in this ground acted as some sort of sink, absorbing what his ancestors had done in those dim and bloody days. And then, somewhere under the surface, it had somehow taken those tendencies, those traits, and transferred them into this other medium, this subterranean monster that seemed not only sentient, but downright malevolent.

"Jake?" He followed her eyes and saw that his arms had broken out in gooseflesh. "What should we do?"

"I think," he said, "we should get the hell out of here."

Warren held himself warily, shoulders tensed, his hand wrapped around a chunk of granite. Beyond the rock pad, the drill rig tipped at a hard angle into the sky, the shorn metal of the core tube reflecting the morning sun.

"What happened?" Warren asked. "Where are the others?"

"Cameron's dead. Jaimie's missing," Jake said. "We can't stay here. Some of those shoots, the darker-colored ones, release spores. They're toxic."

Hans, his injured arm tight against his body, glanced up sharply. "Spores?"

"Yes," Rachel said. Jake stepped closer to Warren. "What happened to your face?"

Warren wrinkled his nose. "Nothing. A misunderstanding."

Jake stepped closer. Warren's breath reeked of stomach acid. "What kind of misunderstanding?"

"He left us," Hans said, "about an hour after you guys went after Cameron. Just snuck off in the night without saying a word. Took the flashlight and left."

"Why?" Jake asked.

"To look for you guys," Warren said. "I told them the same thing. You'd been gone for a long time, and I thought you might need some help. They were sleeping, and even if they were awake, they weren't going to help much."

Parkson stepped forward, seeming to grow bolder with Jake present. "I wasn't sleeping, Warren. I watched your flashlight beam, and you headed that way." He jabbed a finger toward the ridgeline above them, then turned to Jake. "He was going to leave us here. Something turned him around, or he'd be miles away right now."

Warren shook his head. "I was looking for them."

"Bullshit."

"Shut up," Jake said. "Both of you. We're all here now, and we're all going to climb out of this valley together."

Parkson looked up at the slope, then down at his foot. "We're climbing to the top?"

He had unlaced his boot, and his swollen foot, encased in the muddy sock, bulged inside the cotton. Jake shifted his gaze from Parkson's foot to the valley slope, a loose detritus of rocks strewn up and down its length. Hans would be able to move fine on his own—it was only his arm that was hurt—but Jake wouldn't be able to help Parkson, or anyone else, if they became ensnared. He briefly considered whittling a crude crutch for Parkson, then dismissed the idea. Even if they had the luxury of time to carve a crutch, the trunk of the young cedar tree on their rock pad was too thick to cut through, the branches too thin to support his weight.

"We have two options," Jake said. "The first is, we go all at once. It'll be slow and dangerous."

"And the other option is leaving me here," Parkson said.

"No," Jake said. He pointed toward the top of the valley, the tips of the balsams pointing up above the ridgeline like jagged green teeth. "I can get up there in no time, if I go by myself."

"What about the spores?" Parkson asked. "What if it releases one of these toxic clouds of spores while you're off making your run to safety? Or the tendrils decide to swarm over us? God knows they're big enough to do it."

"Keep your voice down," Jake said. "It might not even know we're on this rock."

"It's a good idea," Warren said.

I bet you think it is, Jake thought. *Send the Indian off to fetch help.*

"Or maybe it knows and it doesn't care," Jake went on. "Maybe it only cares if we step on the ground. That could be its territory, and as long as we stay on the rocks it'll leave us alone."

"Knows?" Hans said. "*Cares?* What are you talking about?"

"It's intentional," Rachel said. "It's trapping us, baiting us. If we all go up that hill, some of us won't make it." She turned to Jake. "What if you get stuck?"

He patted his side. "I have my knife. I'll keep moving, stay on hard ground."

"What about the knife?" Warren said. "If something happens to you, we're down here without any kind of weapon."

"What a hero," Parkson said. "Maybe you should ask him for his boots, too, just in case. We could use an extra pair."

"Listen," Jake said to Warren. He did not like the man and did not trust him, but he also knew that if there was action required, it would be Warren, not Hans and not Parkson, who would be the most capable of assistance. Rachel would help, too, but Jake was close to a hundred pounds heavier than her, and she would be hard-pressed to pull him free if he became entangled. "If I do something stupid and get caught, I'll toss the knife. If you can pick it up and cut me free, fine. If not, at least you've got a weapon."

"Then what?" Warren asked.

"What do you mean?"

"If I lose my scout," Warren said, "how do we get out of these woods?"

"Once you reach the campsite, you'll have the satellite phone, right? Call in for help. Jaimie might still be out there, and there's two bodies we need to extract. You have plenty of people you could call. An entire government." He paused, catching Warren's eye. "Two governments you could call, maybe."

Warren shook his head, not taking the bait. "What if we have to move faster than that? Maybe it follows us up there, and we have to run. We could wander around for forty years in these godforsaken woods."

Jake glanced up at the sun, arcing over the trees. "This time of year, the sun rises in the southeast, not the east. It sets in the southwest, not due west. You understand?"

Warren nodded and pointed at the sun, still low in the sky, partially obscured by a bank of gold-colored cirrus clouds. "Southeast."

"Head south by southwest." Jake held his hand out on an imaginary straight line, then moved it forty-five degrees to the right. "You might not come out at the same place we went in. You almost certainly won't, actually. But if you keep on a southwest line, you'll hit the Little Glutton River, somewhere near the Braids. It's where the river splits up into a dozen channels, and the floodplain is covered with willows. Don't cross it—it's all sand and silt, and the river is going to be high with all of this rain. Turn left, follow the river down until you reach a gravel road. Take another left, and you'll find your van at the Gissammee trailhead. You'll be on the road for ten miles. Someone may come along and give you a ride."

"That's it?"

"Follow the setting sun. Once you reach the river you'll be fine."

"Quit it," Rachel said. "We're not going to leave you to die out there."

Jake eyed the route up the side of the valley. He could see the path he would take, more or less. It was mostly rocks for the first fifty yards, then the long flat stretch he would need to sprint across. Then, where the slope curved upward into the ancient cut of the river bottom, the going would be slower; he would have to pick his way through the saplings, and hope that he had left the underground presence behind him, or that it was too slow to follow him. He flexed his legs. His hips and knees ached with pain gnawing at his joints, sending shoots of pain down the lengths of his femurs, his tibias, all the way into the metatarsals. But he could still move, goddammit. Better than most.

"Jake?" Rachel said again.

"What?"

"We aren't going to leave you out there."

"I'll be okay. If, *if*, I get stuck, it'll probably be too late to do anything about it. Find a way out, find a way through. Don't . . ." he paused, unsure what to say, unsure what words had almost come out of his mouth. An image arose in his mind of those long green walls, the fluorescent lighting, the nurses and doctors and interns and sometimes visitors—not many visitors. He remembered the sound of his footsteps on the linoleum, everything restricted to a narrow band on the color spectrum. Even the light through the windows in the room was bland, bland on the brightest summer day, the beep of the machine, the damn machine, the tubes and sensors and . . . no. *Stop there. Stop before you let your eyes travel down the tubes and the sensors, down to Deserae.*

He touched Rachel's arm with the tips of his fingers. "Don't waste your life on me."

He jumped down onto the spray of loose rocks at the base of the pad, his hand pressed against his knife, and started running toward the top.

Chapter 9

They moved like a pack of wolves, the pace somewhere just south of a trot, spread out in a rough line in the aspen forest. Henry was by far the oldest man, sixty-three that past spring, still fit and light on his feet but definitely the anchor, the one who held the rest of them back from an even quicker pace. He was in the center of the line, and the wings moved forward ahead of him, Henry at the point of the inverted V. It was late afternoon, and they had been moving at this pace for most of the day. Henry knew that they were pushing him, as he would have pushed them fifteen years ago, and felt the bright, hard edge of hatred and envy of their youth, their pushiness, fueling his legs.

He hated Garney the least, because he was the heaviest and the slowest of the younger men. Although they might leave Henry to pick his way through the woods and catch up with them at nightfall, Darius would not leave two men behind. Two men could form a temporary bond when left behind, forming a group within the group. And two men could, if they were so inclined, find a kindred soul, swell their ranks to include a third:

a majority. Those were the kinds of situations Darius would avoid in his own team, exploit in others.

Don't give him too much credit, Henry thought, arming sweat off his brow as he plodded onward. *He's tired, too.*

He could see Darius out on the far-left wing, wending his way through the big white trunks of the aspens. He seemed tired but not exhausted, which was how Henry was starting to assess his own condition. Garney was positioned between them, his shirt completely soaked with sweat. To Henry's right, Weasel slipped through the woods, a thin and ugly little man who Henry distrusted more than anyone besides Darius, and maybe more than Darius. On the right edge was Billy, effortless as he moved through the aspen and hazel brush. Billy was a relation, a nephew once removed, the son of Woolsy Martineau. Woolsy had died in a snowbank outside his cabin in his thirty-second year, when Billy was just a pup. He had stashed a bottle of whiskey outside, to hide it from Tammy, Billy's mother, and after an argument he had slammed the door shut behind him, gone outside, and drank half the bottle in one long, furious pull. It had been twenty-five degrees below zero that night, and the whiskey the same temperature. His esophagus had frozen instantly and he went into cardiac arrest, clutching the bottle as he died, ten feet from his angry wife and the two-year-old son who slept in his homemade bed.

They were all armed, and Henry was no exception. He carried his Winchester Model 94 30-30 caliber in a leather sling on his back, and in the bottom of his waxed canvas backpack he had a small Walther .38 caliber semiautomatic, the bullets in the factory box wrapped inside an old cotton shirt. The shirt was in turn sealed inside two plastic baggies. He had a knife and a hatchet and his mess kit and a bedroll, and nothing in his pack or on his person made any noise at all. Except for his breath, which was turning into a pant.

Garney, despite Darius's objections, was armed only with his Mathews compound bow, the six carbon arrows with expandable broadheads secured in the hunting quiver attached to the bow's frame. Weasel and Billy were armed with moose hunting rifles, and Henry knew what that could do to a man, had seen it once on a hunt near the Burned Lakes, a strange country where wildfire had scorched the thin earth atop the bedrock decades ago. The fire had moved through the region hot and fast, and many of the pines still stood, baked into statues, the branches burned to stubs, the trunks sooty and hard. The soil had been burned so thoroughly that nothing could grow, not trees nor shrubs nor even the ubiquitous purple fireweed. The moose loved it because there was a certain type of grass that flourished along the water's edge, where the fire had not touched. Henry's group had gone in after the tracks of a young bull, lost it on the burned and flinty ground, and split up. Late that evening, one of Henry's hunting partners had mistaken his other friend for a moose and shot him as he moved through the black trees. The hole was the size of a dime going in, and on the far side there was no hole, just the absent half of a rib cage, the shattered ribs curving around the pink mass of jellied lungs. They left the man there, cooling among the blackened pines, and reported him lost in the great wilderness, and there was no search party and they never hunted there again.

Now Henry wished they were headed to the haunted landscape of the Burned Lakes, or to the great unnamed morass of swamp downstream, anywhere but their current destination. Its name came through his mind and he was tempted to mouth it, to feel it on his lips. He had been there before, and Darius had used the previous trip as the basis for his request for Henry to accompany them. Henry had agreed because there was something in Darius's dark brown eyes, a hint of fear. The fear had intrigued Henry. Darius's men were the *Okitchawa*, yesterday's warriors, and they fancied themselves sacred protectors of the wilderness. Or some damn thing. They did have a tendency to make visitors feel unwelcome, that much was true. Perhaps the other things they had claimed (or that other people had claimed of them) were true as well. They were hard men, and Henry counted himself amongst that classification and yet he disliked them and distanced himself from them, not only because of their youth but because of their inability to reason, to see the larger picture. They were still caught in the youthful daydream that they knew enough, within a day or two, about every situation to be able to take immediate and just action. They saw Henry and the others around Highbanks as listless observers, timid and powerless to stop the trespasses, whether it was the constant intrusions of the loggers from the Crown or hunters from the States. More recently it had been an increased focus on what was below the ground, with more planes overhead and more surveyors in the woods every year.

The *Okitchawa*, and Darius in particular, were adamant that their ancestors would never have allowed these encroachments, that they would have protected the resources of the land for their people at all costs. So they took the role of protectors upon themselves, and if they got scent of an outsider, they followed the trail to its bloody end. *Must have got lost in the woods* was the explanation most people gave for the missing outsiders, and they remained truly lost. No bodies had been recovered, even after several massive manhunts.

"This place gives us life," Darius had said, speaking at the First Dance ceremony the year before, right after several surveyors had disappeared into the green, yawning maw of the wilderness. "If we don't keep it clean, if we don't remember the sacrifices of the old ones, we pollute our own souls." He said nothing else, and he didn't have to.

The *Okitchawa* were right, in a way, Henry supposed. But life was different now, and just because there had been old ways of doing things didn't mean they were the right ways.

So why come here? he asked himself. He did not like the encroachments either, but he felt no desire to spill blood.

And the answer came to him, in a single word:

Asiskiwiw. A fearful place, to be sure. But also a place where someone like himself might find the connection he had sought for so long, something that had nothing to do with resources, or intruders. It was, he supposed, a pilgrimage.

He came to a stop, readjusting his rifle strap. On either side of him the other men were paused, sucking in the midmorning breeze on the top of a rise. Garney had his head back, hands on his wide hips, little rolls bunched up at the base of his neck. Weasel hacked and coughed and lit a cigarette, pausing first to rip the filter from the end. Darius, on the left, breathed more easily, as did Billy on the right. Henry felt his calf muscles bunching and tightening, the electrical quiver of muscles used far beyond their normal range. He pulled the leather bota from his pack and drank deeply of the lukewarm water, squirting it down the back of his throat.

"Better save your water, old man," Garney said.

Henry pulled the bota back, letting the water wash over his face. He shook himself to clear his eyes and then turned to Garney. "Braids are at the bottom of the hill. You can refill there."

Garney peered downward, where the more open aspen forest gave way to a tangled mass of alder brush, purple-skinned branches with dark green leaves. "I don't see anything."

"There are none so blind," Henry said, "as those who will not listen."

"Huh?"

"Ears," Henry said, tapping the side of his head. "Quit panting so much and listen."

Below them came the burbling sound of running water. They began picking their way through the alders. The mosquitoes were thick, but did not form the constant swarms of June or July; they were beginning to die off. Everywhere around him Henry saw the signs of autumn, the yellowing patches of big leaf aster on the forest floor, the fading of the alder leaves. He could even smell it in the air, the slow funk of a season's decay bubbling up around his boots. It was his least favorite time of the year, the transition between the richness of the summer and the cool, clear days of autumn.

They converged, funneling into a single line along the lone game trail, and emerged from the thicket. The river in front of them was big and fast and complex. Swollen by the summer rains, it had carved a dozen paths through the silty river bottom, some of them little more than rivulets, others faster and deeper. Willows had sprouted on the numerous islands, thickly clumped, none taller than a man. Henry looked upstream, then downstream. The braided river channels twined and connected and diverged as far as the eye could see, the brown water carving into the edges of the silt. There would be other places to cross, Henry knew, but it would mean traversing an immense swamp on both sides of the river.

Weasel hawked a glob of phlegm into the running water at their feet and watched it speed downstream. "How we getting through this shit?"

"One step at a time," Darius said. He was scanning the horizon on the far side of the river, the skyline featureless except for trees and a few lower clouds. "Check your backpacks, fill your skins. We'll wipe the guns down when we get across."

"How deep is it?" Billy asked. He was looking at the turbid water, which gave no indication of what lay beneath the surface.

"Dunno." Henry pulled a coil of rope from his pack and spread the loops out with his fingers, looking for kinks. "The Braids change every year."

"I don't swim too good." Billy was still studying the river, chewing on his lower lip, sweat running down the sides of his face.

Henry grunted. He had known the Martineaus for decades and he had known Billy for all his life, had seen his name appear on the honor rolls, disappearing from those thinly-populated ranks between his sophomore and junior year of high school, only to return on the A honor roll his senior year. Henry had been in the audience when Billy had delivered a halting but powerful salutatorian address, had been there to wish him farewell when he drove off to Regina to play football and study economics, or perhaps engineering. That Billy had been bright and committed and often unsure of himself, and Henry had liked him quite a lot. This new Billy, the one who had fallen in with the *Okitchawa*, the one who smiled all the time and seemed to have no cares in the world, the slick one, the cool Billy, Billy-*Dawg*, disgusted Henry. It was as though Billy had decided if he couldn't be a college boy he was going to be a thug, no middle ground. Leave all those good and justifiable worries behind him, be confident in what he had and where he was going. Like all the damned rest of them.

"What are you thinking about?" Billy asked.

"People," Henry replied, tying the end of the rope into a loop and passing the length back through it to form a noose. "People who worry about the wrong things."

"People?" Garney said. "You should be thinking about how we get across this river, old man."

Let me guess, Henry thought. *You don't swim too good, neither.*

"Here's the deal," Henry said, noticing that he had their full attention, even Weasel's. "Everybody needs a wading stick. Try to get one with a fork on the bottom. It'll keep it from slipping on any rocks below the surface. Then I'm going to give one end of the rope to Garney, tie the other end onto my waist, and go to that island." He pointed to a long crescent-shaped pile of silt on the far side of one of the main channels, covered with willows. "We'll avoid the smaller islands, the ones without bushes. They're liable to break apart if we climb on them, turn into quicksand. Understand?"

Four impassive sets of brown eyes looked back at him. Henry went on. "Once I make it across, the next guy—Weasel, he's the smallest—follows, holding on to the rope. He helps me hold the rope while the next guy goes across. We work smallest to largest in case somebody gets swept away. If you slip, or start going under, just hold on to the rope. We'll pull you in."

"That the plan?" Garney asked. "What about the next guy, the one after the idiot that just got swept downstream? He goes across without a rope?"

"Yes," Darius replied. "Just like Henry is planning to do, except he doesn't whine about it." He fixed Garney with his gaze. "Go cut your stick."

Garney mumbled something and turned away. Darius called out to him and Garney turned around, his knife in his hand.

"Cut one for me and Henry while you're at it." He held Garney with his gaze. "You have a problem with that?"

Garney turned away without comment, and a moment later the air was filled with dull thuds as they hacked at the small birch trees that lined the river. Darius watched them for a bit, then turned back to Henry, looking at him through those low-hanging eyelids, the look of a boxer who had been hit too much.

"Elsie said you should come with us. Your old girlfriend. Did you know that?"

Henry shrugged. Elsie had been almost fifty years old, quite a bit older than Henry, when they had dated.

Still, she was accommodating to almost any favor he requested, as long as he repaid her in turn. It was not long after they went their different ways that she had shacked up with some trapper for a couple winters and, if rumor was true, suffered a series of miscarriages that had turned her from a middle-aged woman into her current state in a few short years. Yet she had not changed much since then; it was as though she had taken her next thirty years of aging in one big swallow.

"Elsie told me," Darius said, "you went into this forest once, looking for a vision."

"I have gone into the woods many times," Henry said. "For many reasons."

"Don't play games," Darius said, rubbing at the pink scar in his eyebrow. "I'll leave your carcass out here for the ravens to pick apart."

"I'm not playing any games." He hated the whiny, almost subservient tone of his voice. Darius was one of the few people he had ever met who genuinely scared him, and not just because Darius was stronger and faster than Henry. When Darius said things, like how he would leave Henry's body out here as carrion, he meant every word. Despite whatever help Henry might be able to provide, Darius would not hesitate to gut him, or anyone else, if he was provoked. In another place in the world, Henry was certain Darius would either be in prison or a mental hospital.

"She said you had no visions."

"I did not."

"Elsie spoke highly of you," Darius said.

"We were friends once."

"I'm not talking about when you used to fuck her,"

Darius said. "She said you would help me see, once we got to Asiskiwiw."

From the riverbank someone gave a muted curse, and they turned to watch Garney kick at a birch sapling, sending it to the ground. "The valley has been quiet for many years," Henry said, "and the stories were old when I was a child. There may be nothing there."

"You don't believe that. I see it in your scared old man's face."

Henry shrugged. "When I went, I saw nothing."

It was true. For five days he had fasted on the top of the ridge overlooking Asiskiwiw, trying to block out all physical sensation—the dew soaking into his knees, the bugs trundling across his body, the rustling of the breeze, and the animals in the forest at his back. Deeper and deeper, all thought gone. But he had seen nothing with his eyes closed, and when he opened his eyes there was just a long, barren valley filled with odd rock formations, marked by a sluggish river at the bottom. In the mornings, the bluffs on the far side of the valley would catch the rising sun, and he would take some time to explore the rock faces with his eyes, tracing the lichen-crusted precipices, the narrow hogback ridge that cut down the middle of the bluffs. That was all he had seen.

And as for what he had heard, in the end he decided it was nothing, just auditory hallucinations, his mind seeking to fill in the void caused by his absence from other human beings. There were whispers, soft and cajoling, a warm voice filled with laughter, always deep in the night, asking and suggesting, never commanding, inviting him down to the softer ground at the bottom of the valley. For it was there he would find his vision, the voice promised; it was there where Henry Redsky would at last join the ranks of *maskihkîwiyini-wiw*, of those who saw.

"What are you thinking about?"

Henry waved at a hovering mosquito, then gestured in front of him, at the dark clouds that had started to form on the western horizon. "The river," he said. "It's not getting any lower. Let's get moving."

The river bottom was silt, the fine sediment giving way under his boots as he labored out into the middle of the first channel. It was better walking than the slime-covered rocks on the Big Glutton, which only required a minor misstep to send you sprawling into the muscular current. Still, he had to keep his feet moving to keep from sinking in, and the water was cold, even after the atypically warm summer. The current was fast, and though it only reached his waist, by midstream his progress was painfully slow. Before each step, he dug his wading stick into the crumbly bottom, wedged his boot against it, and put his next foot out a step. The rope dragged in the current, threatening to pull him downstream.

Finally, he slogged out of the first channel and onto the island. He pushed aside the screen of willows and crossed to the far side to survey the rest of the river. The other braids were narrower, with the exception of the final channel, which ran along the far bank. Instead of frothing and foaming like the other river segments, it was smooth and fast, marked only by swirling boils.

He backtracked, picking up the slack in the rope, and studied the men on the other side.

"Come on," he shouted.

Weasel stepped into the river, pausing for a moment when the cold water hit him, then started across.

Weasel was a small man, not much larger than a teenage boy, and he didn't know how to wade in a current. He turned sideways, facing upstream and keeping both hands on the rope, taking the brunt of the force of the current on his body. He was panting by the time he made it across, and did not release the rope until both of his feet were on the silty bank of the island. Billy crossed next, and after a moment's discussion, Garney transferred his end of the rope to Darius and splashed across the river. After Garney was on the bank, Darius slipped the end of the rope around his waist and waded into the river. Henry gathered up the loose rope in big coils as Darius splashed up to join them.

Darius pushed through the willows and started wading across the next channel. The water never rose above Darius's knees, and the rest of the men exchanged quick glances and followed Darius, using the wading sticks, as Henry had. They crossed the next several braids easily. The last island was shaped like a teardrop, filled bank to bank with a dense mat of willows. They paused, catching their breath for the final crossing. Henry knelt for a second to examine some bear tracks pressed into the silt. The big rear paw prints were almost humanoid, over ten inches long. A large bear. It had wandered the edge of the island and then crossed back to where they had just come from, looking for god knew what. Beyond them, the last channel surged past, the boils breaking and swirling on the surface.

"Go ahead," Henry said, waving an arm.

Darius studied the current. "This one might be trouble."

"Yes," Henry said. The river had not been nearly this high the last time he had been here. It was almost at spring levels, and nobody crossed the Braids before July or after September. The bear tracks affected him a little too, as they always did. The bear was no danger to them, and he was not scared of being attacked. But it had been here recently, and in all likelihood it had known they were there for some time, watching them with its pig eyes, scenting them with its great wet muzzle.

"Can we cross this?" Billy asked.

"Give me the rope," Henry said. "We'll need it on this one. Tighten down your slings and packs. We might get a little wet."

The channel rushed along the far bank for as far as the eye could see. Much of the power of the river was diffused in the rest of the braids, but the main artery was here. The far bank was steep, leveling off several feet up at a grassy swale ringed by large paper birches. It looked like a park, or some foreign land, and Henry tried to imagine standing there on the high ground, in the grass, with the river behind them.

"Wait a sec," Garney said. "The guy who goes first, it seems bad, but he's got the rope around him. The other guys can pull him back in."

"Yes," Henry said.

Garney turned to the others. "The last guy, he's tied up too. But the other guys, they lose their hold on the rope, they don't got nothing."

Darius stepped up close to Garney. "Spit it out." His voice was cold. "What do you want?"

"I'm just saying, maybe we should figure out a different way."

"Listen," Henry said. "I'll go in whatever order you guys want me to. But somebody has to make it across first with the rope. They might have to swim for it."

He was looking at Darius when he spoke, and the others were looking at him, too. Darius didn't look particularly concerned, just impatient, but Henry noticed that his eyes kept flitting to the river, just like everyone else's were. *He's going to volunteer to go first,* Henry thought. *He can't swim worth a shit, but he's got to prove he's the big man, the leader of the Okitchawa, the great—*

"Henry's the best swimmer," Darius said. "He goes first. Garney goes last."

Henry stepped into the river. The water was up to his waist before he had gone ten steps, and now he could feel the stones under his boots, coated with summer slime. He moved carefully, wedging his boots against the sides of the rocks. The water seemed colder in this channel, making his breath short. It crept up his ribs, and he felt his body wanting to lift. He was going to have to swim for it and was bracing himself for the full immersion in the cold water when he bumped into something hard and rounded. He prodded it with his wading stick, feeling out the contours as the river tugged and pulled at him.

It was a big log, submerged crossways in the current. He could not see it in the silty water, but it was only several feet down, probably a massive pine that had been carried here from the old forests to the northeast. Now that he knew it was there, he could see a long line of boils on the surface marking its location, the displaced water flowing under and over the log all the way to the far bank. He scraped his wading stick along the top of the log. It still had bark on it, and would not be nearly as slippery as the bottom.

Moving very slowly, he climbed onto the log and straightened. The river only came to mid-thigh, and although the current was still pushing against him, the force was much less. He prodded some more with the wading stick, delineating the rounded edges of the log, and took a step forward. The log was steady under his feet. He took another step, his heels digging into the bark. It had started to sprinkle rain, and the river surface dimpled around him.

Don't rush, he thought. *Be an old man and shuffle.*

It was very hard to do, because the bank was growing closer and closer, and he knew that it would only take six or seven big strides to reach it. But he moved slowly, and the log held firm, and in a minute he stepped onto the steep, crumbling bank. He held up a hand for Weasel to wait, then scrambled up the bank and looped the rope around a large birch. When he was done, the rope hung down loosely like a suspension cable just upstream of the series of boils, almost directly over the submerged log.

Weasel went under twice before he reached the log, the little man sputtering and blowing. Even when he was under, his hands were moving, pulling him along the rope. Weasel finally clawed his way back onto the log, shook his head to clear the water from his eyes, and nearly ran across the log to the far side. Billy went next, his normally sinuous movement made jerky and uncertain by his fear. His progress was more thoughtful than Weasel's, and it took him five solid minutes to make the crossing. Darius crossed easily, and Henry could tell he had been studying those who had gone before, avoiding the areas where others had slipped. He did not clutch the rope as Billy and Weasel had, instead running his hand along it, ready to use it if needed but not relying on it.

Just like he's using me, Henry thought. He had already decided they would take another route on the return trip, a longer but easier path. There would be no need to hurry on the way home, and there would be little argument from the others.

Darius stepped onto the bank. On the far side of the channel, Garney wrapped two loops of rope around his waist. He waded into the river, jaw clenched.

Henry was already mapping the rest of the trip to Asiskiwiw, less than a half day's journey once they crossed the river. There had been the remnants of a path when he had ventured there decades earlier, not much more than a game trail, marked by ancient blazes on some of the oldest pines. At several junctures, there were small piles of stones stacked on top of each other, the ages-old marker that could mean anything, from a simple trail marker to a warning to stay away. The trail was likely to have completely grown over by now, but the land itself would point the way; Resurrection Valley was marked by the high bluffs to the north, and the river that drained it could always be traced upstream. That was easier said than done, for the river only resembled a true stream for a short stretch before it spread out into a swampy morass.

He was still thinking about the path to the valley when Garney, who had just gained the log—and who looked like he was finally convinced he might make the crossing—fell. He went down in one movement, no teetering or attempt to regain his balance, his feet just swept from under him. He plunged into the river on the upstream side of the log and disappeared. A large section of waterlogged bark surfaced downstream, rolling over in the current and sinking once again.

A piece of bark came off under his feet, Henry thought. *Shit.* The effect would be like a banana peel.

The back of Garney's head appeared a second later, his face down and just inches above the surface, the cords in his neck quivering as he struggled to keep his mouth and nose above the water. Henry and Billy yanked in the slack, pausing when they felt resistance, then pulling again. Garney's head dipped down and they heard him scream something into the water, just inches from his mouth.

"He's stuck," Henry said, pressing the coil of rope into Billy's chest. "Keep this tight."

He jumped into the river, on the upstream side of the log, and splashed toward Garney. He could feel nubs of limbs, broken off by the log's rolling journey down the river, banging against his feet. The water swarmed over him, up to his waist, then his ribs, shoving him against the log. The tangle of limbs grew as he approached Garney, and Henry could feel other debris lodged against them, a rat's nest of waterlogged sticks, the force of the river wedging them ever tighter against the log.

Garney was sucking in great breaths of air, his entire body straining with effort to keep his face above the rushing water. Henry stepped through the mess of large broken-off limbs under the water, then leaned down to shout over the sound of the river.

"Where are you caught?"

Garney took a deep breath and coughed out something Henry couldn't hear. He repeated the question, and this time he could make out enough of the word to understand; his ankle was wedged under the log.

Henry dove. The river current filled his ears with its frantic and swarming music. He followed Garney's leg down to where it disappeared under the slick black mass of the log. There was little light, and the water was so turbid that he could not see anything, so he let his hands see for him, tracing the contours of the ankle and the branch that had entrapped it. His hands found the culprit, a small tree that had been caught against the larger pine log. It was forked, and when Garney had fallen his foot had slipped into the open V. The force of the river was pushing his leg under the bigger log, pulling Garney with it.

Henry pushed himself back up. Garney was being pulled closer to the water, his breath now bubbling against the surface. Several veins had broken on his neck from the effort of keeping his head above water, and Henry knew he only had a minute left, perhaps seconds. He dove down again, ignoring Garney's grasping hands.

Henry grasped the forked sapling and pulled back. A stream of bubbles swirled out of his mouth as he pulled, his adrenaline-soaked muscles working to pull the sapling up and away, the current fighting him every inch. After a few seconds he released his hold and surfaced again.

"Help me!" he yelled at the cluster of men on the bank. "I need someone to help me!"

Weasel looked at Henry stupidly, then turned to

Darius, whose eyes were narrowed in a strange, hateful expression. Then Billy jumped into the river and started splashing toward him. The sound of Garney's breathing had grown muted, and when Henry looked down he saw that Garney's mouth was underwater: He was relegated to breathing through his nostrils.

"We only have time for one more try," Henry said. "I pull back, you yank his ankle free."

They went under in unison, and Henry took the tree in his hands and planted his feet against the trunk of the log. He straightened, and the forked sapling pulled back again those same scant inches. He felt Billy heaving on Garney's ankle next to him. Garney's leg remained wedged, and Billy let go of it and joined Henry, pulling the forked tree back, two inches, three inches, a full foot. The tree slid back, and the dark, frantic presence of Garney slashed toward the surface. Henry let go of the tree and clawed after him

Garney and Billy were already almost to the shore. Henry waded after them, the tangle of limbs and debris under his feet like clutching hands. He stumbled onto the shore, and Darius reached down and hauled him onto dry land.

He lay there hacking. To his side Garney and Billy were retching out the sour river water. Henry felt as though there was no strength left in any part of him— just enough juice to clear his lungs and power his still-hammering heart. Also to process the sound of the river, which did not sound animate or threatening or lovely. It just sounded like a river that had almost killed them.

After a while he pushed himself onto one elbow.

The rain was coming down harder now, a cool late summer shower. "I know another way across when we come home," he said. "If anyone is interested."

Weasel and Garney looked at him. Henry had always liked to tease when things were very serious, and even though they weren't getting it, didn't appreciate that he was trying to lighten the mood, he liked the look in their eyes, serious, washed clean of the confidence—and the contempt—he'd seen there earlier.

There was silence for a long time. Eventually Garney sat up, then reached down to help Billy do the same.

"We should take it easy for the rest of the day," Darius offered.

There was no response. When Billy answered Henry realized that he had been waiting for him to speak; they all had been waiting for Billy. "No," he said. He was dripping wet and still breathing hard, the rain running down his face. "Let's finish this."

Chapter 10

Jake stood at the top of the ridge, bent over with his hands at his hips. His breath was coming in ragged gasps, and there was a sharp pain in his side as though he'd been stabbed. In front of him the tents were a bright jumble of colors, still covered in dew from the night before. There was no smoke from the fire, but he could smell it as he sucked in breath after breath, the sharp, acrid scent of the blackened embers. It was a welcome smell after the constant boggy odor of the river bottom. The rain clouds had not arrived yet, but he could see the front coming, a low bank of dark clouds scuttling in from the west.

Below and behind him, no more than the length of three football fields, the rest of his party was huddled on the rock pad. There were still several seams of mud from where the ground had opened up the day before. From up here it looked, if not peaceful, then at least unremarkable. If they had been unhurt, it would be just as easy for each of them to do what he had done, weave across the valley floor and up the slope, staying on rocks where possible, until the ground steepened and grew hard under his feet. Then up to this place, this wooded highland forest that was so much safer, so much more accommodating, than the muddy valley below.

A thought circled his mind, gaining traction with each breath.

Leave them.

There was nothing hostile in the thought. Other than Warren, he didn't dislike any of the survivors below. They were all different people with different faults, none of them saints nor devils. It was not their fault that this, whatever *this* was, had happened. They had drilled into it, yes, but similar acts of intrusion the world over had been met with shrugging acceptance by the ground. Of course, those places were not Asiskiwiw.

He straightened and filled his lungs with the cool, pre-rain air. Asiskiwiw, the muddy valley, also known as Resurrection Valley. The former name had been around for a long, long time, ever since Jake's father's people had drifted south and east to this place, where the moose and caribou were thick and the rivers were full of fish. The other name, the English version, was newer, a reflection of the Christian religion that had infiltrated the region with the French, then later the British fur traders.

Below him a shout drifted up, cutting off his thoughts. One of the members of the party—he thought it was likely Warren—waved his arms over his head. Yes, it was Warren, and he could see Jake standing there on top of the ridge, above the panic and out of danger. The shout came again, undecipherable but the meaning was clear: Get your ass moving, Trueblood.

Leave them.

Turn and walk into the woods. Leave them with

their drill rig and their wounded and dead bodies—let them clean up their own mess. It was early, barely autumn. He knew of several old trapper cabins that he could overwinter in, including one he had built himself, less than fifteen miles away. He had his rifle, and it would be a lean winter, with nothing but moose and rabbit, but he knew how to do it, which parts of the animal he had to eat to keep from starving, eyes and brains and internal organs, all the nutrients and fats socked away deep inside the animal. He could do it. Just disappear in the green, yawning maw of the woods, and let these people from the Department of Defense and the research laboratories fight their way out of the valley, then sort through the problems they had created.

Go, he thought again. *Get your rifle out of the tent and go.*

He had his breath back now, and he turned and walked to his tent. He paused outside the flap, studying the scuffs in the pine needles. He was not as good a tracker as others, but he could tell a day-old sign from an hours-old sign. He frowned and then stepped inside his tent.

His rifle was still there. The cartridges were untouched. He thumbed several rounds into his rifle, knowing it was foolish, that he could no more shoot his way out of this danger than he could sprout wings and fly away from it. He filled the Winchester's magazine anyway; it made him feel better. Then he opened his pack and fished out his pills and swallowed them. His bota was still half full of water, and he drank deeply to wash down the pills. He hadn't realized how thirsty he was.

He lowered the bota, swished the remaining water

around, and then took another drink. The rest of them would be very thirsty, and if he went back down he would need to grab the rest of the canteens and botas, perhaps some food as well.

Are you really going back down there?

No. He would make the call on the satellite phone himself. Once he was able to get them some help, he would walk away.

He slung his rifle over his shoulder and went into Warren's tent. The plastic box containing the two satellite phones was in the corner of his tent. Jake took them outside and snapped the locks open. The phones were a matching pair of Motorolas, each one fitted with a small, thick antenna. He didn't know what number to call, but he supposed they would have a few numbers programmed into the internal memory, like a normal cell phone. He pressed the power button, then pressed it again. He frowned, then held the button down for a few seconds. The screen still didn't light up. He tried the other one, with similar results.

A security function? He flipped the phone over, inspected the back, then turned it over again. He felt like a clueless backwoods jerk, unable to operate a piece of modern technology. He would have to bring it down to them, watch them do something simple, like press the power button twice . . .

He thumbed the on/off button twice, then three times. He held it down for five seconds, then ten, then punched it in quickly and released it. There was nothing from the phone, almost as though the batteries were completely—

He flipped the phone over in his hand, unscrewed the tab for the batteries, and pried the cover loose with his thumbnail. The battery compartment was empty except for the connecting wire and terminal connections. He quickly unscrewed the other phone and saw its battery was gone, too. He slid a finger under the foam of the phone case, wondering where the batteries could be. Perhaps Warren had been charging them with the small solar panel.

He went back into Warren's tent. The solar panel was in the corner, still wrapped in the thick cardboard Warren had used to protect it on the way in, the charging cord wrapped in neat coils. No batteries. He searched around the tent, pawing through Warren's clothes and sleeping bag. There was no way Warren had forgotten the batteries; Jake had watched him call in their progress to his boss, or bosses, the afternoon they had arrived on site.

He stood at the threshold of the tent, staring at the ground. He had trampled on whatever sign there might be here. Had the ground outside Warren's tent looked disturbed before he entered the first time? He thought maybe it had. He went to Greer's tent, a light purple job, more colorful than the rest. Yes, there were footprints there, too, the impression of a heel. Hard to tell how fresh, but Greer wore sandals when not working so as not to track dirt from his work boots into his tent. Jake went to Parkson's tent next, which was pitched on harder ground. There were no footprints outside his tent.

He left us, Jake remembered Hans had said. *Just snuck off in the night without saying a word.*

You son of a bitch.

He circled the camp, but he saw no sign on the hard ground. If Warren had taken the batteries, they were either with him or hidden somewhere in the woods. Jake could spend days searching for them, and unless they were someplace obvious, it would be fruitless. What would make a man do something like this? To venture, in the dark, through that lethal labyrinth of tendrils and mucky ground, only to remove their ability to save themselves? Jake could understand part of Warren's motive. Greer was dead. Four of them had disappeared into the night, and the other two on the rock pad with him were injured. If Warren was responsible for the group's safety, he would have a lot to answer for when he made that call. And any help would come from the air, which would be problematic; it would alert the natives to their presence. Jake had no illusions about their supposed permission to be here; this was a clandestine operation, carried out by foreign government agents.

But Warren had gone back down, which meant that there was something down there worth severing their one link to the outside world for, something worth the risk to his own life and those of the others—something he couldn't get to in the dark, but would likely try for as soon as he had a chance.

The samples.

Jake started back down the valley slope.

"Batteries are dead."

"They're what?" Parkson said. "Jesus *Christ*."

Jake stood on the rock pad, feeling the hostility of the group growing, centering on him, the bearer of bad news. They had been trapped on the same piece of rocky real estate for the past eighteen hours. In that time they had seen Greer die, his body infested, and then witnessed Cameron being dragged off. Jamie was gone. They wanted help, and they wanted it delivered. Jake didn't blame them, especially Parkson, with his injured right ankle. It would take Parkson a half hour to make it to the top of the valley, perhaps an hour.

"You're sure the batteries are dead?" Rachel said.

"No," Jake said. "But the phones wouldn't turn on, no matter what I tried."

He waited. The group looked at him, then Warren. Nobody spoke. Jake made a concentrated effort to not look at Warren, to simply survey the ground between the rock pad and their tents.

"Jake," Rachel said. "Why didn't you bring the phones down here? One of us might have been able to get them to work."

"I didn't want to lose them," he said, "in case I, you know. Got trapped."

She closed her eyes, bit her lower lip. "You could have brought one down."

He feigned a look of self-disgust. "You're right, I'm sorry." He brightened. "But we can make it back up there, try to get them working."

"What?" Hans said.

"We walk up," Jake said. He felt the first splatters of rain and turned his face to the sky. The clouds were a light gray above him, darker just to the west, the colder air being sucked into the low-pressure system. "Slow and steady." He motioned at the ground. "It's either asleep or it's full. We stay on the same path, we have a good chance of getting out of here."

"Full?" Parkson said.

Nobody answered him. They were silent for a

minute, all of them looking where Jake was looking, at the top of the ridge. The ground between was littered with rocks. Warren tensed, seemed about to speak, when Rachel cried out.

"Oh my god," she said. "Look!"

A hundred yards to the south, a lone figure was stumbling toward them. She weaved through the rocks, banging her shins on the larger rocks. Her head was hanging down, her jaw slack. It was Jaimie, moving with a curious shambling gait, as though she were trying to run with legs that had fallen asleep. As they watched, she banged into a large rock, almost fell, then straightened and kept coming on. Even from this distance they could see there was something wrong with her face.

"Jake?" Rachel asked. "That is Jaimie . . . right?"

"Stay here," Jake said. He stepped down from the rock pad and called out. She came toward him, head hanging down, wheeling as though trying to avoid the raindrops. Jake went out to meet her, stopping when she was twenty feet away. She had lost her shoes, and her socks were worn away to her ankles, the tattered wool stained with blood. Her toenails were splintered and torn, and Jake winced as he watched her step on a sharp rock. Jaimie herself didn't flinch, just left a red, smeared footprint on the stone and took her next step.

"Jaimie?"

She stopped but did not look up. Her arms hung limply at her sides, and there were bits of twigs and lichens in her hair. She was bleeding from both ears, and her crotch was stained dark. He could smell her even from a distance; a musty, coppery smell.

"Jaimie?"

She mumbled something, then took another step forward, like a scared child finally fessing up to some infraction. Or maybe . . .

Maybe . . .

Maybe that's what she wants me to think. Just a harmless child seeing the error of her ways.

He couldn't banish the thought, the feeling that she wanted him to come to her, to wrap his arms around her. "Jaimie, what happened?" He stepped closer, his nose wrinkling. "Jaimie, can you talk?"

She whispered something at the ground.

"You what?"

"I ran with it," she said, her voice muffled. She looked up, and there were streaks of blood coming from her eyes, the sclera marked with burst blood vessels. She had stuffed some moss in her mouth, and her tongue moved around it as she talked. "It was in my head. I *ran* with it."

"With what?" Jake asked, the question popping out before he had time to wish it back in.

She looked at him, her crimson eyes crinkling as though he were in on some joke with her. Then she grimaced and pushed a broken tooth out of her mouth with her tongue. She let it drop to the ground, the enamel stained pink. Jake looked from the tooth to her mangled feet and back to the tooth. He didn't want to look at her face again.

"Come on," he said. "Let's get you cleaned up."

She didn't respond, and when Jake started back toward the pad she stayed where she was, motionless except for the movement of her tongue in her moss-filled mouth. "Come on, Jaimie," he said.

She was singing. The words were very soft, muffled

and indecipherable. It was some sort of nursery song, a child's song. He felt his neck and arms break out in gooseflesh. The air seemed darker, and not just from the approaching clouds. Her matted and dirty hair swung as she sang, the words chuffing out. Her voice rose as the song went along. Now Jake could make it out:

> *Rock-a-bye baby, in the treetops.*
> *When the wind blows, the cradle will rock,*
> *When the bough breaks, the cradle will fall,*
> *And down will come baby,*
> *Cradle and all.*

She paused, then crooned the same five awful lines again. Blood and spit dripped from her mouth as she sang, and she had begun to wobble as the pitch of her voice climbed. A gob of bloody moss tumbled out of her mouth and she stuffed it back in, almost greedily. She started on the first verse again, pausing on *in the treetops.*

"In the treetops," she sang, her voice rising in an awful mixture of elation and horror. "In the *tree*tops, in the *tree*tops!"

Then her voice trailed off and she pitched to the ground, her head striking the edge of one of the boulders. Still Jake stood where he was, watching her chest heave and fall. She was unconscious, her blood-filled eyes mercifully closed.

"Jake?" Rachel asked from behind him. She moved up next to him, watching Jaimie breathe. "The spores," she said. "They're causing her to hallucinate."

"Yes," Jake said. "Has to be."

"What is it?" she asked, her hand on his arm. "You know something, don't you?"

He looked at Rachel, then back to Jaimie. Old stories, the kind they used to tell each other when they were kids, flickered through his mind, an evil far worse than what promethium might or might not do. Stories of the monster that lurked in the deepest part of the forest, in the most wild of places. A monster that might eat you, or might instead compel you to run with it, to course over the ground so fast and so far that you were lifted up. Jake's eyes traveled down to Jaimie's battered feet. The monster might make you run with it until your feet felt like they were on fire. Run with it above the treetops.

They were old stories. He compared them to the new story, the one Rachel told of some rare element, one that infused non-sentient life forms with the properties of animate creatures. An element that saturated the valley's sediments, something so valuable that it made it worthwhile for Warren to put himself back into this desperate situation.

"We need to get out of here."

"You said that already," Rachel said.

"I know," Jake said. "But I really, really mean it this time."

He went over to Jaimie and hooked his arms under her arms. Rachel lifted Jaimie's legs, gripping her at the knees and avoiding her damaged feet. Jaimie smelled very bad, and there was something more than the odor of old blood, some thicker smell. It reminded Jake of a wolverine den he had found once when he was a kid, the rank smell that stuck to his clothes for weeks afterward. It was a smell of wildness, not the good smell of the pines or sweet crushed grass, but the low smell of the swamp, the smell of scavenger's breath.

They hauled her over to the others, breathing in the awful odor. They reached the rock pad and set Jaimie down. Everyone was looking down, staring at her ruined feet, which were actually in worse shape than her face . . . but only when her eyes were closed. When they were open, Jake thought . . . or when she sang . . .

"One way or another"—Jake said, trying to breathe through his mouth. He leaned down and picked Jaimie up again—"we're getting the hell out of this valley."

They were halfway across the open stretch, just below the start of the slope and the beginnings of the trees, when the wind stopped. The sky rumbled above them, and for a brief moment, nothing moved, the leaves on the saplings on the side slopes above them not even fluttering. Then the wind returned, the sky cracked open with a jagged bolt of lightning, and the downpour began.

The rain came down in fat drops, icy cold, the first taste of the winter that would soon turn this country white. Jake repositioned his hold on Jaimie's arms, and in front of him Warren did the same with her legs. They staggered forward, boots sinking into the ground. The soil was still wet from the day before, and the rain pooled on top of the surface, quickly turning what had been a passable stretch into a morass. They slogged forward, Rachel supporting Parkson. Hans scurried after them, holding his injured arm tight against his body.

Thunder cracked above them again, coming faster

and faster until it was a near-constant cadence. The rain poured down, harder than Jake had ever seen. Thunderstorms were rare this far north; the air usually lacked the necessary energy to do much more than drizzle rain. He could hear the big drops slapping the river's surface far behind them, spattering against the rocks in the boulder field they had just left. They moved forward one step at a time, Jaimie's butt bouncing and sliding across the muck and scattered rocks. They were slowing with every step, the soft ground between the rocks coming up to their ankles. Warren called back something over his shoulder, his words lost in the thunder and pouring rain.

"What?"

"Drag her!" Warren shouted.

Jake nodded, and Warren dropped her feet and joined Jake. They each hooked an arm under one of her armpits and started pulling, sluicing Jaimie's limp body across the open ground. They let Rachel and Parkson go out a few yards ahead of them, scouting for the best ground. Hans took their cue, hopping from rock to rock. It was raining so hard it was difficult to see more than a few yards ahead, and the ground was almost completely covered in water. Even the slopes of the valley appeared to be spread over with sheets of water, draining acres of runoff into the valley.

Ahead of them, Hans tripped and pitched headfirst into the water. Jake saw him go down and waited for him to come back up.

"Come on!" he shouted at Warren. Overhead, lightning cracked across the gray clouds.

They charged forward, Jaimie's battered heels leaving twin furrows behind them. Rachel and Parkson had stopped a few yards ahead, and they almost ran into them. In front of them, a yawning fissure had opened in the ground. The muddy water was pouring into it, clumps of sod breaking off and tumbling down. Hans was deep inside the crevasse, twisting and rolling as he tried to free himself from the writhing mass of tendrils that lined the sidewalls. The ground continued to separate in front of them, opening and deepening. Hans slipped deeper into the hole, his mouth covered with mud as he flailed, only managing to work himself deeper into the cut. The tendrils seemed to be passing Hans's body downward, transferring him further into the earth.

Jake stood at the edge, feeling his boots starting to slide into the hole. One of Hans's hands broke free from the writhing nest, a glint of gold from his wedding ring. A tendril snaked out from the sidewall and wrapped around his hand, yanking it downward. The little circle of gold disappeared. Hans was five feet deep. Ten. Water continued to slosh and froth into the crevasse, cascading over the twisting and seeking tendrils. Then Hans was gone, just a vague shape underneath the muddy latticework of the tendrils.

"Get back!" Warren shouted as the earth started to slip away under their feet. "Jesus, man, come on!"

They yanked Jaimie around and stumbled after Rachel and Parkson, who were retreating to the north. They only went a few yards before stopping again. The same fissure that had swallowed Hans was curving around them, blocking their path to the top of the valley. Jake dropped Jaimie and spun around. All around them, the fissure was opening up, the water pouring into it, the rocks and boulders tumbling down in a series of small and large splashes. He saw tendrils pushing at the opposite sides of the opening, widening the gap even as it extended its length.

Rachel pointed to the northeast and shouted something. There was a narrow path near a section of rocky ground, the bedrock forming a slender bridge back toward the river.

"Go!" Jake shouted.

She sprinted for it. Parkson thrashed his way after her, his foot below his injured ankle wobbling and flopping. Jake and Warren followed, holding Jaimie's wrists and yanking her roughly along the ground. Her weight increased suddenly and their forward momentum slowed, then stopped. They turned. Jaimie had slipped down into the chasm at their heels, and her legs were snared by several tendrils. She had regained consciousness at some point, and the addled expression she'd possessed earlier, that strange combination of confusion and cunning, had disappeared. It was Jaimie, really Jaimie, her bloodshot eyes opening in fear and then pain as a large tendril snaked out of the earth and wrapped around her waist.

Then Jake was falling, the ground giving way under him, Warren flailing for balance at his side. Jake sensed rather than saw something coming at him through the slimy ground. His boot kicked out into the air and found something solid to push off, one thought searing across his mind—*God, please let that not have been Jaimie's forehead*. He kicked himself away from the chasm, back up and over the edge. Whiplike lengths fell on his back, his sides. One of them clutched briefly at his ankle, then slid off, the mud too slick to allow it to gain purchase. Then he was up and out of the collapsing hole, scrambling forward, first on all fours and then straightening and sprinting, Warren splashing after him. They could see Rachel ahead, the standing water over her ankles, Parkson flailing badly behind her.

They scrambled across the ridge of bedrock after them, the soil falling away on either side. Rachel was running back down into the valley toward the river, now swollen and discolored. Jake glanced behind him. The entire length of the bottomland was split open, split lengthwise with the yawning fissure. The ridge of bedrock they had just crossed extended all the way to the thick rim of cattails that flanked the river. The same spine seemed to extend underneath the river to the far side, where a fan-shaped series of ledges in the bluff spread out in a sunrise pattern before narrowing to a single razorback, which led up at an angle through the otherwise vertical bluffs.

Jake ran, his boots slipping and sliding on the rain-slickened rocks. The ground continued to fall away on either side, and tendrils reached out of the earth, brushing against his feet, his shins.

Rachel plunged through the cattails and splashed into the river. It had risen almost a foot in the past ten minutes, the surface cratered by the huge raindrops. Parkson blundered after her, screaming with pain, his foot flopping from one side to the other. Rachel made it through the cattails, and seconds later her arms were cleaving through the muddy water as she swam for the far side. Parkson seemed foundered in the cattails, the seed heads erupting in clouds of white above him. They coated his muddy body as he thrashed forward, pitching to his knees.

A large tendril lay across the ridge of rock ahead of Jake. He leapt over it, his rifle rising up on its strap and banging down against his shoulder blades. Ahead of him, Parkson gained his feet and stumbled forward into the river.

Jake plunged into the cattails, coughing and hacking from inhaling the cattail fluff. Normally the river was narrow, just forty yards across, with little current. Now it was closer to sixty yards, and the current was up.

He lifted one boot out of the water, severing the laces with his knife. He pulled the boot off, then did the same with his other foot. Warren waded past him and dove into the stained water, swimming toward the far shore with powerful strokes.

Behind them, something slithered through the cattail stalks.

Jake yanked a piece of shoelace free from the eyelets and used it to tie the boots together. He swung the tethered boots over his neck and started dog-paddling.

The rain was still coming down very hard, the water splashing up into Jake's eyes and nose. Rachel was nearly to the other side. Parkson was halfway across, swimming awkwardly, his body tilted to one side as he favored his good leg. Warren moved through the water with ease, overtaking Parkson, already closing in on the far shore. Jake continued his dog-paddle. He fought to control his breathing, to let his lungs fill with buoyant air.

Ahead of him, Rachel had reached shallow water on the far side, the water up to her hips. Parkson warbled something to her, some desperate entreaty Jake couldn't hear but didn't need to. Parkson was drowning, or he thought he was. Rachel shouted something at Warren, who was just getting his feet under him. Warren ignored her, staggering onto the rocky shore and collapsing against the side of the rock bluff.

Rachel dove back in. She reached Parkson and positioned herself behind him, one arm looping over his left shoulder. Parkson clawed at her, pushing himself up by pushing her down. Rachel tried to slide away, and Parkson reached out, wrapping his hand in her hair, and pulled her in close. They both went under, and then Parkson's head emerged, sputtering, his hands pushing down in the water. Jake swam harder.

When he reached them, Rachel was still underwater, her legs and arms flailing under the surface. Parkson was only barely above the surface. When he saw Jake he reached out, hands spread like claws. Jake hit him in the face, once, twice, three times, and Parkson let go of Rachel. Jake pulled her up, going under himself with the effort. His boots banged against the back of his neck, the cord tight against it.

Rachel's fist struck the top of Jake's head. He saw a thumb coming at him and turned away, taking it high on the cheek instead of his eye. He parried another blow.

"Rachel!"

She blinked, caught herself from throwing another punch. She retched up a mouthful of river water.

"Shore," she said.

"Go," he said. "Right . . . behind you."

Parkson was a few yards away, thrashing at the surface but not making any progress toward shore, his breath coming in whimpers. Jake dog-paddled closer and caught his eye, white with panic. Jake held out his hand. Parkson reached out tentatively, then his eyes widened even more. Jake spun clumsily in the water to see what had alarmed Parkson.

Something was rushing toward them just under the surface of the water, its length extending all the way back to the shore. The water bulged above it as it closed in on them, twenty yards away, then fifteen. The surging water was three feet high, falling away to reveal a massive tentacle, larger than any they'd seen, washed pale gray by the river. Ten yards away now, and Jake could see the tip of it undulating just under the surface, like a hound dog casting its head back and forth for a scent. Jake was directly between the tentacle and Parkson, both of them still dog-paddling to stay afloat, staring.

Five yards. The tendril was slowing as it got farther out from shore, losing some momentum, but still moving faster than either of them could swim.

Three yards.

Jake let his arms and legs go still. He sank, drifting in the current. The tentacle brushed against his back. He drifted a few more feet, motionless, down and downstream, the tentacle a giant wedge-shaped shadow above him. Wait, wait. No movement, not a twitch. Be the rabbit in the briar, the whitetail buck in the thicket. Finally the need for breath overrode all other thoughts, and he kicked for the surface.

He broke the surface and spun around. Parkson was perfectly still, his hands pressed down hard against something that was not moving. He locked eyes with Jake, lips pressed into a thin gray line, and then he was yanked under the surface in a massive swirl.

Jake put his head down and swam toward shore, no longer dog-paddling, his head under water more than it was above. He breathed in sips of air mixed with water, fighting the urge to hack it back out. Eventually his feet kicked against gravel, and he scrambled onto the bank. Rachel grabbed his hand and pulled him up, toward the hogback ridge and away from the narrow cobble beach. Warren was already ten feet above them, and he reached down to help Rachel onto the thin shelf of rock where he had stopped. Both of them pulled Jake up, his rifle clanging against the rock.

He coughed out water, looking at the river through bleary eyes.

Something was twisting and turning at mid-river, leaving a trail of swirling wakes on the surface. Parkson's hand broke the surface, then part of his shoulder and neck. A second later his shoulder disappeared and the water went still.

Jake pushed himself up on one elbow. "Is he—"

Parkson's head emerged out of the water, eyes blank. He slowly settled into the water, pausing when his mouth was at the water's surface. A trail of bubbles blew from his mouth, then another.

"He's breathing," Warren said. "It looks like he's trying to say something."

"We have to go back in," Rachel said.

Jake reached up to his shoulder and unslung the Winchester. His boots were gone. He brought the gun up, ignoring Rachel's cry, then slapping her hand when she tried to push the barrel away. He swung the barrel back over and lined up the shot, the front sight a small bronzed point of light, nestling down into the rear notch. He squeezed the trigger, the gun bucking under him as the water exploded two inches to the right of Parkson's ear. River water fountained down on Parkson's face with the raindrops, splashing into his open eyes.

"What are you *doing*?"

Jake turned to Rachel. "He didn't blink."

"What do you mean?" Warren said. He was looking at Jake's gun as though he had just recognized it as more than a chunk of steel and wood.

"You know what I mean," Jake said. "It wants us to go in and save him. Just like Greer."

And Jake heard Greer's words again, his larynx flexing and twisting under that awful manipulation: *Helllp meeeeeee . . .*

"So now what?" Warren was talking to Jake, but he was looking at the far side of the valley, at the epicenter of the split and muddy ground encircling the crumpled remains of the tarp lean-to containing the samples of promethium. Jake gazed up the length of the hogback ridge. It ran at a forty-degree angle for almost a mile, ending in a notch at the top that reminded him of the gap in the Winchester's sights. There was a Resurrection Valley, and there was also, high up on this far side, a Resurrection Pass. The spine of rock that led to the pass was folded up and out of the bedrock like hands steepled in prayer, a knife's-edge of granite thrust out of the earth by subterranean forces unimaginable.

He looked down at his stocking feet, then up to Rachel. She nodded, motioned him forward. Above them, more lightning crackled across the gray sky.

Chapter 11

"I seen it," Pierre had said, lying on his narrow bed. "I seen what the Whitigo done to them people."

He twisted in his bed, grimacing as he spoke, perhaps from the cancer, which had joined dementia in the battle for which affliction could wreak the most havoc on his bent body. Perhaps the grimace came from the memory. It didn't matter to Henry, who wasn't sure what was more horrifying, the story itself, or whether this awful tale indicated what was left of his father's mind.

"I seen it," Pierre said again from his deathbed. "And no matter how much I tried, I can't never unsee it."

Henry lay at the top of the bluff, elbows pressed against the rocky ground, thoughts of his long-dead father coming to a halt with the sound of the rifle shot below them.

They had been here for an hour, worming their way

to the rim of the valley, reconning just like they would when they were out hunting. The forest behind them was thick with balsam fir, and the needles had drifted down over many decades to form a dense carpet on the rocks. The rain filtered through the needles, and the ground wasn't too wet. A northwest breeze had developed, the first wind of autumn shaking the last of the rain out of the pine needles.

Below them, a battlefield. Henry did not know how else to characterize it. The ground on the far side of the river was split and marred; it looked like a giant child had slashed the valley open with his equally enormous sword. The gashes were filled with muddy water, and one ran almost the length of the valley, zigzagging among the rock formations at the base of the far slope. The drill rig no longer smoldered, but they could see the scorched grass around it, and a few yards away some sort of shelter that had fallen down. Henry could make out the bright domes of several tents on the far ridgeline, above the mess.

Almost straight below them, three figures scrambled up the narrow spine of rock that led to the pass. The hogback would bring them to just a few feet away from where Henry and the rest lay waiting underneath the balsams. Henry could not make out their faces or tell who they might be, but the fact that they had crossed the swollen river and were moving away from their tents told a story, too.

"Twenty bucks," Garney said. "I can get them with three shots. Boom, boom, boom. Weasel, gimme your .308."

"Shut up," Darius said. "No guns, not yet."

Yes, Henry thought. *Let's have some patience.* They

needed to know who these people were, what they
wanted, what they had done. He was surprised at the
damage they had done to the valley in such a short
amount of time, especially since he could see no
heavy machinery.

If it was even these people who did this, Henry
thought, the moisture wicking up from the pine needles into his still-damp clothes.

His thoughts returned to his father, to the last story
he had told Henry. It was not long after the Great War,
but before Henry's father had gone to Holland with the
Second Armored to fight the Huns in World War II.
There had been a string of incredibly harsh winters in
the Highbanks area. Back then it had been just a loose
collection of rough cabins and shelters, a few whites
around but mostly just the Swampy Cree. The winters
had started early and ended late, sometimes lasting
into May or even June before the grass turned green.
And while there were always a few who experienced
the awful sickness sometimes referred to by the in-
nocuous term *cabin fever*—a certain percentage who
could not withstand the mental toll that these winters
brought—it was during this time that there was an unusual amount of killings, an uptick in gruesome mur-
ders. Of things worse than murder.

It was unclear whether Pierre's account was based
in fact or was a product of his dementia; all Henry
knew was that nobody, not even his own mother, had
heard it before.

Pierre had been in his teens. It was late April, and he
had been making his way through the snow-covered

woods, his rifle at the ready. The winters had been hard on the moose numbers, and the caribou had migrated far to the south, so it was not only long, cold nights and lack of warmth that weighed on the people, it was hunger. Raw, screaming hunger, almost all of the people emaciated, able to count not only ribs with their shirts off but also the indentations and bumps along sternum and clavicles, able to identify healed broken bones as easily as with an X-ray. A technology, even at that early age of the technological era, which was already being used to identify illnesses. But even this emerging technology would not have been able to diagnose the malady Pierre was about to witness.

He was far out in the forest on this day when he smelled charred meat. It was not a smell Pierre could have ignored if he tried; he had been physically unable to slow himself in his headlong charge to find the source of the scent. He plunged forward on his snowshoes, tripping several times before making it to the small clearing where a low, rough cabin sat soaking in the April sunshine, smoke seeping out of a crude stone chimney. The snow around the cabin was littered with frozen turds and yellow with urine, and the ammonia smell was finally enough to cause Pierre to pause, to survey where he was. He was old enough to understand that just because a person had found game did not necessarily mean that person would be willing to share. Or that such a person would welcome company of any kind, especially when that person lived so far out in the bush.

But the smell of meat was divine, even with the bitter tang of several months of piss soaking into the ground, and Pierre was, quite literally, starving. He hallooed the cabin, stopping halfway across the clearing to shout again. There was no welcoming shout, but neither was there any warning or indication he should retreat. He paused outside the door and could hear someone moving inside. He knocked on the door and the movements stopped, then started again.

The door creaked open, and whatever Pierre had expected, the sight of a grizzled, ruddy-cheeked, smiling, five-foot-two white man was very low on that list. Pierre had seen the man before in Highbanks: Claude Depere, a French-Canadian trapper, a Canuck, who had married a local woman and raised five hellacious children over the next decade, children who terrorized Pierre and the other children on those rare occasions when they came to the smattering of dwellings on the banks of the river for a festival. But now the cabin was empty, except for Claude and the smell of people who had been crammed into the same space for the past six months, that heavy and cloying odor overlain by the smell coming from the frying pan suspended over the hearth fire.

"Oh, you smell da bacon?" There was a lingering French cadence in his English, which softened the harsher clipped tones of his wife's language. "Smells good, eh boy? Yeah, you come in then, is good."

Pierre unstrapped his snowshoes and went in. He allowed Claude to guide him to the rough-hewn table and sat, watching as the Canuck danced around the frying pan, poking a slab of meat with his hunting knife. The sizzling was a musical sound; what little game Pierre's family had found over the past few months had been winter lean, and it had been months since Pierre had felt the liquid energy of fatted game in his belly. The table was streaked with blood and gore from the butchering that had taken place, and such was Pierre's condition that the smears of blood and curls of yellowing fat did not in any way affect his appetite. Had he been alone, he might not have hesitated to reach down and scrape some of that dried meat from the planks of the table and put it in his mouth.

"I was glad I didn't," Pierre said, seventy years later, twisting in his bed. "Was I glad? Sure I was."

At the fire, Claude stopped suddenly and whirled around to face Pierre, his knife stuck in the slab of meat in the pan. His good-natured grin was gone, and his expression had narrowed so that he resembled a marten, hard on the scent of a hare. "You ain't been running with that big old friend o' mine, has you, boy?"

Pierre's natural curiosity, which otherwise would have prompted him to ask exactly who this big friend was, was overshadowed by his desire to eat. He retracted a finger, which had crept toward a meat scrap, and just shook his head. "No, I'm all alone."

Claude's forehead smoothed. "Well, dat's good then, ain't it? Sometimes, you never know, it could be that he talk to other people . . ."

Claude's voice trailed off, and for a moment Pierre sensed a bit of protectiveness in Claude's tone, as though he suspected his lover had been out cavorting with another. Which led Pierre to his next thought, and despite his desire to avoid any further delays—his mouth was filling repeatedly with saliva, which he had to swallow down every few seconds—he knew he had to ask the question. Claude might be friendly, but if that horde of Depere children threw open the door to discover him eating their dinner (not true bacon, which would be moldy and inedible this late in the year if it

had somehow been saved; rather, bacon being the re-
gional term for young moose that still had a layer of
milk fat) any one of them would be as likely to slit his
throat as say hello.

"Is your family here?"

Claude paused for a second, the tip of the knife deep
into the slab of meat. "They around, yeah, but don't
you worry, boy. We had us a good winter, they grow
plenty fat." He lifted the chunk of meat out of the pan
and held it aloft, the drippings smoking when they hit
the pan. "How much you want?"

Pierre started to answer, when his eyes caught sight
of something that made his insides tighten, like sucking in a great lungful of January air. Hanging on a
hook near the back corner were several shirts, ranging
in size from what would about fit the youngest Depere
child—a rough-mouthed cur of seven—to the oldest,
Rainey, who at the ripe age of fifteen was already suspected of raping two local girls. There were gashes in
the clothes, and the gashes were lined with rusty stains.
Pierre's eyes drifted down to the cot, which was just a
mass of balsam boughs covered by a wool blanket.
There was a dress arranged neatly atop the blanket, a
worn and torn dress made from flour sacks and stitched
together with rawhide in places. The stains on this
dress were brighter red, the same color as on the table
in front of him.

"Well come on now, boy." Claude grinned, and
Pierre saw that his few remaining teeth were stained a
deep yellow-green, as dead and rotted as stumps in the
swamp. "You can't have the whole thing, that ain't fair
no how no way."

"Is it . . ."

Claude's grin faltered. "What, boy?"

Pierre watched Claude's face, saw the shrewdness and insanity swirling in his muddy eyes. "Your friend," Pierre said, grasping for a different tact. "Maybe you should save some for him."

Claude paused, and for a moment Pierre considered running, just running blindly, because he thought the little wild-eyed man was going to pluck the knife out of the roast and throw it at him. Instead, Claude leaned back and began to laugh into the soot-streaked rafters. "Oh, he don't like this kind of meat, no how no way. Not this old bacon, and with a char on it to boot." Then his gaze narrowed again, and his laughter stopped as abruptly as it had started. "Did he say something to you?" Claude stepped closer to him, still holding the roast aloft. "Did he say he wanted some?"

Pierre stood. He wasn't sure how it happened, but his rifle was pointed at Claude's chest, and neither of them seemed overly surprised at this development. He began to back away and Claude followed, the juices from the meat running down his wrist and soaking into the stained cuff of his buckskin shirt.

"Did he, boy? You been running with him, ain't you? Come down here to tempt me, say something bad about him?"

Pierre reached behind him and lifted the hasp on the door. "I don't know who you're talking about."

"I think things, sometimes," Claude said, the words suddenly dreamy, coming out soft and lispy through his rotted teeth. "Like maybe I shouldn't o' listened, shouldn't o' made da bacon so close to home. Maybe I think them things, boy, but I ain't never *said* them, not never. He been . . . he been good to me, he has.

Like a brother. And Lordy, the things we saw, way up there . . ."

Pierre leaned back, and the door creaked open. A wedge of sunlight fell across the cabin's packed dirt floor. Claude stepped back, his eyes dilating. "I ain't never said no bad words, you tell him dat."

Pierre nodded, backed out onto the stoop, and tucked his snowshoes under his arm. He retreated slowly, walking backward with his eyes on the front door, waiting for the little man to come charging out, or for the long barrel of Claude's hunting rifle to poke through one of the narrow slits that passed for windows on either side of the doorway. The snow was still two feet deep, but it had been warm for days, and the snowshoe trail in the sunny, foul-smelling clearing was packed down. It supported his weight enough that he could move without his snowshoes. Still, when he told his wife and son the story seven decades later, he said that it seemed like hours before he was able to reach the safety of the balsams, followed by an eternity as he strapped the willow-and-sinew snowshoes onto his boots, crouched over in the snow, rifle at the ready, looking up every few seconds expecting to see the little Canuck coming out after him, his yellow-green teeth bared.

"Coming for more bacon," Pierre had croaked. "He was thinking about it, sure he was."

That was the end of the story. When Henry asked what became of the man, Pierre waved it off as of no consequence. Several men went out to the cabin in the clearing, led by Pierre, but by that time Claude was gone. They made a perfunctory circle around the cabin, and to the east, near a low bog with the moss poking out of the snow, they found the butchered remains of all five Depere children, as well as his wife. The latter had been selectively butchered; "only the choicest cuts," is how Pierre had related it. They also found Claude's boot prints, headed north, and the men followed them, but only for a while. After a mile or so another set of tracks joined Claude's—rough-shaped, enormous prints that were hard to identify in the rapidly melting snow. The men of the party halted their pursuit shortly thereafter and turned back toward the village, pausing only to burn down Claude's cabin.

"I wish that was the end," Pierre had said. "But that old Canuck wasn't the only one who seen the *Whitigo* that winter, and the next year it was even worse. Came to be, there wasn't a babe left in any cabin from Highbanks to Sawtee, and the next winter he come awful early. It started right after the leaves fell."

Pierre reached out a trembling hand. Henry, a man of thirty with his own hand suddenly trembling, gave him a glass of water.

Pierre drank, his Adam's apple bobbing in his scrawny neck. "'Twas the next spring we knew it wasn't going to leave us alone. That we had to do something, had to put it to bed."

"Put it to bed?" Henry had asked.

"Sure, sure," Pierre said, his good-natured term for agreement. *Shore, shore.* Even his eyes had lost some of their cloudiness. "When the Whitigo runs with folks that much, it's because it's ready to go sleep. Wants to store up what it needs for a long rest, like a bear. But sometimes it gets . . . distracted. So you got to help put it to sleep."

"Sleep," Henry said. He meant it to sound a bit scornful. His father was dying, yes. His father was losing his mind, yes. But that didn't mean he could talk nonsense. Henry sure hadn't been able to, even as a babe.

"Sleep," Pierre affirmed. "You can't have it doing that other thing."

Henry had avoided drinking out of the same glass, or eating off the same plate, once his father's dementia had set in, for a completely unfounded reason: he was scared that whatever had infested his father's mind could be transferred to him. He knew it wasn't true, but it was a terribly strong taboo in his own mind, as shameful as it was. Now he reached out and drank the rest of his father's water in three long swallows.

"What other thing?"

Pierre's eyes were already starting to lose focus, reverting to that addled, faraway look. But before he lost that brief flame of acuity, one of his eyes had drooped down into a long, deliberate wink.

"Staying awake."

The three people were making slow but steady progress, now less than a quarter mile away. Two of them were bent over, hands on their hips; the third was standing, scanning the valley floor and the swollen river below. It was strange watching people exert themselves from a distance, Henry thought, especially when they're people you mean to kill. You expect them to keep coming on, immune to exhaustion. But they were people, and they were perhaps not even bad people, although the scene below seemed to indicate they were, at the very least, careless people. Intruders. Henry was not averse to killing them.

He was not sure they should kill them here, however.

His father's story had not ended with those three cryptic words, *It stays awake.* Three days before he died, Pierre told Henry the rest of the story, how they had supposedly put the *Whitigo* to bed, the story so strange and awful that Henry had never repeated it. It was the story of a gift, of a sacrifice. Sacrifices were not part of the Cree spiritual ways, for the most part. But this was a special case, and the people were desperate.

"Whatever you give it," Pierre had said, "it makes it bigger, faster. Give it life, and it makes that life frantic."

Pierre's eyes had glinted cunningly in his bed. "But we didn't give it life, did we, boy? We gave it something else entire."

Henry scrunched his way along the pine needles, being careful not to silhouette himself on the ridgeline, and hunkered next to Darius. "We should take them deep into the woods. Get away from this place."

Darius flicked his eyes sideways and grunted noncommitally.

Henry jutted his chin at the leaning, scorched remains of the drill rig. "They called this in, Darius. More people are on the way."

"We'll see. Now be quiet."

Henry moved away. Darius would do what he would do, and the others would follow. Henry glanced over to Billy, who had been watching their exchange. Billy didn't know anything about this place, didn't know anything about anything worth knowing. But he wasn't a dumb person, Henry thought. *Not at all. You're scared of Darius and you're scared of this place, even though you don't know why.*

"Stash your rifles," Darius said. "Here they come."

Chapter 12

Jake was three quarters of the way up the ascent when he felt the first trickle of blood on his feet. Ahead of him, Warren and Rachel moved up the narrow ridge of stone at a measured pace, using their hands as well as their feet to climb. It was not a difficult path except when you were barefoot. He considered wrapping something around his feet, then decided to wait until he reached the top. At least he could feel the rocks with his toes and heels, could anchor himself by digging his toes into the small crevices. It was a long tumble back to the bottom of the valley.

He paused on a small, flat bench and inspected his feet. The blood wasn't from a serious wound, just a ruptured blister on the pad of his big toe. His socks had worn away, and he kept thinking of Jaimie, of her mutilated feet. She had somehow worn through boots—good ones, too; Jake had seen the Red Wing insignia—and her lightweight socks, and then the skin on the bottoms of her feet. Running, she had said, but where? And with whom?

"Almost there," Warren called out from above. "Easy, now. We don't want to rush it."

Our fearless leader, Jake thought. *Back in control.* The thought didn't have much venom behind it. There were, he thought, worse things to deal with than this particular asshole.

Rachel looked down at Jake and saw him inspecting the bottoms of his feet. "How bad?"

"Fine," Jake said. He twisted his socks around, so the unworn tops were now on the bottom. It would help sop up the blood, keep his footing from getting any more slippery. No need to think about the consequences. Lose his footing and slide back down there, leg busted. Or spine. Lay there on that little shelf of a beach between the river and the bluff, and wait.

"Do you think it can climb up here?" he asked.

She glanced downward. There was no movement, but the cuts in the earth had not closed over, and the vegetation was marked by dozens of muddy washes where the larger tendrils had carved tracks. "I don't know," she said.

"Is there more than one?"

She shrugged. "It could be just the one. That honey mushroom I mentioned, in the Willamette Valley? It extends for miles."

He thought about that for a moment, all those tendrils leading back to something at the core, a central mass deep in the spongy earth. "Rachel?"

"Yes?"

"Let's keep going."

Warren was already climbing again, sending the occasional pebble cascading down on them. The grade was steepening a bit near the top, and Jake winced as he wedged his foot into a fissure and pushed upward. Above him, Rachel's legs flexed and bunched. In another place and time he supposed he would have been more appreciative of the view.

Concentrate, Jake. Get to the top, then allow yourself the luxury of distraction. Not a second sooner. He slipped a fraction of an inch, then wedged his toe into a crack in the rock. *Or,* he thought, *how about you just skip the distractions?*

Warren said something ahead of them, his voice muffled. Jake glanced up. He couldn't see Warren, who had reached the lip of the bluff and pulled himself over. Ten more yards to go. Warren spoke again, his voice indistinct as it deflected back over the open valley. Rachel paused as she swung herself over the lip, her elbows on the flat ground at chest level, her head framed in the gray sky between two large balsams. She stayed like that for a moment, then swung her leg over and disappeared from his view.

Something was wrong. The alternative was to stay here, clinging to the lichen-covered rocks, or retreat down to the valley.

He reached the lip, paused for a second, and then swung himself over. The first thing he saw when he looked up from where he lay on a bed of balsam needles was that there were way too many legs in his view. He looked up and saw an old Cree man peering down at him, his lined face impassive, his eyes assessing, cool to the point of coldness. Behind him, four other men, all Cree with the exception of a small, pale man, were arranged in a loose semicircle, with Warren and Rachel in the middle.

Well, he thought. *They aren't tendrils, at least.*

Jake pushed himself to his feet and faced the older man. The wind was blowing toward him and he could smell the men's wet clothes, their wet hair. Warren, his face red with exertion, was tight-lipped, his eyes flitting from man to man.

Jake wiped away the balsam needles that were stuck to his cheek. They cascaded down the front of his shirt and fell soundlessly to the forest floor.

"Hey, Uncle Henry."

The old man's face didn't change expression. "Hello, Jake."

He wasn't really an uncle.

When Jake had been seven years old, he woke in the middle of the night to the sound of his mother screaming. She was screaming at his father, and Jake, though no stranger to the occasional argument between his parents, had never heard anything quite this intense. It was a one-sided argument, and Dawn, his mother, was beseeching Martin, Jake's father, not to do something. Jake couldn't understand what it was, only that his father could not do it, according to his mother, at least, who was shrieking over and over again the same plea:

"Don't! Please Martin, don't!"

He had scrambled to his feet, his blankets pooling behind him. It was mid-February, the worst of the long winter months, and the house was cold. The wood fire in the Franklin stove had dwindled to embers, and the wooden floorboards were cold on his bare feet. Outside, the night was blue-black, sprinkled with brilliant cold pinpricks of light from the northern constellations. Ten feet away, through the uninsulated interior walls that separated his bedroom from theirs, Jake's father was doing whatever it was his mother did not want him to, and Jake, only seven, was torn, unsure of what might or might not be happening in his parents' bedroom, and equally unsure of his own ability to step in and assist. But as his mind cleared and he registered the emotion in his mother's voice as what it was—terror, not outrage—he raced out his doorway and through the next, and found out that what Martin was doing was convulsing on his bed, his mother shaking his shoulders to stop him from doing what he was very nearly done with. Which was dying, at the age of thirty-one, from a brain aneurysm. And so Jake began his new life of being a son without a father, standing in a shaft of starlight filtering through the window and watching his mother shake his father's shoulders as the lights in Martin's blood-soaked brain blinked out one by one.

He and his mother went through hard times after that, and although others did their best to help, there was not much in the community to share. Martin had worked in the timber camps, and he had also been a good hunter and an excellent trapper; Jake could still remember the silky marten pelts hanging on the wall, the occasional wolf or wolverine, the beautiful, tawny lynx hides. He knew his father loved the animals and did not like to kill them, but he liked to understand them, and catching them in his snares and leghold traps was one way of knowing the world in which they lived. It had not made perfect sense to Jake, not until he grew a bit older, but he had understood that the pelts brought in money. Money helped with store-bought food, and clothes, and sometimes Christmas presents.

After Martin died there was no life insurance and no income, and when Jake turned nine his mother had conceded to several months of what passed for courtship and married Darren Lecoux, known locally as Coop.

Coop had broken his right leg while working on the BNSF rail gang in southern Ontario a few years earlier. Apparently, it was negligence on the railroad's part; the gang boss had sent Coop and his coworker in to uncouple a section of cars without informing the trainmaster and the brakeman that maintenance was being performed. It was cold, and the diesel engines were still running, and when the trainmaster put the engine in reverse, the hitch of the newly uncoupled car had caught Coop's leg just above the knee, pulverizing the femur so quickly that there had been no pain, just the absence of structural strength, and Coop had fallen down onto the cold tracks, the skin on his cheek freezing to the rail before his good friend Max could pry him out of the way of the rolling car. The damage to his face had required skin grafts, and the damage to his leg had required eight surgeries, all so that Coop might be able to limp his way through the rest of his life.

So there was a check, every month, and while Coop was not rich by most standards outside of Highbanks, he had a nice home, a nice truck, and even a Phowler johnboat with a surface-drive outboard that only required six inches of draft and could navigate all the backwaters and shallow streams up and down the Big and Little Glutton Rivers. He also had a fine collection of semiautomatic shotguns and bolt action rifles, which Jake was forbidden to use and would not have used if he had been granted access. He had kept his father's rifles and the lone shotgun in the small closet of his new bedroom, and although they were older and of inferior quality to Coop's, they were rust free and the barrels were not pitted nor scored. Coop's arsenal, in comparison, was corroded and scratched, although the inherent quality of the firearms—and his ability to get into the backwaters where game wasn't nearly as wary— meant his lack of attention to detail did not matter much.

His mother was a good-looking woman, and for a while Coop had seemed a decent, if somewhat reserved, stepfather who was pleased with his catch (Dawn) if not the baggage (Jake). It was not until the great gears of the railroad bureaucracy got around to grinding away at Coop's situation that things began to change. It seemed a Pinkerton detective had been dispatched to gauge Coop's level of disability. The agent had been disguised as a tourist hunter, and Coop had taken the man's five hundred dollars to deposit him on a sandbar where moose were known to cross the river. He had taken another five hundred to help haul the man's moose back into Highbanks, and a photograph of Coop straining to lift the hindquarters of the bull moose over the gunnels of his johnboat had accompanied the letter informing him that his 75 percent disability had been reduced to 15 percent.

Jake measured their deteriorating home life by the lines of color under his mother's eyes. First it was just smudges of magenta from the all-night arguing sessions, then darker purple and black, the yellow bruises sometimes framing the more recent, vibrantly colored shiners. Empty cases of Silver Wolf vodka, which sold for six dollars, Canadian, for a 1.75 liter bottle, stacked up in the garage. Jake tried to help, his efforts culminating in a stint at the juvenile detention center in Potowatik. That had been the result of holding his skinning knife to Coop's throat one night, the blade smeared with blood from skinning muskrats, Jake promising Coop that he would slide the point in right now if Coop didn't promise to stop hitting his mother now and forevermore. Words to that effect. Coop had agreed, and the next morning the constable had been drinking coffee at the kitchen table with his mother when Jake came in from his trapline.

Jake had come back from Potowatik with a very clear plan, and he was on his best behavior. He had learned in the detention center that he had a very deep pool of patience he could rely on, as long as it helped to deliver results. It was what had made him one of the best trappers around, and so what if the money from his lines, the early waterline for mink and the long landline he ran through the bitter winter, so what if that all went to his mother as her part of the rent? That the house was paid for didn't matter; there was a cost to life, and Jake understood this now, or thought he did.

Henry was Dawn's sister's ex-husband. He was not truly a friend of the family, but he had been good friends with Martin. He had been there when Jake, at age six, had leveled the little single-shot Rossi .410 at a ruffed grouse and made his first kill. Henry saw the change when Jake returned from Potowatik, saw something in Jake's pleasant new behavior that Coop missed. Jake was never sure if his mother was as oblivious to his intentions as it seemed, or if she was simply waiting. Waiting for him to do something that his father would have wanted his son to do long ago.

That fall, as Jake paddled up to check his pocket set

for mink at the mouth of a small feeder stream, his plans nearly complete, he was surprised to see Henry sitting on the bank. Jake paused ten yards out in the river, feathering his paddle in the current. He had only a lone muskrat in the bow of the canoe; as his mind dwelled on plans for revenge, the concentration needed for making an animal place its paw on a one-inch circle of steel that formed a trap's pan had waned.

"You didn't catch nothing in this one," Henry had said, motioning toward the pocket set, a hole Jake had dug in the bank, baited with a chunk of fish and guarded with a $1\frac{1}{2}$ coilspring trap. "But you got a nice buck mink in that blind set, down behind the big rock downriver."

Jake, now sixteen and broad-shouldered like his father, stared impassively at Henry, giving him the stink-eye, but not as upset as he would normally be. A year or two earlier he would have been furious at Henry, at anyone, for mussing up his sets. Mink did not have a great sense of smell, but other creatures did, and occasionally he pulled in a red fox or a fisher on his waterline. And everybody knew it was terribly bad manners—some thought downright criminal—to mess with another man's trapline.

"What are you doing here?"

Henry stood. "What you mean is, how'd I know where you set your traps."

Jake frowned, started to reply, then stayed silent. He was normally a very good trapper; he took a lot of pelts and made a lot of money. There were others, mostly boys but a few men as well, who tried to follow him, perhaps to learn his secrets, perhaps to steal what he had taken. They were unsuccessful. Now, sitting in his canoe with the sun barely over the eastern horizon, he watched Henry, a man he knew and respected, and felt as though a great spotlight had been trained on him.

"I know how trappers think," Henry said. He motioned to the trap at his feet. "This one's okay, it'll take some fur. But that blind set—the one by the boulder? That's craft, right there. That old boar mink, he thought he was all nice and safe where the boulder separated from the bank. Crawl back there, get him a mouse or a frog and—wham!" Henry snapped his fingers. "You get them when they aren't expecting it, just like all the good ones do. Right? Yeah, you're a good trapper, Jake. Martin would be proud."

Jake could feel the river, pulsing against the aluminum at his feet, vibrating up through the canoe's ribs.

"You stick with animals, Jake," Henry said. He leaned down and brushed the dirt from his knees. "Mink and muskrats and fox. I can't see like Elsie, but I see something bad in your eyes, the way you clench your fists around certain men." He held up a hand. "Don't say nothing, just listen. I don't care what your life is like, if you go through with it I'll tell on you. Do you understand? I'll tell on you."

After a moment Jake let the river carry him downstream. His arms felt numb as he dipped the paddle in, drifting down the river, a boy-man who was simultaneously furious, confused, and terrified. Not terrified that Henry would do anything, or say anything, because Jake hadn't actually *done* anything wrong, except, perhaps, in his heart. But in a way that was enough, because in his heart and his mind and his soul he had already committed to murdering his stepfather. The truly frightening part was that he had been so sure his well-thought-out plans were confined to his own mind that he had believed the consequences would be minimal, that nobody would even *suspect*, much less know. It was the great fear that comes to many teenagers when they realize that grown-ups are not nearly so dumb as they seem to be, and it came to Jake fairly early in his life and all at once, and on a subject that had consumed his past eighteen months.

I'll tell on you. It was a childish threat, and yet it had resonated deeply. As Henry must have known it would.

When Jake reached the blind set there was indeed a dead mink in the Conibear 120, the bodycatch trap's jaws nestled around the big boar's throat. The animal was bent into an arch from rigor mortis, and its beady black eyes were open, tacky from the air. Jake pulled the trap free, the mink still attached, and went on to pull the rest of the fifty-one traps he had laid along clay banks of the streams and marshes of the northern wilderness.

Three days later he left Highbanks.

Jake didn't know the other men with Henry, and he avoided making eye contact with them. He wasn't terribly surprised. Even without the smoke from the drill rig fire, it was only a matter of time before Warren's activities would be found out. Hence the desire to get in and out, Jake supposed.

"You lost your boots," Henry said.

Jake looked down. What was left of his socks was smeared with dirt and blood. He looked up. "What are you doing out here, Henry?"

Henry shook his head. "This is the point where I tell you—we're the ones asking the questions."

"You know this guy, Henry?" This question came from the man with a scar running through his eyebrow. They weren't armed, but Jake could see the indents on their jackets where their rifle straps had been placed not very long ago. The absence of rifles, the thought that they might have hidden them, worried him more than if the four men had been carrying. This far out in the brush, almost everyone carried a rifle. He shifted a little, feeling the Winchester slide across his back. He had repositioned his sling on the climb up to run across his body, the strap running from his left shoulder across to his right hip. Instead of being able to simply shrug the rifle off his shoulder, he would have to pull it over his head,.

"He's a Trueblood," Henry said. "I used to run with his old man. His ma is Dawn Lecoux."

"That old white lady?"

"Yes," Henry said. He turned back to Jake, his eyes flitting over the valley behind them. "What are you doing out here with them, Jake?"

Jake glanced at the other four men. The one with the scar called Darius he didn't know, and he didn't know the beefy one. The younger man, Billy, was a Martineau, and the small, vicious-looking man stepping lightly from foot to foot he *did* know. Weasel had threatened to cut Jake's throat once, when Jake was about five years old and had stepped out onto the muddy road by his house to retrieve a wooden arrow. Weasel had been driving his ATV down the road at about fifty kilometers per hour, a bottle of Labatt's in one hand, the other pressed to the throttle. He had to brake hard and swerve into the ditch to avoid hitting Jake, nearly rolling the four-wheeler, his beer bottle shattering on the muddy road.

"Carve yer goddamn Adam's apple out, kid," Weasel had said.

"Answer him," Darius said. "What are you doing out here?"

Jake looked behind him, into the river valley. The river had come up several feet already, the soil too saturated to absorb any more moisture. The valley floor was scarred and marked by long, muddy fissures, but there was no movement. Darius stepped forward, unexpectedly quick for a large man. There was no time for Jake to do anything, not with his knife or his rifle. He expected some sort of violence, and it would be almost refreshing at this point; he might get his ass beat, if not by Darius then by his buddies, but at least that was something he could get his hands around.

Darius looked at him from a distance of two feet, and Jake saw something else mixed in with the latent violence of the man: intelligence, and a healthy dose of curiosity. "You know what they call this valley in Cree, *True*blood?" His voice was low, not much louder than a whisper.

"Sure. Asiskiwiw."

"The muddy valley," Darius said. "You're their guide, eh? What you guiding them for?"

Jake stood eye-to-eye with Darius. There was no way to back up, because the edge of the cliff was just a few yards behind him. And he didn't want to retreat, Jake realized. He was sick of running, more than a little tired of getting pushed around. He studied Darius's face, then smiled.

"Something funny?"

"When you shoot up, say at a helicopter, it shrinks the relief distance." Jake pantomimed bringing a rifle to his shoulder, jerking it up into the gray sky. Darius didn't flinch. Jake brought the imaginary rifle down and rubbed at his eyebrow. "We learned that at Dwyer Hill. You've got to adjust for a target flying overhead when you got a scoped rifle, pull your head back a little more than you would with a shotgun. It's not like duck hunting."

"Dwyer Hill?" Darius asked.

"Sure."

"It's a training base," Henry said behind him. "For Joint Task Force 2 special ops. It was in the papers. K-Bar, all of that."

"You were with K-Bar?"

Jake nodded, not sure why he brought it up. Dwyer Hill. He was surprised at the memories the name brought back. Not the bad memories—those came later. But the good ones, when they were all in it together, running and hiking and crawling, dehydrated and exhausted and sometimes triumphant. Later they were dehydrated and exhausted again, but that was when the killing had begun, deaths on both sides. Rather than triumph, he'd felt a slow deadening, his core calcifying in the world of blood and sand and shit.

"You think that you were some special forces asshole scares me?"

"Scare you?" Jake said. "I was just trying to teach you how to shoot."

Darius laughed and took a step back. "You aren't going to provoke me that easy, Special Ops. We got all kinds of time, though . . ." His words trailed off, and he made a motion to his men. "I'd prefer not to waste any more. What was his mom's name again, Henry? Dawn?"

Henry nodded, slowly.

"An old lady back in my village," Darius mused. "What you guiding them for, Trueblood?"

Jake felt a series of emotions swirl through him when Darius said his mother's name. First came anger, cold and focusing, at the implied threat to his mother. Close on the heels of the anger was a deep sense of irony. He had spent the last five years deliberately distancing himself from everything and everybody. Even taking this job was a way of separating himself from his upbringing, working for a group that knew nothing about this land, a group that he had always suspected wasn't playing by the rules. Now he was here, at the perfect place and time to be able to take unencumbered action, and the people he had run up against knew his mother, were threatening to hurt her if he didn't cooperate. And if he was reading Darius's eyes correctly, it wasn't an idle threat.

Nor, he supposed, was the threat confined to just his mother.

He glanced at Rachel, tense and watchful where she still sat on the ground. He could tuck and roll and have the Winchester up and firing in a few seconds—if he didn't get tangled up. This group, as vicious as they looked, probably hadn't taken any fire in their lives. They might panic. But they would probably only panic after he started firing, and maybe only after he hit one of them. Part of him marveled at the ease with which his mind reverted back to the logistics around killing, just fell back into step with it, like walking with an old acquaintance. Not an old friend, maybe, but close. He wished he had a bit more real estate to work with.

"He's with us," Rachel said. "Our guide."

"Rachel," Warren warned.

She went on. "We have a mineral lease for exploration. Our drill rig is down there. You probably saw the smoke."

"You have a lease," Darius said. "From who?"

Rachel turned to Warren. He shook his head.

Darius motioned to Billy, and the younger man pulled an object from his belt—it wasn't a pistol, but rather a short war club Jake recalled being referred to as a *mistik*—and brought it down hard between Warren's shoulder blades. Warren staggered forward and fell to his knees, his eyes widening in pain. *Here we go,* Jake thought. *Welcome to our little woodsy corner of the world, Mr. Campbell. How do you like the view?*

"You want another?" Billy asked.

"It's . . ." Warren started to say, trying to catch his breath. "It's from the provincial government."

"Oh yeah?" Darius said. "That's real nice, I'm happy for you. There's some guy from Winnipeg with you, can show us this provincial lease? 'Cause I seem to remember, we're supposed to have some say in the matter. What they call us down there, First Nations?" Jake noticed that he had quite suddenly and neatly been excised from the conversation. That was fine. He was just a guide, after all, and the brains of the outfit was sitting over there in the pine needles.

"It's all legit," Warren said.

"I think we better start having a better conversation," Darius said. "Because I'm getting frustrated. Three people for an exploratory lease? Billy, you got something sharper than that *mistik* in your pack? He ain't listening too good."

Billy drew a hunting knife out of his backpack, the blade bright as he tapped it against the side of his leg. Warren's throat convulsed once, twice, but his lips remained set. Billy leaned down, the blade glittering.

"There were five more of us," Rachel said.

Billy paused, the knife a foot from Warren's face. Darius held up a hand to Billy and turned to her. "Where are they?"

"There was an earthquake," she said. "A bad one. That's when the drill rig tipped over and caught on fire." She went on in a rush. "The ground split open, blocked us from going back to our campsite. Some of the people fell into the openings, and one man, Greer, hit his head. Another man drowned crossing the river, less than an hour ago. We're the only ones left."

"An earthquake?" Garney said. "Darius, let me use Billy's knife. I'll cut through the bullshit real quick."

Good thing she left a few choice parts out, Jake thought. *They'd really want to do some cutting.*

"Not now," Darius said, turning to address Jake. "You understand that if somebody pops up out of the woodwork, or we cut the tracks of somebody else, the girl pays."

"We're all that's left."

Darius walked over to Warren and toed him in the ribs. Warren jerked as though shocked with an electric prod. He glared up at Darius, his expression bright with hate. He had been trying to reach the spot between his shoulder blades where he'd been struck with the *mistik* and couldn't quite reach it, much to the amusement of

Weasel and Garney. "The girl pays," Darius repeated. "That's a core drilling rig. For samples?"

Warren blinked. "Yes."

"And you have an exploration lease?"

Warren paused, wiped the sweat from his brow. "Yes."

Darius nodded, walked over to Rachel, and punched her in the face. She crumpled, and when Jake looked up he saw that Billy had the knife raised slightly. Rachel twisted in the pine needles, gasping. Darius watched her squirm for a moment, then held up a hand. Billy tossed him the knife and Darius knelt over Rachel, his hand curling into the blond hair on the back of her head.

"The lease?"

Warren's face had gone pale. "I don't have one."

"What did you find?"

When Warren didn't answer right away, Darius pressed a forearm across the back of Rachel's neck, smashing her face into the forest floor. He wiped aside her spray of hair and positioned the tip of the knife on the back of her neck, twisting the blade back and forth lightly, almost playfully. Rachel let out a low moan of pain, her fists clenched around handfuls of pine needles.

"I . . ."

Darius looked up. "Well?"

"We didn't find anything," Warren said. "The earthquake destroyed the rig before we could extract samples."

Darius shook his head, as though disappointed, then turned to look at Jake. "Unsling your carbine, Special

Ops." He turned his head a fraction of an inch. "Henry, he plays hero, you shoot him in the belly."

Jake cut his eyes to the left. A few yards away, Henry had pulled a Walther pistol out of his backpack. The muzzle, which had been trained on Jake's chest, dropped a fraction of an inch. Jake shrugged off the Winchester rifle, keeping his fingers away from the trigger. He held the rifle out in front of him and laid it down on the pine needles, the muzzle facing into the trees.

"The knife," Darius said.

Jake pulled his knife, the handle streaked with mud and gore, out of its sheath. He tossed it to the ground next to the rifle.

Darius pressed his own knife deeper into the back of Rachel's neck, his mouth set in concentration. Jake cut his eyes to Warren, who was shaking his head rapidly, trying to protest, to stall. Rachel let out a muffled scream, her legs thrashing. Darius's hand applied more pressure, his tongue poking out of the corner of his mouth.

"They have samples," Jake said. "I saw them."

Darius turned to him. The muscles and ligaments in his forearm stood out like cables. "Samples of what?"

"I don't know," Jake said. "But they found what they were looking for."

Darius turned down to look at the back of Rachel's neck. There was a thin trickle of blood curving down, and she had gone very still. He cocked his head to the side, staring at the blood as it trickled a path through the pine needles. He was breathing heavily, not from exertion.

"Darius." Henry was still looking at Jake as he spoke, the muzzle of the gun never wavering. "She might be useful."

Darius paused, still watching the trickle of blood where it welled out of Rachel's skin. Then, abruptly, he stood and turned to Jake. "Okay." His breathing had returned to almost normal. "Now you guide us," Darius said, pointing down into the valley. "Down there, across the river and over to your camp. Understand?"

Before Jake could answer Garney stepped forward. "You serious? We don't need to cross another goddamn river."

Darius stared at the large man. Garney swallowed once, twice, then cast his eyes downward but did not retreat. Jake alternated glances at the other men. Billy seemed disappointed, either by the lack of action or by the prospect of going down into the valley. Probably both. Weasel had drifted out of sight, somewhere off to the side of the semicircle. Henry seemed lost in thought, his forehead set in deep lines as he glanced down into the valley and then back at Jake. The Winchester was only a few feet away, and Jake only needed a second or two of distraction. Where was Weasel?

"What would you have us do?" Darius asked.

Garney toed a line in the pine needles. "We already did it. We found them, stopped them. Now we just need to finish up."

Darius rubbed at the side of his face. "And the samples? The data they might have collected already?"

"What do you mean?"

"They didn't come in here blind. They found something, by satellite or maybe from all those planes we've been seeing. You think there won't be others?"

"But they can't just start mining," Garney said. "They're here illegally."

"Yes," Darius said, the contempt thick in his voice. "That will stop them. "

"Garney's right." Weasel's voice came from behind Jake, just a few yards away. "Finish it right here. Look at that rig—they didn't get nothing out of the ground."

"We don't know that," Darius said, still patient, waiting for the others to come around. Billy got it, Jake could tell. The younger man's face had lost all sense of playfulness, and he kept looking down into the valley, same as Henry. Stopping them—Rachel, Warren, and himself—didn't end the project. Someone would come looking for them, would find the samples . . . and maybe would find out just how effective the promethium was in animating tissue. If anything, that would give them even more reason to want to pull this particular form of promethium out of the wet ground. Biomedical applications, military enhancements . . . the sky was the limit.

Keep looking at the river like that, Jake thought. *I'll take that little popgun away from you, Uncle, and see what happens next.*

"We don't have any samples," Warren said. "We didn't log anything, either. There's no reason to go down there."

"Darius?"

"What, Henry?"

"You're right," Henry said. He was still looking down at the valley. "We need to go down. Whatever is there . . ." he paused, looking from Warren to Rachel, then to Jake. "It doesn't belong to them."

Darius cocked an eyebrow. "You're with me, old man?"

"Yes," Henry said. "But we go in and out, fast as we can. All of us, in and out. Understand?"

"In and out," Darius said. "Yes, okay."

Jake stared at the man he used to call Uncle. There was murder in his eyes, murder in all their eyes. Behind him, Weasel stepped lightly in the pine needles, his breath coming in quick little pants, waiting for the nod. On the forest floor, Rachel had twisted her head and was looking at Jake, the side of her neck covered in blood. Warren was on his knees, staring at the knife still in Darius's hand.

Henry took a step closer. There seemed to be, at least for the moment, some kind of transfer of power in the group from Darius to Henry. "What *did* they find, Jake?"

Overhead, the wind blew softly through the balsams. Jake could almost hear Jaimie's monotone chant in the breeze: *In the treetops, in the treetops.*

"Just samples," he said. "They collected them yesterday morning, before the earthquake. I know where they put them." He paused, aware that beneath the adrenaline and the fear and the sharp, biting pain of his lacerated feet was the beginning of something thin and tenuous as a cobweb. Up here, the only thing he could expect was a bullet. That was the logical conclusion to this interaction, a knife or a bullet, an orderly end to a disorganized life. But down there, in Asiskiwiw, chaos reigned.

"Sample bottles?" Darius asked.

"Yes," Jake said. "They seemed excited about them.

He"—Jake nodded at Warren—"said something about this being exactly what they were looking for."

Warren seemed about to protest, but stopped himself before he spoke. Something was registering in his eyes, a comprehension.

Just be quiet, Jake thought. *Act pissed and scared. Be your normal asshole self.*

"Where?" Darius asked.

"They're hidden pretty good," Jake said. "Way back in the woods. I don't think I could tell you if I tried."

Darius held his eyes for a long time. "Okay, Special Ops," he said after a minute. "Let's see what you can find us."

Jake went down the hogback first, followed by Darius. Warren and Rachel were positioned between Garney and Weasel, with Billy close behind. It was more difficult for Jake going downhill than it had been going up, partially due to his feet—and partially because they had tied his wrists together.

Henry remained standing at the edge of the cliff for a long time, rubbing his hands over each other as though his fingers were cold, watching them descend. He was chewing on a maple twig, stripping the thin bark off and spitting it aside until the twig was a bright white. After a while, Henry flung the skinned twig to the ground and swung himself over the edge, catching up with the rest of the group just as they were dropping down the last little section of the hogback onto the narrow beach.

The river had gone up several more feet, shrinking the cobble beach to only a few yards wide. The water was the color of chocolate milk, racing downstream and carrying a plethora of logs and branches with it. A bird's nest made of woven grass went spinning by, turning around and around in the current.

"How deep?" Darius asked.

"Over our heads," Jake said. "It was lower than this when we crossed it. I don't know if we can make it across until it drops."

"Try," Darius said. "We'll give you a rope. You make a wrong move, I'll shoot you in the ass." The men had retrieved their rifles from the brush before starting down, and Garney had pulled out his compound bow with the six broadhead arrows. Weasel had taken Jake's Winchester, and it pained Jake to hear his rifle banging carelessly off the rocks on their descent. It had suffered its fair share of dents and scratches over the years, and the bluing had all but disappeared from the barrel and receiver, but those were his marks, and marks from his father.

"This one's loaded with 200-grain Nosler partitions," Darius said, patting his rifle. "Put a hole in you big enough to watch TV through. Give me your rope, Henry."

Jake studied the river, trying not to think about getting shot, or stabbed. Trying to think about how this would work if he crossed first, and alone.

"I thought you wanted me to show you where the sample bottles were," Jake said. "I can't do that if I drown."

"I told you, we have rope," Darius said. "Besides, the girl will tell us if you don't. Garney and Weasel know how to get people to talk."

"She doesn't know where—"

Darius shook his head. "Swim, Special Ops. They taught you that at Dwyer Hill, didn't they?"

"The river will go down," Jake said, speaking loud enough for the others to hear. "A few hours, it'll be down three, four feet, and the current will be way slower than it is now." He held up his wrists. "I'm not going anywhere." As he spoke, a log drifted by in the river, a massive black spruce with limbs and needles still intact. Darius watched it, then turned to look at his men, who were watching the river as well.

"Let's wait," Billy said. "Build a fire, rest a little. We've been running hard."

"That's exactly what he wants," Darius said, jerking his head toward Jake. "Give them time to wiggle free."

Billy snorted. "The day I worry about some wannabe city Indian getting out of my knots is the day I throw my rifle into the Little Glutton. Come on, Darius. A little fire, a little rest, an easy swim in the morning." The rest of the men were nodding behind him.

Jake watched Darius, knowing he had won another small stay, probably worthless, but perhaps not. Before, on top of the cliff, he had postponed the death he'd read in their eyes. Now, he may have done something more; applied a bit of pressure to a crack he hadn't even known was there, a fracture within this group. Darius's eyes remained locked on Billy. Finally he nodded.

"I'll get the firewood," Garney said.

There was little room on the beach to segregate the prisoners (and there was no other way to think of themselves, Jake thought; all three of them were bound hand

and foot), so they all shared in the warmth of the fire as the sun went down. A stash of driftwood had lodged in a small natural alcove a few feet up the side of the bluff face, and the wood had been sheltered from most of the rain. The seasoned wood made for a hot, nearly smokeless fire. Jake positioned himself at various angles on the rocks, trying to let the heat bake some of the pain out of his stiffening joints.

"What's wrong?" Rachel whispered. Above them, on the other side of the river, Venus hung low in the southeastern sky. Warren was a few yards away.

"Nothing."

"You hiss each time you move."

Jake turned to her, the dismissive reply withering in the back of his throat. She was scared, he could see that, but she had hope, too—a foolish hope, but since he clung to one himself he could hardly fault her for it. There was a large mark on her right cheek, and crusted blood had collected at the bottom of her nostrils from where Darius had punched her, and at the base of her collar where he had cut her. Her eyes reflected tiny orange triangles from the campfire.

"My joints."

"Arthritis?"

"I'm not that old." He shifted so he was facing a bit more toward her, a bit more away from the rest of the group. "I went to college after the military, in Minnesota. Some of it, the northern parts especially, are a lot like this." He motioned with his bound hands to indicate the wilderness around them. "Well, not quite like this, but close. My wife . . . my wife and I weren't together anymore, and I stayed out in the woods for a long time. Into the wild, I guess. Not for adventure. A couple weeks, maybe a month. It was early spring, and there were a lot of deer ticks around. I picked off most of them in the evenings. Some of the baby ticks, the nymphs, weren't much bigger than the head of a pin. I missed one."

"Lyme disease?"

He nodded. "I didn't know what was wrong for a few months. Didn't care, either. By that time it had settled into my bones, into my lymph system. Once it's inside you, it's hard to control. I have flare-ups."

"Are you . . . is it bad?"

He shrugged. "There's a new treatment for chronic cases like mine, not much different from chemo. I'd have to be in the hospital for a few weeks."

"Why didn't you go in?"

"I don't know," he said. "I guess I don't like hospitals much."

She was silent, studying his face. "Did you get divorced?"

"No," he said. "She . . . there was an accident."

"I'm sorry, Jake. She died?"

"No," he said. "Not quite."

He waited for the follow-up questions, but they didn't come. Instead, she turned to look at the river, at the dark land beyond it. In the starlight, it looked like a disorganized graveyard, the scattered boulders tilted at strange angles. When she spoke her voice was barely a whisper. "We're going back over there."

"It's all I could think of."

"It was the right thing to do," she said. "But I still don't want to."

Her face looked incredibly delicate, finely drawn in the starlight and flickers from the embers. Vulnerable and courageous at the same time. "Just stay by me," he said. "No matter what."

Before she could reply a shadow fell over them, and Jake twisted around to see Weasel standing a few feet away. He had taken his damp shirt off to dry next to the fire, and his bare torso was almost hairless, thin to the point of gauntness. Jake could see bumps along his ribs where they had been broken, and the raised skin of an appendectomy scar. He was holding a Buck 110 folding knife, the wood handle framed by brass ends. Weasel flicked the knife open, closed it. Opened it again and squatted down, looking at them as he ran the blade up and down his pant leg. Jake looked away. After a while, Weasel straightened and went back to the fire, where Henry and Darius were talking.

"You know where I heard it?" Henry was saying. "That same old lady that you've been running with." He paused. "And I'm not scared, I'm just telling you we should be careful. *Thoughtful*."

"Elsie said something similar to me," Darius murmured.

Henry looked up. "Did she tell you about the old priest, the old *maskih*?"

Darius shook his head. "She didn't say much. Didn't want to talk about it."

Henry poked at the fire with a stick, sending a cloud of sparks drifting upward. The northwest wind had strengthened, and although they could hear it rushing overhead they were sheltered in the lee of the cliff. Garney tossed another chunk of driftwood onto the coals. The wood popped and spat, dried resins and sap making tiny explosions in the seasoned spruce. Billy sat a few yards off, his back to the river. It had already dropped several feet, but the current continued to carry sticks and logs downstream behind him, silhouettes that caught the firelight for an instant before winking out of sight.

"Some people," Henry said, his cadence punctuated by the pops and hisses of the burning wood, "think there are times, and places, where certain actions—violent actions—can cause a reaction. An amplified reaction."

"Fairy tales," Darius said.

"Someone shoots an archduke," Henry said, "and twenty million people die. That's not a fairy tale."

"That's war," Darius said. "And it was about money, and power. Not an amplified reaction."

Henry stared blearily at the fire, his eyelids drooping. *He's tired,* Jake thought, *a tired old man who pushed himself to his limit getting out here. He doesn't want to argue, he doesn't want to debate. He wants to get a bit of sleep, but there's something he wants them to know.* Behind Billy, a large log rolled in the current like an alligator surfacing, and just as quickly disappeared.

"Their people died over there, according to them," Darius said. "Whatever you're worried about has already happened."

"They died. They weren't killed."

"Whatever."

"Did anybody ever try to appease their god by letting someone die of natural causes, Darius? I'm talking about deliberate action. That's what wakes things up, gets their attention."

Darius sighed. "Just tell us, then. Or go to sleep."

Henry tapped the charred end of his stick on a flat rock absently, leaving a series of black marks. He pushed an unburned piece of wood deeper into the fire. Overhead, the wind moaned and sighed. Henry tossed his stick into the fire, the stars blazing above him. "Have any of you ever wondered," he said, "why we never come here anymore?"

Pierre twisted and moaned on his death bed. Then Henry's dying father opened his pain-addled eyes, saw his son sitting next to him, and continued his story.

It was the spring following the third bad winter, and there were only a few children left in Highbanks.

The local community, sparsely populated to begin with, had shrunk by roughly half. Of those who remained, perhaps a quarter were suffering with what researchers would half a century later term Seasonal Affective Disorder. At that time, the whites called it by a simpler term: cabin fever. The Cree had other names for the malady, most lost to history. Regardless of the label it bore, the effects of long periods of cold, darkness, and malnutrition were well known and well feared. Three winters where the snow came early and departed late, three winters where thirty-below-zero temperatures were routinely coupled with winds so intense that any exposed skin felt as though it had been seared by an open flame. In a way, three bad winters were viewed with a bit of relief, as three was the number known to break cycles, the number of change.

But these past few winters had been different for the people who called themselves the Swampy Cree. First and foremost there were the whites, with their foreign language and their often-wondrous tools and their strange ways. There was talk about great palaces and buildings to the south and east, structures that defied description. They brought with them steel and religion and evil vapors that caused many of the Swampy Cree to die, coughing out their lifeblood, their bodies wracked by fever. It was an intrusion, an opening up of their world to forces unknown. And with this intrusion came a deadening of something intangible, a softening. Suddenly, the unbelievably complex challenges like building a fire or killing a moose were now reduced to mere flicks of the wrist.

And during those winters, at the confluence of bad winters and the dwindling of something – of Something—the children had begun to disappear. Only one or two that first year, but even more the next, and by the time the ground had begun to thaw in May of the third year, over twenty children, Cree and white, had disappeared into the green tangle of the Canadian wilderness.

It was the grandparents who were the most scared, even more so than the distraught parents and siblings. For the oldest of them remembered the last cycle, when their cribmates had disappeared, the times when the snow in the spruce was crisscrossed with the great and shaggy tracks of the Whitigo.

But it had never been quite this bad, and the children continued to go missing well into May. Several were pulled back at their doors or shelter flaps by their parents, the children blinking, fully awake and invariably crying because they couldn't go outside, couldn't join their friend who had promised them warmth and food and fun as they had never known. Squirming and writhing in their parent's grasp, stomachs bloated from malnutrition, and their arms and legs thin as twigs, screaming to be let go so they could run barefoot into the woods. And as often as not, when the child was put back to bed and the father awoke from where he lay sleeping in front of the door, to venture outside into the thin and uncertain light of the northern dawn, the tracks would be there. Pressed into the snow, not quite as large as someone wearing snowshoes, but many times larger than the boot prints of a man, indistinct in shape but always with the same smell, the odor of a denned animal mixed with the damp smell of moss. The tracks were spaced ten or twenty feet apart in places, sometimes disappearing for the length of an entire valley only to reappear on the far side.

The local *maskihkîwiyiniwiw*, an aged man named Kiwiw, held a council. It was a fact that the people were dying, he said. He read in the spring winds that another bad winter was coming, perhaps worse than the other three. They could not continue on in this place; they needed to leave their home, to scratch out a new existence somewhere else. But they had settled in this cold, mosquito-infested region for a reason: it was also a place of unbelievable bounty and beauty, and it was just as much a part of their souls as the children they had lost. Yet Kiwiw said it was clear that their home had been usurped, that the great wanderer had either taken offense or had become infatuated with them. Neither scenario was tenable.

At this point there were two versions of how Frederick, the excommunicated priest who had settled in the area a few years earlier, became involved. Some said it was voluntary, that he had witnessed the despair and desperation of his fellow men, that this manifestation of evil had rekindled his soul and his faith. The other story was that some of the men had decided that perhaps the reason they had been the subject of such intense attention in recent years was *because* of Frederick's faith, supposedly discarded long ago but still clinging to the man—along with the near constant odor of cheap whiskey—which may have given offense to the great wanderer. These men had decided that tying Frederick up in the woods, perhaps with a belly wound or two, might be a good way to appease their tormentor.

Wherever the truth lay regarding his entry into the desperate situation, there seemed to be agreement that, for all his faults, Frederick still possessed great oratory skill. Whether it was out of compassion or self-preservation, he used that skill to insert himself into the drama unfolding that spring in an Indian encampment, hundreds of kilometers from the nearest Catholic church.

Frederick told Kiwiw and the elders of the group a story, reading out of a tattered and soiled Bible. It was a story of another group of people tormented by another demon, and he talked of a man who cast that demon into a herd of swine. He had to explain what swine were, as well as many other things, and his command of Cree was tenuous at best, so there was much lost in translation. But he must have made a convincing case, and the elders agreed that it had to be tried, even though none trusted Frederick . . . and what he proposed was terribly risky. Still, there was little choice. Their land had turned sour, perhaps because the old ways were dying, perhaps only because of bad luck. And the Swampy Cree did not want to leave their home.

Two days later, Frederick, Kiwiw, and three elders stood in the bottomlands of Asiskiwiw. They had no swine in Highbanks, and the only domesticated animals were a few scruffy dogs that were now as wild as wolves. The few horses and the lone ox in the region had been butchered and eaten long ago. But the Cree knew of a place where the earth was filled with a presence, a dark and moldy life that had the size and the substance to act as a suitable proxy for a herd of swine. And there, in the center of a muddy valley bordered by a steep rock bluff on one side, a spruce post had been pounded deep into the soft ground. Tied to the post were three emaciated children, two of them crying. The third stared vacantly into the sky, as he had done since his second year. Some of the crueler people in the village simply referred to him as *metoni*, the idiot. In actuality, he was terminally ill with some unnamed brain disease, which robbed him of first his language and now most of his motor skills. He had only months, perhaps weeks, to live. None of this was a comfort to his parents as Kiwiw took him from their arms the evening before, Frederick mumbling something about Abraham behind him as they left.

The evening waned. The sun set; the fingernail moon rose above the balsams ringing the valley, a cold, white curl of light reflecting on the last patches of snow. The two healthy children were still snuffling and occasionally crying out for help, asking for a blanket, for water. The five men stood some distance away, Kiwiw with a staff adorned with raven feathers, Frederick with a canteen of water he had pulled from the Little Glutton River, murmuring over it and making motions with his hands. The Cree watched this, impassive. They were no strangers to ceremony.

Then it was deep in the night and the men were talking, speaking in hushed whispers just loud enough to hear each other over the children's whimpers. They were divided on whether or not they should continue. It was conceded that the wanderer was devious as well as deviant, and such a simple trick, such a simple trap, had been doomed to failure from the start. Their words came out in steaming puffs of air that dissipated a few feet above them. After a particularly heated exchange, Kiwiw noticed that the children had stopped crying. They were all looking to the east, their heads cocked slightly. One of the children smiled, another—the one who was sick—laughed for the first time in over a year. They began pulling at their ropes again, tugging harder and harder, stopping their struggles only long enough to cast their eyes into the blackness of the forest. The night had gone absolutely still and the only sound was the children's struggling, the rough rope scraping against the spruce pole, their breathing growing ragged from exertion.

Then their efforts stopped, and the children settled back to the ground. Above them, at the edge of the forest, something stepped out of the woods.

Three of the Cree men turned and ran. Kiwiw dug his staff into the soft ground and pressed his bony chest against it, wrapping his arms around the thin wood. Frederick watched the creature approach with a rapturous expression, his fingers clenched around his Bible in one hand and the canteen in the other. It seemed made of darkness, a massive shape with a dancer's grace, twisting and winding its way down the valley slope, its long hair catching the weak moonlight in long wisps of silver. It leapt over a boulder, springing so high that Frederick thought it might not come back to earth. But it landed and continued on, and the children giggled and squealed with pleasure.

It stopped a few yards away from them. For a moment, it resembled nothing more than an enormous spring bear, hungry for meat. Frederick blinked several times, for now it seemed to resemble a massive bull moose, perhaps crazy with brainworm. Then a cloud passed over the moon, and the images of bear and moose dissolved into features less distinct, half-formed and wild, framed by long tendrils of hair.

It opened its mouth, and above them a loon cried out, the mad cackle of the fish-eater. The creature turned to the children, who were jostling for position to better see their visitor, then back to Kiwiw and Frederick. It took a step back, suddenly cautious, and one of the children cried out in dismay. The creature paused, looking back at the ragged assortment of children. A long and tortured moan came from above them, far above the trees on either side of the valley, the sound of a creature whose intense desire was struggling against its innate caution.

Then it stepped forward with a rush, crossing over the rough circle Kiwiw had drawn in the soil eleven hours earlier, and bent over the children. A series of wet slopping and grinding noises came from the circle, and Kiwiw shoved Frederick forward.

Frederick shook his head, his movements stiff as he began sprinkling water from his canteen around the edge of the circle Kiwiw had drawn, speaking Latin for the first time in more than a decade. The creature was still huddled over the children. One of the children was laughing, another was crying out in pain. The last seemed to be doing both at once.

The creature straightened just as Frederick came back to his starting point, as though it were going to bolt, but it was a fraction of a second too late. It stopped at the edge of the circle as though chained, the long hair around its mouth caked with gore. Its eyes caught the reflection of the moon, and for a moment Kiwiw thought he saw something Cree, something that resembled his father's proud and haughty features, in its terrible visage.

Frederick spoke in Latin. "In the name of the Father and the Son, I cast thee out." He paused, poured a palmful of water into his hand, and threw it at the creature. It did not react to the water, nor change its appearance to Kiwiw or Frederick. But one of the children at its feet, who had been reaching out to caress its great furry leg, drew his hand back in horror and began to scream.

"I cast thee into the ground, unclean one," Frederick said, "into the dust from whence you came."

With that, Frederick stepped forward and shook out the rest of the contents of the canteen onto the creature's hide. It stood impassively, not struggling nor reacting, until Kiwiw stepped forward. He said something in Cree, his voice as clean and joyful as the song of a spring robin, and struck the creature with his staff.

"Now you take what you have stolen," Kiwiw said. He looked down at the small corpse of the one some in his village called *metoni*. "Take it and run with it."

From above them came another twisted cry, the tone alternating between pain and rage in discordant timbres.

The creature did not disappear but dwindled, shrinking and twisting, the hair changing, what appeared to be a face lengthening and dissolving. It dropped from two legs down to all fours, then back to two legs, then finally settled on four legs. It spun in a tight circle like an ass-shot dog, twisting down next to the children, its jaws popping. It fell to the ground, snorting in ragged breaths. Kiwiw drew a short copper knife from his belt and plunged it deep into the ruff of hair at the base of the creature's head. It slumped to the ground, silent.

When the three elders who had fled returned the next morning, Kiwiw and Frederick sat slumped against the pole. At their feet was an ancient-looking black bear, as emaciated as the children, its ribs pressing against the mangy fur. Its yellowed teeth were worn down to nubs, and the retractable claws were dull and chipped. There was little that was unique about it, save for the knife still buried in the back of its neck. Its gray muzzle was streaked with gore, and in between its back molars were the masticated remains of moss it had been chewing on.

The children were dead.

The men returned to the village, dragging the bodies of the children in a hastily built travois. They left the bear where it was.

Nobody went back to look at the bear, to check on their story, not even the parents of the dead children. It was a well-known fact that black bears would some-times revert to human prey when they grew too old and weak to chase their usual prey. Of course, the attacks had happened largely in winter over the past three years, when bears would be hibernating. Of course, the gaunt carcass slumped near the spruce pole could not make such large tracks in the snow, nor go dozens of yards between strides. But it was a relief to be able to say it was a bear, to say it and mourn and go on living.

They could feel spring in the air for the first time, could feel the lifting of the biting cold.

The following winter would be mild, as would the next several. In a couple of years, the sound of children could be heard again along the banks of the Little Glutton River, and they were not troubled by any more bears.

The fates of Frederick and Kiwiw were largely lost in the tangles of time, but they passed the story on, Kiwiw to the new *maskihkîwiyiniwiw*, and Frederick to the Catholic church in Winnipeg, where he traveled over the course of several months to let them know what had transpired in the great wilderness to the north, of the power of the Lamb even in the savage woods, a power that had been matched, perhaps exceeded, by that unnamed Cree religion. The acolyte and priest who heard his tale were pleasant and accommodating to this stinking, wild-eyed, obviously insane man who claimed to have once been a priest himself, and sent him to the local house for the destitute for a bath and a meal, after which he disappeared and was never heard from again.

The story was spoken of rarely, just enough so that it was remembered, the tale like a hibernating bear that rouses itself just enough to keep from slipping into eternity.

Chapter 13

*M*an, Billy thought, *that old fart's a pretty good bullshitter.*

He lay stretched out on the rocks, the heat from the campfire warming his left side. His rifle lay on the rocks to his right; the rest of their arsenal was next to the fire, drying out to prevent rust. Billy didn't like to leave the guns bunched up, and after his watch he had taken an oily cloth to his rifle, swabbing out the receiver. The inside of the barrel would have to wait until they got back to Highbanks.

Jake and Rachel were a few yards away, sleeping, their toes pointed out over the river, which was dropping rapidly as the night wore on. Warren was closer to Billy, watching him and the fire in alternating glances. Darius, Weasel, and Henry were out cold, their mouths open, their snores coming from way back in their throats. Billy had already done his watch, two hours of tending the fire and watching the three city people, kicking Jake once when he wouldn't stop whispering to Rachel. Then Garney had relieved him, and now

Billy was free to go to sleep, or smoke, or think about old men and their stories.

What the hell was Henry trying to do? Scare them out of taking action?

Maybe it was just cold feet on Henry's part, because he knew Jake when he was just a kid. Billy got it. He didn't care about Trueblood, but looking at the girl it was obvious she wasn't part of some evil empire set on destroying Billy's homeland. She was a scientist who had come along because it was her job, and she probably thought it was going to be wild and remote and exotic. Even Darius has to recognize that, Billy thought. Drop them off in the woods, see if they can make their way out. If not, oh well.

Except, regardless of whether these people survived or not, someone would be back. There was treasure in the ground, so precious these people had tried to fly in under the radar, take a few scoops for free. They couldn't allow that, not if they were going to call themselves *Okitchawa.*

Still, Billy thought, *I wish we didn't have to cross that river.*

He'd expected Darius to react more to Henry's story, to chew on it and stare out into the darkness and say something mystical. Or say nothing, but still look like he had something mystical to say—Darius and his foul old girlfriend, Elsie, tapping into something the rest of them couldn't even fathom. Jesus, what a bunch of bullshit. But no, Darius just went to bed, went right to sleep.

Overhead, a straggler from the Perseids scratched across the sky, blinking in and out of sight in less than a second. Billy watched the sky, waiting for more. Just a little bit of sleep and his mind would clear up. Would reset.

Surgical was the word Darius had used. They had been surgical in their interception of the three capitalists, as if he was some commando. It was probably Jake's veteran status that got him thinking along those lines, Darius with his channeling of energies and ideas, few of them original. He had taken on this whole "protect the Cree land" deal from Elsie, and now it was like his religion. Billy had joined up with them because he wanted to do something, wanted to *be* something.

"It won't help."

Billy turned to look at Warren, a white dude who in his nice flannel shirt *did* look like the establishment, an agent of an evil empire. The kind who a hundred and fifty years ago would slide a piece of paper over for the chief to sign, in exchange for a few copper pots and maybe a few more drinks of devil-water.

Warren jutted his chin out toward the valley. "We don't have any samples, you know that. I see how smart you are."

"Shut up," Billy said.

"But even if we did, so what?" Warren's voice was low, just loud enough for Billy to hear. Garney was staring at the river as though willing it to keep receding. "You think the demand for this stuff is going to go away because you guys don't want it in your backyard?"

Billy propped himself up on his elbow. "You're Warren?"

"Yes, Billy, my name is Warren."

"Warren, you got maybe one more dawn to see." He

let his hand stray toward his sheathed knife. "Maybe not."

"I'm not trying to provoke you."

"You're annoying me," Billy said. "If I have to stand up to make you stop, I'm only going to do it once."

"Then do it," Warren said. His voice was calm, and Billy pushed himself up a bit. Did he really think Billy was making empty threats? No, Billy didn't think he did. There was fear in his eyes, but also a bit of a *piss on it, let's see what happens* attitude. The guy had probably defused a few issues in his time with his nerve and his calm voice, run a manicured hand through manicured hair and said, *Folks, let's stop and think about this a moment.*

"Do it," Warren said. "But you better check with your boss first."

"You said you weren't trying to provoke me."

"Listen," Warren said, leaning forward. "You guys are going to stall out the development of this deposit one, maybe two years. Then they'll be back up here, someone will be. I don't really care—I've made my career, Billy. I have plenty of money, and I'm not a crusader for all the *rah-rah* shit about how critical this is for national defense. We need it bad enough, we'll blow the shit out of China and go take it."

"What are you a crusader for, then?"

"My life, at the moment." He held up his wrists. "Being a covert contractor for the DOD has benefits, Billy. I have millions. Better yet, I can direct research, future explorations. I can make them move away from this area. There are other sleeper deposits out there, other places the United States government can stick its nose into." His eyes gleamed as he locked Billy in his gaze. "You let Darius kill me tomorrow, all of that goes away. Somebody will be back here, and you won't be a rich man. You might even end up in prison."

Billy lay back down. A curl of smoke drifted over him, and he breathed it in, bitter and biting. He pushed himself back up. "That all you got?"

"Money and power?"

"Come on. You think I'm going to let you go, *hope* you do what you say?"

"I never said anything about letting me go off by myself," Warren said. "I couldn't find my way out of these woods alone if I tried. Let me free, then go after me in the morning. Convince them you can do it alone. Then we go back and I get the money for you, set it up so they can't trace it. That's not a problem, happens all the time. I got plenty of experience there. Then, at that point, you decide if you want to kill me and be a rich man, or whether you want to be a man who takes a chance on being great, as well as rich."

"By letting you go."

"Yes."

"I get the money part. Okay, let's say we live in a perfect, trusting world and there's no strings attached," Billy said. "You go off and direct your research elsewhere. Nobody's going to know why the development stopped here."

"You serious about this saving the earth stuff, Billy?"

He shrugged. "Sure."

"You think this is it?" Warren gestured around them, at the fire and the sleeping bodies curled around it like dogs, at the dark river a few yards away. "Direct battle? Come on, you know you're just screwing around, delaying the inevitable. Kidnapping, killing? Those are some hammer-handed tactics. You're better than that."

Billy propped himself into a sitting position and looked around. Garney was slouched over and sleeping on watch, something Darius might kill him for if he discovered it. But Darius and Weasel were out cold, too. Henry, who seemed to never sleep except maybe for a nap in the afternoon sometimes, was out as well. Rachel and Jake were sleeping close together, their breathing deep and regular, hands and legs still neatly trussed. Hammer-handed tactics; yeah, that was about right. Hammer-headed leadership, too. Darius might have some good ideas, but they were wrapped up in his mysticism—what Darius thought of as cold-blooded spiritualism—and he handled adversity by strangling it with his bare hands.

"You're playing the silver-tongued devil, eh?" Billy said. "Man, you better shut up—I could use me a silver tongue. Cut it right out of you."

Warren scooted closer to Billy. "You need to evolve, you need to switch your tactics. You know that, I can see it." Warren's eyes gleamed in the thin orange light of the campfire embers. "What do you call yourself, the *Okitchawa*? What's that, Cree for *ass-kickers*?"

"It means warriors."

"Okay, that could work, or maybe you come up with something a bit less . . . aggressive. So we set you up personally, you have your own wealth. That helps. You inherited it, or got some sort of settlement. Doesn't matter. First thing you do, after you go have some fun for a few months, maybe a year, is you set up a foundation. Native Lands Matter, or you stick with *Okit-*

chawa, whatever." Warren's voice had risen a bit, and Billy had to motion him to keep it down.

"We aren't opposed to resource extraction," Warren went on in a softer voice, and Billy understood Warren was talking for this fictional foundation, explaining their position to a media outlet, a potential funder, a judge. "Okay? We just want to make sure the best science is used to evaluate whether it makes sense to do it *in this particular location*. What the social costs would be, what the impacts would be on the society, on *our way of life*." Billy had the sense that if Warren's hands weren't tied, the man would be gesturing like a lawyer expounding on certain damning facts. "That message, Billy, would drive fear into the hearts of the men who want to use this place. And the best thing? You don't oppose every project. You're not one of these people, 'don't do anything ever.' Some projects are okay, the benefits are worth more than the negatives. That way you build trust, credibility. You build respect. You start to be funded by the government, start getting money from the same corporations you're sticking it to, because they know they need you on their side."

Billy shook his head. "You think I could do something like that?"

"You got the smarts, the looks. The charisma. You fund the best engineers, the best scientists, the best strategists. Dig into the real issues, not just the emotional aspects. Let them do the heavy work, the modeling and statistics. You communicate it to the public, to regulators, to the courts if need be. To the great unwashed masses. You'd win, Billy, more than you'd lose. And even our losses would be magnificent."

Billy was silent, thinking. He knew he should lie

down and go to sleep, or maybe kick Warren in the throat and go to sleep.

"I let you free," he said, slowly, "and you do what? Let me know what's going on? Let me know what fights to pick?"

"Not me," Warren said. "Someone, though. I'd make some recommendations to a few companies that they might want to make a contribution to your organization, call it an act of good faith. I have lots of favors owed me, Billy. The money would roll in, and you would be able to hire who you wanted. I'd give advice, or my person would. You could take it or leave it."

"It all sounds good," Billy said. "Except."

"Yes," Warren said. "Except how do you know I won't just walk away, forget about all this?"

"There you go."

Warren leaned in close. "What would you do if I betrayed you, Billy?"

"You know what I'd do. *If* you were here, *if* I could get my hands on you."

Warren nodded. "My wallet's in my left back pocket, Billy. Grab it, please."

"If I want to take your money, I don't need an invite."

"I know," Warren said. "The wallet, please. There's something I want to show you."

Billy scooted over to Warren, moving slowly so as not to cause the rocks to scrape against each other. He reached into Warren's back pocket and extracted a thin leather wallet. He opened it, pulled out a wad of Canadian and American currency, and held it up to Warren. "You think this is enough?"

"No," Warren said, and his voice was different. Subdued. "The pictures."

Billy frowned, then pulled the two photos from their plastic sheaths. One was of a girl of about sixteen, beautiful and bright-eyed, wearing a sweatshirt with an image of a volleyball being spiked over a net. The sweatshirt read WEST FLAGSTAFF HIGH CHAMPS, and the previous year's date was printed in block lettering underneath. The other was of a boy, perhaps ten or eleven, holding up a brown trout with a streamer fly sticking out of its lip. The boy held a fly rod in the crook of his elbow. Billy turned them over and saw that both had been signed "To Dad," with "Love ya bunches, Kayla" on the back of the girl's picture and the other signed "Tommy the Trout Whisperer."

"So?" Billy put the pictures back into the sheaths. "This supposed to make me feel bad about what we're going to do to you?"

"No," Warren said. "It's your insurance."

Billy glanced at the pictures inside their plastic casing, then up at Warren's face. His visage was almost completely dark, the starlight catching the edge of his nose, the embers from the fire winking in his eyes. But there was something soft inside those hard lines, something that hadn't been there before. And there was a strong resemblance to both of the children in the pictures: the same Roman nose, the same wide-spaced eyes, more pronounced in the boy but there in the girl, too.

"What?"

"They go to West Flagstaff," Warren said. "That's in Arizona. Now you know where they are, what they look like. Keep the wallet, keep the pictures, Billy. If I move my kids to a different town, to a different country, there's a chance that you will use your money to take your revenge on me that way." Warren went on, before Billy could talk. "I don't know if you'd do something like that. It's enough for me to know it's possible, because they are literally the only things in life that I care enough about that I can use as insurance. Look me in the eyes and tell me I'm lying."

Billy looked down at the pictures again, flipping them back and forth. "You'd use your own kids to save your skin?"

"They need me," Warren said softly. "This is the only way I might make it back to them."

Billy closed the wallet and laid it on top of his thigh. It had been a long day and a longer night, and the dawn was coming on, finally, a slight gray fraying at the edges of the black horizon. The darkest part of the night was behind them and now there would be a new dawn, new choices. He let his eyes wander over the men sleeping by the dying campfire. Hard men who were able to make hard choices. That was what had appealed to Billy, not because he lacked the ability himself but because it was something, perhaps one of the few things, he admired about himself. It was good to be around those you admired. But hard choices weren't always the right choices.

Remember that, he thought. *If you lead people someday, remember that they will admire you for the hard decisions, and they'll leave you for the wrong ones.*

He looked at Darius, who sounded like he was choking on his snores. Garney was asleep, his chin down on his chest. Behind them the river burbled and whispered.

"What do you think, Billy?"

"I think you're still annoying me," Billy said, pulling his knife from its sheath. "We're going to have to do something about that."

"Hell," Weasel said. "I don't believe it."

They stood looking at the shrunken river, the top of the sun just peeking over the horizon. They could see two distinct waterlines on the far shore. The higher one was from the flood of the day before, the vegetation on the far shoreline flattened and muddy. Logs and driftwood were deposited along the edge, some weathered and worn from years of aging, others splintered and fresh, the yellow wood hinting at the force of the flood in the upper watershed. The second waterline was much lower, marked by dark brown sediment. It extended several feet down, the green-slimed sediment covering the rocks. Water wept out of the banks from the saturated soil and trickled down to the river, which had shrunk to a mere thirty yards wide.

Their rifles, all except the one Billy had slept next to, were gone.

Garney's bow remained, as did Henry's Walther pistol. Billy still had his *mistik*, and they all had their knives. But the rest of the long rifles, Weasel's and Darius's moose hunting rifles as well as Henry's and Jake's 30-30s, which had been placed next to the fire to dry out and prevent rust, were as gone as Warren. Billy's .308 was slung over his shoulder.

"We're outgunned," Weasel said. "He could get up in a high spot and pick us off, one by one."

"Spread out," Henry said. He had been the first one up, and had awakened the rest of them to alert them

Warren had escaped. "See if you can cut his track.
Weasel and Garney upstream, Darius and Billy downstream. I'll stay with these two."

Weasel spat between his boots and glared at Garney. "I gotta be next to him, I'll cut his belly open.
Come on, Billy." They started upstream, moving along
the edge of the narrow beach.

Garney waited while Darius knelt where Warren
had been, passing a hand over the rocks as if he was
trying to see if there was any residual heat left from
Warren's body. Then he reached down and plucked up
something very small from between the pebbles, a tiny
fiber of rope, less than a centimeter long. He peered at
the end of it, then studied the rocks nearby, letting his
eyes roam over the sharper edges for several minutes.
Finally, he let the fiber drop and looked up at the bluff,
at the spine of rock that snaked above them.

"I'd like to find him," Darius said mildly. "I'd like
to talk to him a bit about how he escaped."

"Darius, I'm sorry," Garney said. "I was just so exhausted—"

"It's over now. Come on."

They had only gone a little way downriver when
Weasel whooped from upstream. Darius and Garney
ran up to join them. Henry yanked Rachel and Jake to
their feet and prodded them forward, marching them
up the gravel beach with his Walther. Weasel was pointing at a set of tracks on the far side of the river. Someone had tried to cover them up, smearing the boot prints
with his hands and throwing some cattails over others.
It may have looked good in the dark, Jake thought, but
it's not fooling anyone now. He looked at Billy, who
was studying the tracks intently.

"He went after the samples," Billy said.

"Of course he did," Weasel said. "Where the hell else would he go?"

"I thought he . . ." Billy said, looking up the face of the bluff. The spine of rock they had used to traverse the cliff face was the only way to reach the top. "Yes?" Darius said.

Billy looked down, quickly. "Nothing. I just would have thought he'd go the other way. Up the bluff."

"Well," Darius said. "It looks like he didn't."

Darius walked into the mud of the shrunken river-bed, and the rest followed. The river bottom was soft on the edges, but the flood had scoured the rest of the channel and the footing was firm, the water only up to their shoulders at the midpoint. The river was cold and smelled different than it had the day before—cleaner, not as stagnant.

When they climbed, shivering, out of the mud on the far side, the old smell returned, the fetid, putrescent odor seeping out of the ground. The fissures and mud-pots were much as they had been. In the distance, the canted drill rig looked like some relic from a ruined past, as out of place as a circle of stones in a farm field. There was a vague suggestion of a mound where Greer had died, but nothing to indicate the body of a man.

Warren's tracks petered out on the rocky ground in front of them.

"The samples," Darius said to Jake. "Where?"

Jake pointed his chin to the left, where the crumpled remains of the lean-to were, just yards from the drill rig. "Let's start there," he said. "Most of the other samples are up above."

Darius pulled Jake's hands up to inspect the knots.

After a moment he let them drop, seemed about to order one of the others to do something, and instead dropped into a crouch at Jake's feet. He pulled a hank of rope out of his pack and quickly trussed Jake's ankles, cinching the knots hard but leaving a few feet of slack in between his feet.

"Go," Darius said.

Jake shuffled forward. His natural pace had been halved, and he thought of the old shows he had watched as a kid, the prison movies with the inmates mincing their way to the cafeteria, to the yard, sometimes holding the ball of their ball and chain, sometimes just with the chain between their ankles. There was something awful in that, in the shortening of the natural stride, more humiliating than wrist chains.

They moved in a single file across the valley floor, the *Okitchawa* treading softly with the rhythm of natural hunters. By comparison, Jake was noisy, dragging his feet over the wet ground, bringing his heels down hard on the earth. Rachel was watching him with alarm, and when he caught her eye she shook her head, almost imperceptible, but the meaning clear enough.

No, Jake.

Well. He might not be able to run, but she would. And he had not harbored a grand strategy, no plans for both of them to escape. He just needed a distraction, a moment when Darius and Weasel, the two natural-born killers, were not focused on them.

What had Henry said in his story? It was like a bear?

Like a sleeping bear.

Okay, then. Time to wake it up.

He climbed onto a large, flat boulder, then down onto the soft ground again. He glanced back at Rachel, avoiding her face and instead glancing at her legs, her feet. They were skirting the edge of the largest fissure, the one that had turned them back toward the river the day before. There was a way around the fissure at the far end, an escape route they had missed in their hasty flight—or perhaps the fissure had stopped expanding once they had changed course. It didn't matter, it was there now and it was the natural route he would need to take. Billy prodded Rachel onto the rock and then followed her up, pausing for a second to glance into the fissure, where rocks were sandwiched between strata of red clay.

"Goddamn," Billy said. "There really was an earthquake."

The rest of the group was already off the boulder, on the softer ground. Jake's ankles dragged across each other and he pitched forward, hitting the mud with his elbows.

"Get up," Darius said from behind him.

Jake rolled to his side, kicking his feet against the ground and sending a muddy spray of water into the air. Weasel stepped back, annoyed. Jake twisted around, jerking his feet some more, throwing a tantrum because he couldn't get up. Letting all the anger flow into his muscles, his bare feet thudding into the ground again and again.

Come on, come on.

"Quit fucking around and get up," Darius said.

It will take what you have, Jake thought, pounding his heel into the muck, *and amplify it. But you only have indifference, Jake. You have separation from those you love. You are unresponsive, and it will be too—*

He felt the ground shudder underneath him.

"What the hell," Weasel said, backing up a step. He glanced at Henry, then Darius. Billy shrugged his rifle off his shoulder. Ahead of them, Garney notched an arrow onto his bow. The ground shimmied again, and muddy water squeezed out of the earth around them, the puddles shaking with ripples. Henry hopped back onto the rock, and Darius did the same. Billy had taken hold of Rachel and had her in a loose headlock, his eyes casting around him at the shuddering ground. There was a wet sucking noise, and the ground began to separate underneath him.

"Jake! To your ri—"

The rest of Rachel's cry was cut off by Billy's tightening forearm, but Jake sensed the presence slithering out of the ground and rolled away, something cold and wet sliding across his shoulder. He kept rolling, feeling the presence pursuing him over the wet and broken ground, the chasm widening behind him. His head struck a rock and his vision went dark, then cleared enough to see the tendril, which had emerged from the far side of the chasm. It had changed direction and was going after something else.

Of all the people in the group, only Garney had stood his ground. The rest had retreated to the rocks, separating like a flock of ducks after a shotgun blast. Now they were spread out on either side of the chasm, clinging to rocks as the ground shuddered under them. Garney stood at the edge of the chasm, his bow at full draw, the string pressed against the side of his face. The tendril in front of him was grayish red, the color of cheap meat at the butcher shop. It paused a few yards from Garney, as though momentarily perplexed by this man who stood his ground. Garney squinted, his left eye closed, his arms steady.

He murmured something, his lips moving against the bowstring, and the tendril surged forward. There was a ripping sound from the chasm as it pulled itself apart, tearing off from the base of the tendril anchored in the sidewall. It fell three yards in front of Garney's mud-splattered boots, twisting and rolling in the muck.

"What . . . ?" Weasel said. "Wait. What . . . ?"

Garney, who had tracked its progress the entire time with the tip of his arrow, released the string. The broadhead sliced through the tendril two feet back from its tip, dead center. About, Jake supposed, where the brain would be—if it had a brain. The arrow went through the tendril, skewering it to the earth. Behind it, the torn end of the tendril thrashed. Garney looked up, his face calm and deadly. He gave Darius half a nod, and then another tendril rose out of the chasm from behind him and punched through his body.

The front of Garney's shirt blossomed outward and tore. The gore-streaked tip that emerged immediately reversed course, curving around in a tight circle to reenter Garney's stomach, just a few inches from the exit wound. Garney's eyes bugged out, his mouth open but soundless, the loop of the tendril pressed across his blood-soaked abdomen. Then the tendril twisted and pulled at the same time, ripping Garney backward. His screams followed him down into the chasm, his raspy cries bouncing off the muddy walls, still clutching the bow in one hand.

Jake scrambled to his feet. Darius and Weasel were already running for the top of the valley, dodging and darting between tendrils and the labyrinth of holes and cracks. Billy was still on the rock, his forearm around Rachel's throat. Henry was watching the earth, seemingly transfixed. There were no tendrils around them for the moment, but several more were creeping out of the chasm.

Jake drew his knees up and looped his arms over them, his fingers brushing at the knots at his ankles. He felt along the coils of rope until he found one of the ends, tracing it backward. He dug his fingernails in, twisting and pressing. He cursed under his breath as a fingernail peeled back, and then dug back in, using the lubrication of the blood to wedge his fingers deeper into the knot. The tension dissolved incrementally under his fingertips, but the progress was slow, slow. Something scraped behind him and he paused, his fingertips pressed into the knot, his breath held tightly inside his hammering chest. The scraping stopped, whatever was behind him pausing less than three feet away.

Go, he thought. *Go on.*

The scraping came again, repositioning itself on the rocks, as though it had heard his thoughts.

It senses you. Maybe not your body heat, but your panic—your frenzy to live.

Jake let his mind go, let it drift away to the only place he could think of that felt the least like life. Down the tiled hallway, past the bulletin boards, the air itself sterile, smelling slightly of alcohol, of the air purification system itself. Beeps and buzzes punctuating the low hum of nurses' voices. Fluorescent lights buzzing, the cold light. Past room 213, past room 215. Occasionally a doctor or nurse with head down, bustling off to someplace more important.

Take a right and there it was, the short little hallway. The Dead End, he called it in his mind. There was an enormous red and blue checkered painting at the far end, next to the elevators. At first he hated the picture for what it tried to do, its obscene attempt to bring color and life into this place, and then he did not hate it anymore because he understood the intent behind it, and it became one of the many things he tolerated. But he still did not like it. Take in the picture, then inhale a breath of the artificial air, so different from the taste of air inside the forest, the air here antiseptic, yet it felt dirty when he drew it into his lungs. Then exhale, and there it was, room 217, and from inside its ten-by-twelve space, there was a beeping that came at intervals of somewhere between fifty-seven and sixty-one beeps a minute. In a way it was one of the worst parts, hearing that beeping, so steady and regular, and thinking, well, that sounds okay, so maybe the rest . . .

Then inside the doorway and there she was, the shell of what had been, not so long ago, the embodiment of life itself. Sit down, reach out and feel the warm skin. It had grown looser over the months as the weight had shrunk from her body. Eventually he would let his eyes move from the pale skin to the gown they had dressed her in that day, either green or light blue. Green had been her favorite, the color of poplar leaves when they first emerged, the gown a pallid cousin to that vibrant spring color. From the gown, over the slight bump where the sensors were attached, over the neck—still lovely—still almost as lovely as it had been all those years ago in the coffee shop. The face had grown gaunt and it looked different, the angular cheekbones too sharp now, the lips thin. The eyes a darker blue than they had been, and vacant. Just vacant. Once, and only once, he had pinched the skin on her arm hard, wanting to see if he could clear some of that vacancy for a moment. Her mouth had twitched and the pace of the beeping had intensified for a few seconds, but that was all, there was no change in her eyes. He had left a small bruise on her forearm.

Then the confession, the same words every time.

I'm sorry, Deserae. I'm so sorry.

His apologies were not for the bruise, not for his absences, not even for his role in how she had ended up here. That last part just sad and stupid, a moment's distraction in the car and then they were flying through the air, glass shattering, metal crumpling. Her screams in his right ear, her blood on his face, his wrists.

The apologies were for his cowardice. For his retreat. First there had been his self-imposed exile, his distancing from his childhood home. She had cajoled and demanded more from him, had insisted he be brave enough to feel pain. They had been working their way north, taking months, years, but always getting closer to his home. There had been no hurry. They thought there had been no hurry. And now she was gone, and he had reverted to who he had been: a spectator in life.

He opened his eyes, slowly coming back to himself, aware that Billy was shouting in the distance. The tendril he had heard at the base of the rock was gone. He had no idea how long he had been in his self-imposed mental fugue; it could have been hours, but he was pretty certain it had only been minutes, perhaps not even that. His fingers were still halfway inside the knots, and he pried the rest of the cinched rope apart and stood.

Billy and Rachel were retreating seventy-five feet away, stumbling from rock to rock, Billy still holding Rachel. They were caught between two chasms, and several tendrils were working toward them from both directions. The tendrils were thicker and longer than they had been the day before, more deeply colored. It's getting stronger, Jake thought.

Not just stronger, his mind whispered. *It's getting ready for something. For a transformation.*

Darius, Henry, and Weasel had been turned back from their attempt to flee the valley, thwarted by another chasm stretching open in front of them, a mud-smeared grin that widened and widened. They were retreating toward the big rock pad with the lone cedar tree, the only piece of real estate large enough to offer any protection, pausing only to hack at tendrils. Jake looked down at his wrists, still tightly bound, with no way to get his fingers on the knots. He could be of no help to Rachel like this; he couldn't even protect himself. But if he could sneak his way down the valley, he could be out of Billy's rifle range in minutes. Retreat, then come back for her. There was nothing else to do.

Retreat and then come back, eventually.

In the back of his mind he heard the beeping, its regular and monotonous tone.

He stepped onto the soft ground. His feet were still numb from being cinched so tightly, and they bumped and dragged over the ground. He stumbled along the edge of the chasm, not looking at the writhing lengths working out of the edges of the ground below him, feeling the earth sliding away under his feet. Clumps of earth fell into the fissure as he walked, and he looked down as a large clod tumbled down the chasm and hit one of the tendrils. The tendril paused for a moment, trembling, then plunged back into the sidewall.

Go on, Jake thought. *Go tell your buddies there's fresh meat up here.*

He reached the section of tendril that Garney had shot with his arrow. It had turned nearly black. Jake knelt next to the shriveled form, the reek of decomposition already wafting from the severed end. He grasped the arrow with his tethered hands and yanked the shaft free. The broadhead was the old two-bladed style, very sharp. He sat down, blocking out the slithering noises coming from the fissure beside him, trying to block out Garney's voice as well, choked and pain-filled, issuing from deep in the earth.

He positioned the feathered end of the carbon arrow between his feet, then angled it back, the front of the shaft nestled in the notch between his knees. The broadhead was only a few inches from his face. He brought his wrists over the blade and touched the rope to it. A few fibers separated.

He lifted his wrists and repeated the motion. The blade was streaked with black gore from the tendril.

Rachel screamed. Jake jerked, the broadhead sliding across the rope and nicking his wrist.

Tendrils were swarming toward Billy and Rachel, the small rock patch crawling with them. Billy spun left and then right, Rachel's hair flying as Billy jerked her around. Another large tendril emerged from the fissure, moving steadily toward them. For all its size it gave the impression not of vigor but of rottenness, as though it might fall apart at any moment, the flesh ready to disintegrate.

But before it disintegrates, Jake thought, it wants to see what happens.

He sensed Billy's intention in his frantic look, in the sudden tensing of his shoulders. "No!" Jake yelled, at the same time pulling his wrists hard over the broadhead. The rope separated under the blade.

Billy shoved Rachel forward, toward the mass of approaching tendrils. She tumbled to the ground, breaking her fall with her tied hands. In front of her, the black tendril rose, trembling, higher into the air. Rachel scrambled to her feet, a tendril shooting forward to loop around her ankle. It yanked her back to the ground, and this time she hit the rock on her side, the air whooshing out of her. She gave a breathless cry of pain as more tendrils surged toward her, crawling along the rock in an intertwined mass, their progress slowed only by their own numbers, so intent on this new prize that they were unwilling to make room for their brethren.

Billy ran toward the chasm, his feet digging into the crumbling edge, and launched his body into the air. The chasm was ten feet across, and he hit the lip of the far side at chest level, his legs dangling into the earth. His rifle was slung across his back and a tendril crept out of the crevasse, twisting along the leather strap, and yanked downward. Billy yelled and kicked back with his legs, his fingers digging furrows into the earth. He slid backward, then at the last moment twisted his shoulders and ducked, letting the rifle sling slide off his shoulder. He scrambled back up over the lip, still kicking at the tendrils around his legs, and staggered toward the rock pad.

Rachel was being pulled into the other fissure, her hands clawing at the rock. Jake picked up the arrow.

"Rachel! Hold on!"

She looked up, her eyes wide, fingers trying to hook into the rock. Then she disappeared over the edge: first her legs, then her torso, then those enormous, terror-stricken eyes, and finally her fingers, still scrabbling for a hold on the broken ground.

Jake slid headfirst to the lip of the chasm. Rachel was several feet down, a swarm of tendrils surrounding her. In the background, a large, dark presence loomed, a despot on its earthy throne. Gone were the creeping, almost brainless movements of earlier; these tendrils surrounded her tenderly, carefully wrapping around her legs and her body, twining their way around her arms and her chest. The other victims had been meat, but this was something else: a prize.

Jake got to his feet. She was already too far down to reach, and he felt panic seize him, a full paralysis of mind and body. For a moment his mind was blank as she was pulled deeper into the darkness. Then he heard a beep in his mind, the sound of a pulse echoing on a hospital monitor, the sound of slow, drawn-out death, and his paralysis broke. He dove straight down into the chasm, arms spread wide like a linebacker, and hit Rachel's midsection with his chest. He still had the arrow in his right hand, and he kept it far out to the side, wrapping up Rachel with his left arm. The tendrils around her snapped under the sudden force of the impact, and she and Jake plummeted down deeper into the hole, bouncing against the sides of the sodden earth. There were more tendrils farther down that slowed their descent, but these seemed to be inanimate, simple obstructions rather than the seeking, clutching lengths of the tendrils above. Finally they came to a halt at the bottom of the chasm, prostrate and entangled with each other, but for the moment free of growths sprouting from the sides of the chasm. Far above them was a wedge of gray sky, framed by a latticework of writhing tendrils. The large, dark tendril was slumped over, damaged by Jake's crashing entrance into its world.

Jake spat out a mouthful of mud. One of the tendrils above them twisted toward them, the tip cocked at a slight angle.

"No," he whispered, then punched through the waxy flesh with his arrow. The tendril withdrew. He got to his feet, his knees braced against the sidewall, and jabbed the broadhead into another tendril. It slithered back into the earth. The tendrils seemed less aggressive down here. Or perhaps they were momentarily confused, as any animal would be when the prey turned around and charged instead of fleeing. Whatever the source of the hesitation, Jake was certain it wouldn't last.

Rachel got to her feet. She was scratched and bloody, her fingernails splintered. She kicked off a section of torn tendril from one foot, then got the other foot free. She looked up at the sky, then kicked a toehold into the soft earth two feet up. "Come on, Jake," she said. "Let's go up."

Chapter 14

Billy pulled himself onto the rock pad, kicking at the tendrils on his calves, his ankles. The last fifty yards had been a nightmare sprint, the ground simultaneously dissolving and coming alive, the cracks and holes opening up wider and wider, the narrow bridges of drier ground between them turning softer with each step. The rest of his group had watched him zig and zag, Darius and Weasel leaning down to help him onto the pad. Each man had his knife out, and after they pulled him onto the rock pad they turned back to back, watching all sides of their sanctuary.

"You lost your rifle," Darius said.

Billy ignored him and crawled over to Henry, who was on his back, wheezing and clutching his left arm. Billy shook Henry's shoulder. "Is this what you were talking about?"

Henry turned his eyes to Billy. "Just," he said. "Just need . . . a . . . second."

"Look at that," Darius said. "I don't believe it."

Rachel was climbing out of the fissure, mud-streaked, her forearms crossed by red welts. She paused at the lip, then turned to pull Jake up. They stood on wobbly legs and regarded Darius and the others, less than fifty yards away. Jake had an arrow clenched in his hand. There was movement in the chasm behind them, but for the moment none of the tendrils were going after them. They, like Darius, seemed to be uncertain how to react to this development, to two people who had literally climbed out of their graves.

Darius reached down and yanked Henry's Walther from his belt. Other than their knives, it was the only weapon they had left; Garney's bow had disappeared along with him into the chasm.

"No," Henry wheezed. "No killing. It will . . . make it . . . worse."

Darius brought the pistol up. "Get over here," he called out, "or I'll shoot both of you, right where you stand."

Jake said something to Rachel, then held up his hand not holding the arrow and extended his middle finger. After a moment Rachel joined him, her arm thrust high into the sky. The blood had mixed with the mud on their bodies and it looked a bit like war paint. Their eyes and teeth—they were smiling, grinning actually—were very bright.

"They think I'm bluffing," Darius said. He pulled the trigger, the gun bucking in his hand. A spray of mud and rocks exploded just to the left of Jake. Jake and Rachel turned and ran, running crossways, Jake in the lead as they skirted the edge of the fissure. Darius tracked Jake with the Walther, his finger pressing against the trigger. The fissure curved toward Darius before tapering off enough for them to jump across it. Their current route would bring them closer, within thirty yards, a much better range for the short-barreled Walther.

The sights of the pistol were a foot in front of Jake as he ran. Darius's finger depressed slowly, making sure he kept the lead in front of Jake's chest.

"No!" Henry pushed himself up and staggered toward Darius. Weasel stuck out a leg and Henry pitched forward, but the momentary distraction was enough to cause Darius to squeeze the trigger before he was ready. The gun bucked and Jake paused, staggering a little, then continued on. Darius fired and fired again, too furious to aim correctly, sending slugs screaming into the air around them. Jake leapt across the chasm, then turned to catch Rachel. His chest was broadside now, twice the target it had been.

"There we go," Darius said, and squeezed the trigger. This time, instead of firing, the Walther gave a small click.

He spun back to Henry. "Where are the bullets?"

Henry looked up through a skein of long, graying hair. "It's too late, Darius."

Darius stepped forward and kicked Henry in the jaw. Henry's head snapped back and he turned over on the rock, his eyes glazed. "'Bring the old man,' she said." Darius spat out the words, his nostrils flaring. "'He'll bring you wisdom.'" He kicked Henry in the ribs, rolling him over.

Darius set the Walther down on the rock and ripped open Henry's backpack. He dug through the coils of rope, a small tarp, all the other crap Henry had brought with him. At the bottom was a ziplock bag holding two cloth bundles. Darius tore it open, spilling out a handful of 30-30 cartridges. He opened the other bundle, plucking out several small, short rounds.

Jake and Rachel's progress through the fissures was slow, and the tendrils that lay along the ground slowed them even more. They hadn't gained much distance and were still within range for a few more seconds. Darius slapped at the stony surface for the pistol, not letting them out of his sight.

The rock was bare. He looked down, then up.

"No," Darius said.

Henry had pushed himself into a sitting position, and he held the Walther in his right hand. His left was curled like it was broken, the fingers like claws. "Don't spill blood here, Darius."

"You wouldn't dare."

Henry drew his arm back. His face was ashen. "It took a sacrifice to put it to sleep, Darius. It wants another sacrifice to wake up, to *consolidate*. It needs something *intentional*. Can't you feel it?"

"I don't feel anything," Darius said. "Give me the pistol!"

Henry's eyes locked on Darius, suddenly fierce. He flung the pistol into the distance, the little Walther spinning in the air and then skipping across the ground. It came to rest thirty yards away in a seam of mud. Within seconds a large tendril crawled to it, testing it for warmth, for movement, pressing it deeper into the ground.

Henry climbed to his feet. "You want to do something," he said, "you do it with your own gun."

Darius pulled his knife from his sheath. "You're going to go get that."

"It's gone," Henry said. "Just like your rifle is gone.

Stolen from you while you were sleeping." He paused, looking into the gray sky. When he turned back to Darius his eyes were calm. "Sleeping like a baby. A stupid little baby."

Darius crossed the rock pad and seized Henry by the arm, bringing the knife to Henry's stomach. "You know why we make babies, old man?" He plunged the knife into Henry's belly all the way to the hilt, then ripped it crossways. A torrent of blood splashed onto their feet. Henry looked downward at the pool of blood spreading across the lichen-crusted rock. "To replace old men," Darius said, shoving Henry off the edge of the rock pad.

Henry landed with a splat. Dozens of tendrils swarmed out of the soil, weaving around his bloody torso. Several more crawled over Henry's face, touching and pressing, moving lightly, almost tenderly. The ground was suddenly hidden beneath a mat of intertwining serpentine shapes that formed into a loose cocoon around Henry, pressing over his stomach wound.

Something rippled underground, a massive heaving that reverberated through the rock. The tendrils contracted around Henry, pulling him tighter to the earth. Everything went very still.

Across the river, Jake and Rachel paused, dripping river water from their clothes at the base of the cliff. The only movement was a solitary yellow aspen leaf, floating down the river they had just crossed.

The ground opened slowly, dilating around Henry's body. Several rocks popped free at the edges and tumbled into the darkness. Henry Redsky followed, not so much falling as being handed down from one set of shifting tendrils to another. A low sound came out of the earth, something that could have been human, could have been animal. Or it could have been the earth itself, a gravelly whisper of rock sliding across rock.

Billy stood at the edge of the rock pad. Henry's lips were still moving under his shroud of tendrils, the pupils of his eyes expanding as the light grew dimmer. The earth rumbled again, the tendrils coming out of the sidewalls interlaced with their counterparts on the far side. Very slowly, the earth came back together.

This time, the earth stayed still. Most of the remaining tendrils retreated back into the ground, until the valley looked as it had a half hour earlier.

After ten minutes of silence, Billy stepped off the rock pad, pausing at the mudpot where Henry had flung the Walther. He inserted his hand into the mud, wincing, but nothing happened. The tendrils had all retreated. But the ground was not entirely still, not entirely dormant. It was rocking slightly, a gentle back and forth, like a jaw chewing.

"I can't find it," he said. He looked up. Rachel and Jake were already a quarter of the way up the spine of rock. Jake had paused to watch Billy, one of his hands grasping an outcropping. Then he turned and continued to climb.

"The gun is gone, Darius," Billy said.

"We don't need it," Darius said. There was still a lone tendril atop the ground, limp and motionless. Darius walked toward it and it slowly slithered back into the earth.

Billy watched it disappear, thinking of Henry down there, somewhere. "It's not hunting anymore," he said.

"No," Darius said. He was still holding his bloody knife, and he wiped it on the side of his pants, one side and then the other, leaving a scarlet chevron on the denim. He sheathed the knife, took one last distrustful glance at the ground, and then nodded toward Jake and Rachel, who had started to climb again. "But we are."

Chapter 15

The time for running was over.

His feet were bleeding badly. His joint pain was escalating, the flare-ups in his hips and shoulders pulsing with pain. Everything he had done to his body over the past week had been just begging for this kind of reaction. He placed one foot ahead of him, grimacing as the rock pressed against the battered flesh. Behind him were a series of bloody footprints on the hogback.

Don't think about Lyme's, he thought. Don't think about your feet. Then what? The girl, maybe. The one ahead of you, the one who keeps looking back to make sure you're okay. What about the thing that's in the ground, the thing that seemed to not only swallow Henry, but seemed to . . . savor . . . him? Try not to think about that, either. That's all, just try not to. That part is behind us.

He dug his fingers into a small concavity and leveraged himself a few more feet up the bluff. A dislodged stone bounced down the side, coming to rest on the gravel beach far below them. He had unscrewed the broadhead from the arrow and could feel it lying flat against his leg. If he twisted or flexed wrong, the blade would cut him, but there didn't seem to be any better storage options.

"Okay?" Rachel asked. He couldn't make out her features; the gray sky was getting darker by the moment, and her face was lost in the shadows.

"I'm fine," Jake said. "Keep going."

She looked out behind them. "They're crossing the river."

"I know," he said. "We need to get to the top."

"Then what?"

"Then we rest. Come on, Rachel."

Ten minutes later they reached the top. She helped pull him over the edge, and they lay there panting, muscles shaking. It was cold, and he could feel the heat of her very distinctly as they lay side by side. After a moment, she got up and knelt next to his feet, squinting. "Don't," he said when she started to tear of a section of her shirt for a bandage. "It's going to get cold tonight."

"We have to do something," she said. "You're bleeding like crazy."

He withdrew the broadhead from his pocket and handed it to her, then motioned towards the cuff of his jeans. "Slice off the bottoms, about a foot long." She bent to the work, carefully cutting through the thick denim and then sliding the sections down and over his battered feet. She paused to inspect the bandages-slash-moccasins, frowning. "We need to tie them on," she said. She cut a long strip from her shirt, then cut that into four smaller strips and tied the bundles of denim into place, cinching them tightly. "How bad does it hurt?"

"Not bad," he lied. He got on all fours and climbed to the edge of the cliff and carefully poked his head over the side.

They had made it to the base of the cliff and were staring up at them. Darius saw Jake immediately and turned and said something to Weasel, who looked up and nodded.

Jake pried a fist-sized rock from the ground and let it tumble down the cliff. The men at the bottom scrambled out of the way, the rock smashing into the gravel beach a few feet away from them and sending out a spray of smaller rocks. Jake pulled another stone out of the ground and hefted it in his hand, letting them see it. Rachel brought a couple more rocks over and set them by him, including a larger rock, almost the size of Jake's head. He considered sending it down to make a point, then decided to save it. If they were stupid enough to begin climbing, he would make the big rock his first drop. No more warnings.

"A stalemate," Rachel said.

"For now." He looked up at her. At some point she had taken a moment to wipe away the worst of the blood and the mud, but her lip was swollen and there was a large bruise on one side of her face. He supposed he didn't look very good himself, but he liked the look in her eyes, the set of her mouth. "They're going to try to kill us, Rachel. Maybe not today or tonight, but tomorrow for sure."

"Why?"

"Because they've made up their mind to do it," he said. "They've already lost two of their men. They won't let it go."

"It wasn't our fault."

"No," he said. "But we're the reason they came out here. The reason why all of this"—he gestured below them—"happened."

"Jake," she said, "I had no idea there could be this kind of reaction. You have to believe me. I saw trials in the lab, but it was with algae and bacteria. The promethium affected them, yes, transferred some properties. Like a virus using the DNA of its host, the kind of methods we use for genetic therapy, but enhanced. Still, it was nothing like this, nothing to suggest—"

He held up a hand. "Rachel?"

"Yes?"

"Calm down. I believe you."

She swallowed, searching his face. "You knew there was something strange about this place, too."

"Yes," he said. "Legends." He paused, a small smile creasing his lips. "But nothing like this."

From somewhere below them, the earth shuddered. It was not the steady rumbling of earlier. These were a series of convulsions spaced a few seconds apart, as if the earth were retching, trying to dispel something caught in its throat. They crawled to the edge of the bluff and peered out over the darkening valley, the river a pale ribbon of light. On the far side, something was moving, a writhing mass of shadows next to the rock pad. It grew larger, seemed to contract, then grew again.

Not retching, Jake thought. *More like giving birth.*

Below them, Weasel's voice drifted up, angry and frightened. Jake dropped another rock over the edge in case they were having second thoughts, sending it careening toward them. It landed between the men and the river, but they hardly seemed to notice. All eyes were locked on the far side of the water, the epicenter of the convulsing earth.

"Rachel?"

"Yes."

"It could move before."

"Yes."

"But it was tethered to something, wasn't it?"

She looked at him. "There would have been a central mass," she said. "The tendrils are just the fruiting bodies. I can't be sure."

"It could move, but it couldn't . . . travel."

"No," she said.

His eyes remained locked on the cluster of twisting shadows, the vague details becoming less distinct as the last of the light faded. In seconds it was not much more than a darker shape in the blackness covering the valley bottom, easy to lose sight of. "Those legends about this place, the ones I heard when I was a kid?" he said. "They were about the great wanderer. The Whitigo, the old man of the woods. Not really a man."

She was silent. The earth shuddered again, and then again, sending pebbles cascading down the bluff.

"It was a moss eater, Rachel. This great big old beast who could move through the woods and the sky—he ate moss. Most of the time. Sometimes, though, it craved something different. Flesh. But only young, innocent flesh."

"Jake, let's not wig ourselves out, okay?"

"Do you know what the greatest punishment for a wanderer is, Rachel?"

"Jake, come on—"

"Prison," Jake said. "Being locked in one place. No change of scenery, no new people to meet, to torment.

The same thing, day after day." He turned to her. "It would be a terrible thing."

From below them, the earth gave a final shudder and something ripped open, with a sound of fabric—or perhaps flesh—rent apart. Wind sighed through the branches above them.

"We need to go, Jake. Now."

"There are three of them coming after us, Rachel. I can't outrun them with my feet in the shape they're in. There's a Cree village called Highbanks about ten miles from here. There's a constable there, or at least there used to be. He can call in to Potowatik for more help."

"Help for what?"

"To arrest Darius," Jake said after a while. "He killed Henry."

"Jake—"

"If we both go, they'll come up through the pass right behind us. All of them. If I stay here, I can delay them, maybe stop them. You go for help, Rachel. I'll hold them off."

Below them, Weasel's voice came again, pleading this time. Darkness had descended fully, and the starlight was minimal. Jake knew that later his eyes would grow acclimated to the darkness and he would be able to see fairly well. Well enough to drop a rock on his pursuers? Perhaps, perhaps not. But Resurrection Pass was not the only way out of the valley for them. They could go around the cliff and flank him, it would just take a bit longer. That was okay, too. It would allow Rachel to build up her head start.

"Can I find it?" she asked. Her pulse was visible on

the side of her neck, beating rapidly against the thin skin. "Highbanks?"

"Yes," he said. He gave her directions, pointed out the stars and constellations she needed to orient herself.

"If they make it up the pass, it'll be three against one."

"Yes," he said. "I'll be ready for them."

"With your arrow? Even if you build a bow—"

"There are other ways, Rachel. To slow people down, to stop them. All of this," he paused, waved a hand at the forest, "is still my home as much as theirs. With a little luck, I'll catch up to you."

She seemed about to say something, and instead looked up at the sky again. Below them, the three men had stopped arguing. He listened for sounds of them climbing up the rock, but the night was quiet. He wormed back over the edge and peered down. The river still held some light, the stars reflecting off the slow current. The men were gone. Jake craned his head, listening, and thought he heard splashing far upriver.

"They're circling around," he said. "Go, Rachel."

"How do I get there? Tell me again."

He laid out the route as best he could. The river bisected her path at a right angle, so she would hit it at some point. He studied the landscape in his head. Eventually, the river looped back around and would lead her to the village, and for a moment he considered telling her to just follow the river. But that route was three times longer and would require her to cross more streams and another small river, plus make her go through one of the most treacherous swamps he had ever en-

countered—miles of sucking bog and floating mats of
vegetation. In the end, he told her that if she got lost she
should simply follow a stream, any stream, to a river,
then the river to civilization. And to stay on high ground
when she could. It sounded better than it worked, he
knew. Countless men and women had followed some
unnamed river to their death in this country.

When he was done, she turned and studied the tangled wilderness behind them and then turned back to
him. "Are you going to kill them?"

"I'm going to slow them down," he said.

"If you do—"

"Only if I have to."

"If you do," she said, then seemed to pause and re-
focus on his face. "If you have to kill them, Jake, do it
quick. Then come find me."

She disappeared into the wilderness.

The clouds had finally parted, the sky above ablaze
with distant stars. He was glad for the direction it
would give her, but with the clouds gone it had turned
colder, and he knew the night would be frigid—the
first night of autumn, regardless of what the calendar
said.

If they came for him, they would come soon. It was
a few hours at most before they would work their way
around the northern edges of the bluff. Then they
would either retreat or circle back for him. Or build a
fire, wait him out for the night, and come at him when
they were rested and warm and he was weak and cold.
He thought of the convulsing earth, spasming as it vom-

ited out something, *something,* onto the cold rocks of the valley floor. No, they would not build a fire tonight.

Jake lay in his position, flexing his toes and fingers to keep the circulation going. When he moved, if he moved, it would have to be very fast, and the cold was becoming a serious issue, the hard northwest wind of autumn cutting into his body, so cold that he sometimes thought he could smell the vast frozen tundra to the north, a place where the soil never completely thawed. It was different country from this, even colder and far more open. Some of his people lived there, and he had visited once and had not liked it. It was too bright and too windy, and there was nowhere to escape the sun or the wind. The woods were better, and this place he had chosen was deep in the heart of the forest, where Jake lay nestled in a tangle of blowdown, where the worst of the wind could not reach. But it was still very cold.

He'd reopened some of his wounds, some deliberately and some from his exertions. They were minor lacerations for the most part, and he had been trained to avoid letting the pain take precedence in his thoughts. It could not be ignored, and anyone who said so was a fool. It was simply about making sure you kept the pain in the proper perspective; suffer through the little pain to prevent the big pain. But it still hurt, and so he needed to think of other things.

Where was Rachel?

It would be dark in the woods, and she wouldn't be able to see the fading light in the west, like you could see it when you were in more open country or on a lake. She would have to rely on the stars as he had told her, and yet the forest was thick, so thick. The branches would block her sight and it would be hard to keep in a straight line. *And you are doing a great job analyzing the situation,* he thought. *It is very helpful to try and figure out what she might or might not be doing, instead of listening to what might or might not be coming through these deadfalls. Focus.*

He was shivering. He supposed the shivering would be bad enough in an hour that he would have to leave this spot and move around to prevent hypothermia. Already he was stiffening, and he would be unable to move like he would need to. He grasped the short spear he had carved, using the broadhead, between his bloody fingers, his index finger and thumb marked with dozens of nicks from the short blade. The spear had taken a long time to whittle, and he had concealed the shavings in a pile of woody detritus at the bottom of a dead spruce, where a woodpecker had left a series of exploratory holes. The other shavings, for the hidden triggers, the sharpened sticks he had carefully crafted, those shavings he had buried in the forest duff behind the biggest tangle of fallen and semi-fallen trees. The wind subsided for a moment. He heard something move in the silence, the softest of footfalls. It was repeated, and then, just before the wind picked up, the murmur of a voice. He tightened his grip on the spear, told himself once more to be patient. They were three and he was one. They had knives, and he had what would best be described as a sharp stick.

The narrow opening through the blowdown of dead spruce and cedars created a tunnel, like the dark gullet of some grotesque beast, the fractured tree limbs like broken fangs. There were thousands of such blowdowns in these woods, mostly victims of ice storms in the spring. He blinked. There was a shape in the tunnel, crouched over, its gaze alternating between the ground and the path ahead. It took a few steps toward him, then stopped and studied the ground again, like an animal tending to its serious and unknown business of the night.

It was Weasel. He was whispering to someone behind him, and the wind carried his words to Jake in a series of vowels and consonants, as hard to decipher as the shape of the man, now just twenty yards in front of him.

"St . . . leedin. Ryin . . . iggle into . . . brush."

The shape behind Weasel was much heavier and taller. Darius. Billy must be behind them, or perhaps circling behind Jake. Jake urged Weasel and Darius to continue forward in his mind, *rah-rah*ing them on, telling them there was nothing to worry about, just a half-blood city Indian with bad feet and no weapons. Still they waited. There was no flashlight beam, and he knew that even if they had flashlights with them, they would be loath to turn them on. They knew he was waiting for them, a hunter being driven into a corner by other hunters. A flashlight was a beacon.

He hoped that was what they thought, hunters against a hunter. Because although he had learned to kill at an early age, he had been a trapper long before he had become a hunter.

Move, he thought. *Move.*

The two shapes merged together in the darkness, then separated, slowly advancing along his blood trail, the trail he had left for them. It led from the small campfire he had cobbled together, then just as quickly smothered, knowing the smoke and embers would draw in his pursuers. *If* they chose to pursue him, which Jake had not been sure of; he suspected they might just flee back toward Highbanks. But Darius was nothing if not tenacious. The trail leading from the campfire to the blowdown was difficult but not impossible to see, a line of scuffed and bloody marks from his feet. He had not thought how it might look in the dark with no flashlight, and realized Weasel must be a first-rate tracker.

Come on, he thought. *Don't think about how obvious it is. Just look at the trail, at the pitiful picture it paints. Your poor old city Indian, bleeding and trying to hide. Outnumbered and now outmaneuvered.*

Weasel drew near. Twenty-five feet, twenty, the acrid smell of him pushing ahead on the wind. Darius was ten feet behind, his head swiveling constantly, looking everywhere except where Weasel was looking. The starlight was sprinkled throughout the gnarled tangle of canted tree trunks and broken limbs. Jake had to fight to control his breathing, had to keep from clenching his fist on the spear. He wanted to lunge, to ram the stick through Weasel's scrawny throat.

Weasel passed by almost close enough to touch, barely glancing at the three logs, fallen close together with a triangular space between them, a narrow cave suspended three feet off the ground. The two big spruces were on the bottom, forming the cave floor. The other was on top, the heavy tangle of limbs covering everything except Jake's eyes, peering out like the eyes of the wolverine, which was what he needed to be now: mean and tough, vicious enough to drive a young grizzly off its feed, the glutton of the northwoods. The wolverine was the trapper's nemesis, a scuttling beast that would follow your trail and eat everything you had caught along the line. A maddening creature, one damn near impossible to figure out.

"He's nestled in real deep," Weasel whispered. "There's a blood mark between those big logs up there."

"Go on," Darius said. "You see him, let me know."

Weasel stepped forward, Darius pausing just a few yards away from Jake. Jake couldn't risk turning his head to watch, so he listened, listened to Weasel weave through the tangle, listened to Darius's light breathing. Overhead the wind shrieked and blew the last bit of warmth from the air.

Come on, he thought again. *It's exactly what you think. Some pitiful guy you tracked down, huddled underneath the big blowdown. It must have looked like safety to him, to this pitiful guy. All those logs crashed together like a flattened tipi. Looks good, doesn't it, Weasel? You won't even have to try to conceal my body once you finish me off—it's already buried under there.*

He was no longer cold.

Weasel paused, then circled around the cluster of giant tilted logs. Then he returned, his footfalls a series of light scratches under the sound of the wind.

"He's under there," Weasel said. "I can see part of his leg. Nestled up underneath." Weasel sounded simultaneously apologetic and excited when he spoke next. "You can't fit, Darius."

Jake did one quick assessment of his body. There was one throb from his hip, almost as though it said, *I'm hurting, buddy, but ready when you are.* His toes and fingers were singing with hot blood, and he could feel the battle haze creeping in on his mind, crowding out all other thoughts.

"Fine," Darius said, motioning with his knife. "Go bleed him out and let's get going."

The jumble of logs was thirty feet from where Jake lay. Darius was roughly halfway between Jake and the blowdown. The trees had fallen into a clump, leaving a bit of open space around them, as close to a natural clearing as there was in this mess of logs and leaning timbers. Weasel surveyed the blowdown again, trying to determine the best route in. Finally, he dropped to his hands and knees, then pulled several loose branches away from a dark triangle at the base of the pile. He inspected the ends in the dim light, holding up the severed tips, then tossed them aside.

Jake drew in a breath, flexing his legs.

Yes.

Weasel wiggled into the blowdown, his knife held out in front of him. Darius moved a few steps closer, watching Weasel and then swiveling his head from side to side. Jake had seen moose do the same thing walking into a shooting lane, feeling something tickling at the base of their brain, the sensation of being watched.

"He blocked it off," Weasel said from inside the tangle, his voice muffled. "Gotta kick through it."

"Hurry up." Darius was looking above him, at the top of another tangle of fallen trees, where one of the branches was rubbing against a tilted trunk, moaning in the wind.

It's not even me he's looking for, Jake realized. *It's the other, the dark shape from the valley. The one that drove them away from the base of the cliff.*

"You ready for me in there, Jake? I got something for you."

There was a splintering sound from inside the tangle. Then another, and the pile of logs shifted, one of the massive trunks that had been precariously balanced crashing down, its branches snapping, sending wood and bark flying. The ground shuddered briefly, and for a moment the forest was quiet. Then Weasel began to scream, his voice exploding out of the tangle of branches.

"My legs! My goddamn legs!"

Darius started forward instinctively, then stopped short. He whipped his head around and stared at his backtrail, rotating his knife so it was held flat to the ground, the faintest silver light reflecting off the blade from the stars. He looked at the tangle of logs around him, all the storm-felled trees lying at odd angles, studying each one closely. His breath came out in smoking clouds, evaporating over his head.

"Help me, Darius!" Weasel screamed. "My legs are pinned! Jesus! Jesus Christ," his voice trailed off for a moment and he groaned in pain, then took in several ragged breaths. When he spoke again, it was in almost a normal voice. "Darius, get me out of here."

Darius took a step back, still holding the knife out in front of him, and swiveled back around. Weasel began to scream again, louder and louder, beseeching Darius to come in and lift the crushing weight of the logs off his legs. Darius continued his visual reconnaissance, and after a minute his eyes locked on Jake's resting place. In the starlight Jake thought he saw Darius's eyes narrow briefly, his shoulders tense. Jake bunched his legs under him, not wanting to emerge quite yet, but that was fine, it was what it was. He almost started forward, then caught himself as a branch broke above and behind Darius.

Darius spun around, the knife tracing an arc through the air in a warding-off gesture. A dark shape emerged from the tangle on the far side of the blowdown and slid to the ground, panting.

So Billy did circle around, Jake thought. *They were going to flush me out of here like a rabbit.*

"What the hell's going on?" Billy asked. More screaming issued from inside the blowdown. Billy bent over it. "Weasel?"

"Get me out of here!"

Billy straightened and looked at Darius. "Why are you just standing there?"

"He's out here, somewhere." Darius motioned to the blowdowns with his knife, jabbing it in the direction of the thickest spots.

"Who?"

"He's out there," Darius said. "Waiting."

Billy blew out a disgusted breath and turned back to the deadfall. He pulled a flashlight out and poked the beam into the tangle. He traced the light up one log, down another, and then repeated the pattern on Weasel's legs. The limbs and needles threw out a series of clawing shadows on the deadfalls behind them, and for a moment Jake saw the shadow of Weasel's outstretched hand through the tangle, reaching out for Billy.

"It's not as bad as it could be," Billy said at last. "His legs fell between a couple smaller logs. The one that fell on top of him is resting on those two. He doesn't have the full weight on him. We just got to pry it up an inch or two to get him free."

Billy bent down and picked up a limb from the

ground, as thick as his wrist and about six feet long. He wedged it under the log resting on Weasel's legs, using one of the smaller logs as the fulcrum, and pushed down lightly. "This might work. Come on, Darius."

Darius looked around him again and then shook his head. "Leave him."

"What?"

"Leave him there. We need to go."

Weasel began to scream again, a stream of curses directed at Darius. Billy waited for Darius to join him, but he stood where he was, his knife still held out in front of him. Billy muttered something under his breath, wedged the flashlight into the crotch of a branch, and shoved the limb deeper under the log. There was an enormous dead spruce tree tilted above him, the roots mostly ripped free of the earth. Billy pushed on it, testing its stability. It swayed slightly, then returned to center.

"You're going to have to pull yourself out, Weasel," Billy said. "Can you drag yourself out with your arms?"

Weasel croaked something in the affirmative. Billy pushed down hard with his lever, the limb cracking but not breaking. Weasel groaned again, but this time the timbre was different, a bit of relief mixed in with the pain. Billy pushed down even harder, and the pile of logs shifted again. "Almost there," Billy grunted. "Give me a hand, Darius!"

Darius did not move, and Billy finally took the extra step he needed, two feet deeper into the log pile, to improve his leverage, the two feet Jake had been urging him to take in his mind. Billy's boot crunched on something and the log above him, the canted log that Billy had tested a moment ago to ensure it would not fall on him, came alive. A tension-loaded limb, held back by the number-four deadfall trigger, an ancient and deadly catalyst that could hold back such tremendous weight or energy, a trigger Jake had whittled so painstakingly that evening—the same style trigger Jake had used to kill his first snowshoe hare—that tension-loaded limb whistled forward in a perfect arc, its length marked with yellow scars where the smaller branches had been trimmed away, and struck Billy three inches below his left collarbone. Billy stumbled backward as the limb rebounded in the opposite direction, waving back and forth in the light from the flashlight.

Billy staggered back several feet, his shoulders slumped, his breath whistling oddly. Weasel called out something to him and Billy turned his head a fraction of an inch.

"Billy?" Darius said.

Billy's hand crept up to his chest and touched the dark spot blooming there, pressing his fingers against it. He looked at the darkness on his fingers, cocked his head to the side, and slumped to the ground. The flashlight had fallen, and the beam was now pointed toward the log pile. In the light that spilled from the ground up to the dark sky, Jake watched the branch that had struck Billy finally rock to a stop. The eight-inch shaft Jake had affixed to it at a right angle was still there, the broadhead from Garney's arrow dripping blood into the log pile. From the ground, Billy exhaled. The exhale went on for a very long time, finally ending in a quiet rattle, almost lost in the wind.

Darius watched him for a second. Then he turned to

face the spot where Jake still lay. "Come on, then," he said.

Jake wormed his way off the logs and stepped into the clear, the stick held flat against his leg. He'd been trained in hand-to-hand combat. That training had been with other weapons, and it had been when he was younger and wearing good boots and not scraps of denim on his feet—the rest of his pants were under the log pile, the legs that had lured Weasel in to Jake's trap. Despite all of those things, the battle haze had descended fully on him now, and he had to hold himself back from rushing forward. Darius waited for him, a dark silhouette with the tangled shadows of the dead-fall behind him.

"The one-two punch," Darius said. He had dropped his knife hand to his side, and they stood looking at each other from a distance of twenty feet. "I'm impressed. Did the first one trigger the second?"

Jake took a step forward. "Separate," he said. "Each one was independent of the other."

Darius glanced at Billy's crumpled form. "It went into his heart."

"Yes," Jake said. He moved forward several more feet. "I was just hoping to catch a lung."

"Lucky."

"You can stop talking now."

"Luck runs out," Darius said. Jake took another step forward, Darius's features coming into focus: the bent nose, the hooded eyes, with the lighter scar tissue slicing through his eyebrow. The flashlight was fading, but there was still plenty of light. Plenty.

"Yes," Jake said, "it does."

Darius looked at him. "They're all dead." Behind them, Weasel gave a whining gasp. "Or dying."

"I'm not done yet."

"Are there any more traps out here?"

"No," Jake said. "No more traps."

"Then I could walk away?"

Jake lifted the stick away from his body, letting the faint and yellowing glow from the flashlight wash across it. "Theoretically."

Darius dropped his knife, and the blade stuck into the ground with a scratching whisper. "Then let me."

"What?"

"Henry was right," Darius said. "There's been enough death."

Jake strode several steps forward, grasping the spear in both hands, feeling the solid, deadly weight of it, the heft and balance exactly right, perfectly in tune with his thoughts, his emotions. He was enraged rather than pacified by this sudden cowardice. When he was a few yards from Darius he leapt forward, moving with a speed he had not used in years, a speed he thought had departed him and that he now found diminished but certainly not gone. It was a speed he had used to great effect in various ways, and with which he now moved towards Darius's right side and swung the spear like a baseball bat. Darius brought his hand up at the last moment. There were two cracks. The impact drove through Darius's forearm and struck him on the side of his head. He took one awkward side step and fell to the ground.

Jake was on him immediately, his knee pressed into Darius's sternum. The spear had cracked and broken, but in the light Jake could see that it had fractured in such a way that, although it was shorter, it was also sharper. The end was like a stiletto, tapering to a point, which he pressed into the hollow of Darius's throat. Darius was stunned, the side of his face bleeding. Had he not brought his arm up, Jake would have crushed his skull.

"Come on," Jake said. "Open your eyes."

Darius's eyelids fluttered. Jake gave him a moment to focus, testing Darius's body with his knee, ready to plunge the sharpened end of the spear into his throat at the first flexing of muscle. But not wanting to, not quite yet.

"Come on," Jake said. "Can you feel it?"

Darius tried to swallow, and his Adam's apple pressed against the point of the wood. Jake held the spear where it was, and a line of blood trickled out from the cartilage. Darius mumbled something and one of his arms twitched, scratching in the leaves and pine needles.

"Can you feel it?" Jake said again. "What you wanted for me, for Rachel." He pressed the point of the stick deeper into the hollow of his throat. "What you gave Henry."

Darius's eyes opened all the way. His left hand, the unbroken one, continued to scratch and twist in the forest floor. For a moment, Jake allowed himself the luxury of seeing himself through Darius's eyes, to peer upward at the stars with this monstrous dark shape over him. To feel the point of the stick on his throat, the awful throb on the side of his face—waiting, waiting— not understanding how it had come to this and certain it was a mistake, somehow. But knowing also that mistakes happen.

"This is what you wanted," Jake whispered, twisting the stick a bit, enlarging the hole he had started. Darius's eyes opened a bit more, his breathing tightening. "This is what they felt."

Darius's lips parted, a grimace or perhaps a smile, and a second before Jake plunged the stick into his neck he heard his name. It came from above him, whispering down through the pine needles from the cold starlight above.

"Jaaake . . ."

He paused, one hand still wrapped in the collar of Darius's shirt, his knee still pressed against his sternum, the hot throb of his own pulse in his ears.

"Jaaake." This time his name was followed by laughter. Something moved through the air above him, the crackling of branches, as though something were descending from the treetops, drifting down to the jumble of the blowdown.

From inside the logjam Weasel gave a whimpering sob and then fell silent.

Jake looked up. There was a silhouette atop one of the other blowdowns, a shape that blotted out a portion of the night's stars. The light from the dying flashlight did not reach it and Jake was glad for that, glad that whatever stood there was hidden from view. He looked, and although it was hidden in the darkness of the Canadian night, Jake knew that it looked back at him. Looked and watched and waited. And he understood, with an insight so clean and terrifying that it could not be anything but the truth, that this man, if it was a man, had spoken not to stop him or forewarn him, but only so that Jake would acknowledge its presence before he proceeded. So that he would know he killed with an audience, and that the audience approved.

Suddenly he was cold again, the adrenaline and the red haze gone, his arms breaking out in gooseflesh. His muscles felt suddenly stiff, clumsy with pain, all the pain and aching that had gone away now flaring up in a complete and sudden return, as though in response to this presence, like a ship signaling back to a lighthouse beacon. Pain signaling to pain, cold reflecting back to cold. Jake's breath plumed out into the dark sky and passed over his eyes in a veil of white smoke. Then his breath evaporated. The shape was still there.

"Jaaake."

His name again, so soft it could have been the wind, could have been the moan of the limb rubbing against the larger trunk of the spruce.

Go ahead, he thought. Kill Darius, make him pay for the pain. Make him pay for the terror he had inflicted on the group, for the killing . . .

There was movement underneath him, and before he could react he felt searing pain along his side. He fell away, rolling along the ground as Darius's knife sliced through the air inches from him. All of his movements felt nightmarishly slow, the knife intensely animate by comparison, seeking to burrow in through his ribs for warmth and sustenance. He rolled twice more and came up holding the stick in front of him, but Darius was not on him. Blood was coursing down Jake's back, and he could feel the laceration tearing open even more as he scrambled to stand. Darius was on his feet, his broken right arm held against his chest.

That's why I'm still alive, Jake thought. The first cut had gone along his ribs but not through them, and the other attempts had missed him cleanly. *He was stabbing with his left hand.*

Darius still had the knife in his hand, but he wasn't looking at Jake. His head was tilted upward, toward the silhouette perched atop the tangle of blowdown. The shape was still, except for a slight movement around it, a shimmering Jake thought might be clothes, or perhaps hair. The flashlight beam did not touch it, the light slowly extinguishing.

Darius walked over to the log pile, tucked the knife into his belt, and picked up the fallen flashlight. Before Jake could yell at him to stop, before he could shield his eyes, Darius pointed the flashlight beam at the dark figure standing above them.

The countenance upon which the flashlight beam, weak as candlelight, shone was plain and human and familiar. It—he—did not react to the light in any way. The pale yellow beam went trembling across the face and then, reluctantly, descended down the torso. The weak beam of light stopped at the abdomen, encased in the remains of a shirt stained with blood and dirt. Something was writhing under the tattered cloth, greenish black, something that seemed to be rooted inside his stomach and now was twisting in the light, recoiling from it.

Darius jerked the flashlight back up, and as he did, the batteries lost their tenuous connection and the night went dark.

"Hen . . . Henry?"

The shape seemed to float down the log pile. Jake found the movements hard to follow in the darkness and knew that his eyes and perhaps his brain were not processing information correctly, that somehow he was hallucinating or embellishing what was actually happening. But the shape continued to move, and its face had been Henry's and somehow it had not been. Could not have been.

There's life underneath us. Jaimie's words came flooding back to him, poor lost Jaimie. *More life below than above, sometimes.*

The shape reached the base of the blowdown, and now it seemed to merge completely with the darkness, the starlight not reaching it. Darius dropped the flashlight. He said his own name, *Darius*, whispering it in a breath of smoking white vapor. His name was repeated, and this time Jake could not tell if it was Darius who spoke or this other, this impostor in Henry's clothes and Henry's skin, who said it. It came closer, silent, until it was standing very close to Darius. Darius's breath continued to plume out and break across the dark shape that was almost but not quite lost in the shadows of the deadfall, a dark shape whose breath did not smoke, whose chest appeared to be still. But there was movement below the chest, slithering and bulging under the fabric of its shirt.

"Henry, I . . ."

The shape leaned forward and whispered something into Darius's ear. Something—*an arm,* Jake thought, *it has to be an arm*—reached out and caressed the side of Darius's face. It did not look like an arm, though. It looked like a tendril, a tendril that had taken on the shape of an arm, an abomination of a human limb. It pressed against Darius's cheek, slid across his mouth, and then withdrew.

After a moment, Darius tilted his head back to the firmament, as though to howl. Instead he began to laugh, and a moment later the Henry shape joined him, their laughter twisting together and floating up into the star-studded night, wending through the broken limbs and the pine needles and joining with the night wind still howling from the northwest.

Jake watched. If he chose to, he could walk over and join them and they would welcome him in, the joke would be shared with him, and he would laugh too, laugh and laugh as his pain finally and completely left him, the pain in his joints and head and heart. It would all be gone, and there would be something else— not happiness, but the savage pleasure of giving in.

He took a step forward. A branch cracked under his step, and the two figures turned to look at him. In the darkness he could not tell one from another. They laughed again, not in mockery, and one of the shapes beckoned him closer.

"Come."

Jake did not know who spoke. It did not seem to matter.

"Run with us."

There was an honor in the invitation. Not all were worthy, not all would make good company. He understood this; he feared this. Jake planted his foot in the ground, feeling the stick he had stepped on pressing through his hastily made denim shoes, the pain clarifying his jumbled thoughts. Pain, he thought. It's there for a reason. It's there to remind you what happens when you don't pay attention to life. It's what makes you human. His thoughts flashed to Deserae, lying in her hospital bed hundreds of miles away. She was beyond pain. She had felt the sensation when he pinched her, but it had meant nothing to her damaged mind.

But she was with him, her pre-injury presence imprinted in his conscience.

Okay, then. It was not only rare earth elements that could transfer properties. All that was good and joyful and lovely about Deserae was still with him, pressed deep inside. And it was Deserae he heard now, her words whispering in his mind.

Theirs is not your path, Jake. For a moment he could almost smell her light fragrance, could almost feel her warm breath tickling against his ear. *Choose your own way.*

"Run with us." One of the shapes—he thought it was Darius—had stepped closer. There was something smeared across his face. Blood, perhaps, from the blow Jake had given him minutes earlier. But the darkness seemed to be spreading out in a radial pattern rather than dripping downward, a darkness that was blotting out his features one by one.

Not your path.

The other's head was cocked to the side, as though it heard the whisper of Jake's lost love. Before it had seemed relaxed, completely at ease. Now it was tensed, and the slithering noises were intensifying. The Henry shape seemed to be growing and morphing at the same time, twisting and wending up into the night sky.

Jake turned and ran.

Chapter 16

He woke with a start and sat blinking, trying to conjure reason out of the cold and dark air. His lungs burned as though from some deep-seated respiratory infection, and his feet were a throbbing mess, tacky with blood. The light around him was negligible, and although he had hoped for a moment that it was dawn, he knew now it was not. Knew that he had slept for minutes rather than hours, and the night still held the land in her silent, black fist. The only light was that of the stars, burning their thin alien light down upon the land. He was burrowed in under a fallen spruce and he was very cold, and as his consciousness returned, so too did his panic, for he could hear the sound of something making its way along the pine needles of the forest floor.

Something was coming toward him in the woods. Jake pressed himself flat to the ground. He had plunged down creek banks and up creek banks, through swamps and over dry land, and the command to go with them, to *run with them*, had never stopped, had always been right there behind him. Now there was no more strength left in his body and what was coming would come, and it would find him or it would pass him by.

It moved steadily through the woods. It sounded very large, far too large to be Darius or Henry or both of them combined. Perhaps a moose or a caribou or a bear drawn in by the smell of his blood. He could hear it scraping against the trees, pushing through the branches, almost as though it was deliberately making noise, trying to get his heart to thud right out of his chest. There had been two bad times in the desert, once when they had engaged a cell of insurgents outside a small, dusty town that was supposed to be friendly. It had been an even match, one of very few, and any illusions he still had harbored about the advantage of superior fighting tactics and weaponry had fled, along with the rest of his squad, as the slugs whistled around and through them, the sound of copper-jacketed lead punching into flesh like hard rain hitting a lake. Three casualties, and he had not been one, but he had felt death singing in the air and knew his tune was out there, that if he stopped to listen it would find him.

The other time it had been friendly fire, and it had been very, very close, bad communications all the way through, shots fired and ordnance arranged, and then, at the very last moment, called off on Jake's order. He had decided, in the end, that he would rather make a mistake on his side than on the other side, would rather be responsible for the deaths of his own men than those of someone else's.

Ahead of him, something scraped against a spruce and limbs crackled. It sounded very high up, like a falling object crashing through the branches. At the same time, he could hear the sound of feet padding through the grass and brush at ground level, not thudding but *swishing,* the light tread of a hunter. *No,* Jake thought. *Please.*

It came on.

It was within thirty yards. He peered out through the latticework of branches and needles and saw nothing but blackness and the sawtooth horizon of treetops, and above that, the faint glow of the Milky Way. His breathing sounded very loud and he could not control it, could not stifle it without threatening to make his next breath all the louder. The woods crackled again, and a large spruce backlit by the starlight lurched forward and then back, the pointed tip bobbing back and forth. The wind sighed, and Jake grimaced at the low and fetid reek in the air. It was the scent of life, but on the ragged edge of decay—the smell of the valley, unmistakable even here, in his nest of pungent evergreens.

Another spruce tipped forward, then another. It was moving in a straight line, the same direction he planned on following when darkness lifted, the one that would lead him to the Big Glutton River and then to Highbanks, a place he had not been in years. It would be far from a safe haven, but it would be where Rachel was and where his mother would be, too. He could not quite bring his mother's face into focus, but he knew she would be older now and perhaps sadder.

But Highbanks, most importantly, was civilization, a place where the chaos of the bush was held at bay. He thought of how the shape had seemed to recoil under the flashlight beam, had seemed to thrive—to grow, perhaps—when it was lost in the shadows of the blowdown.

The brush crackled. Far in the distance a loon gave off its yodeling cry.

It's just Darius and Henry, he thought. *Be quiet and let them pass. Your breathing isn't as loud as you think. Just let them pass.*

His fists were curled into tight balls, pine needles and some twigs pressing into his palms. He felt them biting into his skin and tried to concentrate on the sensation, on the pain. Pain was okay.

"Jake."

The voice came from what sounded like a high spot in one of the tallest trees. The wind had dropped as the night wore on, and the sound of the voice was throaty and musical, a rough and sighing timbre. He seemed to hear much more than his name in the voice; he heard a story, a promise of what could be.

"We could have run. We could have run so far and so fast it would be like flying. We could have roamed for centuries, our sustenance coming from the burning dawns over a thousand smoking swamps, from the darkest of winter nights when trees crack from the cold and there seems to be no warmth left in the world save what we harbor in our own bodies. We will be there when the blood is spilled and eyes grow wide with terror—bird and hare and man—and we will rejoice in this, in all of this."

"Jake."

One moment it sounded like Henry, the next it sounded like Darius. And when it spoke his name for the third time it sounded like neither of them. Jake told himself that it was a trick of the air, that whoever had spoken must have turned away or covered his mouth with a hand. Because the third time, the voice sounded like something that might be coughed out of the mouth of a bear or a lion, his name bastardized by vocal chords not accustomed to human language.

"Jaaaaake."

Three times, Jake thought, his mind going back to Sunday school and the lessons out of the Old Testament, when Samuel had repeatedly been called out by God in the night. *Three times I called out for you.*

He was tempted—tempted to climb out of his sanctuary and just . . . go. There was something incredibly alluring in the call, something entangled with the way he had felt with his father when he was very young, when some of the mysteries of the great north woods had begun to reveal themselves. That was when he had begun to understand that there were secrets to be unlocked, and that unlocking them gave you entry into a sacred world that most would never even guess at, treasures that could not be measured in pelts or antlers alone. But those experiences had been pure, clean, in a way this journey would never be. He knew that.

"No," he murmured into the forest floor. "No."

Laughter hissed out of the woods, simultaneously mocking and disappointed. It was the disappointment that affected him, for whatever it was out there was not acting. It was truly sad to not have him with it. This was not because it needed him; it was, at its core, a creature of abject loneliness. It thrived on the loneliness, and nothing could accompany it for long, but it wanted a partner, someone to run with, if only for a while.

The laughter faded. He waited to hear the thing move, to come toward him or continue on its way. But there was nothing, no sound at all. He waited, and the woods were quiet, quiet, not even the loon calling out again, nothing scurrying in the detritus of the forest floor, not even the buzz of some late-season insect which had weathered the cold front and now sought to fill its belly with hot blood. There was only silence, and on the air the smell of the valley, wafting in puffs and eddies, hinting at a presence that might still be there . . . or that might have departed, leaving only this residue of stink behind.

He lay under the spruce for what seemed like hours and may have been. He did not crane his head upward to stare at the heavens, attempting to try to track the time by the cartwheeling constellations. Neither did he look toward the east for sunrise. He waited, he breathed. From time to time he said *no*, although his name was not called out again.

Some interminable time later the darkness began to lift. As the first gray light filtered through the branches around and above him, he heard something move off through the woods. It moved quickly and in a straight line, due west. As soon as the footsteps faded the birds began to sing around him, the chickadees and then the crows, and finally, just when it was light enough for Jake to move, the jays began to vocalize.

He climbed out from underneath the spruce and brushed the needles from his clothes. He had only the roughest idea where he was, but the sky was clear and the sun was almost up. All he had to do was head southwest and he would find the river, and then he would go upstream or downstream to the Braids. Somewhere along the line he would pick up Rachel's track.

He headed west. The other had passed a bit to his north, and after paralleling that trail for a while, after the sun had risen completely above the horizon, he cut to his right to intercept the trail. After a few minutes he saw the dark side of an overturned leaf on the ground. He looked around him in all directions and knelt, studying the leaf and the exposed soil it had covered. To the west he could see more overturned leaves, nearly impossible to see except here, at ground level. Whatever had passed was dragging its feet slightly, as though injured. It was not Rachel's track.

He stood undecided in the gray morning woods. After a moment, he started down the trail of overturned leaves, occasionally spotting a sliding footprint on the forest floor. For all the creature's sloppy footwork, it was moving in a straight line. After a while Jake began to trot, the fresh pain from his cuts a welcome distraction from the thought pounding in the front of his mind, the question that returned time and time again.

What was he following?

In an hour, he had not caught sight of anything save a few squirrels, chattering at him from high in the spruces. Then he crossed a small gully, and on the top of the other side he saw a body lying flat on the ground next to a decaying log. The person had fallen in such a way that Jake knew he was dead. He knelt beside the corpse and turned it over. Henry's milky eyes stared vacantly up to the pines. There were a few small red ants crawling across his face, and Jake wiped these away with the pads of his thumbs. Henry looked shrunken, and his fingernails and his hair looked much longer, as though he had been a corpse for weeks instead of hours. There was some kind of horrible wound in his abdomen, and his shirt was plastered with black blood. A light gray growth had spread across one of his arms, and Jake studied this for a moment but did not touch it.

He looked around and saw that the trail of shuffling feet ended here. Unlike Jaimie's, Henry's boots were intact, although soaked through and plastered with mud and leaves, the sign of a man who has stumbled, rather than walked, for miles through the woods. *He was just a host,* Jake thought. *Old and weak, with a bad heart. It didn't need him, not once Darius joined up.*

That had been part of the invitation. You didn't just run with it, you ran *for* it, like Jaimie, careening around the valley, her lungs full of its foulness. Running and running, until your feet fell from your legs. But Henry hadn't been able to run.

He stood. The trail did not end here. A broken twig was pressed into a nearby depression of decaying leaves, as though someone had knelt here before Jake, perhaps to lay Henry down, or to take something from him. Jake rose and walked in a circle, expanding outward in an ever-increasing spiral. He had almost given up when he saw a flattened goldenrod, twenty feet from Henry's body. He knelt next to it. Whatever had broken the goldenrod stem had left a large depression, too big for a footprint, although to Jake that's what it looked like. Thirty feet ahead of it was the only other sign: a spray of needles had fallen from a large spruce. There was a broken limb halfway up the tree.

Jake looked from the ground to the tree and back to the ground. Then he went back to Henry's body and began to unlace his boots.

Jake's pants were still in the blowdown, stuffed with leaves to replicate his legs, the final temptation that had led Weasel into the trap. He pulled Henry's pants loose after his boots and stepped into them. The pants were a good fit, as were the boots. The pants were smeared with mud and blood, and the boot leather had been soaked by Henry's passage through the woods. Jake took a few steps, wincing, his feet rebelling against this new pressure.

"Pain is okay," he said aloud, his voice shocking in the stillness. "But it's getting pretty damn old."

He cinched Henry's belt tight. There was a slight bulge in the side of a pantleg, and Jake reached into the front pocket and withdrew a small jackknife, identical to the one Jake had used as a trapper. There was a small nick near the base of the blade. He remembered holding the edge of a blade—this blade—to the throat of his stepfather, the same nick caked with gore from skinning muskrats. He remembered Coop's mewling protests, the thick funky odor of the muskrat blood drying on the knife blade, how Coop's veins throbbed just below the edge of the knife, only a few centimeters of thin air between skin and steel.

You've come full circle, Jake thought, sliding the knife back into his pocket. *You and me both.*

He started toward Highbanks. It was eight o'clock in the morning.

*   *   *

He reached the river in the early afternoon and made his way down the Braids. The sun had come up, briefly warming him, and then clouds had come scudding in from the west, and he knew it would rain again soon. The mudflats that normally ran along the riverbank were covered by the water. There were no tracks of any kind. The river was swollen, and Jake stood looking at it, wondering if Rachel had really swum this cold river alone and gone up the other side. The alternative was that she had missed it and was lost somewhere behind him.

He turned and walked back upriver. The Braids were three quarters of a mile in length, and by the time he had reached the upper end, the river had risen another inch. All of the rain from the day before was just now reaching the larger rivers, and they would continue to climb until all of the small sandbars and islands would be covered with water, until the rapids downstream would sound like thunder.

"Rachel." He had meant to shout it, but his voice came out a hoarse whisper. He breathed in deeply and tried again. "Rachel!"

The sound of the river swallowed her name. He yelled twice more and waited for a return call, but there was nothing. After a few minutes, he knelt down and started to unlace Henry's boots. Then he retied them and stepped into the river. He had had enough of bare feet.

The water was icy. It pressed into his myriad wounds, his breath shortening with every step. It was deeper than he thought, and soon he was swimming again, his boots kicking in the heavy current. He very nearly missed the first sandbar, entering the calmer water of its downstream eddy just in time to avoid being swept into the next braid. He stood and wiped the water from his eyes, panting. The next island was almost directly across from him, and he walked to the upper end of his current sandbar, then waded upstream at a quartering angle until the current was to his waist. Then he pushed off, swimming hard for the island. He reached it at the middle of its length. He crossed the island and repeated, his breath coming in ragged gasps by the time he crawled up the far bank.

He sat in the mud of the riverbank. It was only eight miles to Highbanks, and for the first time he wondered what he would do when he reached it, what warnings he would give that might be heeded.

He pressed a finger against one side of his nose and blew, then repeated the process, clearing his nostrils of river water. It didn't matter. Rachel, when he found her, would need no convincing. His mother . . . well.

Concentrate, Jake.

He climbed up the bank and made his way through the alder thicket that flanked the western edge of the river. The ground grew higher, and soon the alder swamp gave way to poplar highlands. There was a disturbance in the higher ground, a long scrape of upended leaves, the dark forest loam forming a ragged scar on the earth. He stood at the edge of the disturbance, dripping river water from his tattered clothes. He squatted on his knees and studied the sharp edges of the smaller boot heels and the other imprints, larger, from which it was impossible to discern shape or size or direction, as amorphous as the bush around him and the shifting clouds above him. The tracks became somewhat clearer at the end of the disturbance, leading toward Highbanks in great leaping strides.

Jake stood. There was a single hair caught in a fold of bark at the base of one of the poplars, an ashy-blond hair ten inches long. He looked at the hair but did not remove it from the tree trunk.

It was only a hair. The rest of her was somewhere up ahead.

Chapter 17

When Jake reached Highbanks it was dusk, and the first houses he passed were dark: rectangular windows limned with aluminum frames, the metal catching the glow of the rising moon, the panes black. To Jake, the village had a sense of being not only vacant but abandoned, and long-abandoned at that. The trail in the woods had petered out a mile back, fading as the light in the woods grew dim. He strode up to the first trailer house and pounded on the thin door.

In the silence that ensued he heard some faraway thudding, barely audible—felt it more than heard it. It was a sound he mistook for his own heart, and he was surprised to hear it beating so slowly. He pressed a thumb to his wrist and found the throb; his pulse was still hammering along, from the exertion of his final push to Highbanks and the knowledge that the end of the trail was very, very close. He cocked his head, the thudding finally making sense: they were drums, coming from the other side of town.

He stepped down from the porch. There were other houses in sight, two trailers on the left. Farther down, on the right side of the road, was a stick-built cabin, the typical A-frame construction used to ward off snow buildup on the roof. It looked even shabbier than the aging trailer houses. It had been his childhood home, before they had sold it and moved in with Coop.

He started trotting down the main road. It was just a dirt road mixed with some coarse gravel, but it felt like a superhighway after all his trudging through the underbrush. He reached the center of the village, stopping for a moment to rip one of the posters tacked to the side of the community center building free. The flyer was for the First Dance, Highbanks' annual pow-wow, the time when all the parents from miles around brought their children in for their first taste of bear meat, their first hesitant steps in the packed earth around the central fire. It was tonight, Jake realized—the biggest festival of the year, the time to celebrate the end of the growing season, the beginning of the killing season.

And as it had since he had crossed the Braids, the question—the Question—returned. Not what to do when he found Darius. That was simple—he would finish the job he had started the night before. If he still could.

Because *that* was the Question—*How can you kill what's already dead?*

He let the flyer drop from his hands, the sound of the drums now making perfect sense. He thought about Henry's story about how the people had ended the plague of cannibalism and madness more than a century earlier, the story of how they had put the old monster to sleep. Now that monster was locked in Darius's addled mind, his brain and body infested with the poisonous, half-dead presence trapped for decades in the soils beneath Resurrection Valley.

And now the great wanderer had found a medium. But it wasn't a complete override of Darius, Jake realized. Whatever the underlying mechanism—the distillation of violent instincts in the promethium, hopping from an underground fungus to one person, then the next, or a possession from the old demon of the north woods—it did not discard what was there. It took what was bad and used it. *Amplified* it. Jake glanced around, looking for a car or an ATV he might commandeer, but all the rigs in Highbanks, large and small, would be parked at the dancing ground. The headlights would be turned on to keep the area well lit, to keep the toddlers from wandering off into the woods. Jake ran down the road, pausing when someone shuffled out from a building ahead of him.

"Hey!" he called out. "Hey!"

The person continued on, not even sparing him a backward glance. Jake ran forward, calling out as he went. Still the figure shuffled along, neck bent and shoulders bowed, wrapped in a long dark green cloak. Jake grabbed him by the shoulder and turned him around, an old man, his eyes widening in shock. There was an ancient, yellowed hearing aid in his ear. He looked to be full-blooded Cree and very old, his face filled with multiple and finely-formed lines, his eyes rheumy. He looked familiar but Jake couldn't place him, a man who would have been advanced in years when Jake left here, decades ago.

"Have you seen Darius?" he asked, speaking very slowly.

The old man blinked twice. He tapped his ear and shook his head.

"The *Okitchawa*," Jake said.

The old man's befuddled expression cleared, and he grinned at Jake, revealing a mouth entirely devoid of teeth.

"Yes," he said, in a croaking lisp, the Cree words coming back to Jake with a certain tickle in his cortex, the old rhythm of his first language. "The dance!"

"You saw Darius at the dance?"

The old man nodded. "Everyone. At the dance."

Jake turned to go. The old man clawed at him, his fingernails scratching at Jake's soiled shirt. "Everyone is there," he said, his tone insistent. "Everything. Why I'm going. It's been . . ." his eyes wandered off, searching the darkened woods for something, "a lifetime," he said at last, his voice now shaking with terror, or perhaps elation. "Lifetimes since the old ways have held sway."

"What?"

The old man's mouth curled into his toothless grin again. "Go. They wait for you." Jake turned and ran. The sound of the drums grew louder, the tempo faster. Jake could see flashes of fire through the trees now, the flames from the big fire almost reaching the tops of the balsam trees, thirty feet up.

He slowed as he reached the edge of the clearing and veered off into the woods, the silhouettes of dancing people flickering through the trees. The firelight bounced off of dozens of cars. The new fingernail moon had slipped behind some thin clouds, and the wind was picking up once again, sending the clouds racing across the moon's crescent face. Jake could feel the faint heat from the fire even here. Closer to the fire the men and boys would be dressed in summer clothes, some in not much more than loincloths.

The beating of the drums was constant and the dancers moved as they always did, the adults nearest the fire, the children dancing in their shadows, even the two- and three-year-olds learning the rhythms of the dance. It had always amazed Jake and it still amazed him now—even caught deep in his dread, his mind working around the Question—to see how the toddlers could abandon their inherent clumsiness for brief moments, dancing in the twisting and flexing shadows of their fathers and uncles. On the outside were the old men, the elders, forming an outer ring. The First Dance for some, the last for others.

The wind picked up suddenly, and the flames blew sideways, causing the men on the downwind side to flare outward from the intense heat. Jake waited for the gust to blow itself out, but the wind continued to blow, quickly reaching a gale-force-level intensity, as though a low-pressure system had plopped down in the woods opposite him. The drum beats slowed, then stopped. The massive bonfire was nearly horizontal and people were scrambling out of its way, scooping up children and snatching blankets.

Jake stepped to the edge of the clearing. He was plainly visible, but nobody looked his way. They were all focused on the suddenly out-of-control fire, the intense heat. Already, the grass on the downwind side was scorched black. The flames roared with the wind, dancing and darting toward a cluster of people. One of the children screamed, and as though waiting for the cue, several others joined in, their high cries swept from their mouths by the ferocious wind. The fire roared, a captive beast almost out of its cage.

Then the wind stopped, and the flames that had sprawled out along the ground shrank back within the rock boundary of the fire ring. Some of the adults glanced at each other uneasily, several looking at Jake.

He paid them no attention. Darius and Rachel had appeared at the edge of the scorched grass on the far side of the fire, Darius's hand clenched around Rachel's upper arm. Behind them was another man, a strangely bloated man, half bent over, his face hidden from view.

Darius's face was scratched and bruised, and his eyes seemed to be composed entirely of reflected firelight, as did Rachel's. There was something on his face, a growth, spreading from his right cheek to cover part of his nose and the side of his mouth. Neither seemed to recognize Jake, wedged within the group of Highbanks villagers staring at them. The other man was bent over and clutching himself, as though suffering from intestinal distress.

"Darius?"

An old lady moved out from the edge of the crowd. She was wrapped in a coarse shawl emblazoned with bright orange and pink chevrons. Her long gray hair had been tied in a bun, but the wind had pulled most of it free, and it now formed a tangled snarl around her small head. She was no more than five feet tall and couldn't have weighed more than ninety pounds, but people withdrew as she strode forward. Her face was pinched and lined, the eyes hooded. Elsie. She was the only person Jake recognized, outside of Darius and Rachel.

She stopped a dozen feet away from Darius and drew up to her full height. "Darius, what have you brought us?"

Darius opened his mouth as if to speak, but instead he pushed something out of his mouth with his tongue. It landed with a small splat at his feet, a green glob of sodden moss. Elsie recoiled, and then she caught herself and squared her shoulders.

"You let that girl go," Elsie said. "She doesn't need to be held onto."

Darius grinned, and the spaces between his teeth were colored dark green. He shook Rachel slightly. "We ran," he whispered, his voice lisping and guttural at the same time. "Ran *faasst*."

Something rippled under the growth on his cheek, swelling and then subsiding. His hair was longer than it had been just the day before, Jake realized. More hair puffed out of his shirt, long tangled lengths that were matted with the same growth covering his face. His eyes were wild, dancing in the light of the fire.

Elsie took a step forward. "You did good, Darius. You found them. Now you . . . you rest."

Darius cocked his head, then turned to the other man, the bloated man with his face smeared with dirt. At first Jake did not recognize him, and then he did, picking out his features. Warren Campbell crabbed his way into the firelight. His once neatly combed gray hair was filled with leaves and plastered with mud. His eyes darted from the group back to Darius, not in fear but with some strange combination of cunning and subservience. Behind them the pine boughs scratched against each other in the wind, which was increasing in intensity again.

"Eat," Darius said, his voice phlegmy and rough. "Show them your hunger."

Warren fell to the ground and began grubbing in the packed dirt, his fingers hooked into the earth. He started cramming soil and leaves into his mouth, making loud smacking noises. His teeth grinded away at the small stones in the soil, chewing up the pulpy leaves and sod.

Jake watched, horrified. He had thought that the infestation was limited to one person, one medium at a time. But Warren was affected, too, and the greed that he had possessed for the samples was running rampant. Now his desire to take from the earth was manifested in this primal urge to consume. *Soon enough,* Jake thought, *he'll eat so much dirt his belly will burst.*

"I'm hungry, too," Darius said. A little of the old mischievous gleam came into his eyes. "Not for dirt."

"Darius," Elsie said. "You and your friend got into something. Some bad plants, maybe. You . . . you need to get some rest, let your mind clear up."

"He was lost," Darius said, his voice a scratching whisper. "Forgot who he was. I—we . . . reminded him."

"Who's we, Darius?"

He grinned, a green smear of teeth. "You know, Elsie. You know."

"What would you have us do?" Elsie asked, her voice little more than a whisper.

Darius took a step forward, dragging Rachel with him. She was pale, her face slack, and Jake still couldn't tell if she was in shock or under the spell of the same affliction as the rest of them. Warren hopped after Darius, his mouth caked with dirt.

"Give us one," Darius said, his voice barely audible above the crackling of the fire. His eyes roamed over the children, tucked behind the legs of their parents. "One to run and play with."

"No," Elsie said.

The purple bruise stood out in dark relief on Darius's temple, the place where Jake had struck him the night before. Jake could even see the small hole in the hollow of his throat where he had pressed and twisted the splintered end of the shattered stick against his trachea. Jake should have finished it then and there instead of gloating, instead of savoring Darius's terror.

"Just one," Darius said. "And we will cast our eyes elsewhere."

"No," Elsie said. "Not that. Never that."

You outran yourself, Jake thought, watching Darius. *Whatever is driving you, it went faster and further than you realized. It's already leapfrogged beyond all reason. Now you stand alone, and you demand choices that make sense only to you—or to whatever is wrapped inside your brain, whatever transferred from the ground to poor dying Henry, who was too weak to run, or didn't want to. And then from Henry to you. Yes, you embraced it, and you ran with it, you certainly did. But you ran too fast, went too far.*

"Just one," Darius said. "One of your own accord. We need . . . we need something *fresh*."

Several of the children had begun to cry. Elsie glanced behind her, then stepped forward, her voice firm. "Be gone," she said. "Leave us."

"We will come back," Darius said, and again his face bulged and twisted under the growth. His jaw seemed to lengthen, to resemble a snout in the flickering light. "And when we do, it will be more than one that we take."

"You're not taking anyone," Jake said. "Not one child." He stepped forward. "Not Rachel."

Darius's hand moved to the back of Rachel's neck. His lips parted, and a strange growling noise came from his throat, the cords of muscle in his neck twisting in the firelight. Jake was reminded of Greer, of his plea for help through his stiffening vocal cords. Was Darius really still in there, somewhere? It hardly seemed to matter.

Jake stepped forward, separating from the rest of the crowd and passing by Elsie. The heat was intense this close to the fire, and he could feel it baking into his bones, loosening his joints, the sweat pouring out of him and stinging his eyes. He stopped ten feet away from Darius. The wind was picking up again and it touched the sweat, made Jake hyperaware of the coolness on his hot skin. A few feet away Warren shuffled closer to the fire, then away, his bloated face smeared with dirt.

"Leave her."

"You have not seen it," Darius breathed. "Not yet. It is more than you would imagine. Greater and stronger and faster . . ." His eyes rolled back in his head, his green-stained teeth spreading open in a wolf's smile.

"Rachel!" Jake called out.

Her head had been down. Now Darius tilted her head up and she looked at Jake with dulled and vacuous eyes. "She ran with us," Darius said, "as did he." Darius turned and regarded Warren, who was mumbling something fast and incomprehensible under his breath, his eyes alternating between the ground and the bluish core of the bonfire. "We had fun with him."

"You've breathed in something, Darius," Jake said. "It's affecting your brain."

Darius grinned. He had no weapon that Jake could see, but something about the way he held Rachel's neck caused Jake to hold back.

Darius turned toward Jake. "Tell them," he said. "Tell them what we found sleeping under the soil out there. It's not a bad thing to have found."

"Darius," Jake said, "it's time for you to go."

"Yes," Elsie said. "Go, but leave the girl." She had reappeared out of the shadows, surrounded by several other women. To Jake's surprise, he saw his mother was with them, older than he had imagined but still beautiful, her hair streaked with gray and the skin around her eyes crinkled into a fine bird's nest of lines. Other women stepped forward, and the men followed, standing behind Elsie and Dawn Trueblood and the rest of the women. Someone had begun to murmur, a low singsong chant that several others picked up on.

"One," Darius insisted.

"Leave us," Elsie said, and to Jake it seemed as though she spoke not to Darius but to something behind his shoulder.

Darius stood looking at them. The wind was increasing steadily, ratcheting upward into gale force. Then he leaned forward and murmured something into Warren's ear.

Warren shrieked, in horror or exultation it was impossible to tell, and flung himself forward. Jake sprang to the side, and Warren charged into the middle of the bonfire, stumbling over the tilted logs. Immediately, the smell of singed hair washed over them, and there was a series of small popping noises as his skin boiled and split. He exited the flames, arms outstretched and his clothes burning brightly, a plump scarecrow lit afire and come to life. He stumbled toward Jake, his shirt dripping off of him in burning ropes, his eyes filmed over from the incredible heat. His arms were spread wide as if in embrace, the dirt on his face cracking and peeling away to reveal bright pink skin.

There was a press of people at Jake's back, with nowhere for him to turn. Warren's milky eyes locked on Jake, his arms still spread wide, and he lurched forward again. Jake backpedaled, bumping into several people and almost tripping. He caught himself, casting his eyes around him, trying to avoid that burning visage steadily approaching. All around him people were fleeing, scooping up children and retreating from the madness of the scene. He was caught in the middle, Warren so close now Jake could feel the heat from his blazing clothes.

Ah hell, Jake thought. *I was done running anyway.*

He lowered his shoulder and tackled Warren at the waist, hearing the bigger man's breath come out of him in a soft *whoomf,* the flames from his burning hair and clothes licking around Jake's head and arms. He drove his legs forward, raising his body up as he went, Warren's arms seeking purchase on his back. Warren's feet lifted off the ground, and Jake surged forward with all his strength and then let go. Warren went flying backward into the fire, the flames closing over him. He landed flat on his back in between several logs, the flames white hot above the red embers. Warren managed a sitting position, his mouth open and working but there was no sound, just the roar of the flames and the stench of burning flesh. The rest of the huge logs, stacked up tipi style, collapsed over the top of him.

Someone was slapping at Jake. He whirled. Elsie and another woman were putting out the flames that had blossomed on his shirt.

"Mom?"

Dawn Trueblood used her thumb to squash out the last of the burning fabric on his collar. Her eyes were very wet. "Is it really you, Jakey?"

Jakey. He had not heard that in years and suddenly he was five years old again, with a bruised shin. He looked past the scattered bonfire, and in the flickering light caught a glimpse of Darius and Rachel, her upper arm held tight in his grasp, slipping into the shadows of the forest at the edge of the clearing. "I'll explain later," he said. "I need to go get Rachel."

She held his chin in her hand, then nodded. "Go get her," she said. "Then come back to me."

He plunged into the woods, too dark now to see anything besides the outlines of trees, the amorphous shapes of the alder and mountain maple. He didn't need his eyes, though; he could hear Darius ahead of him crashing through the brush. The sound was louder than the howling wind, louder than the sudden rumblings of dozens of cars starting in the clearing behind him. Their headlights came on almost in unison, sending flickering lights racing through the trees. The crashing stayed ahead of Jake and he ran after it, the headlight beams fracturing into slotted bars, the trees casting long shadows out in front of him.

He stopped at the edge of a small meadow. The slumped remains of an ancient shelter stood in the middle, surrounded by twisted trees. The clearing was no more than a quarter acre in size, the thick spruce and fir forest flanking it on all sides. The moon highlighted the edges of the tall grass and shrubs, not frost-burned yet but close, close. The smell of autumn hung thick in the air, mingled with the smoke of the bonfire.

Darius stood in the middle of the clearing, bathed in the meager light from the fingernail moon.

"Where is she?" Jake asked.

Darius looked down at the grass and prodded a lifeless form with his foot. "She ran too far." Behind him, his shadow moved in the backdrop of forest, a giant that twisted and stretched among the trees. Darius's hair had become disheveled in his flight through the woods, and its shadowy silhouette spread, shaggy and wild, across the canopy of the trees. It looked different from the fine hair Darius had had the day before. Now it was coarser, with lichens or something similar stuck in its lengths—or growing from it, just like the moldy patch growing across the skin of his face.

"I'm going to kill you," Jake said. He withdrew the skinning knife from his pocket and clicked it open. "Whatever you are."

There was subtle movement on the ground, and behind and above Darius the shadow nodded its giant, shaggy head.

"I am here."

Jake circled to Darius's right, his eyes darting down to Rachel's slumped form, then back to Darius. He moved through the tall grass, the tiny heft of the skinning knife curving into the fold of his palm. Henry's boots squelched water as he walked, and his breath came and went in steaming clouds, snatched away from his mouth by the wind. By comparison, Darius was quiet, still, waiting for Jake to close in. He seemed contemplative, perhaps even peaceful, as though Jake's threat to kill him had placated, rather than alarmed, Darius.

That's not Darius, he thought. *Don't be thinking that. It's something more, something worse. The distillation of whatever was underground.*

And again the Question raced through his mind: *How can you kill what's already dead?*

In the grass at Darius's feet, Rachel moaned. Jake lurched forward, the old battle haze returning, a red cloud building around the edges of his vision. It was the blinding, exhilarating sensation of letting go, all the pain, all of it, just sliding away, pushed to the back of his mind. He darted forward, cutting toward Darius's uninjured arm, the little skinning knife held low and close to his hip. He would rip the blade upward, would gut Darius as he had gutted countless hares, as he had sliced open hundreds of muskrats. As Darius had gutted Henry.

You just kill it, he thought, and charged in.

He closed with the dark shape, and then he was inside the circle of Darius's arms. The smell of decay and rottenness and plain old Cree, plain old sweaty human, Jake's smell or Darius's or both, was cloying in Jake's nostrils. He could not get a good grip; Darius's torso was twisting and bulging, growing outward and upward into something else, a slithering presence, incredibly strong. For all of that there did not seem to be much fight in him. One quick swipe would be all it took. You killed it by killing it, that was all. It was the only way to make the source of your pain go away, the only way to conquer it.

Jake brought the knife up, his teeth bared.

Not your path, Jake. Deserae's voice again, no longer warm but stern. *Not yours.*

He paused, the point of the knife inches from Darius's navel. A vision of Rachel came back to him now, wiping the blood and mud from her face at the bottom of the chasm after Jake had tackled her, the sky above them laced with writhing tendrils.

Come on, Jake. Let's go up.

He paused. The knife dropped a fraction of an inch. What would happen once he gutted Darius, if he succeeded in killing him? The presence would still have to go somewhere, would still have to run with something. And Rachel was still alive. She might not go willingly, but she would go with it. She would run until she, like Henry, dropped. Or threw herself into some awful death, as Warren had in the bonfire.

"What?" Darius's voice was not much more than a snarl. "What?"

"Take me," Jake said. "I'll run with you."

The shape with which he had wrestled went very still. Something—the back of a hand, perhaps—slid across his face, pressing against his cheeks, dragging over his nose. He could feel the trail it left behind, cool and wet, clinging to his skin. Darius seemed to have grown very tall in front of him, his arms not so much fending off Jake and his little knife as embracing him, pulling the killing hand in close. Now his grip loosened, and Jake forced himself to look up into those eyes, the same haunting look in them that he'd seen in the alpha female wolf, the cunning and bloodlust and inherent wildness all mingled together. But these were mixed in Darius with madness, with a savage inhumanity that made it difficult for Jake to speak his next words.

"Let her . . . let her go," he said. "Take me."

Darius paused, uncertain. This was different, different from Henry, different even from the offering of a child.

It doesn't think I mean it, Jake thought.

He took the knife and pressed it against his wrist, the sharp blade biting into the skin. He drew the knife across his wrist and then held the wrist up, the dark blood bubbling into his palm. The dark shape above him groaned, then leaned down. Something that felt like a muzzle snuffled wetly into his hand, inhaling the blood. Carefully, Jake transferred the knife to his mouth, biting down on the handle. He could taste his blood on the handle, bright and coppery. He drew his other wrist against the blade, pressing deeper, and blood shot from the newly cut wrist into the air, then subsided. There was little pain.

Jake let the knife slip from his teeth. A multi-ended tendril, shaped like a child's hand but matted with coarse fur, pressed against the burbling blood. The pattering sound on the grasses below him slowed, then stopped. The great shaggy head bent forward, whining. Far above him the wind whined in response, echoing the long, greedy call.

"Leave her alone," Jake said.

There was no answer. He drew back, pulling his wrists free. The Darius thing moaned, a low and piteous sound.

"Leave her alone," he said again. "Her and the children."

It moaned again, something that sounded like assent.

"Say it louder."

It looked up at him. The creature was no longer Darius, if it ever had been. It was a conglomeration of what had been Darius and what had been in the ground. The way it looked at Jake was similar to the way the rotten-looking black tendril had regarded him back in the valley, like an old despot, one that lives through others and despises them for it. It opened its mouth, and a single, strangled word came out.

"Ye-es."

Jake's vision was closing in, his head growing faint as his wrists started to ache. He could feel the presence drawing on his blood, ingesting it, making it its own. Soon he would be drained completely dry, and this— whatever it was—would lope off into the woods, recharged and freed. Perhaps Jake would run alongside it, for a while. Either way it would fulfill its part of the bargain. It would leave Rachel alone, would leave the children of Highbanks alone. For Jake had given willingly, and something told him this thing valued that above all else, the surrendering of one's self, the giving over of your will to its own, to be a slave to its desire.

The Darius creature wrapped its arm, its *tentacle,* around Jake's back to pull him closer. His pulse was racing, the pain intensifying as the creature sucked more blood from his wrists.

I'm sorry, Deserae. I'm sorry, Rachel. I'm sorry, Mom.

He was starting to panic as his life drained away. He didn't want to die, he never had. He just hadn't wanted to live. Jake tried to keep still, even as his brain and body began to fight against the Darius thing, to struggle to regain what was his. He pushed at the coarse hair, and his fingers plunged into a damp, twisting mass under the hide. There was nothing there to push against. He tried pulling back, and the tentacle wrapped around his body tightened, drawing him in, in, in.

He forced himself to stop resisting. There would be no pulling away, and in that instant of understanding Jake realized he had been right when he decided it was time to stop running. He had been right earlier when, hemmed in by Warren, he had charged forward. No matter what his choice was, he had to go straight into it. No more backing away, not even in these last few minutes he had left.

Especially not in these last few minutes.

"You want it?" Jake asked. "Take it!"

From deep inside himself he let go of all the pain he had held tight through the years. First was the rootlessness, the sudden orphaning when he had lost his father to the aneurysm, then his mother to Coop. Next were the long years in the military, the nausea and guilt and elation of his first kill, then the slow grinding away, the long months spilling more blood, all the blood soaking into the flinty earth, sanding the edge off his youth, blunting what had been bright and hard and sharp, leaving him calloused, indifferent. There was the terrible last night with Deserae, the twisted, blood-splattered steel, the torn fabric spilling out of the passenger seat. Then room 217, the steady beeping, the eyes vacuous and gone, her mind gone, the rest of her still tethered to a world she could no longer meaningfully exist in. He let the hurt and pain and shame and regret all flow out, letting loose all the controls he had placed around it, mentally cutting away ropes and nets, letting it all go from him into this awful subterranean thing inhaling his essence. It would have all of it.

It whined. It moaned. The suction on his wrists lessened, became hesitant.

Take it, Jake thought. *Take my pain. Let it grow inside you like a virus.*

He had one more thing to give this creature. The chronic mental and emotional pains were not all he had carried. For years now he had harbored his own infestation: the insidious bacteria lodged deep in his joints. He concentrated on the aching that was still there, insulated by the sharper pains in his wrists and his feet. Feeling the pull of the creature connecting to it, deep into his lymph and marrow, the tick-borne malady that caused so much pain that it had driven hundreds, if not thousands, of afflicted people to kill themselves.

The creature gave a strangled cry and staggered

backward. Jake regarded it on wobbling legs, his vision blurring. It had expanded, Darius's compact frame spreading out and becoming wispy and tall, the hair long and thick, the moldy patches digesting and changing his face, until what remained had only the vaguest resemblance to a human being. The legs seemed impossibly long—the lower body of a great runner. Darius's brown eyes now had a greenish tint, and of all his features, only the scar in his eyebrow remained, the patchwork of growth forming around the healed tissue.

But now that great, tall frame, which seemed as though it might continue to expand and expand until it filled the night sky, hunched over. It wrapped its arms around its stomach and bent at the knees, then contorted violently. It grabbed at a great knobby elbow, then its hairy shoulder, its teeth gnashing.

Jake could think of nothing to do with his wrists, so he pressed them together in a bloody smear, the sudden flare of pain making him focus. The creature was still twisting around and around, tearing at its own flesh, gibbering at the sky. Jake saw a thin line of reflected moonlight, the blade of his skinning knife. He needed to cut a tourniquet for his right wrist. The left was not cut nearly as deep, but he had found an artery on the right, and it was pumping out a steady stream of blood. He watched it, mesmerized, then leaned down to pick up the knife. He had already lost too much blood.

Lost lots of stuff, he thought. *Never mind about that. The wrists, Jake.*

He picked up the knife and it squirted from his blood-drenched hands. He scrambled after it, losing sight of the small knife and then finding it again in another spray of moonlight. It was almost impossible to grip, the pain and blood making the slender handle slip from his grasp time and time again. He felt something more than panic, something close to terror, run through him. It could not end like this, bleeding out while he chased his knife across the forest floor. A few yards away the creature gave a long and wavering cry, then fell to the ground, its great hairy feet thrashing in the tall grass.

Then Rachel stirred and sat up, blinking, just a few feet away. She looked from Jake to the struggling creature and then back to Jake. He held out his wrists, a mute gesture, more explanation than appeal. Blood splattered onto the tall grass, dark smears streaking down the yellow blades.

"Jake," she said. "Your belt."

He looked down stupidly. A second later she was there next to him, her fingers fumbling to unbuckle Henry's simple leather belt. He held out his right hand and she cinched the belt tight around his arm, placing the end of the strap in his mouth while she unbuckled her own belt and placed it on his other arm. She took the loose end and wound it around his forearm, grunting as she pulled, then tucked the end under one of the loops. She peered at the wounds for a second, nodded to herself, then used his knife to cut several long strips from his shirt to use as bandages.

"It was in my head," she said. "My body. I felt it, Jake. I *tasted* it."

He murmured a reply and let his eyelids drop. She slapped him hard across the face and his eyes opened, her face coming back into focus. "No," she said. "Stay with me, Jake. I can't carry you out of here if you faint."

There was a scuffling noise behind them. Slowly they turned to regard the creature, which had shrunk in on itself, the long legs and arms now contorted, bent at sharp angles. It was dragging itself along the ground, giving off a high, whining cry as it made for the far side of the clearing. It was mostly hidden in the tall grass, a dark shape scuttling back for the cover of the woods. Behind them, flashlights had slashed through the woods, men's voices bouncing between the tree trunks.

"The knife," he said. "I need to finish it."

"I'll do it."

"No." He held out his bandaged hand. Rachel ignored him and strode forward. She caught the creature at the edge of the woods, planting her boot in the middle of its knobby back. It seemed almost insubstantial, not much more than a great, fragile spider with several broken legs. It looked up at them, its green eyes full of pain and loathing, one of the tentacles waving weakly in the air. Rachel drew the knife back.

She can kill it, Jake realized. *She can end it. It's caught between forms, and the medicine I gave it was bitter. Bitter.*

He strode forward and brought his bandaged forearm up, blocking the downward motion that Rachel meant for the back of the creature's neck. She turned to him, ready to fight at first, and then perplexed when she saw his face and understood he wasn't under its spell. He lowered his bandaged arm, the blood from his cut pattering slowly onto the grass. The creature was watching him, lips curled back to reveal its green-yellow teeth, fuzzy with mold. Rachel fell back a step, staring at the creature. She looked horrified, as though she had not yet seen what it was, had not truly understood what had been inside her until this very moment.

"Go, then," Jake said. "You've taken it from me. Now run with it."

It regarded him for a long moment, the hate and pain and anger in its expression mixing with something else. Not fear, not respect, but an acknowledgment, the barest tip of its misshapen head. One creature of the dark woods nodding to the other.

"Go."

They watched as it dragged itself into the shadows of the trees, seeming to meld with the darkness. There were a dozen flashlight beams coming their way, the men in front already breaking into the clearing. Jake felt a surge of pride in the people of his hometown, people he barely knew, yet who were part of his family. They might not be coming for him, or not just for him, but they were coming. They were beating the darkness back into the night, bringing light with them. He tilted a little, suddenly dizzy again, and Rachel was there, under his shoulder, looking up at him with curiosity.

"Jake?"

He looked down. "I know."

"It looked like you, Jake. For a second it looked like your face."

"It's okay."

"Are you sure?"

He looked once more into the woods. His wrists

were throbbing with a deep, biting pain. Every part of him seemed to hurt in some way and yet . . . and yet it felt different now. The sear of a clean cut. The knot of people had almost reached them, the flashlight beams dancing across the tall, blood-smeared grass.

"No," he said. "But I have hope." He looked up at the night sky, at the Little Dipper scooping away at the darkness. Rachel's hand pressed against his lower back, supporting him. "I have hope."

Chapter 18

He still hated the painting.

Jake stood in the hallway, looking at the red and blue abstract, the bright glare of color. He rubbed a finger over the bump of skin on one wrist, then the other. It was becoming a habit, the tracing of the scar tissue, as though the knobby skin and flesh were his very own rabbit's foot.

He was the only one in the hallway except for a custodian, swirling his mop in a steady, monotonous swishing motion at the far end, and the occasional nurse. It was after visiting hours, but nobody seemed to care that he was here. He had signed in to the epidemiology lab three hours earlier. After his appointment, he had gone to the pharmacy and filled his prescription—extra-strength doxycycline—then hung out in the cafeteria, drinking black coffee through the dinner hour, until it was only he and an old man, eighty-five or ninety years old. The old man was staring at a newspaper, the sports section of the *St. Paul Pioneer Press*, but did not turn a page in the hour Jake was there with him.

Now Jake craned his head, listening for the beeping.

He had things to say, and this visit was, if not something he had looked forward to, then at least something not as terrible as it had been before. Before, his thoughts had alternated between regret and the intense desire to end the beeping, to pick up a pillow and put an end to it, knowing he was too cowardly to do such a thing.

His phone buzzed in his pocket. He pulled it free and looked down at the text.

You okay?

It was Rachel. She was in Arlington, and would be for several more months as her government contract wound down. There seemed to be waning interest in promethium, at least on the surface; the exploratory team's trespasses had made the national news in both the United States and Canada. The Canadian Parliament had responded quickly and decisively, banning all mineral exports to the U.S. and declaring an area of a thousand square kilometers around Resurrection Valley to be the newly formed Amiki National Refuge, off-limits to timber harvesting and mineral extraction. Rachel, although she had been cleared of any criminal wrongdoing, was told she would face stiff civil penalties and jail time if she attempted to enter Canada again in her lifetime. She had laughed a bit at the restriction, much to the chagrin of the Mountie telling her about it, a dark-haired man with a serious gray jacket and black tie, a guy who looked more like an undertaker than an officer of the law.

"That's fine," she had said. "I've seen enough of it."

The Canadian forensics team had gone into Resurrection Valley, removing the drill rig and the rest of the materials they had left behind. Jake and Rachel waited for their report, expecting to hear something about the devastation—perhaps something about the corpses in the valley, or Billy's or Weasel's body in the forest—but whatever the forensics team found remained secret. Or perhaps, Jake thought, there was nothing there of interest anymore. Perhaps it had all decayed, gone back into the earth. He'd heard some rumors about payments to families of the deceased, large checks enclosed in cards expressing sincere condolences. It all seemed not to matter very much anymore to him, although he knew Jaimie's and Greer's families were demanding more answers.

I'm fine, he texted back. The phone was new, the technology a bit jarring. The world had moved along while he was in the woods. *Going in to see her now.*

He walked through the door. Deserae had lost weight since he'd last visited her, her face hollow and sunken. Her eyes were closed and the hair along her temples had started to turn gray. She was a year younger than Jake. He pushed a lock of hair back behind her ear and took her hand in his own. It was cool to the touch, unresponsive. He listened to the beeping, he looked at her face. He felt the lifeless weight of her hand in his own. He was thinking of one of their favorite lines in literature, back when they were young and in love and would read to each other. His tastes were different from hers, but she had liked this book, had imagined herself with cropped hair in the Spanish countryside behind enemy lines, or sometimes as the stout, fierce woman dealing with her traitorous husband—a husband who had deserted them and betrayed them, and then, in the darkest part of his retreat, returned. Deserae would recite variations of the lines to him, usually in jest, and he could hear the lines from *For Whom the Bell Tolls*, her voice still with him. It always would be, and not so long ago he thought that was a curse. Now it felt like, if not a blessing, then at least a comfort.

I believe thou art back. . . . I believe it. But,
hombre, thou wert a long way gone.

"I'm sorry," he said, and his voice seemed out of place in this room. "I went away, not just from you, but from everyone. Myself. I'll try not to do it again."

He held onto her hand, remembering again that first night they had met, the night of the swirling snow-flakes in Rice Park. The way she drank her coffee, the way her eyes, so bright and dark, had watched him as he spoke, the sudden flash of her smile. That had been the first time he had seen her, and he closed his eyes now, feeling the tears coming down and making no effort to brush them away, just letting them course down his cheeks. It wasn't fair. She should still be here, should still be flashing him that brilliant smile. Perhaps they would still be reading to each other, late at night, edging into middle age but still holding on to the best parts of their youth. Yet he had been lucky, so lucky, to have the time he had with her. That part had been more than fair; that part had been a blessing. A miracle, even. And miracles, like nightmares, were part of his life.

He sat with his head down, his palm warming her hand. After a while he heard footsteps behind and he turned, his eyes red, wiping at his cheeks with the sleeve of his shirt.

RESURRECTION PASS · 359

The nurse who stood in the doorway was an older white woman, plump, with a kind face. She held a scanner of some sort in one hand. "It's okay," she said in a quiet voice. "Take your time saying good-bye."

Jake placed Deserae's hand back on the bed, then leaned down and kissed her cheek. He straightened.

"Thank you," he said. "I'm good."

"You sure?"

He smiled at her and moved through the doorway. Jake Trueblood walked past the red and blue painting, nodding at it as he went. The light coming through the windows suggested it was late evening, not quite sunset. Yes, he was good, as good as he could be at this moment. He was also done with saying good-bye, at least for a while. Now it was time to say hello, and he knew exactly where he was going to start.

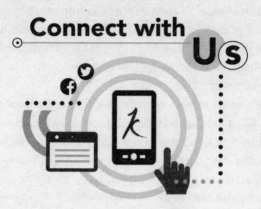